THE
SEVERED REALM

THE RIVEN GATES
VOLUME TWO

BY

MICHAEL G. MANNING

Cover by Amalia Chitulescu
Map Artwork by Maxime Plasse
Editing by Grace Bryan Butler and Keri Karandrakis
© 2018 by Michael G. Manning
Printed in the United States of America

ISBN: 978-1-943481-26-2

For more information about the Mageborn series check out the author's Facebook page:

https://www.facebook.com/MagebornAuthor

or visit the website:

http://www.magebornbooks.com/

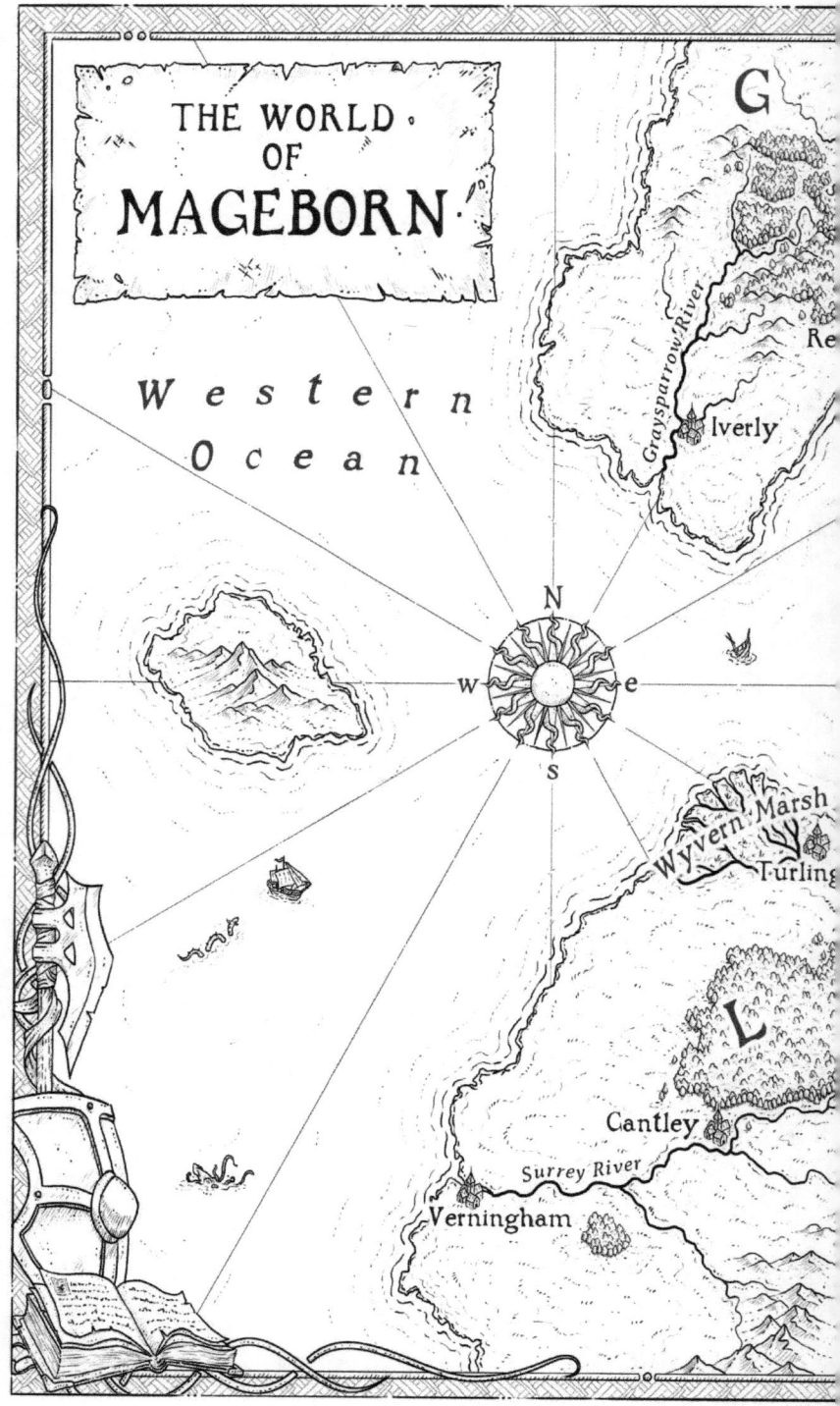

DUNBAR

O
D
D
I
N

SURENCIA

Vergil River

ensa

Northern
Wastes

f

n

Shepherd's Rest

Glenmae River

Cameron

Arundel

Lancaster

Elentirs

Formby
Marsh

vern

Trent River

H   I   O   N

River

ALBAMARL

ensa

PLASSE
2015

outhern   Desert

 # CHAPTER 1

It had been more than two weeks since the funeral, and despite Chad Grayson and his liquid encouragement, I hadn't done much. Most of the Thornbear family had moved to Albamarl and were now staying in the Hightower residence within the city's massive bailey. Only Gram Thornbear remained in Cameron, but as Chad had predicted, I had my suspicions he might be considering asking me to release him from my service.

Gram's fiancée, Alyssa, was still working for me as maid, but her probation would end soon, and I had no doubt she would follow Gram wherever he went. I had intended to talk to Rose before the move, to apologize, but she had been gone before I had recovered from Chad's 'counseling.'

My family was still in mourning for their mother, but my youngest, Irene, seemed to be taking it the hardest. She still felt responsible for her failure to save Penny from the monsters that had wounded her, and it didn't help that her closest friend, Carissa Thornbear, had moved away.

Chad and Cyhan both had dragons now, but I saw very little of them. They had taken to the wilderness, ostensibly to 'patrol,' but I had a feeling they were up to more than that. My intuition told me that Cyhan was probably helping the hunter adjust to his dragon-bond. Cyhan had never had a dragon before either, but he had had an earth-bond once, so he was already acquainted with the difficulties that came with having extreme physical strength.

Matthew had been keeping himself locked away, losing himself in whatever project he was currently working on. I hadn't spoken more than a couple of sentences to him since Penny's death. He had made it clear that he held me responsible for Penny's death, and the wound was too fresh for me to approach him. I would have worried more about him, but Karen kept a good eye on him. She was still traveling, expanding her horizons during the day, but she stayed with us in the evenings. More specifically, she slept in his room.

I wasn't sure how Penny would have felt about that. We had both worried he might never find someone, and my wife had liked Karen, but she might have balked at allowing them to be so intimate without some sort of official betrothal.

Moira had spent the first week after the funeral in her room, refusing to engage with anyone, but after that she had come to some sort of decision. I wished I knew what it was. She had left for the city of Halam. I thought she might be helping her friend, Gerold, the new King of Dunbar, but I had no real idea.

My youngest son, Conall, now Sir Conall, was in Albamarl. Of all my children, I thought perhaps he blamed me the least, but he was hiding from himself. He had been named the Queen's Champion for his service, saving her life during a recent assassination attempt, and as a result was a minor celebrity among the members of the Queen's Court. As a younger son, and a middle child, he probably welcomed the attention brought on by his newfound fame.

Irene kept herself busy with Castle Cameron, and her resolve served to keep the people organized and motivated. She spent most of her days there, using her power to assist in the removal of tons of stone rubble that stood in the way of rebuilding our ancestral home. They had finished clearing the last of it yesterday, and now she was moving on to the outer wall, which had also been partly demolished.

The obvious conclusion one could draw from all of this was that I was a terrible father. If someone had said that to me a few weeks ago, I would have argued with them, but now I was inclined to agree. Penny had been the glue that held our family together; that was painfully apparent now that she was gone. If I had been a good parent, it was only because of her influence.

Today would be different, though. I had spent the last few days consulting my memories of what Castle Cameron had been like previously and sketching new plans. The new keep would be larger and stronger, with a better layout. The old one had been originally constructed over three hundred years ago, and later owners had added to it and remodeled parts, resulting in a somewhat chaotic floorplan.

Building a castle, or even just rebuilding one, was an undertaking that would ordinarily consume years and thousands upon thousands of hours of labor. Building the keep I had planned would be impossible, if it were left to traditional techniques and stone masonry. But I didn't plan to build it—I wanted to try something new. I would *grow* it.

I couldn't help but remember something I had once been told by the shade of Moira Centyr, *"Listen to me, son of Illeniel, and I will tell you what I learned at great cost, once, long ago, ages before you were born. The ability to destroy is the least form of power, though it is the first form that any power will take. Even an infant is able to destroy things, weak though it may be. Using your talent to build, to create, or to restore, those are the greater forms of power; and those forms require time and cultivation to mature."*

I had later helped her to regain some of her humanity, giving her a body of flesh and blood, and she was now married to Gareth Gaelyn. Unfortunately, she and I were no longer friends, but I still treasured what she had taught me. My life might have turned out better if I had paid closer attention to that particular bit of wisdom; for example, if I had spent more time finishing Penny's armor instead of running off to destroy ANSIS.

Today I would create something new, build something stronger than what I had allowed to be destroyed.

"Are you sure about this, Dad?" asked Irene, looking up at me worriedly. "I've never been your miellte before." The word miellte meant 'watcher,' and it was the traditional term for a wizard tasked with keeping an archmage from losing his mind while using metamagic.

I had used my gift without taking such precautions too many times to count, but there was no reason for me to take risks when help was at hand. "You'll be fine," I told her. "Just watch me, and if I seem to be drifting too far, talk to me. Our minds will be linked, so I will hear your thoughts no matter what. You remember the spells I taught you?"

She nodded, and then added, "But I've only been a mage for a few weeks."

4

"Doesn't matter," I replied. "Being a miellte isn't a job that requires a lot of skill. The most important thing is the relationship between the archmage and the person acting as miellte. Being my daughter makes you almost perfect for the task."

"Why?"

"Because I love you. It will make the connection stronger. No matter how lost I become, I'm less likely to ignore your warnings," I answered calmly.

I could see the fear in her eyes, the self-doubt. She had lost her mother, and now she feared losing me as well. If I did screw this up, she would be far worse off, but my hope was that if we succeeded she would regain some of her confidence. "Are we ready?" I asked.

Irene's eyes unfocused for a moment as she used her magesight to search our surroundings once more. "The courtyard is clear," she answered.

Taking her hand in mine, I linked my mind with hers, and then turned my thoughts inward, opening the gates of perception and letting the voices of the world seep into my soul. Within me, etched with crystalline perfection, were the plans I had laid out for the new keep. Ignoring all the other voices, I focused on the drumbeat of the earth, absorbing it, making it mine.

My awareness expanded, sinking into the ground. To accomplish what I wanted would require delicacy and precision. Deep below the castle was the Ironheart Chamber, the prison-trap I had once used to trap Karenth, the god of justice. Much of his power was still contained there, and it was important that I not allow the work I was doing now to disturb it. If the enchantment was damaged, it might explode, destroying not just my castle, but the entire region.

Farther down was the molten sea that would provide the raw materials for my new castle, but that sea wasn't yet suitable. I made it a part of myself, and then began to draw it up, filtering it with the knowledge contained in the frail flesh and blood brain that stood on the surface. Iron, nickel, copper—these were things I could use.

The ground began to shake, evidence of a lack of control. Smoothing the rough edges of my mind, I brought the shaking to a stop. I had to be fluid, flawless, and perfect as I poured the blood of the earth into the shapes I desired.

***

Irene stood beside her father, feeling small. She was not particularly short for a girl her age, but standing next to him made her feel diminutive. Once the bond between their minds formed, she felt better, safer, but that illusion vanished quickly as his mind grew distant, changing into something alien. She saw it all through his eyes, but being human, much of it was incomprehensible to her.

Her father's hand grew hot, so hot it began to burn her skin, and she gasped when she turned her eyes on him and saw that his body was changing, turning to stone. He had forewarned her of this, so she chanted a quick spell to protect herself from the searing heat.

The ground trembled for a minute or two before becoming still again, and then she saw a blazing white fountain erupt from the center of where the keep had once stood. It sizzled as it came into contact with the air, throwing sparks in all directions and filling the air with an acrid odor. Irene chanted another spell, building a shield that would not only protect her from stray sparks but also filter the air and keep it clean enough to breathe.

Her father's mind was nearly gone. The stone statue standing beside her was merely a remnant—it contained only the tiniest amount of whatever it was he had become—but she clung to it, not just with her hand, but with her heart and mind. *I'm still here, Father. Don't forget me.*

There was no response, but the glowing fountain of liquid metal rose higher, climbing into the air like a golden serpent. It snaked back and forth, and parts of it began to solidify into reddish-orange metal shapes. More continued to pour forth from the earth, as the bones of a massive structure slowly formed in front of her.

Minutes passed into hours as it grew into a towering construction of heat and metal. She grew tired and her legs grew weak. As the day wore on, she sank to her knees, still holding onto the statue and wishing she had thought to pee before they had started.

Eventually the metal stopped, and a crackling sound filled the air as a new substance emerged. This new substance was a bright orange, flecked with black—liquid stone. It flowed up and around the metal framework and filled the spaces in between. The sun gradually dropped below the horizon while the keep continued to take shape.

The moon was high in the sky when the stone portion was finished, and Irene felt certain they were almost done, but it wasn't over. She wanted to cry when sand and soil began to rise from a dozen points around the new keep, flowing in to smother the burning rock. *Father, I'm tired. I can't keep this up,* she entreated him silently, but again, there was no response.

The sand and earth buried everything, but it didn't stay still. It moved, shifting and pressing on the leviathan of stone beneath it. The moon set, and darkness covered the world, but her inhuman father's work went on ceaselessly.

At some point, Irene's desire to relieve herself had disappeared, gradually replaced by sensations of thirst and hunger. Something was wrong. She knew it. It shouldn't have taken this long. She still felt the presence of a strange intellect in the stone, but she couldn't say for certain that it was her father anymore. If he was gone, it was her fault. It had been her job to keep him anchored to his humanity.

Dawn had come by the time the sand started receding, disappearing into the earth, leaving behind a gleaming black edifice. It hardly mattered to Irene. Sitting on the ground next to the pillar of stone that had once been her father, she felt hopeless. Her arm was numb and aching from being held raised over her head for hours, but the real pain was in her heart.

She had failed. *Mom, I'm sorry. I couldn't do it. Now he's gone too.* The world went silent as she bowed her head and closed her eyes. After a time, she lapsed into unconsciousness.

Sometime later, someone found her. Irene felt herself lifted, cradled in strong arms. Long hair tickled her face, and when she opened her eyes she finally understood. *I'm dreaming.*

Her mother was carrying her, a look of concern on her face. Irene stared up at her, thinking, *If this is a dream, let me stay asleep a while longer.*

Eventually Penny stopped and knelt, setting Irene down on a cold stone floor. "Sorry, sweetheart, I wanted to take you home, but I couldn't find the way. It looks like the old entrance is gone. The keep is completely changed. Rest here until your father returns."

"I lost him, Momma. He can't come back," said Irene sadly. "I lost both of you."

"Don't be silly," said Penny, stroking her daughter's hair. "He'll be back, I promise you. You did well."

"This is just a dream, isn't it?" said Irene.

Penny nodded. "Yes, but sometimes dreams are just as important as the real world." She sat down next to her daughter. "Have you eaten?"

Irene shook her head. "No."

Her mother scowled and then sighed. "Your father—I'd love to give him a stern talking to right now. Tell him I said he'd better take better care of you."

Irene sniffed, trying not to cry. "He's not doing so well, Mom. Things aren't the same since, since you…"

"Shhh, I know. But he still needs to snap out of it. He has a lot of people to help him, if he would let them. What are your brothers and sisters doing?"

Irene started talking, giving her mother a summary of what had been happening, describing the distance that had grown between her siblings. The more she talked, the more agitated her mother became.

Eventually, Penny stopped her. "So they've just dumped everything on you? That isn't right. The oldest should be the one to step up first!"

"Well, Matthew is—"

"I know exactly how he is, but what about Moira?" Penny paused and then growled softly to herself. Then she spoke again, "I know what you need to do."

"What?" asked Irene, hopeful again.

"Talk to Rose. She knows how to handle them, and she has more than enough spine to slap your father into shape," said Penny.

"She's gone," said Irene, tears welling again. "They got into an argument, I think. She moved back to Albamarl with Carissa and Elise."

Penny looked thoughtful. "Hmmm. He told me they had a fight, but I didn't think it was that serious. You need to go to the capital, then. Talk to her, explain things, just as you did with me. She'll understand."

"I don't think so, Mom. She won't listen to me…"

"Then tell her *I* said it, and if she doesn't fix it, then I'll haunt her!" snapped Penny.

"But this is a dream. I can't…"

Penny put a finger over her daughter's lips. "I already told you. Sometimes dreams are more important than what we think is real. Trust me."

After that she held her daughter, the two of them leaning against the cold stone wall until Irene drifted off again.

 # CHAPTER 2

I woke up cold, stiff, and sore. My right arm had gone to sleep, and my back was explaining to the rest of me that it wasn't going to take this sort of treatment anymore. Glancing around, I realized I was in the bailey. *How the hell did I get here?*

My last good memory was of the construction of the castle. I had gone deep into the mind of the earth—too deep, perhaps. Usually I could at least recall the return, but this time it was just a blank after a certain point.

Irene was leaning against me. Had she brought us here after I finished? It bothered me that I didn't know. I tried to ease out from under her, but as soon as I moved, she groaned and opened her eyes. "Dad?"

"Yeah, it's me," I told her. "Did it turn out like I planned?"

"I'm not sure."

"How did we wind up in the bailey?" I asked.

She frowned. "I had a strange dream."

I grinned at her. "So, you dreamed us here?"

Irene shook her head. "I don't think so. I was carried—that was you, right?"

I shrugged. "Maybe. I get really weird when I go that deep. I don't remember much. Let's go home."

The heat radiating from the new keep engulfed us as soon as we left the bailey. It felt similar to being in an oven, or at least as I imagined it would feel if I were ever inside an oven. That was one of the few forms of torture I hadn't been subjected to yet. *Give it time,* I thought. *Sooner or later someone will find a way to remedy that gap in my education.*

We hurried into the transfer house and took the newest circle back to our hidden home in the mountains. Lynaralla found us within moments of entering the house.

"Welcome home," said the She'Har girl.

There was something odd about her appearance, but it took me a moment to figure out what it was. "Lynaralla, why are you wearing an apron?"

"It seemed prudent to wear the proper protective gear for the task," she answered.

A more thorough inspection revealed that the ends of her long, silver tresses were stained and stuck together with a mysterious brown substance. Adding that to my available information, including the strange smell in the air, I came to the obvious conclusion. "Have you been…cooking?"

The smile she put on her face was so awkward that it made me shiver. "Yes. I started yesterday but you never returned, and Matthew and Moira never appeared either. I was forced to throw it out, which may be for the best. I don't think it was very good."

"Where was Alyssa?" I asked, concern growing in my heart for what I would find in the kitchen.

"She still hasn't returned," said Lynaralla.

Irene broke in, "You gave her leave to visit her father for a few days, remember?"

"Oh," I said noncommittally. "Let's see what we have."

My newly adopted daughter led us into the kitchen, and the normalcy of the scene I found there made me immediately suspicious. I had expected the place to be wrecked. Most new cooks make stupendous messes, but our kitchen appeared pristine. *Perhaps she used magic to clean as she went,* I thought.

The food itself didn't seem frightening. Small chunks of meat were smothered by a thin, brown gravy and accompanied by an assortment of root vegetables.

"None of it is burned," announced Lynaralla proudly.

"It looks edible," I murmured. *She's already a step ahead of Rose if it isn't scorched.*

"Sit at the table," said the She'Har girl. "I will bring plates."

A few minutes later, Irene and I were seated in the dining room, with two plates in front of us. I glanced at Irene and gestured with my fork, indicating she should take a bite.

"After you," she told me with suppressed mirth in her features.

I said nothing, but the daggers in my eyes conveyed my feeling. Traitor. Fork in hand, I speared a small piece of meat and lifted it to my mouth. Surprisingly, it was tender, though the seasoning was entirely lacking. It could be eaten, though. I took another bite, but the texture made me wary, so I spit it back out and examined it.

Of course, it's tender. It's raw! The exterior had been lightly seared, but beyond that no further cooking had occurred. "The meat needs to be cooked more," I said aloud. Then another thought came to me. "Speaking of which, what kind of meat is this? I don't remember having anything other than eggs and salt pork on hand when I left the other day."

Lynaralla made another attempt at a smile, botching it even worse than the first time. "I had to be resourceful. I hunted for this myself."

Oh, no. "But what animal did it come from?" I asked, fearful of the answer.

"At first, I thought I might capture a deer or some rabbits, but then I remembered Alyssa complaining that rats had gotten into the root cellar, so I decided to solve two problems at once," Lynaralla said proudly.

I dropped my fork and carried my cup of water to the outside door with me, where I began rinsing and spitting to clear every trace of her 'food' from my mouth. That done, I returned and began a careful lecture regarding which animals humans consider appropriate for eating. I didn't bother showing disgust or being dramatic, for it wouldn't have done anything to reinforce my words. The She'Har could be very literal, often comically so, but they were excellent listeners. So long as I spelled out in great detail what was and wasn't for eating, she would remember.

After I had finished that, I moved on to lesser matters. "Do you know where the salt is?"

"Isn't that just for preserving meat?" she asked.

I sighed. "Tell you what, tomorrow morning I will teach you to cook."

In the past, we had had almost half our meals in the main hall of the castle, but until the keep was finished, that was no longer an option. Penny had done a lot of our cooking at home, but while I didn't brag, I was probably the best cook in the family. Matthew and Moira were pretty well versed in the subject as well, while Irene and Conall were ignorant of everything other than knowing how to peel vegetables and wash dishes.

In the weeks since my wife's death, however, none of us had felt up to taking on the task. Alyssa had done most of it, when any of us bothered to show up.

I gathered up the food and discarded all of it. Then I made a simple dish of carrots and turnips. It wasn't much, but there wasn't much to work with. It settled our stomachs at least.

The next morning found Lynaralla and me in the kitchen together. She was meticulous in her movements, which I took as a good sign. I doubted she would ever be very creative, but attention to detail was important in cooking. Even if she didn't become a great chef, she could definitely become a proficient cook.

It was almost comical how serious her face was when she put on the apron, but before we went any further, I stopped her. "You need to tie your hair back as well. You got food in it yesterday."

She nodded and then pointed at me. "Where is your apron?"

I rarely wore one. I had a reputation for getting food all over my clothing while eating, but for some reason I had much better luck while cooking. "I won't need one. I'm here to teach. You'll do everything. Now pay attention." I pointed to an object on the counter. "This is the salt mill. Salt is the most important seasoning when you cook. Too little and your food will be bland, too much, and it may not even be edible."

"Will it be required for eggs?"

"Definitely," I told her. "Eggs can be served without it, and they're still decent, but a little salt will make them shine."

"Does everything need salt?" she asked intently.

"Damn near it," I answered. "Even salad benefits from a tiny bit of salt right before you serve it, but let's focus on breakfast for now."

Breakfast went well, and Karen even managed to coax Matthew into joining us for Lynaralla's first exhibition of her new skills. As I sat at the table, Irene, Lynaralla, and Karen filled the room with light conversation, and for the first time in weeks, the house didn't feel quite as empty. Matthew glanced at me at one point, and as our eyes met, I could see a similar feeling in his features.

Maybe we could survive this.

Then Sir Harold showed up, entering the room from the hall that led to the portal to Albamarl. He looked almost apologetic, but then he straightened and said in a formal voice, "Your Excellency, forgive the intrusion. Queen Ariadne requires your presence."

I found the entire performance irritating. I hadn't built the portal to the Queen's chambers so she could send messengers to drag me out on a whim. "Tell her I'll stop by this afternoon," I responded.

"My lord, I am afraid that this isn't a request. She demands you attend her forthwith."

Forthwith? I doubted Harold had ever used the word before Dorian had found him, seen his potential, and decided to train him. He had come a long way. That thought did nothing to keep me from being ticked off at the demand. What was Ariadne thinking? I shoveled another egg into my mouth and stood. "Very well. I am ever the loyal servant." Crossing over, I began to lead him toward the portal.

Harold looked uncomfortable. "You might want to change your attire, my lord."

I shook my head. "Of course not! If the Queen needs me, it must be urgent. Who am I to delay for such a trivial matter?"

Irene caught my elbow. "I'd like to come too."

I gave her a curious stare. "I don't mind, but why?"

"I haven't seen Carissa in a while."

Carissa Thornbear, Lady Rose's daughter, was Irene's closest friend, and the two of them hadn't seen each other since Penny's funeral. I simply nodded.

***

One nice thing about the portal was that it led directly into the Queen of Lothion's private chambers, which meant I would likely get to see her privately before being dragged into whatever dog and pony show was planned for me.

I wasn't disappointed. She was waiting for me in the front sitting room.

"Mordecai," she said as I entered. Harold quickly bowed and led Irene from the room, leaving us alone.

"Your Majesty," I responded, taking a knee. "You wished to see me?"

"Get up," she commanded. "It's just the two of us. You know better than that."

I kept my eyes on the floor. "As your humble servant, it is always wise to show deference," I replied. "How else should I answer such an urgent summons?"

"Damn it, Mort! Get up and talk to me. I don't have long before the council meeting. I need to know what is happening."

Relenting, I stood and following her direction, took a seat. "I've already told you what happened."

"There are a lot of rumors about the day of the attack on Albamarl," said Ariadne.

I shrugged. "I'm not particularly worried about my reputation."

The Queen looked irritated. "And what of mine? Do you think a monarch need not worry about such things? Lancaster rule was founded in large part on your support. How well do you think it will last if the nobility rebel against me?"

"Whatever they think of me, Ari, my actions are not yours."

"We're cousins!" she snapped. "Over the years they've held their tongues because of that fact, but recent events are too much. The close ties between our families are no secret. If we cannot find some reasonable answer to these rumors, I may not be able to shield you."

"I'm perfectly fine being a scape-goat," I said angrily. "I've done it before. I still have the scars to prove it. If there's that much pressure on you, take my title. Give it to my son. Then they won't be able to accuse you of shielding me for your own purposes."

"That isn't the point, Mort! You've been through enough. I know you're in pain. Losing Penny hurt all of us. I couldn't do that to you. And even if I could, cutting my own legs out from under me wouldn't strengthen my position," she said sadly.

Frustrated, I asked, "Then what do you want from me?"

"First, give me the full story. I need to know exactly what you did, and why. If I know that, I can at least give the reasoning and pretend I had some strategy, even if things didn't go entirely as planned."

She was right. I couldn't argue against her point, so I gave her a detailed explanation without leaving out anything. When I finished, she sat still, a pensive look on her face.

"So, in the middle of the night, as soon as you learned their location, you went to destroy one of these 'nests' and sent your children to eliminate the other? You didn't even give it a day's thought or consideration?"

Well, when you say it like that, it sounds stupid. I nodded.

"You didn't expect the sort of reprisals we saw?"

"I did send Conall here, Ari, and I gave dragons to your knights. It isn't as though I didn't expect *something* to happen. I just didn't realize how strong the response would be," I said defensively.

"How many more dragons are there?"

I hesitated. "I plan to bestow another seven or eight, once Harold gives me his list of candidates."

Ariadne's eyes narrowed. "That isn't what I asked."

"More than ten," I told her.

"How many?"

"Listen, Ariadne, I've never shared that information with anyone. I think it's important to keep our enemies guessing."

"I'm not your enemy, Mordecai. I'm your cousin. Don't you think I should know?" she said with calm resolve.

"Not necessarily, no," I said flatly. "The dragons were my creation. Created with the power I took from the gods with my own two hands. They belong to me. I decide who they go to."

"Mordecai," she said, her voice taking on a dangerous tone. "I'm your Queen. I shouldn't have to remind you that you hold your lands in service to me—to Lothion."

"The land, yes," I answered. "But the dragons are mine. They were not granted to me. I *made* them."

"And if I command you to give them up?" she asked coldly.

There was steel in my voice. "I wouldn't recommend you take such a course, *Your Majesty.*" After a second, I added, "Why this sudden paranoia about the dragons? You've never pushed the issue before."

Her eyes bored into me, but then she relaxed, letting the tension flow from her shoulders as she exhaled. "From what you've just told me, I can make the claim that I authorized your actions. But while that will remove the blame from your shoulders, it will make me look somewhat foolish. I need to show the lords that I have a plan for Lothion's defense. The dragons make an excellent case in that regard, but I can't even answer basic questions about them. How can I admit that I don't even know how many there are?"

I remained silent, thinking. Finally, I said, "Tell them there are at least ten, but that you won't say more on the subject. Let them think *you* are keeping it a secret."

Ariadne rose from her seat. "Very well. We'll play it your way."

I gave her a grateful smile. "Thanks, Ari."

She nodded and then hesitated a moment. "Have you discovered anything about Roland?"

Roland was her brother, the Duke of Lancaster.

I shook my head. "Nothing yet, but I haven't given up."

She pulled me to my feet and then hugged me. It was a slightly awkward gesture, given that she was dressed in the robes of state and wore her crown. The attire wasn't really made for such things, and I had to be careful not to lose an eye on the spikes on her crown. Then she spoke softly into my shoulder, "I'm sorry about Penny. I know this hasn't been easy for you."

The Queen of Lothion pushed me away. "I have to face the council now. They've waited long enough."

I started to follow her, but she waved me away. "I can't take you in there looking like a peasant farmer. Go home. I can deal with this alone."

"Ari…"

"Not another word. This is the least I can do. Take care of your family."

 CHAPTER 3

Irene intended to go to the great bailey that guarded the gates to Albamarl, since that was the location of the traditional Hightower residence, but she encountered Benchley in the palace hall first.

The chamberlain bowed as soon as he spotted her. "Lady Irene, it is an honor to see you."

Straightening her back, she answered, "Benchley, right?"

"At your service."

"Could you tell me where I might find Lady Hightower?"

Benchley nodded. "Certainly. Lady Hightower is currently in the council chamber with the other lords, awaiting the Queen's presence."

"Oh," she said, disappointed.

He smiled at her. "Let me take you there. If the meeting hasn't started yet, you may have some time to talk to her before it begins."

A short walk later, she found herself outside the door to the council chamber. Her brother, Conall, stood guard outside it, along with one of the regular palace guards. Benchley went inside to inform Rose while Irene waited. "What are you doing here?" she asked her brother.

"What does it look like?" answered Conall. He looked awkwardly self-conscious in his armor, which consisted of a gilt-edged breastplate over mail. The royal arms were emblazoned on the breastplate.

Irene eyed him critically up and down. "Shouldn't you have the Cameron arms on your breastplate? You aren't a palace guard."

Conall glared at her. "Father's never given me any armor with our arms on it, not that it matters."

"We have surcoats," countered Irene. "You should be wearing one over that, to represent our family."

"Why is this such a big deal to you?" asked Conall, irritated.

The guard beside Conall was doing his best to pretend he couldn't hear them, but it was obvious he was uncomfortable. Irene didn't care. "Noblemen are supposed to wear their own arms, even when in service to the Queen. You're a Cameron."

"I'm a younger son of a count," said Conall. "I'm not the heir. Technically, I'm nobody."

"You're my brother. Doesn't that mean anything to you? Are you ashamed of your family now?" Irene was seething, but before she could say more, the doors opened and Lady Rose stepped out.

"Did you just come to annoy me?" asked Conall.

"Father told me to tell you to come home," Irene lied. "He hasn't seen you in over a week. Have you even thought about how he's feeling right now? How I'm feeling?" Her voice was gradually rising in pitch and volume.

Rose put a hand on her shoulder. "Let's talk somewhere else, Irene. I don't have much time." She glanced at Conall. "You can argue with your brother afterward."

Irene followed her down the hall, looking over her shoulder to give her brother a dirty look as they went.

Rose opened a door that led into a small antechamber and offered her a seat. "How are you holding up?"

She took a deep breath, wishing she could imitate Rose's perfect composure. "You need to come back," she said at last.

Rose arched one brow. "Did your father send you to tell me that?"

Fidgeting, Irene stared at the tiled floor. "No."

"Then why are you saying it?"

"Because it's true," said Irene, her frustration showing in her voice. "Everything is falling apart. No one talks anymore. Moira's gone off somewhere, Matthew keeps himself locked away most of the time, and Conall is here pretending to be a hero. It isn't right!"

Rose gave her a sad smile. "You miss Carissa, don't you?"

"No. Yes. That's not the point! Aren't you listening? I'm worried about Dad. He needs help," she replied.

Taking a deep breath, Rose answered, "Irene, after something like this, your mother's death, people often deal with their grief in different ways. I know it seems like the end of the world right now, but things will get better."

Unable to contain her feelings, tears began to spill down Irene's cheeks. "Don't you care about us anymore? We need you! It isn't alright. Dad nearly killed himself the other day doing something stupid. He needs you. Why won't you come back?"

Leaning forward, Rose took her hand and patted her cheek. "You know I care about your family. Believe it or not, I'm working very hard right now to help your father. He has a lot of enemies in the capital, and he needs me to figure out what they're plotting." Then she paused before continuing, "And besides that, I don't think he wants me there right now. He's hurting, and my presence may only make it worse for him."

"That's not true," protested Irene.

"Why don't you come stay here with Carissa for a few days?" suggested Rose. "She would love to see you."

"No," growled Irene. "You have to come home. She said so. Please!"

Rose frowned. "Who said so?"

Irene bit her lip, unsure how to answer.

"Who said so, Irene?" asked Rose again.

"Mom!" she blurted out.

Overcome for a moment, Rose dabbed at her eyes with the sleeve of her gown. "Oh, Rennie, I know this is hard, but you have to be reasonable."

"She did say it. I swear!" insisted Irene. "I saw her. She told me to tell you she would haunt you if you didn't come slap some sense into my dad."

Rose's eyes were glistening, but she smiled at Irene's remark. "That sounds like her. Was this a dream you had?"

"Yes, but it was real! It was really her. She said some dreams are more important than real life," explained Irene.

Standing up, Rose drew Irene into her arms and hugged her tightly. "You miss her a lot, don't you?"

Irene continued to argue, but Rose was unyielding. After a few minutes, Benchley appeared to warn them that the Queen was on her way, and Rose left. She made one concession as she stepped away: "I'll visit soon, Rennie. Don't worry."

***

When Rose returned to the council chamber, she scanned the room with a seemingly casual glance. Gregory, Duke of Cantley, sat chatting amiably with Count Malvern, while Tyrion appeared to be entertaining Earl Balistair and Count Airedale with a humorous anecdote. Leomund, the Prince-Consort, sat quiet, not involved in any of the other conversations. *Not surprising,* thought Rose, *since he isn't well liked.*

She crossed the room, and as she walked, she drank in her environment, absorbing the details. It was the habit of a lifetime, one that she had learned at the feet of her father, though she had quickly exceeded him in ability. Almost subliminally, she noted the clothing worn by the other nobles, their expressions as they talked with one another, and which faces they looked at when they weren't talking.

All these things gave away valuable information, some of which was intended to be seen, and some which was meant to be private. Knowing the difference was crucial. Those skilled at the game could pretend to give away things unintentionally as a means of misdirection.

The men in this room were the most powerful nobles in Lothion, and they were well trained in the arts of politics and diplomacy, but none compared to Rose Thornbear when it came to reading a room.

A privacy ward protected them from eavesdroppers, but it couldn't shield them from Rose's discerning gaze. Magic was useful for many things, but ultimately it was human intellect that was most important when it came to gathering and understanding information.

Three seats were notably vacant, those that should be occupied by Lancaster, Tremont, and Cameron.

Tremont's vacancy was an old problem. The late Andrew Tremont's land had been ravaged by shiggreth and had yet to be resettled. While the title was still available, it hadn't been given out since it was currently next to worthless.

Lancaster was a more troubling vacancy. That seat was held by the Queen's brother, Roland, who had been missing for several weeks, along with Lancaster itself.

The seat for the Count di' Cameron had been empty for more than ten years, since Mordecai held the Council of Lords in general disdain. His refusal to attend had begun after his public humiliation when he had been flogged for his involvement in the destruction of Tremont's lands and people. That alone would have made him unpopular, but the fact that his opinion still counted for more in the Queen's eyes than did that of the entire council made them even more resentful.

Tyrion took notice of her entrance and meandered over to talk to her before she could resume her seat. Unlike the other noblemen in the room, he eschewed excessive embroidery and ornamentation in his attire. The archmage made do with simple linen trousers and a soft leather vest over a loose, white shirt. He also left an unacceptable number of buttons undone, exposing a muscled chest covered with exotic tattoos.

Everything about him seemed to shout his overwhelming masculinity to the room, and when he drew close, Rose could smell his scent. It didn't carry the flowery notes so popular in the perfumes used by the aristocracy; in fact, she couldn't detect any hint of deliberate artifice. It was just the smell of a very healthy and recently bathed male.

It reminded her of Dorian, and that made her uncomfortable.

"You look particularly lovely today, Lady Hightower," said the Duke of the Wester Isles.

Rose wasn't interested in flattery, but for some reason she felt a faint thrill as the deep notes of his voice passed over her. She ignored her reaction as she replied, "One does what one can, Your Grace. I see your attire remains as…rustic…as ever."

If the reproach in her remark bothered him, he gave no sign of it. "I am what I am, Lady Hightower. Dressing myself in today's finery would be as pointless as putting a wolf in sheep's clothes." There was humor in his voice.

Nicely done, thought Rose. "A nice sentiment, Your Grace, though it ignores the fact that clothing is more than simply fashion. It has a practical purpose."

Tyrion grinned. "I am not well acquainted with social conventions, Lady Hightower. If I pretend to greater sophistication than I possess, it will not aid my purpose. Instead, I think it better to admit to both my strength and my weakness. The plainness of my wardrobe is a simple statement of my character. I cannot pretend to subtlety, but candor can also be a virtue in politics."

"Purpose and intent are the key points, Lord Tyrion," said Rose. "Seeking to reinforce the impression of one's integrity through plain clothing may also be a sign of artifice, if the purpose of such a display is in the service of deceit."

The Duke opened his arms wide, as if surrendering. "I cannot compete with you in a war of words, Lady Hightower, nor would I wish to. The truth is that I was born in a simpler time. I am not adroit enough to attempt such deliberate tactics. Candor is my only weapon; my clothes reflect that."

"If probity is indeed your main quality, you should have no trouble sharing your intentions, Lord Tyrion. I find it curious that you have entered the world of politics. What is your real purpose here?" asked Rose.

"Simple I may be," said Tyrion, "but even men such as I have more than one purpose. My main goal is the preservation of our civilization. I once fought to free mankind from the tyranny of the She'Har. Now I seek to keep it free from the corruption of ANSIS."

Rose looked down demurely, before returning her gaze to Tyrion's visage. She used the opportunity to scan the room, taking note of those watching her conversation, as well as those pretending not to be interested. "It is worth noting, Your Grace, that in the end you became the enemy you fought against. It would be a tragedy if such a thing happened again."

Tyrion's muscles tensed, and Rose felt his anger like a flash of heat against her skin. After a second, he responded, "I cannot help the past, but I hope in the future, my actions will dispel your mistrust."

Rose's gaze remained steady. "Then we hope for the same thing, Your Grace."

Leaning in, Tyrion spoke in her ear, his lips so close that she felt his breath on her neck. "I am not your enemy. I know little of hope, but I know much of desire, and I believe we both desire the same thing."

She struggled to repress a shiver at his closeness, but then he continued, "Rejoice, Lady Hightower, for I always take that which I desire, and you *will* be pleased." Then he withdrew, heading to his own seat.

Rose nearly gasped, for her pulse had quickened, and she felt a flush of heat in places better left unspoken. Unconsciously her hand went to her bosom, to make sure that Mordecai's enchanted pendant was still there. It was. *What was that? He shouldn't be able to affect my emotions,* she thought.

She sat down, her mind racing as she tried to make sense of what had happened. As a result, she remained silent until Benchley stepped in to announce the Queen's arrival.

After Ariadne entered, the usual routine of rising, bowing, and waiting for her to take her seat followed. Minutes later, the meeting was underway, but it wasn't long before the Duke of Cantley brought up the subject that was on everyone's mind.

"What about the absent Count di' Cameron? Has he made an accounting of what happened yet?" asked Gregory Cantley.

The Queen's cool gaze swept across the table before she answered, "He has little to account for, Your Grace. He consulted with me before the events of that night. His actions were made with my approval."

Prince Leomund's eyes seemed to bulge at that pronouncement. "You said nothing of this before."

"You doubt my words, *husband?*" asked Ariadne calmly.

The Prince-Consort's eyes shifted nervously, and Rose noted that they lingered on Count Airedale for a second longer than anyone else. Then he answered, "Of course not, my Queen. I was merely surprised."

Leomund has made a friend, noted Rose mentally. *David Airedale will bear watching in the future.*

"Begging your pardon, Majesty," said Tyrion, breaking in, "but he only speaks what we are all wondering. Your announcement is sudden, and we cannot be blamed for thinking you might merely be seeking to protect your cousin, the Count." His eyes never left the Queen's face as he spoke, though several members of the council drew sharp intakes of air at his brazenness.

"My response to you is the same, Lord Tyrion," said Ariadne. "I approved the Count di' Cameron's plan before it was put into effect. It was my mistake in underestimating the enemy."

Tyrion smiled. "I wouldn't be so critical of yourself, Your Majesty. A ruler's decisions are only as good as the information available to her. Speaking as a wizard, we have many means of attaining information that are not possible for those without magic. My descendant should have been more thorough in his investigation before he presented you with his proposed course of action."

Count Malvern spoke up, "With all due respect, Lord Tyrion, you are very new to this council to be criticizing Lord Cameron. I have personally witnessed his efforts to gain more knowledge of our enemy. I cannot think what more he could have done."

Airedale responded immediately, "Times have changed, Malvern. Mordecai is no longer the only wizard in Lothion. To be frank, our Queen has options now. It would seem prudent to me that we make use of them. Lord Illeniel is an excellent example of this; Lord Gaelyn is another. Their talents could be put to good use for the realm."

"Which is precisely why both of them are now counted among the nobility of Lothion," observed Ariadne wryly. "We are not blind to the gifts that lie before us."

Lady Rose lifted a finger. "If I may?" After the Queen nodded, she went on, "Lord Tyrion, your arrival in the capital the night of the attack was fortuitous, almost unbelievably so. Would you care to explain?"

Tyrion nodded. "I would be glad to. As all of you are aware, the people I represent are not human. The She'Har have many assets that could prove valuable to the kingdom in dealing with the threat of ANSIS. One of these is a method of detecting and locating the enemy. I was testing this when I learned that our enemy was moving on the capital."

"Shouldn't you have warned the Queen then?" asked Rose.

He shook his head. "There was no time. I had only just learned of it when the attack was about to commence. I came as quickly as I could."

"We would hear more of these 'assets' you mentioned," said the Queen. "How were you able to learn of the attack?"

Tyrion smiled. "May I be permitted to use a small display of magic? Nothing dangerous, just an illusion. It will make the explanation much simpler."

Ariadne nodded, and he lifted a hand, holding it out toward the center of the table. A second later, a small creature appeared in the air. It looked very similar to a honey bee. "This is one of the krytek," began Tyrion. "For those unfamiliar with the She'Har, we are able to produce temporary soldiers to protect our groves. The general term for them is 'krytek,' but it can seem confusing to outsiders because they can take an almost infinite number of forms. We can tailor them to whatever purpose is needed. The one you see presented in this illusion is designed to detect ANSIS. Because it is small it can be produced in vast numbers, and as you can see, it has wings, which gives it a wonderful amount of mobility."

"When you say 'temporary,'" questioned Ariadne, "what exactly does that mean?"

"They live for three months," answered Tyrion. "The limit is built into them when they are created to avoid a host of problems that might arise if we created new species and released them on a whim. Krytek are created by father-trees, while our mother-trees produce actual She'Har children who do not have this time limit and are expected to propagate our race."

Lord Balistair lifted his hand. "What you have shown us is incredible, but I have a question. Once these little insects of yours detect the enemy, how do they pass this information along? If you are proposing to send them flying across the length and breadth of Lothion, there will be hundreds of miles between them."

"An excellent question," said Tyrion. A second figure appeared beside the bee, one with a human semblance. "The first krytek I showed you, the detectors, have a limited magical ability and minimal intelligence. They can use this not only to locate the enemy, but also communicate what they have found to their companion krytek. What I propose is to create a number of human-appearing krytek to work alongside your guardsmen."

Rose frowned. "When you say, 'human-appearing,' you mean…"

"They would look exactly like any other citizen of the kingdom. They could be dressed in the same armor and liveries as your normal guardsmen, to avoid alarming the populace. In truth, I could give them any appearance, but I think this would be the best choice to avoid creating a panic. These krytek would receive information from the smaller ones and be capable of coordinating with your own forces," explained Tyrion.

"Couldn't normal She'Har do the same thing?" questioned Rose.

"There are too few," said Tyrion. "Lyralliantha's tree is still very young, and because of that, quite small. The number of children, in the case of a mother-tree, or krytek, in the case of a father-tree, that can be produced is directly limited by the size of the tree. Human-sized creatures require a significant investment of time and energy. Because of this, only a few She'Har children have been created thus far. My tree is very old and quite large, so producing swarms of these detectors and a decent number of human-sized coordinators is not a problem."

"It sounds like an excellent idea," said the Queen. "How long would it take to implement?"

"As you can guess, I have produced some of the smaller krytek. The larger coordinators are almost ready. They can begin working with your people within the week, once I transport them from my home," said Tyrion.

Malvern frowned. "You produced an army without consulting your Queen?"

"They only live a few months," explained Tyrion. "And when I began, I was not yet a vassal of the Queen. Rest assured, I only have benign intentions in regard to our kingdom."

"And when the three months has passed, what then?" asked Cantley.

"I will continue creating them during that time," explained the new Duke of the Wester Isles. "Once the threat has passed, or when the Queen decides it is no longer necessary, I will stop."

The discussion went on for some time, but Rose didn't contribute much more. Instead, she listened, and more importantly, she watched. The details of Tyrion's proposal she filed away, but that was only a fraction of what she learned. The most important things she learned were unspoken. Glimmers and hints of backroom conversations that could only be seen by watching the faces of those who were now speaking.

Leomund and Airedale have gotten closer, while Tyrion obviously approached Cantley and Airedale before this meeting, she noted. What concerned her even more, though, was the fact that she could tell that Ariadne and Tyrion also seemed to have developed a previous rapport. *How did I miss that?* she wondered.

In contrast to the others, Cantley and Malvern hadn't known anything about what would be discussed. From his words, Malvern seemed to have a friendly attitude toward Mordecai, but Cantley was somewhat hostile.

In the end, she didn't like her conclusions. Tyrion was firming up his ties with the others, and while he spoke warmly of his descendant, it was clear that he intended to use the distrust the others felt for Lord Cameron to strengthen his own position. That left only the Queen, and perhaps Lord Malvern, on Mordecai's side of the equation.

And the Queen was clearly smitten with Tyrion. Rose could see it in Ariadne's eyes when she looked at the man.

Before the meeting was adjourned and everyone began to leave, Rose had already made a mental list of fresh orders for her subordinates. Everyone in the room bore close watching, but some of them would need particular attention if she was to learn their full intentions.

 # CHAPTER 4

I returned home alone. Irene was still in the capital, though I presumed she'd be along after a while, unless she chose to spend some time with Carissa Thornbear.

The house was empty. Completely empty. Alyssa was still away, and Matthew and Karen were both absent. If she had taken him somewhere, he could be literally anywhere in the world.

It was probably the first time I had been in the house without anyone else present since Penny's death. I had thought I was used to the empty feeling that now predominated there, but the feeling was so intense now it made me want to run, to get out.

This isn't healthy, I thought. I needed to stay busy.

There was plenty to do. I had a newly created castle to work on. It was still far too hot for anyone to enter without protection, but I could try to accelerate the cooling process. Otherwise it might take a year for the heat stored in all that stone to dissipate. Unfortunately, moving that much water would require me to use my abilities as an archmage again, and without Irene there I didn't dare.

I still had enchanting projects in my workshop to finish, so I decided to see if I could find something there to keep my mind off of things. I set off, but on my way, I passed through the living room. There on the table was a large bottle of amber liquid, a gift from Chad Grayson.

It was tempting to sit down and have a drink—or ten. I had done a lot of drinking over the past week, primarily at the Muddy Pig, with Cyhan and Chad. Drinking alone had never been very appealing to me.

But now it was.

I stood still for a long moment, staring at the bottle, before continuing on my way. Now was not the time to get drunk. Passing through the kitchen, I went out the back door and walked through the garden. Even the damned vegetables made me think of her.

Finally, I reached my workshop, my quiet sanctuary. I hadn't been inside in weeks, but I had no worry about it. It was the one place that was all *me,* and only me. There, I pursued personal projects. Penny had almost never been inside, and she certainly hadn't decorated it. If there was one place that would have few reminders of what I had lost, that would be it.

The enchanted globes set into the ceiling lit themselves as I entered, casting a cheerful, warm glow over the room. One wall was dominated by books, mainly my notebooks, sketches, and personal logs. I kept them not as much for myself as for my descendants. My memory was such that I never needed to refer back to them.

Another wall held a long table, covered with a miscellany of old projects and special tools, as well as raw materials. It was a sort of storage area, a random jumble of things set aside to avoid cluttering my main workspace, which was the main table in the center of the room.

On that table was a set of nearly completed plate armor. Lying beside the armor was the prosthetic arm that was also very close to finished. Both had been meant for Penny.

Damn it!

My emotions rose and slammed into me like a giant wave, destroying my equilibrium. Without thinking, I turned and left the workshop, quickly shutting the door behind me. Trying not to remember what I had seen, I went back into my house, walked to the living room, and grabbed the bottle. Then I sat down and began to drink.

Through it all, I diligently tried to keep my mind blank—and failed utterly. Using my legendary focus, I tried to keep my attention on one thing. *Pour, drink, swallow...*

After the burn subsided from each drink, I poured another, ignoring the feelings of rebellion that arose from my abused gut. *Penny would not approve of this,* I thought idly.

My anger built at that thought, and the empty glass in my hand began to vibrate. I threw it across the room to shatter against the stone mantle of the fireplace. "That was self-defense," I muttered roughly. "If I hadn't thrown it, it would have shattered in my hands."

I don't need a glass anyway, I realized. Lifting the bottle in one hand, I gave a sad chuckle. "I have the bottle." It was still half full, so I raised it to my lips, hoping to remedy that problem. I choked.

Good thing Chad wasn't here to see that, I thought, setting the bottle down again as I struggled to maintain control over my rebelling stomach. The only good thing about the burning and nausea was that it made it easier not to think about my inner suffering. The alcohol was beginning to make itself more evident as my world devolved into a comfortable blur.

Fifteen minutes and I'm already this drunk. When the rest of it hits, I'm going to be smashed. I felt a momentary sense of worry. I hadn't been this intoxicated in—well, a very long time. Probably sometime before I had discovered my abilities as an archmage.

"At least no one is home, in case I start melting things," I slurred. My eyes lit upon the broken glass, and it occurred to me that someone might step on it and cut themselves. Reaching out with my power, I tried to gather the fragments but only succeeded in scattering them further. *Shit.*

The low table in the center of the room seemed to sway on legs that were now rubbery. I tried to stand and quickly gave up on the idea, since it felt as though the house was beginning to get into rough waves. Everything was swaying from side to side.

The glass still bothered me, though. I needed to do something about that. Since my control had degenerated, it made more sense that I do something simpler. Opening my mind, I tried to slip into the mind of the stone. That would probably clear my senses.

I thought.

It did *something.* Though, whether it was what I intended, I was no longer sure. The broken fragments melted into the floor, which was a plus, but everything else began to melt as well. The walls of the house sagged, and the furniture around me was drooping. Lifting my hand, I watched my fingers as they dripped toward the ground, and I began to laugh. Had anyone else ever seen something so hysterical? I doubted it.

An indefinable period of madness ensued, in which the room whirled and shifted. The shadows came to life, and Dorian and Marcus appeared, dancing a slow waltz together across the room. The table that should have been in their way had long since vanished.

At some point, Irene showed up, looking concerned as she stared down at me. "Dad! What are you doing?"

I tried to answer, but my tongue rolled out of my mouth and somehow was long enough to reach my lap. Needless to say, it made speaking intelligibly impossible.

Irene looked around in alarm, no doubt surprised to see the chairs wrestling in the corner. I wanted to tell her not to worry, since it was a friendly squabble between our furniture family members, but again, my words failed me. I stared up at her, my vision blurry, hoping she would relax.

And then her face began to slide downward on one side, as though her bones were turning to jelly. Her mouth opened, and a scream of horror filled my ears.

Oh no! What have I done? Helpless to control myself, I realized too late that my daughter had fallen victim to my reckless whims. Trapped within myself, I could only cry out silently, *Penny!*

And then the world melted away.

***

Some time later, I woke. I was in bed, and despite my recent indulgence I had not the faintest sign of a headache. Cautiously, I lifted my head and moved it back and forth, just to make sure my hangover wasn't waiting to ambush me. Nothing.

No pain, no nausea, and the world stayed comfortably solid, without the slightest sign of swaying or spinning. *What happened?*

And then I remembered. Bolting out of the bed, I threw open the bedroom door and ran down the hall to Irene's room. I found her sleeping inside, quiet and angelic in her slumber. There was no sign of the horrific melting I had seen before.

Did I imagine it? That didn't seem likely. Alcohol had never made me hallucinate, not that I had ever had so much to drink before. Closing her door quietly, I went to the living room, wondering what I would find.

Everything looked normal, if scrupulously clean. The table was back in its place, and the chairs had untangled themselves. Nothing had changed, other than it looked as though someone had given the room a thorough cleaning. The dust was gone, and the floor had been swept, or possibly even mopped. Had Alyssa returned early?

My magesight found no evidence of anyone else in the house. Puzzled, I reached up and rubbed my beard, only to find it gone. *Huh?*

Back to the bedroom, I sought out the mirror above Penny's dressing table. As my hand and magesight had already confirmed, I was freshly shaven. I generally preferred to keep a well-groomed goatee on my chin, as well as a moustache, but both were gone. Over the past few weeks I hadn't kept up with my grooming, which had resulted in a thick, itchy scruff over the rest of my cheeks, but all of that was gone now. Even my hair had been neatly trimmed.

"This really is weird," I said to myself. "Who gets drunk, cleans the house, and shaves?" In fact, I had been bathed as well. My nose was picking up the faint notes of the rose-scented bath oils that Penny kept in our bathroom. The thought of someone grooming, undressing, and bathing me, all while I was unconscious—well, it was unsettling to say the least. The only person I could think of who might be capable of it was Alyssa, and she was nowhere to be found. Surely my daughter hadn't done all this before going to bed. If so, I would be even more embarrassed.

An empty bottle of McDaniel's finest sat on the dressing table, and beneath it I saw a sheet of paper. Putting the bottle to one side, I lifted the sheet and examined it. It bore a short line of words so badly written as to be almost illegible. I recognized the handwriting immediately, for there was only one person I knew with such bad penmanship. Penny.

You're an idiot. Endanger our children again, and I'll make sure you don't wake up next time.

My vision blurred. *Forgive me, Penny.* Standing up, I squared my shoulders and sought out my clothes. Naturally, I found them laid out for me, neatly ordered and looking suspiciously smooth, as though they had been pressed.

Trying not to think about what it all meant, I went to the kitchen. It was late morning already, and Irene would likely be hungry when she woke. There wasn't much to work with, but there were fresh eggs in the yard and some hard bread in the pantry, so I did my best. Eggs and toast with butter were never a bad thing.

Irene wandered in, having smelled the results. "Dad?"

I gave her a brave smile. "Good morning."

Her face held an odd expression. "How did I wind up in bed?" she asked after a minute.

I shrugged. "I had too much to drink last night, so my memory is foggy. I might have tucked you in."

"The living room," she mumbled. "I thought you lost control." An unpleasant memory passed through her mind, and she shuddered. "I don't know what happened after that."

Facing her squarely, I apologized, "I'm sorry about last night. I never should have let myself drink so much. I certainly never wanted you to see me like that. I won't let it happen again."

Irene looked uncertain, but then she noticed my bare chin. "You look better today, but I'm not used to seeing you without your beard. You look funny."

Somebody's idea of a joke, I thought ruefully. "I had an accident with the razor and decided to start fresh. Give it a week, and it will look better."

We ate in silence after that, both of us lost in our private thoughts. I still couldn't believe the note I had found, or the other evidence I had seen, but for some reason it shocked me less than I would have thought it would. I had been a wreck for over two weeks now, and this latest revelation, rather than reinforcing my grief, somehow gave me a feeling of peace.

Glancing up, I found myself staring into Irene's blue eyes. She was studying me with quiet intensity. "What?" I asked.

"What are you planning to do today?" she asked.

My first impulse was to tell her I would finish one of my projects—alone—but I stopped myself. That wouldn't do. I needed to turn over a new leaf. My daughter was still new to her power, and she had much to learn. It wasn't the time for me to retreat into my private world.

"We," I said with special emphasis, "will be doing some enchanting today."

"I know next to nothing about enchanting," said Irene frankly. "Should I change my clothes?" As per her usual, she was wearing a dress that was more a thing of fashion than practicality.

"Probably," I answered with a nod.

Fifteen minutes later, she met me in my workshop wearing a pair of linen breeches and an old shirt. "Where did you get those?" I asked, indicating her clothes.

"They're Conall's," she replied matter-of-factly, as though borrowing her brother's clothes was something she did every day.

I shrugged and got down to business, handing her a thin metal rod. "This is what you'll be working on," I told her.

"Great. What's it for?"

"You're going to make a rune channel, one of the all-around most versatile tools a wizard can have," I explained. "With it, you can channel power with greater intensity and defeat protections that raw magic simply can't overcome, such as enchanted defenses or spellwoven shields. It will also increase your range."

"You said it was versatile," complained Irene. "It sounds like it's only versatile as a weapon."

"Well, yes, but it's also invaluable for creating other enchantments."

"How?"

Reaching into my pocket, I pulled out a delicate silver stylus. "This is a rune channel," I told her. "If you look closely, you can see the tiny runes etched along the length."

Irene gaped. "They're so small! How did you make them so fine?"

I smiled. "With a rune channel."

"I don't think you could make them that small with something this size," she said, waving the wand I had given her.

"You're right," I admitted. "To get down to something this size, you have to make a succession of smaller rune channels, but for most purposes, that wand will be the perfect size. You've seen the two that Elaine keeps with her."

"How come you never use a wand?" asked Irene. "I only see you with your staff most of the time."

"The staff suits me most of the time," I explained. "When I need to do small work, I use the stylus. I rarely need anything in between."

My daughter looked thoughtful. "That makes sense. I think I'd rather have a stylus too, and a staff."

"A staff is rather cumbersome to carry around," I declared. "That's one reason Elaine prefers the wands."

"Not if I use a magic bag, like you do," countered Irene.

"Do you have one?" I asked, my eyes glinting with mischief.

She stared at my belt, which held several such pouches, then started to say something but stopped. After a minute, she answered, "I'm guessing you won't just give me one."

I smiled.

We spent the next several hours working on her wand. I wish I could say it was a magical time of father-daughter bonding, but the reality was far more boring. This was the simplest type of enchanting, and I had chosen it because it made learning the fundamentals easier. Years before, I had done rather badly trying to teach Moira, first attempting to teach her the theory, then the practice. The result had been intense boredom for her, and consequently, a lack of interest.

This time I was determined to teach by doing, explaining her failures when asked, and offering helpful advice when it was wanted. It was vastly more interesting for Irene, but for me it meant a lot more time watching and wishing I could speed things up.

During some of the longer periods of empty time, I worked on the armor for Alyssa. Penny's was nearly complete, but since the enchantment hadn't been added to it yet, it was still possible for me to rework the metal, shaping some of the pieces to fit the younger woman's measurements.

I had considered starting completely fresh, rather than using the armor I had made for my wife, but when I really thought it over that seemed foolish. What would I do with Penny's armor? She had never worn it. Would I turn it into a memento, put it up in some sort of shrine? I had enough reminders already. Every square inch of our home was a reminder, full to the brim with the possessions we had collected together over the years. Even the nicks and dents in the furniture reminded me of her.

"Dad?"

Looking up, I saw Irene had a question written on her features. "Mm hmm?"

"Why can't I just resize this?" she asked.

"What do you mean?"

"The enchantment is the same, whether it's on a staff or that little stylus. Why can't I just resize it?" she said, rewording her question.

It was an interesting thought, but the answer was simple. "Because the substrate has to change too,"

I answered. "It supports the runes and provides the proper geometry for them. You might be able to change the size of the runes themselves, but they're etched into a solid material."

"What if you got rid of the solid part, the metal?" she suggested.

I stared at her for a moment, puzzled. *That wouldn't work,* I thought immediately, but then I felt a nagging doubt. *Or would it?*

"You said enchanting was the same as She'Har spellweaving, right?" said Irene. "They don't use materials for their spellweaves."

Spellweaving used different symbols and geometry, but the essence was the same. "But we need them to support the runes until everything is in place," I said automatically, "since our minds can't hold so many separate elements at one time."

Irene held up her nearly finished wand. "The metal is needed to create it, but what if you melted it afterward, let the metal dribble away until only the runes were left?"

Intrigued, I gave it some serious thought. Eventually, I replied, "The runes are intangible. You couldn't hold it with your hand."

Irene looked disappointed. "Oh."

"But," I went on, "if you created a second enchantment to mimic the form of the metal, something solid, like a shield enchantment, it could support the rune channel and enable you to hold it in your hands. You'd have to make both before you removed the metal."

"So, it *could* be done," said Irene, pleased.

"We'd need to add elements to control the size, allowing it to expand and contract according to need,"

I said, warming to the problem. Clearing the armor off my work table, I waved at her to bring her wand over. "Let's try something…"

The rest of the day blurred away as we worked. Lunch was forgotten, and it wasn't until well after dark that our stomachs were finally able to force us to stop.

 # CHAPTER 5

The next day I spent several hours teaching Lynaralla the basics of breakfast, paying special attention to how I worded the information I gave her. It paid to be careful—otherwise there might be another raw rat incident, or something even more horrifying that I hadn't yet imagined.

Alyssa returned from her break looking in even better health than usual. Knowing her father, I imagined that their idea of quality time had probably involved a lot of sweating and probably weapons for added excitement. I had recently granted her and Cyhan both dragons, but while he was used to the benefits and perils of enhanced strength, she wasn't, so their training had likely had a lot to do with adjusting to being so strong you could break your own bones if you mishandled the opening of a door.

I turned Lynaralla's cooking lesson over to Alyssa, since Matthew and Karen showed up shortly after Alyssa did.

"Where have you been?" I asked my son, fully aware that with Karen's ability to teleport at will, he could have traveled the world several times over without me even knowing he had left his room.

"We went to Lancaster," he answered promptly. "Well, where Lancaster used to be anyway."

That response might have worried me a few weeks earlier, when the region was covered in primeval forest and inhabited by a dozen varieties of deadly animals, but

I had taken care of that problem already. The area was a volcanic nightmare now. Not an active volcano mind you, a temporary one. I had used my metamagic to draw magma from the depths of the earth, and now the place was a wasteland of rapidly cooling igneous rock.

"I'm assuming you learned something," I prompted. Matthew wasn't the sort to mention his doings unless he had something to tell about them.

He nodded. "Zephyr flew Karen and me around the entire perimeter. There's a dimensional boundary that surrounds it, sort of an interface between our world and whatever world that place came from. The site near Cantley had the same boundary, and both were hexagons of identical size as best I can tell. The one in the northern wastes was the same as well."

I whistled—or tried to; my whistling skills were rudimentary at best. "At least they fit some sort of pattern. If we could just figure out what it means."

"That's not the worst of it," said Matthew, glancing at Karen and then back at me. "At the points of the hexagons, I noticed more boundary interface lines pointing outward from each hexagon. It was so faint I didn't notice it at first, but once I followed one, I realized they form a honeycomb pattern."

My conscious mind seized up while my subconscious processed what he had said, but Karen broke the silence, "He *wanted* to cross over one of the boundaries, to see what was on the other side, but I convinced him we needed to talk to you first." The tone of her words made it plain what she thought of that idea.

I was grateful that she had talked him out of it, while simultaneously amused by her irritation. My son might just survive in this crazy world if he could keep from driving Karen away. That thought made me remember Penny. She had always struggled to knock some sense into me. *What will I do without her?*

Matthew ignored the remark and went on, "Karen took us all over Lothion, and knowing what to look for, I spotted similar faint dimensional boundaries everywhere we went."

Frowning, I stared at him. "So, you're implying that…"

"I think the entire world is covered with a honeycomb pattern of dimensional boundaries," said Matthew, finishing my thought for me.

I blinked. My son and I locked gazes for a long minute, as we both considered the implications. The hexagonal shapes were key, for they indicated a tie to She'Har spellweaving. Finally, I said, "We knew they created a pocket dimension to protect themselves from ANSIS, but this—this is unbelievable."

"It beggars the imagination," agreed Matthew. "But now that I've seen it, it makes some sense."

"Hey!" broke in Karen. "I appreciate that you two are having a moment, but it would help if you explained some things for those of us who don't have the benefit of a headful of ancient alien knowledge."

I turned to her. "When the She'Har first came to this world, it was to escape from ANSIS, but they knew that they would eventually be found, since their enemy had acquired the ability to bridge the divide between different dimensions," I began.

Karen nodded; she had already heard this part.

I went on, "We thought that they had created a separate dimension, to prevent this one from being directly reachable, putting powerful guardians there to keep ANSIS from progressing farther if they did enter that extra dimension. They named those guardians the 'kionthara,' which means 'gatekeepers' in our language, though the people of our world called them the Dark Gods."

"But now we know that isn't what they did at all," said Matthew, breaking in.

I nodded. "Now that I think about it, that story just wasn't possible. The amount of power it would take to create a pocket dimension large enough to encapsulate our world—it just isn't practical. No, that isn't the right word. Practical doesn't cover it—it's orders of magnitude from being practical. It was impossible. They could never get enough power to do something that big."

"So, what *did* they do?" asked Karen.

"They took this dimension and split it into two parts," I answered.

Matthew shook his head. "Not the entire dimension, just this world. The entire thing would be equally impossible."

That made sense. "Alright, so probably just this world," I agreed. "They didn't create a new dimension at all. They divided up this world into hexagonal pieces, and then used them to create the *appearance* of a separate dimension within the original. Sort of."

Karen looked very confused. "But Matthew found the borders. If it's all part of the same dimension, how could he cross into the other one? There have to be two. Right?"

"Not two—thousands, maybe tens of thousands," corrected Matt. "They divided the world, using a massive spellweave. Half of the hexagonal shaped cells were hidden inside small pocket dimensions that would fit them. The other half were left in the original dimension. The interfaces are designed such that the thousands of small pocket dimensions are connected, so they seem like one world. Those same interfaces stitched the pieces left behind together into another world, but the two are actually the same. It's just been divided into pieces and put back together differently."

"That's insane," declared Karen, and I was inclined to agree with her. "Do you really know this? Or are you just making up wild theories?"

"Well," I admitted, "at this point it's really just a theory."

"But it makes sense," put in Matthew. "We need more information." Looking at me, he asked, "Have you started reading the Erollith sculptures they brought back yet?"

The question embarrassed me a little. It had been weeks, but I hadn't spent more than a few minutes looking at them. Penny's death had derailed my plans in that regard. It's hard to study anything when you're grieving. "I've barely begun," I told them. "There's so much that it could take me years to read through it all."

Irene wandered in. She had been in the kitchen watching Alyssa and Lynaralla but had finally gotten bored. When her eyes landed on Matthew, her face brightened. "Look who has returned. I was starting to wonder if you still lived here."

Matthew rolled his eyes. "I was only gone for a couple of days."

"I haven't seen you in a week," groused Irene. "You never leave your room." Then she gave Karen a pointed look until the young woman began to blush.

"That's not—" stammered Karen. "It isn't what you…"

I wanted to laugh, but I kept my tone serious. "Don't bully her, Rennie. She may be your only hope of becoming an aunt." Karen's blush went from delicate to purple as the blood rushed to her blue-tinted cheeks.

"Dad!" warned Matthew, uncharacteristically protective. Secretly, I approved of his reaction.

"Alright, alright, I won't tease her," I said, submitting quickly.

Irene broke the awkward silence by changing the subject. "Dad started teaching me enchanting today," she said proudly.

Her brother frowned slightly. "You almost sound as if you enjoyed it. Moira used to say she thought she might die from boredom."

Irene smiled in that special way she had, the one that seemed to light up a room. In some ways she reminded me more of Penny than any of my other children. "It was a little boring at first, but after we got started, I realized it's actually quite interesting."

Matthew was surprised. "If this is your first day, you must've been working on rune channels, and you found them interesting?" He had been the only one of my kids who had really taken to enchanting, but now I could see his interest piqued by the fact that he might not be alone.

"You should see what she came up with," I put in. "She thought of something that never occurred to either of us."

"Oh really?" said Matthew. "I need to see this."

We went to the workshop then, and Karen and I stood off to one side while Irene proudly showed her brother what she had been working on, explaining her idea and how we were trying to implement it. I watched my son's initial skepticism turn to enthusiasm as he quickly realized she really was on to something new. Karen glanced at me helplessly; she still hadn't learned much on the topic of enchanting, so all of it was over her head currently.

For myself, I found my heart swelling with pride as I watched the two of them conversing. Ordinarily, Matthew had little use for his younger sister, but she had impressed him, bringing a new perspective to his favorite subject. *I wish you could see this, Penny,* I reflected, but even the sadness of that thought couldn't dim my joy at the moment.

Eventually, Karen remarked on the fact that she still hadn't begun learning enchanting, and Matthew was forced to begin explaining the subject. That led to an extended discussion between the four of us, and while I thought my son's teaching style was rough, I was surprised by his patience with their questions. After a while, I went back to working on Alyssa's armor and left the three of them to what had essentially become a small class on enchanting.

The afternoon passed pleasantly, and for the first time in weeks I didn't feel as though I was drowning in grief. When Alyssa came out later to inform us that it was time for the evening meal, I forced her to wait while I double checked some of my previous measurements. Then we called a break and went to eat.

Moira showed up in the middle of supper, and the conversation turned to exactly where she had been and what she had been doing over the past week. She seemed mildly embarrassed about her weeklong retreat from the family, but no one was tactless enough to confront her about it. Once the food was finished, Alyssa started to clear the table, and the rest of us retreated to the living room.

"Did you learn anything of interest in Dunbar?" I asked.

My oldest daughter shook her head. "Not really. The World Road is operating as expected, and Halam is probably on the verge of a boom in business now that they can trade freely with Lothion and Gododdin, but you expected that. Gerold is settling into his role as king, and while there were a few hiccups, I think the government will remain stable."

That caught my interest, and I watched her face carefully, wondering if she had broken the rules again and 'adjusted' anyone who might have been chafing under the rule of their new king. Gerold had been a minor noble before her intervention in the neighboring kingdom. Then Moira had killed their king and used her abilities to place her friend in power.

She caught my eye, and understanding my question, gave a subtle shake of her head to indicate that she had behaved herself. I was glad for that, since I couldn't really ask the question in front of the entire family.

"Where is Conall?" asked Moira, having noticed his absence at dinner.

I sighed, but Irene leapt to answer the question, "He's still in Albamarl, playing champion for the Queen."

"He isn't playing," corrected Matthew. "As much as I hate to admit it, he acted very bravely protecting the Queen during the attack."

"That still doesn't excuse him for abandoning his family after..." Irene's voice tapered off. No one wanted to say it. *After Mom died.*

Moira stepped in diplomatically, "We're all dealing with it in our own way. I can't say much. I've been hiding in Dunbar for a week."

Matthew's face grew smug. "Thank goodness I stayed home to keep an eye on Dad."

While technically true—he *had* been here for most of the week—the statement was an outrageous boast, since he had kept himself locked up in his own world the entire time. Irene immediately protested, "You! You and Karen were in your room most of the time, doing whatever you pleased!"

Karen blushed yet again. "It wasn't like that! He was as upset as everyone else."

"I was not," argued Matt. "I was reminiscing quietly. Mourning, if you want to call it that."

Karen's eyes flashed momentarily, and she started to open her mouth, but she shut it quickly again and pursed her lips.

She almost said he was crying, Moira sent to me mentally, *but she stopped herself to avoid embarrassing him.*

The conversation moved on to more pleasant topics after that. Matthew and I played a few rounds of chess while the others played cards. In short, it was nice. It was the best evening at home any of us had had since losing Penny. We played and talked, and finally, when it grew late, everyone went to bed.

My happiness died there, as soon as the door closed behind me and I was confronted with the empty room. It was still and quiet, like a tomb.

I undressed and sank into bed, extinguishing the magical lights with a soft word and letting the darkness enfold me. Our marriage bed had become a place of cold loneliness. After an unknown period, I fell asleep.

 **C**HAPTER 6

The next morning I woke with more than my usual energy, at least more than I'd had recently. After washing my face, I dressed and went to the kitchen, where I found Alyssa already making a start at breakfast. "Morning," she greeted me.

"Morning," I returned, and then I stepped up and made myself useful.

"You don't have to do that," she reminded me as I put a pot of water over the fire for the porridge. "It's my job, after all."

Looking at her from the side of my eye, I answered, "The nice thing about being the master of the house is that I can do whatever I want. Today I want to help."

Alyssa dipped her head respectfully. "Thank you."

Before breakfast was ready, I felt a new presence enter the house through the portal that led to the Queen's chambers in Albamarl. A second later, I recognized the aythar of the newcomer. It was Rose.

Is she here for breakfast? I wondered. It didn't seem likely. We hadn't seen each other since the funeral, and considering how I had spoken to her the last time we talked, I wasn't sure I was looking forward to seeing her. *I should apologize.*

"You look industrious," said Rose as she entered the kitchen. My back was turned, as I had long ago learned to pretend not to notice people until they spoke or came into my line of sight. It made people uncomfortable if I was always waiting for them when they entered a room.

"Rose," I said, turning around. "Uh—are you here for breakfast?"

"If you have enough," she replied politely. "I mainly came to say hello to everyone. I've been gone awhile, after all." She was clad in a powder-blue gown that shimmered with silver embroidery and a modest lace trim. It matched her hair and eyes perfectly, but then everything she wore always seemed to suit her. It never ceased to amaze me that anyone could be so well dressed at such an early hour. I did well to have clothes on.

"I'm sure there's enough," I said immediately, while Alyssa discreetly added an extra handful of oats to the porridge.

"Good morning," said Irene, yawning as she entered. Then her eyes lit on our visitor. "Rose!" She hugged Rose tightly. "You came!"

"What?" I asked.

Irene flushed slightly, but Rose answered quickly, "Rennie reminded me I should visit, when she came to the capital yesterday."

I should have suspected that my daughter had arranged the visit, but it surprised me anyway. Probably because I had been so self-absorbed lately.

"Well, of course, you're always welcome," I told her, trying to keep my voice natural, but I could tell I sounded slightly stiff.

Breakfast was quick, and the chatter fairly subdued, in contrast to the previous evening's warmth. It was partly because it was morning, and none of us were really morning people, but I thought it was also Rose's presence.

She had been my wife's closest friend, and seeing her now after her absence made us all feel as though Penny might show up at any moment to chat with her.

After it was over Matthew, Lynaralla, Irene, and Karen went to my workshop to continue the lessons on enchanting and begin sorting through the Erollith sculptures. Alyssa started her routine cleaning duties, and Rose and I were left alone.

We had been friends for decades, been through unimaginable dangers together, and helped raise each other's children, yet the silence that stretched out between us was almost painful. I found myself toying with the teacup in my hand, and when I finally looked up, I was caught by Rose's piercing blue eyes.

I held her gaze without looking away for an unknown time. There was compassion in those eyes, a shared sorrow, and no small amount of sympathy, but her lips remained firmly pressed together. She said nothing.

At last I found my tongue, and said what was long overdue, "I'm sorry."

Considering the situation, the stress I had been under, the grief of losing my wife, many people would have just let me off the hook for my previous bad behavior with a simple 'don't worry about it.' Rose wasn't one of those people. No matter how badly I had been hurting, my words had been completely out of line.

She responded with honesty, "Thank you, but your apology is not accepted—not yet, anyway."

"I shouldn't have said those things," I added. "I didn't really mean them."

Rose sighed. "You know what they say about 'truth in wine'? The same applies to when people are overwrought.

We say things we shouldn't, but that doesn't mean they aren't true, or sometimes that we didn't *wish* they were true."

In a fit of anger, I had told her that now that Penny and all our shared friends were dead, there was no *us*, referring to our long-time friendship. There was obviously no way that could be true, so what was she implying? Who was I kidding? I knew exactly what I had meant. I had been referring to the unspoken attraction that had long underlain our friendship. Remaining friends with Rose, even if nothing ever came of it, felt like a betrayal of my wife. It wasn't Rose's fault, but I had lashed out at her because of it.

Now she had done it, she had put the ugly truth in front of me. How could I respond to that? "Uh, Rose, I honestly didn't mean it. I was just—"

She held up one finger, stopping me. "No, Mordecai, let's not brush this under the rug. You meant exactly what you said, so let's deal with that."

"It wasn't fair of me to—"

"No, it wasn't fair, but that's not the point," countered Rose. "The point is that you're afraid that now that Penny is gone I'll take this as some sort of opportunity. Do you honestly think that I've been a widow all these years because I was sitting around waiting for *you*, like some vulture? That I've been waiting in the wings, pretending to be Penelope's friend, pretending to love your children, pretending to be your friend, all so I could someday snap you up as my reward?"

"Well, no, of course not," I muttered, unsure what to say. I hadn't really looked at it from that angle, but now that she phrased it that way, it was obvious that deep down, that's exactly what I had been thinking, consciously or otherwise.

Rose's carefully controlled demeanor was beginning to show signs of stress. Her fingers trembled, and her eyes were growing puffy. "That's exactly what you implied. Do you have any idea how hard it was to remain here after Dorian died? How painful it was to watch you and Penny, when my own family was shattered? I didn't do that for some stupid romantic interest! I did it for Penny, I did it for Gram and Carissa, I did it for you and your children as well. And until your words the other day, I've never regretted it."

Well damn, I really am a jerk, I thought. Rose's eyes were damp, but I couldn't decide whether she was about to cry or come at me with her claws out. With Penny, I had never been uncertain—it was always claws. Well, sometimes it was tears and claws, but claws were always in there somewhere. After a moment, I realized my mouth had fallen slightly agape. I was mute, without a clue what I could say to make things better.

Rose helped, turning her head to hide her tears. She waved one hand at me. "I'm done. Now you can say what you wanted to say."

Feeling awkward and incredibly stupid, I got the words out again, "I'm sorry."

"Apology accepted," she answered.

She started to dab at her face with her sleeves, but I caught her wrist and fished a handkerchief from my pocket. "Here, use this."

"Thank you," she said, sniffing. Then I started to hug her, but she shot me a warning glance.

I froze, and then said, "I'm not making any assumptions. We're still friends, right?"

She nodded and then embraced me. "We're not just friends, we're family. You'd better not forget it in the future."

"I won't," I assured her.

After a brief moment, she pushed me away. "There are some other things I need to talk to you about, privately."

I looked around to remind her we were already alone. "Go ahead," I told her.

"You're certain no one can hear us?" she asked.

"Not much is certain in a houseful of wizards," I observed.

Rose walked into the hallway and led me to my bedroom. "There's still a privacy ward on it, right?"

I nodded and opened the door to let her in, shutting the door behind us. "We have complete privacy," I assured her, before amending my statement, "unless Moira's planted one of her tiny spellbeasts in here again. What are you so nervous about?"

Smoothing her skirts self-consciously, Rose took a deep breath. "It's not that I don't want your children to hear this, but I'd rather you know first." Her eyes briefly scanned the room as she spoke.

Knowing Rose as well as I did, I wondered what conclusions she might draw from the state of my room. At the moment, it was uncommonly tidy, as a result of whatever had happened the night before. I walked to the dressing table and picked up Penny's note and carefully folded it up, placing it in my pocket. Whatever Rose might guess, I wasn't ready to talk about it.

Rose was kind enough to keep her conclusions to herself. Instead, she kept to her subject. "Tyrion is making serious inroads in Lothion's politics."

"He's already ingratiated himself as the savior of the capital," I agreed. "It's to be expected that he'll have his time in the light."

"Unfortunately, he does not seem to be as inept at politics as I expected, based on your previous descriptions of him," said Rose. "He has already made several allies among the other peers, particularly with the Prince-Consort."

"Leomund?" Somehow, I wasn't surprised. "Birds of a feather, they say."

Rose frowned at me. "There's more to this than can be seen at a first glance. Have you heard any of the rumors concerning Leomund?"

"I know he's an asshole," I said glibly. "But that isn't a rumor. It's established fact."

"His hunting trips are well known to be a polite excuse to get away from the capital," said Rose. "But the game he hunts walks on two legs rather than four."

"Oh, that."

She arched her brows in surprise. "You already knew?"

I felt mildly gratified to have known something before Rose. "Ari told me a month ago. She isn't particularly concerned about it. In fact, I think she would rather he stay out of the palace entirely. There's no love lost between the two of them."

Agitated by my lack of worry, Rose walked to my wardrobe and looked inside, examining the clothes hanging there. "It's far more serious than that, Mordecai. This isn't some landed noble cheating on his wife. It's the Prince-Consort, and his dalliances weaken the Queen's position, eroding the faith that the rest of the lords have in her. Surely you see that?"

"Not to make light of it," I began, "but many of them are guilty of the same. Who are they to judge her?"

"She's the Queen," said Rose emphatically, closing the wardrobe and turning back to face me. "Imagine if King Edward's wife had cheated on him, or if Genevieve had slept with other men while James was king?"

Looking at it in that light, it did seem more serious. I was already aware of the double standard. Lords were almost expected to stray beyond the bounds of marital propriety, but their ladies were not.

Rose continued, "As Queen, Ariadne holds the power in their relationship, although Leomund is a man, his position as her subordinate makes his betrayal of their wedding vows far more harmful. Not only that, but the man has not done much to keep his adventures a secret. He practically brags about them among some of the other lords. These aren't discreet affairs with one or two women. As far as I can discover, he's been bringing a wide variety of young women to his hunting lodge."

"Young women?"

"Very young," added Rose. "Scandalously young."

"What would you propose Ariadne do about it?" I asked.

"Ideally, she would send troops to his lodge and catch him in the act. Embarrass him publicly, divorce him, and then imprison him. Technically his betrayal counts as treason, since she is the reigning monarch. Edward would probably have gone as far as beheading his wife if she had been caught in something like this. Either way, she needs to show her strength, but instead she seems content to pretend the problem doesn't exist. And that brings us to our other problem."

"Which is?"

"Tyrion seems to be getting very close to your cousin, and she doesn't seem to mind the attention," said Rose flatly.

That was a bitter pill to swallow. "It probably isn't what you think," I responded hopefully.

"Mort," said Rose, giving me a solid stare. "Think about who is telling you this. Do you really think I would mistake the signs?"

"Is she still wearing the pendant I gave her?" I asked. Rose nodded.

"Then he can't manipulate her emotions. Surely she'll be wise enough to make the right decision on her own."

"Don't be so sure of that, Mordecai," said Rose. "Contrary to your juvenile belief that women are unlikely to stray, my gender is just as prone to hormone-induced stupidity as yours is. Also, there's a chance that your ancestor has found some way around the protection your pendant provides."

That gave me pause. "What do you mean?"

She took a deep breath to steady herself before continuing, "I suspect that Tyrion may have tampered with my emotions before the meeting."

"Tampered?" Immediately my mind flashed to the things Tyrion had done in his youth, and my eyes traveled downward unconsciously to study Rose's dress. It was a silly reflex, as though by studying the state of her dress I could determine whether the fiend had laid a hand on my friend. "What happened?"

"I experienced something I'd rather not describe. I can't definitively say it was caused by his tampering, but at my age I think I have a better handle on my emotions than that. It was entirely unexpected," she said carefully, her cheeks flushing faintly.

Hot rage flashed through me at the thought of Tyrion inducing some sort of artificial lust in Rose. My fists clenched involuntarily, and I struggled to contain my temper. "He'd have to be a Centyr to manage something like that," I muttered.

"Let's not jump to conclusions," cautioned Rose. "I'm not even sure it was tampering."

"Of course it was," I snarled. It had to be, though for a moment I felt a wave of self-doubt wash over me. My ancestor was certainly attractive enough, in a primal sort of way. Perhaps what had happened to Penny, and now Rose, was entirely natural. I took a moment to collect my wits, glancing at Rose with some embarrassment. "Conall is there," I said suddenly.

"Pardon?"

"My son, Conall," I repeated. "I've been a little annoyed about him spending all his time in the capital, but I think now we can use it to our advantage."

Rose caught on quickly, "He wasn't in the meeting, and the room was warded. He could detect any use of magic if he was present, couldn't he?"

I nodded with a grim smile. "I'll talk to him, make sure he knows to take his new role seriously. So long as he stays with Ariadne whenever another mage is around, they won't be able to attempt anything."

"That's an excellent idea," agreed Rose. "Now let me catch you up on Tyrion's proposal during the meeting."

"His proposal?"

She smiled. "We've only discussed my assumptions thus far. Let me tell you about his plan to protect the kingdom from ANSIS."

Rose began talking, and I found myself listening intently. As she described Tyrion's proposed solution to ANSIS, I found myself appreciating his plan. My ancestor certainly didn't lack for big ideas. He might just be instrumental in keeping the world free of invaders, if I didn't kill him first.

 CHAPTER 7

The rest of the day I spent delving into the secrets held within the Erollith sculptures that Lynaralla had brought back, and after Irene and Karen had gotten tired of learning enchanting, Matthew and Lynaralla joined me, since they were the only others who could read them. The three of us split up, reading separate sculptures, but even after hours of work it felt as though we were only barely scratching the surface.

There were more than fifty of the sculptures in the storeroom attached to my workshop, and each one represented days or weeks of work to read. It would take me more than a year to get through them all, and even with the three of us working, it would take months.

It wouldn't have been so bad if we had had some way of knowing what we could skip, but to know that, we would have had to know exactly what we were looking for. The clues to what the Illeniel She'Har had originally done to our world could be hidden within any of the writings.

It was enough to drive a man mad. When I went to bed that night, my frustration was enough to make me forget how empty the bedroom felt—almost.

The next morning, I made an early start, relatively speaking. I intended to go to Albamarl and have a talk with my younger son. I had told the others what I meant to do, and Irene caught me before I could leave through the portal.

"Dad, wait," she said abruptly.

"Hmm?"

She handed me a leather bag stuffed with something bulky and relatively lightweight. "Be nice when you see him."

I narrowed my eyes. "What do you mean?"

Irene studied her feet. "I wasn't very kind when I saw him last, but I've done some thinking since then. I think you should be supportive. Conall may seem like he's running away, but he actually craves approval. He's trying to prove himself."

Reaching out, I lifted her chin to look in her eyes. "And?"

"If you yell at him, he'll be less likely to come home," she added. "Mom always said you catch more flies with honey than vinegar."

Actually, I was pretty sure I had been the one to use that phrase more frequently, but it was a common saying, so I wasn't about to quibble over it. "What's in the bag?"

"Surcoats," answered Irene. "They're Matthew's, but he never uses them. I yelled at him the other day for not wearing them while he represents the family as the Queen's Champion. If you give them to him, and tell him you're proud of him, he'll probably wear them."

I stared at my daughter in open admiration. *When did she become so wise?* I wondered. She certainly didn't get that kind of maturity from me. I had been pretty wild and reckless until my mid-twenties. Taking the bag from her hands, I dragged her into a hug. "Thank you, Rennie. This is a brilliant idea. I don't know what I'd do without you."

"Don't tell him the surcoats were my idea," she cautioned.

I smirked. "He's going to know they're Matthew's."

"Tell him Matthew suggested it," she said with a grin.

"Does Matthew know you've robbed him?"

"I'll tell him in the workshop later. He'll go along with it," she said confidently.

With that, I left, stepping through the portal into Ariadne's private suite. She wasn't present, so I made my way out and went in search of my wayward son. By some luck, Harold was the first person I encountered whom I knew. "Harold!" I greeted him.

Since there was no one else in the corridor, he returned my greeting just as informally. "Mordecai!" If there had been others present, we'd have been forced to stick to more formal forms of address. "What brings you here today?" he asked.

Smiling, I got right to the point. "I'm looking for my son."

"You mean the esteemed Queen's Champion, Sir Conall?" he asked with mock seriousness.

"The same."

"He's in the training yard," replied Sir Harold. "I'll walk with you."

"Training yard?" I said querulously. "Do you have him swinging at the pells? I know he's a knight now, but I don't think it would serve anyone's interests if he wastes his talents with a sword when he's a wizard."

"Tyrion is giving him some pointers," said Harold.

"What?" I burst out.

"It's not what you think. Come see," said Harold placatingly.

It took me a moment to regain my composure, and then I followed him through the palace until we reached the training yard. The entire place was a web of privacy wards and magical barriers set up by Gareth

Gaelyn and Elaine Prathion years ago, so I wasn't able to spot my son with my magesight until we left the building and entered the yard.

What I saw angered and surprised me. I didn't know what to think. The training field was a wreck: Great divots had been torn out of the ground leaving holes of widely varying sizes, along with corresponding mounds of earth scattered thither and yon. My son stood in the middle of it all, dirty, ragged, and breathing heavily.

But I couldn't see any wounds on him; otherwise my resolve to keep things friendly might have gone out the window.

Tyrion circled him, stalking the perimeter like a predator. For the first few seconds that I watched, things were calm. Nothing was happening. But then my ancestor sent a series of rapid-fire attacks at Conall, bolts of pure force that were so potent they seemed to rip the very air apart.

My son deflected each of them in turn, even though they happened so quickly as to almost be simultaneous. His body twitched slightly, and his arms jerked as though he might try to use his hands to do the deflecting, but it was his power that did the work. An outside observer would have seen little without magesight, but the thunderous cracks and booms as he countered each blow shook the walls around the training field, and more divots appeared in the earth where some of Tyrion's attacks were driven into the ground.

Tyrion had noticed our arrival by then, for he held up one hand to indicate that he was calling a halt to things and then started walking in our direction. Conall walked over as well, meeting my eyes evenly as he came, as though challenging me to disapprove of what he had been doing.

Patience, I need patience, I repeated to myself silently.

Conall reached me first since he was closer to begin with, greeting me once he was within ten feet, "Father."

"I'm glad to see you are well," I said.

"You came yesterday, but I never saw you," he returned. "I wondered if you were avoiding me."

"Not at all," I answered. "I was busy, which is why I came back today—to see how you were doing. Irene said she saw you, though."

Conall grimaced. "It wasn't much of a meeting. She nagged at me the entire time."

Smiling, I joked, "She takes her sisterly duties very seriously."

My son looked at me for a moment, uncertain how to respond. Finally, he gave me a crooked grin. "Yeah, she does," he agreed.

Ahh, the awkwardness of youth, I thought. *I don't miss that phase of life at all.* Thinking on what Irene had said, and what I now saw before me, I couldn't help but think she was right. My son was seeking his independence and ready to show his teeth if necessary, while at the same time what he truly wanted was my acceptance and approval.

Tyrion had reached us by then. "Your cub is turning out to be quite a lion," he observed. "He's more aggressive and confident than any of mine were."

I didn't like the comparison, but now wasn't the time to start another pissing match. "I'm quite proud of him," I said loudly, keeping my eyes on Conall's. "Being made Queen's Champion at such an age is a rare honor, but I never doubted his courage." I did my best to sound sincere, though in truth I would never shake the image of Conall as my little boy.

Harold snorted. "And you were worried we'd have him out here swinging a blade."

Tyrion lifted one arm. "The only blades out here are the ones we make for ourselves."

Don't kill him, don't kill him. I repeated that mantra in my head several times. "If you gentlemen don't mind, I'd like a few minutes alone with my son. I haven't seen him in over a week."

The two other men nodded, and I led Conall back into the palace. As we walked, he said, "You don't mind me practicing with Lord Tyrion, do you?"

I could tell he was nervous, but he was doing his best to hide it. "You know pretty well how your mother and I feel about the man," I answered, then wanted to kick myself for the phrasing. *'Your mother and I.'* It was the habit of a lifetime. "However, I can't stop you from learning. As long as you're careful, I don't mind. Just don't make the mistake of trusting him." *And please don't look up to him,* I added mentally.

Conall nodded. "I haven't forgotten, but I thought it would be foolish not to learn from the best while I have the chance."

I almost choked at that. *The best?* "Tyrion has a long history of violence," I agreed. "He survived hundreds of battles against other mages when he was young, but he also has difficulty knowing when to show restraint. He mortally wounded one of his daughters while training her. Make sure you're careful."

My son piped up, "I think he's matured since then."

It made me want to laugh, listening to him make judgements about the maturity of others, but I kept it to myself. "Learn what you can from him, but don't make the mistake of wanting to emulate him."

"I won't, Dad," said Conall. His voice was sounding more hopeful now. No doubt he had been expecting me to reprimand him or dress him down. Being treated with respect had caught him off-guard. "Where are we going?"

"The Queen's chambers," I replied.

"Why?"

"There's a privacy ward around them," I observed. "The Queen isn't there at the moment. We can talk undisturbed, and afterward I can head home without running into any more old friends."

"Oh," said Conall. "That makes sense, I guess."

Once we had reached Ariadne's sitting room, I offered him the leather bag I had brought.

"What's this?" he asked.

"A present," I answered. "Something I think you need now that you're the Queen's Champion." I gave him a proud smile.

He opened it and immediately recognized the surcoats. "Are these Matthew's?"

"He doesn't need them. You do," I returned. "You need to wear them so everyone in the capital will know the Queen's Champion is a Cameron."

Conall smiled shyly. "Thanks, Dad."

"Don't thank me," I told him. "You earned this position for yourself. Just remember you represent your entire family while you're here."

"I'll make you proud, Dad," said my son.

"I'm already proud," I returned. "But your job is something else I wanted to talk to you about."

"What about it?" he asked.

"Well, originally I had wanted to you to come home. I still have a lot to teach you. You haven't even begun to learn the basics of enchanting yet, but given the present circumstances, I've decided maybe it is for the best for you to stay by the Queen, at least for a while."

Conall frowned. "Because of ANSIS?"

"That's certainly a concern, but it isn't my only concern. My other fear is that someone may try to interfere with the Queen's mind or emotions," I said honestly.

"You mean with magic?"

I nodded.

"But the only wizards in the capital, besides me, are Tyrion and Gareth Gaelyn," protested Conall. "Neither of them would…"

I held up a finger. "Just keep an eye on her. Try not to let her be alone with either of them."

His eyes were wide as he stared back at me. "You don't really think one of them would try something on the Queen?!"

Looking at him seriously, I said, "I'm not making any assumptions when it comes to the Queen's safety. You did well when I sent you here. Extremely well. Remember that your loyalty to the Queen comes first. You are *her* champion. You should take your role very seriously. Even without ANSIS to worry about, she has a multitude of enemies, and most of them are also her vassals. In politics, your enemy will often be standing beside you with a smile on his face."

That wasn't half bad. If Rose had heard me, she might even have been impressed. It wasn't that I was clueless about politics—I just hated the subject, but I had been forced to learn quite a bit about it over the last few decades.

Conall straightened and dipped his head briefly. "You can count on me, Father."

"I am. While you're here, you're my eyes and ears. Try to learn how the court works. Don't take anything for granted," I told him. "And make damn sure that no one with magical abilities is alone with the Queen. For that matter, make sure no one without them is alone with her either, unless one of her guards is with her."

"What if she orders me out of the room?" he asked, warming to his new mission. "Sometimes she wants privacy."

I shrugged. "There's no helping it if she makes it an order, but don't be afraid to let her know your concern if she gives you an order that makes you worry for her safety. The best servants are those who share their minds, and a good liege will respect that."

"Should I tell her about this conversation?"

"No reason not to," I said. "She's your liege, so you can't keep anything important from her anyway. It will make your job easier if she knows what you're thinking." As I told him that, I couldn't help but remember the nightmare I had been for my own guards in the past. *Poor Harold,* I thought. *I nearly gave the poor man a nervous breakdown every time I snuck off.*

At least Ariadne couldn't create illusions, or teleport, and she had been monarch long enough to be well used to the constant presence of servants and guardians. If she were wise she would make good use of the opportunity and keep my son close to her. There was much to be said for the earnest sincerity of youth. She would find no treachery in Conall.

Having said everything, I embraced him again and made my way back home. Of course, the trip home entailed little more than a short walk down a hall and into what had once been a closet, and then I was home. Then I sought out my other children in the workshop and got back to work.

They were doing well on their own, and I didn't feel like reading the Erollith sculptures, so I resolved to finish Alyssa's armor. In another month, her service to me would be done, and she would likely need it, if she intended to stay close to Gram.

 CHAPTER 8

The next week was productive. I finished Alyssa's armor, which she received with more enthusiasm than I had expected. I also included a set of enchanted blades, two long knives, an arming sword, and a spear. If she intended to continue as a warrior, I would make certain she was well armed.

I wondered what Rose would say when she found out I had given her future daughter-in-law a veritable arsenal of magical weapons. The thought brought a smirk to my face. She would just have to deal with it. Being the sort of girl she was, Alyssa would have armed herself anyway, one way or another.

Irene and Karen's skill in enchanting was progressing too. They wouldn't be crafting anything exceptional for a while yet, but they could handle the essentials. In particular, the first enchantment I made certain that Irene knew was how to construct a teleport circle. I tried to get her to memorize the keys for all the important circles, but as with Moira, it proved to be difficult for her to remember them all.

Having learned from my mistakes with both Moira and Elaine, I had her promise to keep a notebook containing all the keys with her. To facilitate that, I had her craft herself a storage pouch that opened into a chest she kept in her room.

Karen learned the basics of circle creation as well, although obviously she didn't really need to use them herself, given her special gift. She was more excited to learn how to create the storage pouch, and she made one at the same time Irene made hers.

Near the end of the week, I returned to Castle Cameron, or what would be Castle Cameron once it was finished. Even after a week, it was still so hot you could feel the heat radiating from it from across the castle yard. With Irene's help as a miellte, I used my abilities once again, this time to draw forth a small river's worth of water from beneath the ground. I encapsulated the entire structure and kept the water inside and around it for several hours to try and remove some of the heat.

Afterward, I was surprised to discover it was still hot. I had underestimated the amount of heat such a massive stone structure could hold.

The next morning, after breakfast, Matthew called me aside. "Dad," he began.

"Mm hmm?" I replied.

"I want to examine the dimensional interfaces," he said simply.

We had talked about them several times over the last week, and he knew I wanted to be included the next time he did anything. Since he was the only one we knew for certain could sense them, I had been very clear I didn't want him to do anything else without me. It was probable that Lynaralla would be able to sense them since she was an Illeniel She'Har, and there was a chance that Conall and Irene might be able to as well, but currently Matthew was the only one who had any experience with such things.

"I'm in," I told him. "Is there anyone else you want to bring along?"

"Just the two of us," he answered. "It's easier if I don't have too many people around. All the talking makes it hard to think."

I almost laughed at that. My son really wasn't much of a people person. "Sounds good. Where do you want to try this?"

"Near Lancaster. It's close, and Zephyr can fly us there pretty quickly."

I could have flown us there twice as quickly without a dragon, but I didn't say that. If anything, I avoided flying too much around my children since I didn't want to encourage them to try it themselves. Losing one of them in some sort of aerial accident was the last thing I wanted. Slightly over an hour later, we were landing near the border of the igneous wasteland that sat where Lancaster had once been.

As I climbed down from Zephyr's broad back, Matthew asked a sudden question, "What happened to the door at home?"

It caught me off-guard. "Pardon?"

"The door," he repeated. "The one that looks like it melted without burning."

"Which door is that?"

"The closet door in the living room," he explained. "The frame is slightly wavy, as though it's been warped somehow, but the door matches it exactly."

I hadn't noticed, and since we rarely used that closet, I doubted anyone else had either, but I had a pretty good idea what had happened to it. "I'm not entirely sure," I stalled.

He went on, "I asked Rennie about it, and she said to ask you."

With a sigh, I decided to confess. "I had too much to drink last week."

"You lost control?" There was no tone of accusation or judgement in his question, but I couldn't help but feel guilty nonetheless.

"I think so," I admitted. "My memory of that night is a little fuzzy."

He shook his head and 'tsk'd,' but didn't say anything else.

When he didn't take up the opportunity, I decided to prod him. "That's all you have to say about it?"

Matthew shrugged. "You do stupid stuff all the time. Sometimes it works out in my favor, so what can I really say?"

"In your favor?"

"You let me travel to an alien world to risk my life for a dragon and a girl I hardly knew. That's not only stupid, it's bad parenting, but I can't complain since it worked out in my favor," he explained.

Flabbergasted, I stared at him. *Bad parenting?* Alright, I had to admit he wasn't wrong on that occasion. "You didn't really give us a choice," I reminded him. "It was let you go or alienate you by refusing and then having you sneak off anyway."

"You *assume* I would have snuck off," he corrected. "I've always been an obedient son. I might have done as I was told. A responsible parent would have ordered me to stay even if there was only a chance it would work."

Glaring at him, I responded, "You're lecturing me? I would say what I did was an example of enlightened parenting! You should be grateful I'm your father, you ungrateful whelp."

An evil smirk turned up one corner of his mouth. "You know I'm putting you on, don't you?" When I didn't answer immediately, he continued, "I'm starting to see where Conall gets his gullibility. I always thought you were smarter. Maybe age *does* make you dumber."

What a little bastard! I thought. Catching his eyes, I stared mutely back at him. I didn't blink, until my eyes began to water from the dry air. Then I turned my face away and gave my shoulders a faint shake as though I was crying.

"Hey! Dad, it was just a joke. Don't take it so seriously," said Matthew hastily, marching around me to check my expression.

Glancing up at him, I grinned. "Sucker."

"I didn't believe your poor acting for a second," he said indignantly.

I clapped him on the shoulder. "Yes, you did. Now we're even. I guess the stupid doesn't fall far from the tree."

"The *stupid* tree," he said, then he started walking. "The interface should be in this direction."

We walked for several hundred yards with Zephyr following behind us as we circled the outer edge of where the primeval forest had been. A strange feeling passed over me, and Matthew stopped, putting one hand up. "I think this is it." He walked back toward me and then stepped forward and back one step a couple of times.

It might have been my imagination, but I thought I could detect a subtle shimmer in the air near the area he was stepping across. "This is it, huh?" I said, holding my hand up as though I would try to touch it.

Matt gave me a strange look. "You can see that?"

"Just barely. I suppose it takes someone with your gift to see it any better."

"Karen couldn't sense it at all," he replied. "I can barely detect it either. I don't think you should be able to feel anything from it."

"Maybe it has something to do with being an archmage," I suggested.

He looked doubtful. "Well, we don't know since you're the only one to look, but I have a feeling that it wouldn't matter."

"Next time, we'll bring the others and see who can sense it and who can't," I told him. "What do you want to do, now that we've found it?"

Stepping up to the invisible boundary, he spread his hands wide, as though he was pressing them against a wall. "Watch." Then his aythar began to move.

It flowed outward from his fingertips, spreading out like oil on water, shimmering through a wide range of colors that weren't really colors at all. Slowly, his magic faded from my magesight, and the air in front of him shifted, as though it were turning into a window, or perhaps a portal. The view was of a heavily shadowed forest, rather than the open plain we were currently standing in.

I let out a low whistle of appreciation. It was the first time I had ever had a chance to witness him using his dimensional abilities. "That's fascinating."

"How much did you see?" asked Matthew.

"Well, I can see an opening to another world."

"Before that," he insisted.

I described what I had seen, which seemed to confuse him even further. "You shouldn't have been able to see that."

"It was just aythar," I replied.

"But it was shifting through different dimensions to find the resonance of this boundary. You shouldn't have sensed anything until the actual portal began to open," he informed me.

Without warning, a massive fist the size of a small tree trunk shot through the opening, reaching toward him. Matthew stepped to one side, neatly avoiding it, and then let his portal collapse, severing the arm near the elbow. It fell to the ground with a heavy thump, blood draining from the severed end. "They really aren't friendly over there, are they?" he intoned calmly.

He hadn't moved quickly. His motion had simply begun early enough to avoid the attack without any need to leap or jerk his body. The entire thing had looked odd to me. It reminded me of the Illeniel krytek from Tyrion's ancient memory. "Did you get a forewarning of danger?" I asked. "Or did you sense it with your magesight through the portal beforehand?"

"I wasn't looking," he admitted. "I was too busy trying to figure out how you were able to sense things you shouldn't be able to. The danger sense thing happens almost unconsciously. Did you feel it too?"

I shook my head.

"Well, it wasn't reaching for you anyway, so even if you had it, it wouldn't warn you, I suppose," he said, still thinking aloud.

"Trust me," I said, "I've been in plenty of danger over the course of my years. If I had this precognitive danger sense of yours, it would have shown up by now."

Matthew didn't seem entirely convinced, but he didn't say anything else about it. Instead, he walked a straight line in the direction of Lancaster, remaining parallel to the nearly invisible boundary. When we had reached the point where it met the edge of the missing part of Lothion, he turned and followed the edge of it for a distance and then held up his hands again.

Once more I saw his aythar flowing outward, and a new portal opened. This time it wasn't a forest in front of us, but a continuation of the road that led from Cameron to Lancaster. The terrain ahead of us was open and sunny.

"I think that's Lancaster ahead of us," said Matthew.

I nodded. "We should have done this weeks ago." My head was swirling with ideas. There was every chance we could rescue the people from Lancaster, including Ariadne's brother Roland and his family.

"The idea occurred to me a few weeks ago," he responded. "But then, well, you know."

Penny's death, I finished mentally. That had thrown all of us into chaos. I couldn't blame him for not bringing it up. We had all been distracted by our family tragedy.

He started to step through the portal, but I stopped him with a hand on his shoulder. "Let's not be rash."

"They've been trapped there for over a month," my son observed. "We could scout the area without too much risk."

The trouble for me was that was exactly what I would have done, if I were alone, but I wasn't prepared to risk any of my family without making better preparations. "Tomorrow morning," I told him. "Another day won't make much difference. We'll bring Gram and a few others."

He looked like he wanted to argue, but after a moment he released the portal and nodded. "Fine."

We returned home and described what we had discovered to the others over lunch. The news excited them, and everyone wanted to come, which wasn't exactly to my liking. I compromised slightly, though. "You can all come to the crossing point, but only a few of you will cross over. Those being Matthew, Karen, Alyssa, Gram, and myself. Irene, Lynaralla, and Moira will remain on this side of the boundary."

"That's not fair," complained Irene. "You're only taking the boys."

I gave her a funny look. "Half of them are female."

"But Karen and Alyssa aren't your daughters. This is familial sexism. You're only letting your sons take risks," argued Irene.

"Conall isn't coming either," I said matter-of-factly.

Alyssa spoke up, ignoring our disagreement. "Gram is in Albamarl, visiting his mother."

"Then I'll go fetch him," I said.

Irene piped up again, "You should just take me instead."

Laughing, I pushed myself away from the table and stood. "Keep arguing, and I'll make you stay home. By the way, it's your day to help Alyssa with the dishes." So saying, I left and went to the portal that would take me to Albamarl. I could hear Irene groaning behind me as I went, while some of the others laughed at her misfortune.

 CHAPTER 9

Back in the Queen's chambers in Albamarl, I surprised Ariadne as she was finishing a private lunch. "Mordecai?"

No one else appeared to be present, so I kept my reply informal. "Hi, Ari. Sorry if I caught you off-guard."

She had her hand over her bosom while she took several deep breaths. "I thought I was alone. You startled me."

Seeing an opportunity to advance my plan, I asked her, "Where is Conall?"

"In the hall," she responded with a frown. "Why?"

"Lady Rose was attacked while alone, in a room that no one thought the enemy could reach. You've made my son your champion—why not keep him close at hand?" I suggested.

Ariadne sighed, then gave me a look of distaste. "I value what little privacy I'm afforded, Mort. Your son has been pushing the same line of reasoning lately. Should I be suspicious of the coincidence?"

I turned my eyes toward the ceiling innocently. "You're the first monarch in several generations to have a wizard in your service. It might be wise to make the most of it."

She pushed away a plate that was still half full. "Did you come to harangue me about my security or did you have a better purpose for your visit?"

"I'm looking for Gram," I explained. "Harassing you was just a side benefit."

"The downsides of having a portal connecting my rooms to your home are starting to become apparent," she said sourly. "I believe he's visiting his mother. Would you like some food before you go?" She gestured at the food on the table before her. Aside from what was unfinished on her plate, there was enough for at least two or three more people in the serving dishes.

Despite having just eaten, it was tempting. I picked up a bun from the table and tore it open before using it to sop up some delicious-looking gravy from a silver tureen filled with beef. My taste buds were not disappointed. "I'm not hungry," I told her.

"One would never guess it," she replied drolly.

Thirsty now, I pointed at her unfinished glass of wine. "Do you want that?" When she shook her head, I picked it up and downed the last of it in a single gulp. "Thanks." Then I leaned over and kissed her soundly on the cheek. "You're my favorite cousin."

The Queen of Lothion let out a disgusted gasp and began wiping away the gravy I had gotten on her cheek. I was already making my way to the door. "I think you should find another way to the palace for when you aren't actually coming to see me," she called to my back.

I turned in a circle as I went. "That's an excellent idea. Conall might be hungry. Do you mind if I send him in to help finish the food?"

She threw up her hands. "You might as well."

I left, chuckling, and made good on my word, telling my son, the noble Sir Conall, that the Queen needed his assistance. Before I could get away from him, my son called out to me. "Dad?"

"Mm hmm?"

He seemed slightly bemused by my sudden appearance. "There's something on your shirt."

Glancing down, I saw a long streak of brown gravy. I gathered most of it onto my finger and stuck it in my mouth, but the damage was already done. *I should have known better than to wear a white shirt,* I thought.

Five minutes later, I was outside the door that led to the rooms currently being used by the Thornbear family. Luckily, they hadn't decided to move into Rose's actual family residence within the capital. Rose's official title was 'the Hightower.' It was her maiden name, and it came from the massive bailey that guarded the main gate to Albamarl, a literal high tower. If she had been there, I'd have had a twenty-minute walk across the city to find her.

A moment after my knock, Elise Thornbear opened the door. "This is a surprise," she said pleasantly when she saw me. Then her eyes traveled down my shirtfront. "I see you've already had lunch."

Nodding, I smiled. "Mm hmm. I thought I'd finish it off with a berry tart. Have any cooling in the window, perchance?"

The old woman laughed and opened the door wider to allow me in. "I stopped baking them over thirty years ago because *someone* kept stealing them," she said, giving me a mock glare.

"If you're implying it was me, I will have to protest. That's slander. The true culprit confessed, as I recall," I told her.

Elise pursed her lips and put her hands on her hips. "Dorian was covering for you and that rapscallion, Marcus," she declared.

I reached back and rubbed my backside. "I can still remember the sting of your switch."

"Not that you learned anything from it," she shot back, and then she gave me a quick hug.

"Elise, is someone here?" said Rose, calling to her mother-in-law from the bedroom.

"Lord Cameron has come to pay us a visit," answered Elise.

"I'll be out in a moment," said Rose, closing her door once more.

What really caught my attention was that there was a man in the room with her. I hadn't heard his voice, but my magesight could easily make him out. Even now he was leaning in, his head close to hers. *What is that about?* My stomach knotted up for some reason, but I refused to consider why.

"Why don't we have a seat?" offered Elise, directing me toward one of several chairs.

My magesight had already told me that Gram wasn't present, and I might have asked where I could find him and excused myself, but I was reluctant to do so now. I accepted her offer and took a seat. My attention was so tightly focused on the happenings in the other room that I nearly missed the chair.

"Are you alright?" asked Elise. "You seem distracted."

She wouldn't have an assignation with her mother-in-law in the next room, I thought. *Rose is far too discreet for that.* It didn't make any sense.

"Mordecai?"

Elise was staring at me. "I'm sorry, what did you say?" I said apologetically.

"I wanted to know if you were alright."

I nodded. "I was just wondering what Rose was up to in the middle of the day." As I replied, the man stepped away and opened a hidden door that led from Rose's bedroom. I couldn't sense him once it closed behind him, as that was the boundary for the privacy ward on the apartments. I hadn't known the door was there.

"I've been wondering that myself," said Elise. "She's been staying in her room a lot of late. I keep thinking she might be ill, but she claims otherwise."

That does not make me feel better. Rose's door opened, and she stepped out, pulling a thin shawl up to cover her shoulders as she exited the room. "I didn't expect to see you again so soon, Mordecai."

"Obviously," I muttered.

"Excuse me?" said Rose, studying my face curiously.

Irritated, I shifted in my chair. "I came to find your son. I wanted to ask for his help with something tomorrow."

"Nothing dangerous, I hope," said Rose.

"It might be, but I have no way of knowing," I admitted. "I'm planning to try and find Roland, and Matthew thinks we need a guardian."

Rose's lips made a flat line for a moment, but eventually she spoke again, "Elise, would you mind stepping out and finding one of the pages? Gram is at the chapterhouse again, I think."

By the 'chapterhouse,' she was referring to the headquarters for the Order of the Thorn. It was located outside the palace itself, so it would take a while for a runner to find Gram and retrieve him, if he was still there.

Elise gave her an odd look but stepped out without saying a word.

Rose turned her attention back to me. "I don't like having you continually drag my son into your dangerous schemes."

"It's a harsh world," I returned. "We all have to deal with things we don't like, don't we?"

Her brows went up and then down again as she fixed a faintly malicious glare on me. "Is something bothering you, Lord Cameron?" She said it in a tone that made it clear she knew what I was agitated about.

I decided not to beat around the bush. "Who was that man?"

"I'm not sure I like your tone," announced Rose.

"Elise didn't seem to know he was there. Should I ask her instead?"

Rose pulled one of the chairs over so that it was beside mine and sat, perching gracefully on the cushioned seat. Then she leaned over and said in a conspiratorial voice, "It isn't that I don't trust her, but Elise is getting a little old for these sorts of things. I prefer not to bother her with my affairs."

My ears grew hot. *Affairs!* Flushing with sudden anger, I turned my head to face her and found myself almost nose to nose with Rose. Her blue eyes were flashing with mischief, and I shifted sideway, almost sliding off my seat.

Rose began to laugh, her delicate peals echoing around the chamber.

"What is it that you find so funny?" I asked.

She laughed harder, squeezing her eyes shut and wiping away mirthful tears. "You," she said, once she had regained her breath.

Escaping my chair, I walked halfway across the room. "None of this strikes me as humorous."

"You never questioned my methods before," said Rose.

"Methods?"

She followed me across the room and stood behind me. "The man was one of my informants. The Queen gave me these rooms because I requested them. The hidden passage makes it far easier to meet with my agents without causing unpleasant rumors."

I turned around, feeling suddenly foolish. "Oh."

"How long have we known each other?" she asked.

A long time. "Decades," I grumbled.

"Then you should know better to trust me by now," said Rose, her eyes glinting with a distant fire. "Just as I knew better than to ask who the woman was who cleaned your room the other day."

That set me back on my heels. Was she implying something? "What?" I responded articulately. "Alyssa has been meticulous about her duties, and entirely *proper* as well, I might add."

"Alyssa doesn't fold your undergarments, nor does she dare touch your jewelry and other personal items," observed Rose pointedly. "She certainly doesn't leave notes on the dresser that you feel the need to hide from me."

I gaped at her, amazed once again by her powers of observation.

Rose poked me in the chest with one finger. "The point, Mordecai, is that I trust you well enough to know better than to leap to foolish conclusions. *That's* why I didn't ask you about it. If it was something that concerned me, I know very well that you would tell me.

"And while we are on the subject, if I *were* to take a lover. It would be none of your business," she finished.

In the span of less than a minute, I had gone from irritated to embarrassed to angry. I stalked back over to my chair and took my seat again. "Of course not."

Rose resumed her seat as well. "Speaking of which, I believe Leomund is meeting his lover today."

"Really?"

She nodded. "He left the capital yesterday for his hunting lodge. The informant who was just here was reporting on whether any of the other lords have decided to take sudden trips. I strongly suspect one or more of them may be involved in whatever the Prince-Consort is up to, but thus far I have been unable to pin down anything definitive. Cantley and Airedale have both left the capital as well, but I have no idea if they're meeting Leomund there or not."

"So, it might not be a lover at all," I posited. "It might be a conspiratorial meeting?"

"Or both," said Rose. "Either way, I'll eventually discover it all. All it takes is time and patience."

And a mind deadlier than a steel trap, I thought silently. "It might be quicker if someone crashed their party unexpectedly."

Rose frowned. "Don't even think about it. If you show up, you might uncover something and still lose any advantage the information might give us at the same time. It's better if we catch them unaware. Then *we* decide whether the knowledge is useful or not, and when or how to use it."

"Very well," I responded, giving an overly formal bow. "I will defer to your wisdom, milady."

The door opened, and Elise entered the room. She looked at both of us and then asked, "Did I miss something?" Gram followed close behind her.

The young knight saw me and dipped his head quickly. "My liege, you needed me?"

"That was quick," I noted. "No need to be so formal. Matthew and I would like you to accompany us tomorrow. We think we may be able to reach Lancaster. We hope to rescue any survivors there."

Gram's eyes grew wide. "You think the Duke might still be alive?"

"I hope so," I said. "With luck, we'll find out tomorrow."

We talked for a while after that. Gram decided to return and spend the night at my house, so he wouldn't cause a delay in the morning. Shortly after that was settled, I made my good-byes and left.

 # CHAPTER 10

I didn't return home after leaving Rose's apartments. Instead, I left the palace and began walking toward my old house in the city. Since Tyrion had claimed it as his own, it was no longer technically mine, which still irked me somewhat—but my factorage was located across the street from it, and I had some business to conduct there.

As I stepped into the street outside the palace, I immediately noticed something odd. My magesight has an extremely long range compared to most wizards. From what I had learned from Moira Centyr, most wizards could detect things with their magesight at a distance of a mile or less. I, on the other hand, had a range that was effective out to around two miles, and most of my children were similar in that regard.

There were other differences, of course. Years ago, Walter Prathion had shown me that despite his shorter range, he was far superior when it came to things like detecting shiggreth, and over the past year I had found out that my son could see things with his gift that I could not—dimensional disturbances, for example, although our experiment near Lancaster had cast some confusion over that issue.

In any case, my exceptional range was picking up a large number of powerful aythar sources within the city. At least fifteen or twenty were strong enough to make me think they were other wizards. There was an even greater number that were far weaker, a number too great for me to easily count, and they were moving.

Wary, I quickened my step and reinforced my shield. *It can't be other mages. There aren't that many in all of Lothion.* The direction of my walk was taking me closer to one of the weaker sources, and just before I reached the corner, a small creature flew around it and buzzed past me. It stopped a few feet away and hovered, apparently interested in me.

I returned its examination and realized it was a small insect-like creature, similar to a dragonfly. Then I remembered what Rose had told me the day before about Tyrion's plan. "This must be one of his ANSIS-detecting krytek," I muttered. A few seconds later it lost interest and resumed flying down the street.

My curiosity aroused, I altered my route to take me close to one of the stronger sources of aythar, even though it was several streets out of my way. I might as well take the opportunity to see the other part of his plan. I was rewarded ten minutes later when a guard patrol came in sight.

It consisted of two men wearing the royal guard uniform, but one of them was a man only in appearance. His aythar and the spellwoven weapon he carried at his side convinced me he must be another of Tyrion's krytek posing as a guard.

The two of them stopped when they saw me approaching, and it was then that I spotted the most obvious difference between them. While the real guardsman fidgeted and fussed with his collar, the krytek remained perfectly still, like a statue. Its eyes followed me closely as I passed.

I touched my brow in greeting, though I wore no hat, and wished them good day.

The guardsman gave a short bow. "Milord," he said, but the krytek said nothing. I could feel their eyes on my back the rest of the way down the street. *That wasn't awkward at all,* I thought to myself.

Still, though it felt weird to be scrutinized, I wouldn't complain if Tyrion's plan kept the city safe from ANSIS. I continued walking, and fifteen minutes later I had reached the factorage. The door was unlocked, since it was still within business hours, so I let myself in without knocking.

David Summerfield looked up from his desk. "Lord Cameron!"

The office was well decorated with fresh flowers, so I assumed he was still in the good graces of the flower girl down the street. "Relax, David, I'm here on business."

My factor offered me his chair and moved to take the one designated for visitors, but I waved him away. "It's your desk, David. Sit behind it." I took the visitor's chair and made myself comfortable.

"What brings you here today, milord?" said David. "I didn't expect you for at least another month."

"I need money," I said flatly. "A lot of it."

"The repairs?" he asked, guessing my reason. "I didn't think you'd need more so soon."

"I've accelerated the construction," I told him. "The main structure is already in place, but it will take a lot of masons, carpenters, and other workmen to turn it into a place where people can live and work."

"The main structure?" said David. "What do you mean? It takes years to build a fortress of that size."

"I grew a new one. But that's beside the point. I'm planning to shift the metals market again, so I thought I'd warn you in advance."

"Which metals?"

"Gold, silver, and a lot of iron," I stated. "It might be best to invest our free capital in other commodities, such as wheat and wool."

He nodded. "The prices will rise considerably if you dilute the value of gold again."

"I'll try to be more moderate," I explained. "I'm not out to bankrupt anyone this time. I don't want to cause too much chaos, but I won't mind if we take a small profit."

"A small profit?" he chuckled. "You could be the richest man in Lothion if you let me move aggressively."

"I only want to restore Castle Cameron and maintain a healthy balance sheet," I told him. "I don't need any more enemies." We spent the next hour hashing out our plans for the next month before we moved on to more casual talk.

"Before I leave, do you know where Prince Leomund's hunting lodge is?"

David seemed surprised at the question. "It's in the royal hunting preserve, a couple of hours to the west of the city. Why do you ask?"

I smiled enigmatically. "Just curious. Do you have more specific directions?"

As it turned out, his files included land surveys that happened to include the area, so he found them and showed me on a map. I didn't bother writing anything down; my memory was pretty handy for situations like this one.

"While you're here," said David before I could leave, "do you know anything about the recent patrols?"

"The city watch?"

He shook his head. "No, since the attack the Royal Guard have taken to the streets. There are patrols everywhere. It has most of the citizens alarmed."

"Are you alarmed?" I asked.

"Anything that's bad for business worries me," responded David. "People have been disappearing. They say the guardsmen are arresting people at random."

Despite the attack, ANSIS was not common knowledge in Lothion. If the citizenry knew that anyone could be harboring a metal parasite that controlled them, well, there would be chaos and possibly even riots. For that reason, Ariadne had chosen not to divulge the truth, but by the same token, it meant that the people had no idea why the Guard was arresting people.

Honestly, I wasn't sure how much I should tell my factor. "The enemy behind the recent attack is thought to have a number of agents and spies in the city. The Guard is probably rounding them up."

"Two days ago, they took Sarah's father," said David. "I'm quite sure he wasn't involved in anything like that. He's a florist!"

"We can't be sure…"

"I knew the man!" said David, raising his voice. "None of the people that have been taken have been seen again. There have been no trials. Families haven't been allowed to visit them. As far as anyone knows, they might as well have been executed and buried."

The ramifications of Tyrion's plan hadn't really struck home with me until then, and I wondered if Ariadne realized how much damage his secret campaign to eliminate ANSIS could do to her reputation. If this continued, there might be a panic. "I'll see what I can find out," I hedged.

"Please do," said David firmly. "And before you go, is the man in your house across the street really your ancestor?"

I grimaced. "Well, technically, now that he's returned, it isn't my house anymore, and yes, he is."

"Rumor has it that he founded Albamarl over two thousand years ago," said David, "but that couldn't possibly be true, could it?"

"Unfortunately, yes," I answered. "And I wish he weren't my ancestor. Is there a point to this?"

David rubbed his chin. "Well, if he founded the city, doesn't that mean he was the first King of Lothion?"

Well, in Tyrion's time there hadn't been a human government of any sort, and it had been his son who had actually laid out the first streets for Albamarl, but that wouldn't make much difference to this argument. "That's dangerous talk, David," I said in a low voice.

He held up his hands. "I'm just repeating what I've been hearing from people in the streets."

"I don't think my ancestor has any interest in making a claim to the throne, and I wouldn't repeat any of that. You could be arrested for treason if the wrong person heard that," I warned him.

"Do you think that's why the Guard has been making people disappear?" asked David, his brows shooting up.

"Absolutely not," I declared. "You have my word on that."

"Then you do know something," said my factor, a conspiratorial grin sneaking across his features.

I fought the urge to cover my face with my hands. If such rumors really were travelling the streets, it couldn't possibly be good for Ariadne. Lothion's monarchy had traditionally been male. My cousin was the first queen regnant in the nation's history. Consequently, there had long been a rather vocal segment of the population that had been against her rule.

Her choice of Leomund for marriage had been based largely on the fact that he was a foreigner, making it unlikely he would gain the support of the nobility and threaten her reign.

But Tyrion was an entirely different story. *Could he have planned this?* I wondered. It seemed far too subtle. *Is that why his krytek are disguised as Royal Guards, to help foment a revolt?*

I was starting to get a headache just thinking about it. This wasn't something I could deal with alone. I needed to talk to Rose. *But first I'll see if I can gather a little information on another front for her first,* I told myself.

***

I was standing in plain sight at the edge of the forest some thirty yards from Leomund's hunting lodge. Though I wasn't hidden, I didn't worry about being seen. "Because I'm doing my best Tyrion impression," I mumbled, smirking to myself. I had covered myself in the illusion of a modestly sized elm to match the trees nearest to me.

It had taken me less than fifteen minutes to reach the area by flying, though I had spent just as much time choosing the perfect observation spot. I was off to one side of the front, so that if any new visitors arrived I could observe them with both my eyes and my magesight.

The lodge itself gave the impression of being a country estate house more than it did a place for hunters to gather, for there was very little about its appearance that could be described as rustic. It was constructed from dressed stone and ornamented with columns at the front entrance, a relatively new fashion that told me the building had probably been built within the last decade if not more recently.

The grounds closest to the house were well tended with a series of delicately sculptured bushes surrounding the ground floor and partially obscuring the windows. In fact, there was a man outside now clipping away at one of them.

Within the building, I had already detected seven servants, four men and three women. One of the women and two of the men were in the kitchen, preparing the evening meal, while the other men were handling other mundane tasks. The second woman was standing in a bedroom on the second floor.

She occupied most of my attention, primarily because her behavior was so strange. At first, I thought she was there to clean the room, but her actions didn't reflect that. She stood at one end of the room without moving, as though she was imitating a statue. I might have thought she was one of the She'Har but for the fact that she did fidget now and then.

Twenty minutes after beginning my observations, Leomund went up to the second floor and entered the bedroom she was in. The woman bowed as he entered, and I began to get a bad feeling.

Leomund didn't disappoint. He said something and then crossed the room before circling her like a predator that could smell blood. The woman remained utterly still the entire time, without even daring to turn her head and look at him.

Then he lifted her skirts and ran his hand up the inside of her leg. She jerked slightly when his hand reached the high point between her legs, but otherwise she didn't fight him. Leomund kept his hand there for a while, until eventually the woman twisted slightly, as though she might try to pull away.

His reaction was instant. Pulling his hand away, he struck her soundly across the cheek, sending her reeling. The woman bumped into the bed frame and fell sideways to land hard on the floor.

At that point, I was probably the angriest elm tree that had ever existed, and I struggled to remain calm. I had known that some lords abused their power by taking liberties with their female servants. I knew it first hand, in fact: my wife, Penny, had once nearly been raped by a visiting nobleman named Devon Tremont, back in the days when she had been a castle maid, and I was just the local blacksmith's son.

But I hadn't expected something like this from Leomund. The man was obnoxious, certainly, but it had never entered my mind that he might be a monster of this unsavory variety. I wanted nothing more than to enter the lodge and do something drastic and permanent to Leomund's manhood, and I might have if he hadn't stopped at that point.

The woman had regained her feet and seemed to be apologizing, but Leomund merely laughed and stalked from the room. She resumed her stoic pose beside the bed, and he went off to occupy himself in what appeared to be a study of some sort.

My chest was heaving in reaction to the adrenaline that had flooded my system, and it took me several minutes to regain my full composure. *Why did he stop?* I wondered. He had saved himself from an unfortunate and painful experience at my hands, but he hadn't known I was here. Was tormenting the maid simply a minor amusement for him?

Pondering these questions, I waited and watched, until another hour had passed. I was considering leaving, but it was then that I detected a carriage approaching along the small lane that led to the hunting lodge.

This was exactly the sort of thing I was here to learn, so I waited. The carriage was drawn by four horses and had a driver and footman, along with a single occupant. By the time it had reached the house, I had identified the man inside from his aythar alone. It was David Airedale.

The Count exited his carriage, and his servants drove it back behind the house to take care of the horses and park it in a small carriage house. Meanwhile Count Airedale was greeted by his host, Leomund, and ushered inside.

Leomund seemed glad to see him, and the two engaged in what appeared to be a lively conversation for a few minutes before settling into the front room for a glass of wine. They remained together there for another quarter of an hour before the Prince motioned for him to follow and led him up to the second floor.

A sick feeling passed over me as they approached the bedroom where the woman still remained, waiting in her statue-like pose. *They couldn't possibly...* I thought.

Airedale seemed surprised when he was shown the woman within, which raised my opinion of him slightly. It went up even more when he shook his head no as the woman began to remove her clothing. The Count almost bolted from the room, while Leomund laughed at his discomfort.

The Prince followed him back downstairs, and I almost relaxed when the count went back to his chair and drink, but Leomund wasn't finished. He was yelling, and after a minute or so, the rest of the servants came to his call. Then they marched, single file, up the stairs. Entering the bedroom where the woman was, they lined up on one side of the room.

"What in the hell are they doing?" I muttered, confused.

Leomund joined them a minute later, while Airedale remained downstairs, looking uncomfortable. The Prince appeared to lecture his servants for several minutes, occasionally pointing at the woman standing by the bed, then he turned and barked an order at her.

She began removing her dress again while the prince rummaged in a chest in one corner of the room. I found myself frozen, unable to comprehend what my magesight was showing me. *Why would he make her strip in front of the other servants?*

I was sick with anger, wavering on the verge of doing something stupid. *What does he have in his hand?* At this range I couldn't be entirely certain— it might have been a short rope, but I didn't think he needed to tie her up. Thus far, his poor maid had been completely submissive.

Then a chill ran down my spine as he uncoiled it in a snake-like motion. It was an item I was intimately familiar with, from my own experience at the whipping post in Albamarl. Leomund brought his arm up and across, and the woman's back arched in pain.

I had no memory of moving, but I dropped my illusion and flew across the intervening space between me and the front door so quickly that I heard her scream at almost the same time I entered the house. The door itself was no more. It existed now as a rain of splinters and fragments that were falling all around me.

Count Airedale stared at me as though I had sprouted horns. "What are you doing here?" he exclaimed, but I had no time to entertain questions. I went to the stairs and flew up them, my feet inches above the steps.

Inside the room, Leomund and his staff were already reacting to the explosive sound of my entrance. One of them opened the door to the bedroom to look out just as I came into view at the end of the hall.

Making a conscious effort, I put my feet back on the ground and marched toward the bedroom. "Get out," I warned the man looking at me. He stumbled into the hall barely in time to avoid me as I stomped in.

"Lord Cameron?" said Leomund in a querulous tone.

I said nothing for several seconds, scanning the room with my eyes. The remaining servants were still, but their faces registered shock and fear. The naked woman stood several feet past Leomund, except I could now see she was no woman at all.

It was a girl, younger than Irene if I had to guess, twelve or thirteen years of age perhaps. She stood close to what might be her adult height, but her breasts were still budding. Blood dripped down her back, following one hip and leg before making a small puddle on the floor.

At first, I didn't react. My mind was in shock as I tried to process the sight, but then Leomund spoke again, his tone mocking, "If I had known you were interested in such things, Mordecai, I would have happily extended an invitation to you."

The voice that answered him was so deep and gravelly I almost didn't recognize it as my own. "One more word and I'll kill you where you stand." Turning my head, I addressed his servants, "Leave."

They didn't need any more encouragement. They scrambled from the room as though their lives depended on it, which I suppose they might. I wasn't sure what I would do either.

"Count Cameron," began the Prince, but he didn't finish. Stepping forward, I drove my fist into his chin with such force that it probably dislocated his jaw at the same time it broke one of the bones in my hand. I had used my power without thinking, increasing my strength and failing to protect my own flesh. The pain was intense. Which somehow made me feel better.

The girl backed away, finding a corner to hide in as the Prince stumbled and fell to the floor, staining his clothing with her fresh blood.

Leomund didn't move. He had fallen limply, unconscious before reaching the ground. That alone saved him from further punishment. The bastard wouldn't feel it.

Breathing heavily, I didn't spare him any more of my attention. I focused my senses on my injured hand and straightened the broken bone fragments before fusing them together. That hurt even more, but the pain seemed to help me clear my head. Then I looked at the girl huddled in the corner.

She flinched when my eyes landed on her. "Please, milord, don't hurt me. I'll do whatever you say." Tears ran down her cheeks even as she tried to straighten her back, presenting her breasts in a way that was so artificial I was certain she had been trained to do so.

My stomach turned at the sight, and I wanted to cry. Only my anger prevented it. "I'm not here to hurt you," I said without moving. "What's your name?"

Considering the circumstances, I wouldn't have been surprised if she had been unable to answer, but she spoke immediately, "Millie, milord."

How long has she been enduring this treatment? The girl was obviously used to accepting commands even while terrified. "And your last name? Where's your family?" I asked.

"I don't have one, milord. They sold me to the Prince when I was still too young to talk," she answered.

My imagination balked at considering what her life might have been like. I picked her dress up from the bed and handed it to her. "Put that back on." She was quick to obey, but I caught her wrist as she lifted it over her head. I had forgotten her wound. "Wait, your back—turn around, and let me look at it."

The way she flinched at my touch tore at my heart, but she turned around obediently, and the sight of her back only made matters worse. Leomund hadn't held back at all. The whip had torn the skin, creating a bright red weal that was still seeping blood. Worse, it was obviously not the first time a whip had been used on her. Millie had a collection of scars that ranged from old to still healing. *What kind of man could do this to a child?*

I wanted to break things, most of all the body of the man lying on the floor nearby. Leomund looked far too peaceful, even sprawled unconscious on the hard floor. *He doesn't deserve to live,* I thought coldly. For a moment, I considered the consequences. If I murdered him I would become a criminal, wanted across Lothion. I would lose my title and lands, and probably my life itself, assuming they could bring me to justice. Even Ariadne couldn't shield me from the law if I killed her husband, regardless of her personal feelings about the bastard. He was a prince.

My son might or might not be allowed to inherit the title. My entire estate could be withdrawn by the crown and passed to another family entirely.

Staring at Leomund, one thing rang true down to my very soul. "If my wife were here, you would already be dead," I muttered. That thought alone almost drove me over the edge. Penny wouldn't blame me, if she were alive. She would have already put her sword through Leomund's black heart. "It might be best to honor her memory by doing what she would have wanted," I said coldly, fingering the dagger on my belt.

Millie began to cry. "Please, sir. Please don't kill him. This place is all I have. If he dies, I'll be thrown out." The words were almost unintelligible through her sobbing, but I still understood her. I wish I hadn't.

I looked into the girl's eyes and felt my own begin to fill with tears. How much had she suffered? She had probably never known anything else but violence and abuse, and now she pled for the life of her abuser.

Wiping my face with my sleeve, I turned away from Leomund and took my hand off my dagger. But for Millie's plea, I would have killed him and said to hell with the price. She had suffered too much, and more violence would only hurt her more, especially if it was done by the hand of a stranger pretending to be her rescuer.

"Shibal," I intoned softly, sending the girl into a deep sleep. I caught her as she fell and laid her gently on the bed, face down. Then I blocked the nerves in her back and sealed her wound before carefully redressing her. I tried not to think of my own daughters as I tugged her dress back into place, but it was difficult. Her body was covered in bruises, some yellowing and others fresh and dark.

Venting my anger at last, I blew the exterior wall of the bedroom apart with a surge of aythar. Then I lifted Millie and cradled her in my arms before taking flight. Within seconds we were gone, and Leomund's hunting lodge was soon beyond sight.

 # Chapter 11

Ten minutes passed before my mind cleared enough for me to consider where I was going. Gauging the sun and the time of day, I realized I was traveling northwest, following a course roughly in the direction of home, but even if I flew at dangerous speeds, it would take at least a couple of hours to get there.

That wouldn't do. The girl I was carrying wouldn't benefit from being hauled across the country in my arms. She needed a bath, a warm bed, and soft blankets. She needed a home, preferably twelve years ago, so she could grow up safe and comfortable. Her biggest concern should be whether there were flowers blooming in the spring, or whether her favorite food was being served at dinner. My vision blurred, and I was forced to shut my thoughts down once again.

Finally coming to my senses, I set down in the seemingly endless forest that stretched from the capital all way to the Elentir Mountains. Reaching into my pouch, I took out my stencil and created a temporary circle to take me home. *To take us home,* I amended mentally.

Alyssa was the first one to spot us after I crossed the threshold of my home and walked down the front hall. "My lord, who is this?" She was carrying a basket full of freshly washed sheets, but she put it down to free up her hands.

"Her name is Millie," I answered softly.

Moira stepped out of her room behind me and looked over my shoulder. "What happened to her? Where did you find her?"

"I found her at Leomund's hunting lodge, near Albamarl. She was one of his servants," I said numbly.

My oldest daughter hissed when she saw the bruises on Millie's thin arms. "She's hurt! Take her into my room. We can put her on the bed in there."

Within minutes, the entire household had gathered in the hallway outside Moira's bedroom. Moira and her alter-ego Myra kept themselves busy tending to Millie while Alyssa ran back and forth, bringing towels and water from the kitchen.

Rather than crowd into the bedroom, I took everyone else into the main room and gave the others an abbreviated version of what I had seen.

"You should have stopped his heart," said Lynaralla, the first to speak after I finished. As always, her voice was calm and even, giving little evidence of the emotions within her.

"Leomund is the Prince-Consort," observed Matthew. "They would try to execute Dad if he did that."

"Why?" asked Lynaralla curiously.

"It's the law," said my son. "Murder isn't allowed, and it's far worse if the person killed is a member of the royal family."

"Stopping his heart would be painless," explained Lynaralla. "Dangerous animals shouldn't be left to endanger others."

Irene nodded in agreement. "You're right, Lynn, but the law would still require Dad to pay for the crime."

"Then your law is foolish," pronounced the She'Har woman. "Torture and abuse cause pain and suffering. Stopping such is a mercy, not a crime."

Irene smiled faintly at Lynaralla's statement, then turned to me. "Do you think the Prince will try to get her back?"

I grimaced. "He can try, but it won't happen."

"Technically she's his property," said Matthew. "If she's a serf, that is. He could accuse you of theft."

I growled, "He can add that to the list. I've already committed assault and destruction of property." All the people in Washbrook and those in Arundel were freemen. Having been raised a commoner, the practice of keeping people in what amounted to slavery was repugnant to me, but it was still allowed in Lothion according to the desires of whatever noble ruled over a particular region.

"What did you destroy now?" asked Gram, standing in the doorway that led to the hall. We had been so wrapped up in our discussion that none of us had noticed his arrival through the portal.

Matthew started to explain, but Alyssa stepped out of Moira's room and ran to embrace her fiancé, forcing us to wait until they had finished their greeting. After they had separated, Matthew caught his friend up on my recent doings, and the conversation resumed.

It didn't really bring us any closer to a solution, but Gram brought up an important point. "You need to report what you saw to the Queen."

I shook my head. "If I go back now, she'll be forced to lock me up until all of this is sorted out. The matter of Lancaster has gone without resolution for far too long. If Roland is still alive, he could be in dire straits. Even if he isn't, there could be a lot of people there that need a rescue."

Gram frowned. "The longer you wait, the worse your case will look. Leomund could accuse you of evading justice. It could undermine your claim that he was torturing the girl."

"There were lots of witnesses," I argued. "Everyone there knew what he was doing to her."

"But will they dare testify against the Prince?" said Matthew.

"We have the girl," I stated. "Her words, and the evidence that lies upon her flesh should be proof enough when combined with my statement."

"She's property," said Matthew sadly. "The law gives Leomund the right to dispose of her however he wishes."

"Torture is still a crime," I said grinding my teeth. "Even the nobility are not allowed to harm their serfs beyond a certain point, even when punishing a crime."

"And what does the law say of striking a prince of the realm?" challenged Gram.

"What would you have done in my place?" I snarled, my frustration bubbling over.

Gram slumped in his chair. "I would already be in prison."

Irene spoke up, "Ari would never lock Dad up for this. It was justice."

Matthew was staring at the floor. "Ariadne wouldn't, but the Queen *must*, otherwise the nobles would rebel."

"Then we'll just put the shield up," declared Irene. "They can't arrest him if they can't get in."

"That would mean civil war," said my son.

I nodded. "He's right. How many people would die if I started a conflict like that?"

"No one," insisted Irene. "The shield would keep them out."

"And what about the farmers?" I asked. "What about the free-holders?"

"They could stay in Washbrook," said Irene.

Ever logical, Matthew pointed out the glaring flaw in her plan. "For how long? How much food do we have for a siege? Think about it, Rennie."

Gram looked at me. "What will you do?"

"You were right," I said. "I have to report this to the Queen, but I'll do so after we handle Lancaster tomorrow. Roland and the people there are too important to wait."

***

The next morning, I stood just outside the area that had once been Lancaster. With me were Gram, Alyssa, Matthew, Karen, Irene, and Lynaralla, although the latter two wouldn't be coming with us across the dimensional boundary. They would be returning home to help Moira with Millie. My purpose for bringing them was to see whether they could also detect Matthew's special translation magic.

Also with us were Gram and Matthew's massive dragons, Grace and Zephyr, and Alyssa's much smaller, newly hatched dragon, Sassy. I still hadn't gotten over the name, but Alyssa insisted it was the most appropriate name for her bond-mate.

Alyssa herself could be described many ways— fierce, loyal, deadly, but sassy wasn't one of them. She was too well composed and respectful of authority for such a term, but she seemed to feel it was a perfect description of her companion, so she had stubbornly stuck with the name.

I directed everyone to observe carefully, and then nodded for Matthew to begin. He held out his hands and aythar flowed outward from his fingers in colorful streamers, pulsing and tracing strange patterns through the air. Before he went any further, I asked, "Can anyone see what he's doing?"

Lynaralla nodded and Irene answered, "Of course."

Karen shook her head negatively. "Nothing." Matthew continued, and the view changed, showing us the road leading to Lancaster. Karen piped up again, "Now I see it."

"Anyone could see it now," said Sassy with no small amount of snark in her voice.

Maybe her name was more apt than I realized, I observed silently. I looked at Irene and Lynaralla. "Do you think you could replicate what he just did?"

"Uh," said Irene uncomfortably.

Lynaralla answered with more confidence. "With practice."

"If we don't return by tomorrow, you may have to bring reinforcements," I told them. "Go home for now."

Irene spoke up, "You're taking the dragons. Are we supposed to walk?"

Lynaralla was tugging on Irene's sleeve to get her attention, but I warned her with a shake of my head. "Is that the only way you have of getting home?" I asked. Lynaralla started to answer for her, but I held up my hand to stop her. "Let her figure it out."

My youngest daughter looked between Lynaralla and me, and then after a moment she had her epiphany. "Oh!" An expression of embarrassment crossed her face. She reached into her new belt pouch and pulled out the little book that contained her notes regarding teleportation circles. "I guess I wasn't thinking."

I pursed my lips but didn't say anything, merely nodding.

Another thought came to her, though. "Wait, I don't have one of those stencils you use."

"You don't need one. You can draw it out yourself. You wrote the circle down as well, didn't you?" I told her.

"I could take them back and return. It would only take a few seconds," suggested Karen helpfully.

"She needs to learn. We can't always rely on you, Karen," I replied.

Irene gave me a sour look as I started to pass through the dimensional boundary. "Aren't you going to at least wait and see if I do it correctly?"

Waiting would take at least ten minutes, if she got it right the first time. "You'll learn faster without me looking over your shoulder," I told her.

Gram seemed uncomfortable. "Is it really alright to leave them alone out here?"

I frowned at him. "Do you really think there's anything out here that could threaten the two of them?"

"I guess you're right," said Gram, embarrassed, while Alyssa took the opportunity to laugh at him.

Striding forward, I went through the portal Matthew had created. The others followed after me, and then Matthew released it. We were on the other side.

The view before us was relatively normal. The road continued on toward Lancaster, just as I remembered it, with the same familiar forest on either side, broken up by small clearings now and then. Behind us, however, was the same looming, primeval forest that I had so recently destroyed. Its trees were larger and more varied, with a thick, almost impenetrable undergrowth of vines and bushes.

We started walking quickly with the larger dragons, Grace and Zephyr, pacing us on either side. The sooner we were away from that wild border, the safer we would be—presumably.

 CHAPTER 12

It was a pleasant walk. Gram and Alyssa took the front, with her dragon Sassy riding on her armored shoulder. Matthew, Karen, and I followed behind them. The road rolled across the terrain, sinking and rising gently as it followed the land.

We could have traveled faster if we had ridden the dragons, but I wanted to go slowly and examine the countryside as we went. After fifteen minutes, we crossed another slight rise and I could see the house I had grown up in off to our left. My mother had sold it a number of years back, and the new owner was also a smith, one who had come to Lancaster to take over the business opportunities arising from my father's death.

The new smith was a young man with a young and sturdily built wife. Sean and Tracy were their names if I had heard correctly, for I hadn't met them in person. My mother had told me they had two sons and another child on the way. By now that meant they had three children, barring unfortunate accidents.

I could tell the house was empty of its residents well before we got close. That wasn't to say it was empty of all life, though. My magesight detected a very large arachnid within, though it was radiating very little aythar. My previous experience in the forest had taught me to pay close attention, but it helped that this horror wasn't underground.

"Do you see it?" I asked the others when we were still fifty yards away.

"Yeah," answered Matthew with a look of distaste on his face.

"See what?" asked Karen.

"In the house," I said, directing her attention by pointing. "In the front room, look closely."

Gram and Alyssa waited patiently, since neither of them had magesight. After a few seconds, Karen jerked and let out a gasp. "Ugh! Oh my god!" she exclaimed. "What is that? It can't be a spider, it's too big. Oh, the legs, blech…" Her face twisted. "I think I'm going to be sick."

"It's different than the ones we encountered before," observed my son. "Bigger, and it's alone."

Grace growled, her throat issuing a deep rumble. "Let me get rid of it."

"The others had a nasty venom," I reminded her. "I'd rather not risk you being bitten."

The dragon snorted, issuing a small blast of flame. "Who said anything about going in there?"

"You're not burning down my childhood home to get rid of a house spider, Grace," I told her firmly.

Karen spoke up in agreement, "It sounds like an excellent plan to me. I'm going to have nightmares for a week just thinking about that thing."

Gram spoke a soft command and two arming swords appeared, one in either hand. "I'll take care of it." Alyssa lifted her spear and moved to stand beside him.

"Lure it outside and I can kill it without damaging the property," I told them.

"I doubt it can hurt us in our armor," said Gram. "I'd feel better if you aren't doing things I can't see or predict. Hold off on the magic unless things get out of control." A second later, as an after-thought, he added, "My lord."

"Fine," I replied.

The rest of us stood close to the road while they approached the house. Inside the house, I felt the spider move. It was right behind the door and it was clearly aware of them. *It's getting ready to pounce,* I realized. Maybe it was related to trapdoor spiders, for the tactic seemed similar.

The two warriors glanced at each other, communicating with a few hand gestures, and then Alyssa stepped off to one side while Gram walked directly toward the door. What happened next was so quick it was a moment before my brain caught up with what my eyes had registered.

The door was pulled open and the massive brown body of the spider emerged, with seemingly countless legs reaching out to grab the young man who stood a few feet away. At nearly the same instant, Alyssa leapt forward from the side, driving her spear deep into the monster's cephalothorax. The young woman didn't have the mass necessary to stop its movement, but she threw it off balance and slowed it significantly.

Meanwhile Gram's swords were moving back and forth, systematically removing the creature's forelegs and mandibles. It fell forward as he darted to one side and began removing the legs on the side opposite Alyssa, who had withdrawn her spear and was now using it to put large holes in the thing's abdomen. The fight appeared to be over almost as soon as it started.

That hadn't stopped Karen from screaming bloody murder the moment she saw the beast spring out of the house. My right ear was still ringing from the force and volume of her yell.

Only a few seconds had passed, and the spider was dying, its few remaining legs twitching. Alyssa thrust her spear into it once more, this time piercing a leathery-looking sac that was anchored underneath the abdomen. Unfortunately, that turned out to be an egg sac, one that was full not of eggs, but of newly hatched baby spiders, each around the size of a coin.

The little spiders poured forth and scattered around their mother, running in every direction, including up the legs of the two warriors that had slain the giant arachnid. For Gram this wasn't a problem—his armor was entirely sealed, only allowing air inside through a carefully controlled enchantment, but Alyssa's armor was of a more traditional design. The joints of her armor were protected by chainmail, but if something ran up the inside of her greaves or vambraces far enough, it might possibly find an entrance through the padding and laces of her arming jacket.

Alyssa reacted quickly, though, leaping ten feet straight up and back before more than a few of the little beasts could begin climbing. Sassy assisted by flying close and sending small bursts of flame to burn away the arachnids.

Grace's response was more thorough, however. As soon as the two warriors were clear of the front of the house, she sent massive gout of flame at the spider carcass and front door, and she didn't relent for nearly ten seconds. The thatching on the roof caught almost immediately, turning the house into a bonfire. Torching my house wasn't enough for her either—after the first gout, she turned her head and incinerated the ground to either side before working her way back to us.

"Damn it, Grace! I told you I didn't want to damage the house!" I yelled at her.

If she was bothered by my rebuke, she didn't show it. The massive dragon turned her head, bringing one reptilian eye around to stare at me. "It was infested. Build a new one."

"It wasn't infested! We killed the spider. I could have dispatched the others without burning the whole house down!"

Grace sat, resting her weight on her haunches as though she was some sort of giant dog. "Better safe than sorry," she rumbled, unrepentant.

I stared at her in disbelief, then stalked away, angrily muttering, "So much for my childhood."

Karen, on the other hand peeked out from her hiding place behind Matthew. "Thank you, Grace. I don't know if I would have ever been able to sleep again if you hadn't done that."

"You're welcome," said the dragon.

"Come on," I called out. "We might as well see if Roland has a need for a pyromaniac dragon."

Several of them laughed, but they followed and we were on our way again. We didn't approach any more of the small houses that dotted the countryside. I figured we had done enough damage for one day. Our purpose was to rescue Lancaster, if there was anyone left, not to sterilize the outskirts.

Half an hour later, we could see the towers of the castle peeking above the trees, so I called a halt. "Sassy, why don't you do a quick flyover? You're small enough you could be mistaken for a hawk if someone or something hostile spots you."

"Your wish is my command, o' wise and grumpy one," responded the small dragon as she leapt into the air.

I glared daggers at the reptile's back as she flew away, then turned to Karen. "While we wait, I have a question for you."

"What is it?"

"Can you teleport from here back to Washbrook, or any other places beyond the boundary we crossed to come here?"

Her answer was immediate. "No," said Karen.

"That was quick," I responded. "You know without even trying?"

She nodded. "It's hard to explain. It's like a map in my head, but I feel it more than see it. Whenever I go somewhere, it gets larger, but as soon as we crossed the boundary, it vanished. The map I have of this place is entirely separate."

I glanced at my son. "But this place is technically still in the same dimension. It's just divided up by artificial boundaries. Shouldn't her teleportation still work?"

Matthew shrugged. "I don't pretend to understand how her gift works, but you're right. That's why I have to make a portal at the boundaries instead of just shifting anywhere like I did when I went to Karen's world. I can open the boundaries, but I can't shift between here and home because they're really still in the same world."

That made sense to me. "I wonder why the animals are so different here than what we're used to."

"How long has your world been split like this?" asked Karen.

Matthew and I glanced at each other. Doing a quick bit of math, I answered, "Close to ten thousand years, probably."

She shrugged. "That's not that long, but if the selection pressures were high enough, it could be enough time for evolution to be responsible."

"Evolution?" I said, frowning.

Matthew patted my shoulder. "I'll explain later. If you search through the knowledge the She'Har preserved from the ancient humans, there's some explanation of it there. The She'Har also had an even more detailed explanation, but it's harder to find since they had a completely different perspective. Basically, it's the idea that living things change over time to better survive."

"The kionthara may have intervened," added Matthew. "They were isolated here for thousands of years, and they were given much of the knowledge the She'Har possessed."

For me, that was easier to wrap my head around. The Dark Gods had become unbelievably cruel during their eons of existence. It would be just like them to tamper with the plants and animals of their home. They had probably done it just for the fun of tormenting the humans that lived here. Sanger's people, the Ungol, had survived living in this environment, and it had obviously made them extremely tough.

Sassy returned while I was still thinking about it. "There's a castle ahead with a large lake beside it," she reported.

"Did you see any people in the castle?" I asked.

"Isn't that what castles are for, people to live in?" said the small dragon acerbically.

I ground my teeth. "Unless the people were all eaten by giant spiders. Did you see anyone or not?"

Sassy turned her head slightly to one side in a gesture that was oddly reminiscent of my dog, Humphrey, when he was deep in thought. "I suppose your question wasn't so dumb after all. I did see a few men walking atop the walls."

"Thank you, Sassy. I'm glad to know you don't think I'm entirely ignorant," I said, sourly. Off to one side I could see Karen covering her mouth as she stifled her laughter. "Did you notice any other significant details while you were scouting?"

"It's much prettier than that black blob you call Castle Cameron. You could learn from whoever built it," remarked Sassy. "At the very least, consider getting a lake and a moat. It's quite scenic."

Gram snorted, but I silenced him with a cold stare. "How about the gates, Sassy, were they open or closed? Did it look like the castle was in a defensive posture?"

"They were closed," said the dragon. "But you should know, buildings don't take postures. They can't move."

Ignoring her comment, I addressed the others, "Let's proceed. We'll approach the gates and see if they'll let us in."

We continued our march down the road, and soon enough the woods on either side fell away as we entered the cleared land that surrounded Castle Lancaster. It was a common-sense matter of defense to keep the area outside the walls clear of trees or large buildings in the event of a war or siege, and Lancaster was no different. In fact, there were usually sheep to be found grazing the area, but I spotted none today. I suspected they had been eaten, either by the castle inhabitants or whatever it was that had forced them to close their gates.

No one hailed us as we stopped in front of the great oaken doors, which I took to be a bad sign. "Hello the gate!" I yelled, using a little magic to amplify my voice.

A voice answered from one of the arrow slits in the gatehouse that overlooked the gate. "Who goes there?"

"I am Lord Cameron, cousin to your lord, Duke Roland. I have come to offer assistance if it is needed."

There was no response, but I could easily detect several men huddled together in the room above the gate, whispering to one another. Eventually one of them replied, "We will have to report this to His Grace. Please wait there."

"Can't you recognize me? I have been here many times," I protested.

"These are dangerous times, milord. I have been ordered not to open the gates without Lord Lancaster's express permission," said the guard.

"Look, I could just fly over the walls if I wanted," I began, but Gram put a hand on my shoulder.

"Just be patient, milord. They are right to be wary. You'll only alarm them if you press the issue or try flying over," he advised me.

Gram was right, of course. So I held my tongue. We waited an eternity, or perhaps ten minutes as a more impartial timekeeper may have observed. Then I detected the original speaker returning with several other men, one of whom I recognized by his aythar. It was Roland.

Relief flooded through me. Until then, I hadn't realized how worried I had really been. If Roland had died, it would have been a terrible blow to the Queen, not to mention me. When he glanced through the arrow slit and saw me, I could see a similar relief in his own features.

"Mort? Is it really you?" asked Roland, calling down to us.

"I'm pretty sure it is," I replied, somewhat sarcastically.

Roland gave the order, and a moment later the drawbridge came down while my ears could detect the heavy grinding of the gears that raised the portcullis operating behind it. As usual, I was momentarily jealous. Castle Cameron had never had a moat, and hence no drawbridge. It seemed unfair. Secretly, I thought perhaps Sassy was right. *Maybe I should create a lake and a moat.*

It was a silly idea, of course. We didn't have a river close by to feed it, so I would have to do some rather unusual engineering to make it happen, and that was aside from the fact that the outer walls and other structures would have to be moved to make room for such an addition. And that was before even considering Washbrook. Would I want to try and enclose the town walls with my moat? The entire thing was impractical. I sighed and discarded the notion.

Once the drawbridge was down, Roland strode across, clad in mail and wearing a steel cap. He stopped in front of me, studying me warily a moment before opening his arms wide and catching me in a giant bear hug. "It really is you! What's happening out there? We've had no contact with anyone for more than two months now. Is Ari safe? What of the kingdom?"

"Everything is fine," I told him. "We've been more worried about you." My words were spoken over his shoulder with a bare minimum of air, for he was squeezing me too tightly for me to breathe normally.

Roland released me and stepped back, casting his eyes at the road behind us. "Let's get inside. It isn't safe out here."

After we were inside, the outer portcullis was again lowered and the drawbridge raised. "So what has happened here these past two months?" I asked.

"I'd rather know what's been happening out there," said Roland. "Why has no one come? The message boxes aren't working either. It's almost as though Lancaster has become an island unto itself."

That was when I realized that Roland had no idea that Lancaster had shifted into what might as well be another world. "It's complicated," I told him. "Why don't you catch me up first?"

My cousin frowned. "You must be hungry. Come inside. You can have the finest dried mutton and salt porridge that Lancaster has to offer." As we walked, he continued, "And as your host, I insist. Guests first, what has been happening?"

Mutton? I shuddered involuntarily. While I could eat it, it was fairly prominent on the list of foods I usually avoided, and being nobility, that meant I never ate it. Unless Penny made it—I knew better than to refuse her offerings, and she had a way of making it more palatable. Once again, I felt a pang of grief as I remembered she was gone.

We sat at the high table in the great hall and drank small beer while the food was brought out. Acquiescing to Roland's demand, I filled him in on everything that had happened over the past two months. The only difficult part was describing what had happened to Penny. Every time I told the story, it felt as though my heart had been torn open again.

When I had finished Roland placed his hand on my arm sympathetically, his eyes damp. "I'm sorry for your loss, Mort. We all loved her. I wish I had been there for you."

I nodded, keeping my eyes on the cup in front of me. If I had met his eyes, I wasn't certain I wouldn't break down. Hearing the soft words of others always made it worse.

Roland called his steward over and sent the man to fetch a bottle of wine, so we could toast to the late Countess. Then began to relate his own tale. "We had no idea we were cut off, trapped in some foreign realm. Not until hearing what you just told me," he said. "Sometime last month, I knew something was off. The farmers and freeholders stopped coming to the castle. The traders never made their scheduled shipments.

"I sent a detachment of men to your estate to inquire if all was well, but none of them returned. A week after that, some of the farmers that live close appeared and asked for sanctuary, claiming that large beasts were devouring their flocks and destroying their fields. I took them in and sent more men to investigate. They also vanished," he explained.

"The message boxes also failed. My letters remained within them, unread, so I sent three more messengers. None of them returned. As you can imagine, I was beginning to become seriously concerned, but it wasn't until the ogre appeared that we closed up the castle and began to treat our situation like a siege."

I leaned forward. "What did it do?"

Roland looked at me curiously. "You've seen it, then? I expected you to react with disbelief when I mentioned it."

I nodded. "In the strange forest I mentioned earlier, the one that appeared where we expected to find Lancaster."

My cousin rubbed at his thick beard. "There's more than one, then. That's poor news."

"I killed that one," I told him. "But I'm sure there are others."

"Well, this one came right down the road, as casual as you please. We still had sheep around the castle at that point, and it picked one right out of the herd and began to eat it like you or I would an apple. Four or five bites and it was gone, feet, wool, head, and all." Roland shuddered. "It stared at the castle but didn't attempt to come in. After a while it wandered off, but the sheep began steadily disappearing after that. None of us were willing to chance looking for them. We've kept the drawbridge up ever since."

"You've been lucky then," said Gram. "There's much worse out there. I doubt anyone outside your walls is still alive."

Roland nodded in agreement. "You mean the spiders? One of them snuck over the wall two weeks ago and tried to take up residence in one of the towers. We lost seven men before we managed to kill it."

"I need to get you to Albamarl," I said suddenly. "Your sister has been worried sick since Lancaster disappeared."

My cousin leaned back, stretching his back. "What I wouldn't give for a nice roast hen and some greens, but if things are as bad as you say out there, I can't see risking my men on the road."

Gram looked at me emphatically, as though he had something to say, but I merely shook my head. "We won't abandon them, Roland—or Lancaster for that matter. I can take you to see Ari and have you back within a day or two. My son and the others can stay here to keep watch over your people."

"What about the ogre?" asked the Duke. "I wouldn't want to meet him on the road, even with you beside me."

The ogre was the least of my worries. I had faced far worse, but it wouldn't do to make light of my cousin's fears. Instead I pointed out the obvious. "We won't take the road," I said smiling.

Roland's eyes grew wide with alarm. "You're out of your damn mind if you think I'm getting in that flying contraption of yours again. I nearly died the last time!"

I smirked at the memory. Years past, I had once taken Roland in an enchanted construct designed to make flying safer. He hadn't come anywhere close to dying, but I hadn't expected him to have such a severe fear of heights. He had vomited all over the interior, and I had been forced to land and render him unconscious to continue. I nodded at Karen. "See that young lady there? She's from another world, and she carries the Mordan gift. We won't have to fly, will we, Karen?"

"Excuse me?" said Karen.

"You can teleport back to where we crossed the boundary, can't you?" I asked.

She nodded. "I believe so."

I turned back to Roland. "See, nothing simpler. She can take us to the border, and we can cross back into Lothion."

The Duke stared at me suspiciously. "And then we'll *walk* back to Albamarl, right?"

"No, then I'll make a circle and take us back to my home. I have a portal there that leads directly to Ariadne's chambers," I explained.

Roland gave me an odd look. "To her chambers? That hardly seems proper. How does the Countess feel about that?" He paused for a moment as he realized his mistake, then lowered his eyes. "Sorry, Mort. I wasn't thinking."

His expression hurt almost as much as hearing him mention my wife, but I kept my expression calm. "It's alright. I do the same thing. It's hard to believe. I don't know if I'll ever get used to it."

My cousin reached for the wine bottle and refilled my glass. "Let's have another toast before we go." He raised his glass, and the rest of us followed his example. "To Penny. May we never forget her kindness and love."

I drained the glass and used my napkin to wipe my cheeks.

 CHAPTER 13

Half an hour later and we stood at the edge of the primeval forest once more, where the faintly shimmering boundary waited. Behind us was the road to Lancaster. Karen, Matthew, and Roland were with me.

"You're sure they'll be fine until we get back?" asked Roland once more. "I dislike leaving my family behind." His wife and son were still in the keep.

"Sir Gram will do well in your place," I reassured him. "And he'll have my son and your seneschal to advise him. We'll be back within a day."

Matthew spoke up, "Let's not get ahead of ourselves. We still don't know if you can open the boundary. If not, I'll have to come with you in order to let you back in afterward."

"Show me again," I told my son. "Slowly."

He nodded. "Compared to crossing dimensions to Karen's world, this is simple." He held his hands out, placing his palms up in the air where the boundary shimmered, almost invisible to my magesight. "Push your aythar outward, like this, and then you have to change it slightly, until you feel it beginning to match the frequency of the boundary." He demonstrated while I watched carefully. Then he dismissed what he had done and told me, "Your turn."

I tried, but while my aythar wiggled around in long streamers, it failed to do anything.

"Not like that," my son admonished me. "You don't move it in that direction. You move it sideways, into a space you can't see with your eyes. Move it in the direction you can feel but can't quite see."

It took me two more tries, but finally I got the feel for it and my aythar seemed to vanish for a second before taking on a shimmer that was altogether different from what I was used to.

"That's it!" said Matthew. "Now, move it outward, tracing the lines hidden there. Once you reach the size you want, you just have to pull and it will come apart, but don't release it after that. You have to maintain the edge or it will collapse back in on itself."

The air opened before me, showing me the road that led back to Cameron, but I lost my hold and it vanished again a second later. It took several more attempts before I had found the knack for keeping it open.

"Now cross over and do it from the other side," said Matthew. "Just to make sure you have it. If I don't see it open again within a couple of minutes, I'll come across and join you."

I held the portal open while Roland crossed, and then I followed him before allowing it to close behind us. We were alone on the road to Cameron, with a volcanic wasteland behind us, the remains of the forest I had destroyed a few weeks before. Turning back, I repeated my new trick and reopened the boundary. Matthew and Karen were there, staring back at us.

"That's amazing, Dad," he told me. "I still don't understand how you're doing it. You shouldn't have the gift. You always told me I had inherited it from Mom."

"I thought you had," I said frankly.

Matthew gave me a funny look, his eyes going slightly out of focus. "We should talk about that when you get back. There's something different about you now."

"What?" I asked, curious.

He shook his head. "Not now. Later, when we're alone." Karen looked at him as though disappointed to be left out of the secret, but she didn't say anything.

"Take care of my wife and son," Roland reminded him.

Matthew dipped his head in agreement, and then I released the boundary, letting the opening dissolve back into nothing once more.

"Ready to see your sister?" I asked. Reaching into my pouch, I pulled out the enchanted stones that, once activated, would become my flying construct.

Roland backed away, fear in his eyes. "You said you would make a teleport circle!"

Laughing, I put away the stones. "Relax. I'm just teasing you." Then I pulled out my stencil and began making a circle to take us to my home.

"You have a nasty sense of humor, Mordecai. Has anyone ever told you that?"

I grinned at him wickedly. "All the time. I blame your brother. He was a bad influence on me."

"I'm not so sure," said Roland. "I've always suspected that Marcus got it from you."

Finished with the circle, I stepped into it and waited until Roland had joined me. "Who knows?" I told him, and then with an effort of will, I took us back to my quiet home in the mountains.

Irene and Lynaralla were glad to see us, but after a brief greeting, I took Roland to the portal in my house. It had been months and he needed to see his sister Ariadne, if for no other reason than her peace of mind. Softly whispering the command word that would keep the portal active for someone not attuned to it, I opened the closet door and led him through into the Queen's chambers.

Several things leapt into my awareness as we entered stepped through the portal. The most immediately apparent was that there were two very powerful sources of aythar close at hand, wizards. There were also several other men in the room. I instinctively strengthened my shield, but a half second later I had identified the other mages by their aythar. My son, Conall, and Gareth Gaelyn were in the corridor on either side of the doorway. Of the other men, one was Sir Harold, while the other two were some of his guardsmen.

All of them looked nervous. Well, except for Gareth, of course. Two thousand years as a dragon had made him difficult to impress with any emotion, other than arrogance.

"He's here," called Harold, notifying the Queen, who sat in the next room.

"I appreciate the welcome," I said wryly. "How did you know I'd be here?"

Harold looked away uncomfortably. "Just a hunch. We've been waiting." Then his eyes fell on the man with me and grew wide.

I smiled. "Well, wait no longer! I'm sure you remember His Grace, Duke Lancaster." I gave a theatrical bow and presented Roland to them.

"Roland?" said Ariadne, still in the other room.

Rather than make her wait any longer, I took the lead and went in, bringing Roland along in my wake. *Why were they guarding the portal?* I wondered. *Did they think I'd bring a threat through it?* But I didn't dwell on it. I was more interested in seeing Ari's face when she was reunited with her brother.

Seconds later, Ariadne and Roland were locked in a strong embrace. The others filed into the room behind, Conall standing on my left while Gareth took my right. The guards spread out around the room and then Harold passed in front of me, stopping to stand between me and the Queen. It almost seemed natural, but their positioning was too calculated to be casual.

The Queen finished her hug and then stared at me, but before she could say anything, Harold began to speak, "Lord Cameron, it is my duty…"

Ariadne put a hand on his shoulder. "Wait, Sir Harold. Let me speak first."

I stared around the room, reading the faces and seeing the tense expressions. "Your Majesty, what exactly is going on?"

Ariadne's face was stern. "Where exactly did you go yesterday, Mort?"

"Actually, I wanted to talk to you about that, privately. I saw something unfortunate," I answered.

"Did you see my husband, Prince Leomund?" she asked.

I nodded. "I went to his hunting lodge. I'll admit I shouldn't have, but I was curious as to who he was meeting there. I know I shouldn't have spied on him, but what I saw was so horrifying I couldn't help but confront him."

The Queen visibly flinched at my words and she took a moment to compose herself before she continued, "Then it was really you, not an illusion or seeming. Did you see Lord Airedale there?"

"I did, though I don't remember if I spoke to him. I went straight up to the room Leomund was in. He was about to whip one of his servants, a young girl," I explained.

"And then?" she asked the question almost as if she didn't want to hear the answer.

I shrugged. "Well, I admit, I lost my temper, but—"

"Father, don't!" exclaimed Conall beside me.

"Sir Conall!" barked Harold. "Remain silent until the Queen is finished with him."

His tone angered me. "Harold, don't speak to my son like that. He didn't mean any harm."

Harold didn't answer, but Ariadne motioned toward me to continue. "Please finish, Lord Cameron." There was resignation in her voice.

Why is she so upset? It made no sense. Obviously Leomund or Airedale had informed them of my assault, but that alone didn't warrant this behavior. Striking the Prince was a crime certainly, but I had had just cause. "As I said, I lost my temper. The girl he was whipping couldn't have been more than twelve years of age. I snapped and struck him so hard it knocked him unconscious."

Ariadne looked shocked. "He was unconscious?"

I nodded. "I know she was his property, but the law doesn't allow even princes to treat a child that way. She had marks all over her body. Who knows how long he's been abusing her, or what things he has done to her? I apologize for saying this, but your husband is a monster."

Angry, the Queen raised her voice, "Then you should have brought him to me! You had evidence of his crime. You had witnesses. You should have left him to the law! I had little love for the man, but this! How can I excuse what you've done?"

All I did was hit him—once. Was that really that bad? "I still have the evidence. I took the girl home with me. Her body is proof enough, and the witnesses are still there. Ask them. Some of them may lie for him, but surely one or two of them can be convinced to tell the truth."

"We have questioned them," said Ariadne. "Their stories match your own, as does Lord Airedale's account."

"Then you know he's a monster," I declared.

"Do you have any remorse at all, Mort?" said Ariadne. "A monster he was, but you killed him in cold blood, while he was lying unconscious."

Had I hit him *that* hard? No, that was impossible. I had checked his heart and breathing before I had left. He had still been alive. My mouth fell open as I looked at the other faces in the room. The coldness in their eyes left no doubt that Leomund was dead. "I didn't kill him!" I blurted out. "He was alive. I knocked him out and tended to the girl. He was still alive when I took her and left."

The Queen looked faintly hopeful. "And she will testify to this?"

"Of course," I began, but then a shadow fell across my heart. "Well, actually I put her to sleep before leaving."

Gareth shook his head in disappointment. "So, you had the kindness to make sure the girl's eyes were closed before you put the dagger through his heart. My heart weeps at your nobility." He didn't try to hide the mockery in his words.

"Dagger? What dagger?" I asked.

Harold glanced respectfully at the Queen before speaking this time. "The Prince-Consort was killed by a single thrust of his own dagger. It was found still standing in his chest."

"Well, I didn't put it there!"

"You dare deny it?" said Gareth in disbelief. "By your own account, and the account of the servants and Lord Airedale, you broke into the lodge, stormed up the stairs, sent everyone away, and assaulted the Prince. You even admit you assaulted him. You expect us to believe he stabbed himself out of guilt after you left? What gall!"

"Damn it, yes!" I shouted. "I've told you nothing but the truth. I struck him and left."

"Enough," said the Queen. "This a matter for a court of justice. Mordecai Illeniel, Count di' Cameron and holder of the Cameron Estate in my stead, you are hereby under arrest, to be held in prison until your case can be decided in a court of law."

I had been down this road once before, and I still had the scars across my back to remember it. I had sacrificed my dignity once, for the sake of the kingdom, but I had no willingness to do so again. Defiant, I looked at the others in the room. "What makes you think you can lock me up?"

Harold put a hand behind him, pushing the Queen, who began to back out of the room.

I glared at him. "You, Harold? You know better. It would take more than you and the entire Royal Guard to take me. Conall alone could handle you and your men."

"Dad," said Conall, drawing my attention, but he wouldn't meet my eyes.

Gareth sneered, "Why do you think your son is here?"

My heart was on fire now. I snarled at Gareth, "Don't even think about getting between me and my son!"

The archmage who had been a dragon laughed cruelly. "He's here to arrest you, fool! I'm just a witness, and extra insurance in case you are stupid enough to do battle with your own son."

I looked at Conall again, and my answer was written in the shame in his eyes. My arrogance, my anger, even my pride died in that moment. *Godsbedamned!* I silently cursed. *How did it come to this?* Slowly, I bowed my head in defeat.

"You finally begin to show some sense," stated Gareth.

Conall stepped forward to stand in front of me. "Father, hold out your hands." In his hands were a pair of milky white manacles made of a material I didn't recognize. They were connected by a three-foot chain and looked suspiciously like the manacles my daughter had described from her time imprisoned in Halam.

"Where did those come from?" I asked. The ones that had been used on Moira had been old, very old.

Gareth snorted. "Do you think you're the only one that can enchant? I was born in the Age of Magic, Mordecai. I've seen things you can only dream of."

"Father, your hands," repeated Conall with more insistence.

"Conall, you don't believe I did this, do you?" I asked him. "You know I wouldn't do this."

At last, he raised his eyes to meet mine. "I know you wouldn't kill someone that didn't deserve it. And I also know that what Leomund was doing was evil. I'm not sure I wouldn't have done the same."

I held out my wrists, and even as Conall snapped the manacles in place I repeated myself, "I didn't kill him, son. Remember that. I should have. I wanted to, but I didn't. I wouldn't lie to you."

"Few will weep over Leomund's death," said Gareth. "But then again, how many will weep for you, Mordecai, when you hang for this?"

"You're a real bastard, Gareth," I shot back. "I'm sure you've been waiting for a day like this."

The other archmage shrugged. "Actually, no. I never thought you'd be this stupid. Much as I dislike you, I didn't think you'd be fool enough to abandon reason and bring so much shame to your family. I certainly won't mourn for you, though."

I growled. "One of these days I'm going to knock that smug look off that red bush you call a face, Gareth. Mark my words."

 # CHAPTER 14

Sunlight glared down on Rose Thornbear as she stepped out of the carriage, creating shimmering highlights in her raven hair that were only improved by the occasional strand of grey among the black. She squinted against the brightness for a few seconds and then began walking purposefully toward the palace carriageway entrance. There were few here to observe her, other than stablemen and palace servants, but she kept her back straight and her shoulders square, proceeding on her way with stately grace.

Rose never slouched, and while she wasn't a tall woman, most who met her for the first time came away with the impression they had met someone taller than themselves. In mind, character, and integrity, she towered over her peers. It was who she was, drummed into her by her father from birth to maturity. *"A Hightower must be as their name suggests, straight, proud, and observant."* She could hear his voice in her mind even now when she thought of his favorite saying.

She kept her steps even and steady, despite her urge to hurry. It wasn't that she had anything important to report, though. In fact, it was the opposite. Most of her day had been a complete waste of time.

That's not entirely true, she reminded herself, mainly out of habit. *All information is useful, even if it isn't immediately apparent why.* That was an element of her personal philosophy, but it did little to ease her current frustration. She had spent the day moving about the city, meeting several of her more reclusive contacts and using the opportunity to make some firsthand observations of Tyrion's new additions to the city's defense.

Her most hopeful transaction had involved some insight into Lord Cantley's personal finances. Considering that most of her sources only provided rumor and gossip, a chance to actually view the personal ledgers of a nobleman was a rare opportunity. Yet it had yielded nothing useful, at least so far as she could tell in the present. Gregory Cantley's finances seemed depressingly mundane.

Rose's other contacts had been similarly unhelpful. She had gained some insight into the reaction of the populace to the Royal Guard's aggressive new methods, but she had already anticipated that result. She wanted more details, and her sources were entirely too vague.

It was at times like this when she was tempted to enlist her mother-in-law's aid. Elise Thornbear had far better contacts among the darker elements of the city, despite her age and high station. But Elise was getting up in years, and she had largely given up her involvement in politics. Rose preferred to leave it that way. Dorian's mother had earned her rest.

When she finally closed the door to her apartment behind her, she let out a long sigh of relief. It might have been a long day, but a cup of tea would make it better. Elise was asleep on the couch in the front room. Rose didn't want to wake her, but then her subconscious brought something to her attention. The older woman's posture wasn't normal.

Did she collapse? Then her nose noted a change in the air, a certain musk that reminded her of…

"Don't worry, she's merely sleeping," said a deep masculine voice behind her.

Despite the suddenness of it, she didn't flinch or startle. Rose had already concluded that he was either in the room or had recently left. "Your Grace, perhaps you weren't aware, but it is considered churlish to enter another's home without invitation. I'm not certain how things were in your time, but in modern society it is also a crime."

The archmage moved around her, stopping to face her. "No one knows I am here, other than you and me. Therefore, it isn't a crime—unless you wish it to be."

Tyrion wore a simple tunic with a wide collar. As her eyes took in his attire, she couldn't help but notice the line of muscle that rose from his shoulder to his neck, and her pulse quickened slightly. *Damn the man. Why is he so… male?* She disciplined her thoughts and made a conscious effort to control her breathing.

He smiled at her hesitation, then leaned closer. "Or would you like to commit a crime, perhaps with me?" Reaching out, he fingered the amulet that hung close to her bosom.

Heat rushed through her, coming from within and extending throughout her body, from her head down to… With an effort of will, she ignored the sensation, as well as his comment. "Why are you here?" she demanded.

The new Duke of the Wester Isles put her pendant back in its place, the back of his fingers brushing lightly across the skin of her chest as he did, sending an electric thrill through Rose's spine. "To save you the trouble of looking for me," he replied.

Rose lifted her eyes to meet his, projecting all the righteous anger she could muster at him with her gaze. "And for what cause would I *ever* seek to find you?"

"Are you playing games with me, Lady Rose?" Tyrion's lips curled, showing his canines. "If so, I find your game enthralling, all the more because I do not know the rules. You know very well why I am here. The real question you should be asking—is what my price will be."

Her heart was beating loudly in her chest, causing the blood to pound in her ears as a flush rose to her cheeks and neck. His eyes were devouring her, and then she felt Tyrion's hand at her waist as he pulled her closer before sliding it down over her backside. "Or perhaps you already know my price, and are aching to pay it?"

Rose felt her knees beginning to tremble and she realized she was starting to lean closer, as though to press her hips against his. Things were about to get horribly out of control. Mind racing, she drew on decades of experience at cooling the ardor of overeager lordlings. "What did you eat?" she asked suddenly.

Tyrion's eyes registered confusion. "Pardon?"

She pulled away from him. "I asked what you have eaten. Whatever it was smells atrocious. Or is that normal for your breath?"

He closed his mouth and stepped farther back, momentarily nonplussed. Rose graced him with a look of pity before adding, "Don't be too worried. It's a problem for many. I understand that chewing mint leaves can help."

Tyrion's confusion turned to irritation. "Are you honestly trying to insult me? Have you no concern whatsoever for current events?"

Rose's expression was one of complete innocence. "Absolutely not, and I have no idea what you're referring to."

"The newest resident of the palace dungeon," said Tyrion, raising his voice.

Rose winced, wrinkling her nose to complete the act. "I'm sorry, Your Grace, but would you mind standing a little farther back? It really is quite pungent." When Tyrion stepped away, she pointed to a chair. "Actually, why not sit over there?" she suggested, before taking another seat for herself—on the opposite side of the tea table.

Once they were seated, she continued, "Now, tell me what you're talking about. I've been absent from the palace all day."

"Then you haven't heard the news?"

Rose arched her brows, indicating how obvious she thought his question was.

"Lord Cameron has been arrested," said Tyrion.

Her heart jumped in her chest, this time for more genuine reasons, but she kept her features calm. "For what reason?"

Tyrion gave her what she assumed he must have thought was a sly look as he answered, "For the murder of Queen's husband." Then he waited, hoping for a reaction from her.

After a few seconds, Rose sighed. "Lord Tyrion, are you going to give me the details, or do you intend to tell the whole thing in short, dramatic statements like some schoolboy trying to impress his peers?"

His cheeks colored with embarrassment, but Tyrion pushed it aside and began to relate the tale. It took several minutes, during which Rose asked no questions, merely waiting whenever he paused, making him feel foolish all over again.

When he had finished, she finally spoke. "Who brought the accusation?"

"Airedale," said Tyrion curtly. "I thought I said that already."

Rose gave him a severe look. "You did not. In fact, you left out a number of pertinent details. Please refrain from making observations and answer my questions. Who were the other witnesses?"

He shrugged. "Some servants that worked there."

"How many?"

Tyrion frowned. "Five, or maybe six. Does it matter—"

She cut him off, "What were their names?"

"How should I know?" he answered, flustered.

Rose ignored his question. "No matter. I'll get those details later. Where is the girl Mordecai rescued?"

Tyrion leaned forward, putting his elbows on his knees and resting his chin on them. Had he realized how tedious Rose's questioning would be, he might not have come. He was regretting it already. "I don't know."

"Did they say whose dagger it was that they found in Leomund's chest?" she asked, relentless in her interrogation.

"His, maybe?"

Indignantly, Rose continued to prod him. "His? Please be more precise, Lord Illeniel. Who do you mean by 'his'? Are you referring to Lord Cameron or the Prince?"

Tyrion shot to his feet. "The Prince! Gods of the forest, woman! Are you planning a prison break or a legal defense?"

Rose glanced up at him, arching one brow imperiously. "It shows your ignorance, Lord Illeniel, that you jump to one solution before considering the other."

160

A low growl rose in the Duke's throat, and he looked ready to tear his own hair out. "Do you want my help or not?!"

Demurely, Rose stood and moved toward the door. "Perhaps, if I decide there is no other course. Otherwise you are useless to me."

His hands clenched into fists as he responded, "You make the mistake of assuming I would help you."

She looked at him dismissively. "Are you referring to your *price* again?" Rose flicked a finger in the direction of his groin, leaving her hand limp as though to indicate her opinion of his manhood. "Don't be ridiculous. You had already decided to help him before you came here. Only a fool would pay you for something you already intend to do. To the contrary, I would caution you not to do anything foolish until I give my blessing. You might only make things worse, while destroying your own position at court." She opened the door and stepped to one side.

Tyrion remained still for several seconds, as though he might refuse to leave, but finally he strode forward into the hall. Then he turned back. "I can't believe…"

"Thank you for the information, Lord Illeniel," said Rose, smiling sweetly as she cut him off. "I'll contact you if I decide to, what were your words again? Oh yes! Commit a crime." Then she firmly but carefully closed the door.

She waited there for several minutes, breathing heavily with her back against the door while she silently prayed that the privacy ward on her apartment was still functioning. Once she was sure he wouldn't try to return, she crossed the room slowly to avoid waking Elise, then went to her bedroom and closed that door as well.

Finally alone, she sank down onto her bed and stared at her hands. They were trembling in reaction to the stress and fear she had been suppressing. Standing up and going to a side table, she picked up the pitcher of water that sat there, fumbling and nearly dropping it as she poured water into her hands to wash her face. An image of Mordecai's face rose in her mind, and she scrubbed her face harder, as though to wash away the tears before they could appear.

Mort, what have you done? she thought, feeling a cold dread fill her heart. She splashed more water on her face, but it failed to take away her fear. Picking up the neatly folded towel that sat beside her washbasin, she took it back to the bed with her and covered her face with it, still fighting her emotions. *More importantly, what will I do?*

Removing her shoes, she let one drop to the floor while holding the other tightly in her small fist. Her grip was so tight she could see it shaking. *You already know the answer to that, Rose,* she thought to herself. She hurled the shoe across the room as hard as she could. Then she answered her own question out loud, her voice coming thick and hoarse from a throat that seemed ready to close up, "Anything."

Rose spent the next half hour regaining her composure. It was a ritual she had gone through many times during her life. She didn't pretend to be emotionless, and on occasion she had even wept in the company of close friends, such as Penny. But it was a rule of her life that she never let others see her when her walls truly crumbled. Only two men had ever seen her at her worst, when she was completely unable to contain her emotions. One of them, her husband, was dead. The other was likely to be hanged in a matter of days.

When she felt ready, she undressed and put away her gown before donning another. Then she let her hair down and carefully brushed it out before she began to braid it again with skillful fingers. It was almost meditative, this ritual of hers. Gradually her doubts and fears faded into the background while her dexterous fingers arranged and pinned the braids into another of her countless styles. That done, she applied a modest amount of rouge to her cheeks and checked her appearance in the mirror.

Returning to the main room, she took a moment to gently arrange her mother-in-law, correcting her unnatural positioning and making sure she could sleep peacefully until the spell had worn off. Then she went to the hearth and put a kettle on to boil water. She was long overdue for her tea.

Through all of it, her mind was in motion, calculating possibilities, and categorizing what she had learned. By the time her tea was ready, she had finished with that and had already begun to decide what her plan of action would be. *One step at a time,* she recited mentally.

 CHAPTER 15

Dungeons, as a general rule, are unpleasant, and the one in the palace in Albamarl was no exception. Personally, I wouldn't have recommended it to anyone, but then people didn't stay in dungeons if they had a choice. That's not to say that all dungeons are filthy, rat-infested holes brimming with foul odors and unsanitary options for waste disposal. The dungeon in Lancaster, for example, was a model dungeon, fairly clean and well maintained.

This one, however, was not in nearly such good condition. Though Ariadne was not known as a cruel queen, and her father, James, had been similarly kind, the ruler before them had been a different sort. During King Edward's reign, the dungeon had seen heavy use and little cleaning. Since his time, the successive monarchs had not needed much beyond the upper level, which they did clean and maintain. The lower levels had been closed up and ignored.

I was not taken to a cell on the upper level. According to Gareth, those noble rooms were not adequate for a mage of my standing and grace. No, I was to be given accommodations to match my abilities, the royal suite as it were. Or rather the arcane suite. No one living had even been aware of the cell he brought me to. It was a relic of the distant past that only he remembered.

Privately, I hoped that that was because he had been stuffed into it at some point, but he refused to answer my questions on the matter.

Gareth, Conall, and I stood at the end of a long corridor on the bottom level, facing a blank wall. The last cells we had passed were more than fifty yards back, and they had been so badly rusted I doubted they were still capable of holding a prisoner, mundane or otherwise. "I guess this is the end of the line," I said, somewhat melodramatically.

Gareth gave me a dubious stare.

"Admit it, you wanted to say that," I said, archly.

"Actually, I was going to tell you not to worry. That what you have seen thus far isn't a good representation of your new home," said Gareth seriously.

Slowly, I closed my eyes, letting the air out of my lungs in a slow exhalation. Gareth wasn't much fun. *The man needs a sense of humor. Maybe it's because he was a dragon for so long?* I quickly discarded that thought. The dragons I had created disproved the theory. Alyssa's dragon, Sassy, dispelled the idea every time she spoke.

Gareth started to relax, a sign he was about to use his ability as an archmage to connect to something beyond himself, but then he stopped. "Before I open the door, let me give you a warning, Mordecai. I'm sure that from the moment those manacles were put on you have been considering how to escape them. I won't deny that it is very possible for you or I to do so, but it will do you no good. Most importantly, you must never use your metaphysical abilities when facing another archmage."

"Worried about your health, Gareth?" I asked him pointedly.

"Yes, but this is about more than just that," he answered frankly. "I've heard about your match with Tyrion and since warned him. Both of you were closer to death than you knew. It is never wise for one of us to fight with another with these powers. Even if we try not to, it is too easy to make a mistake in the heat of battle."

He had roused my curiosity. "What happens?"

Gareth held up his hand and removed his signet ring. "Let us use this ring as an example. If one of us were to make it a part of ourselves, that is well and good. No harm done. If *both* of us attempted to at the same time, it would be the end of us both. The important thing to remember is that it could be anything—the earth, the air, a singular object. No matter how big or small the thing is, if two archmages connect with it at the same time, they become one being."

His speech reminded me of what I had done with Penny, and what I had once done with Elaine. Each time, I had emerged from the experience not entirely sure if my soul was mine, or if we had perhaps switched places. Still, it hadn't worked out badly. "When you say 'one being,' precisely what happens?" I asked.

"I've never seen it. To my knowledge, archmages have always been so rare that it has only happened twice in history, but the records described horrific results. The bodies of the two individuals flow together like water, creating an abomination possessing features of both of them. Their minds are similarly mixed, and the result has always been insanity," he explained.

I prodded him for more information. "What happened to them then? Were they put down?"

The red-bearded mage shook his head. "In both cases they destroyed themselves to put an end to their pain."

"I appreciate the warning," I responded with genuine gratitude.

"I warn you for my own safety, Mordecai. While you are held here, I am sure you will be tempted to escape. For that reason, either Tyrion or myself will be guarding your cell at all times, along with another mage such as your son or one of the She'Har krytek. If you try to escape into the earth or some similar means, we will stop you, and the result would be detrimental to both of us," said Gareth.

I couldn't help but feel some respect for the man, both for his honesty and for the fact that he was quite literally putting his own life on the line to keep me locked up. "Aren't you worried I might do something out of pure spite? If I'm certain to be executed, I have little to lose."

Gareth shook his head negatively. "You have an overdeveloped sense of justice. While I don't particularly like you, I have never known you to harm another for such reasons. In the past, most of your more spectacularly stupid decisions came from ignorance, rather than malice. Hence, I thought it best to inform you of the possibilities."

"And yet, you still believe I killed the Prince?"

"My opinion is irrelevant to the matter," said the archmage. "But yes, I believe it precisely because of that. You have shown a willingness to act on your conception of justice many times in the past, and damn the consequences. This instance appears to be merely another example of that foolishness."

How could I argue with that? Instead, I merely stared at him.

"Another thing," continued Gareth. "My wife is pregnant. In a span of months, I will become a father for the first time."

It wasn't a friendly sharing of happy news. *He's making sure I know that if I get him killed. I'll be robbing his child of its father,* I thought. *As if the risk of harming Conall if he's here on guard wasn't enough.* "Congratulations," I told him. "I will keep that in mind."

Relaxing once more, Gareth opened his mind and spoke to the stone in front of us, making it a part of his very being. It was an interesting moment for me, since I had never had a good opportunity to see it done from an external vantage point. It was surprisingly unimpressive. There was no movement of aythar or other sign that he was doing anything, though I could sense a change in the wall in front of us. Faintly, I heard its unique voice change slightly and it was a struggle not to listen more closely, but I remembered his words.

For an archmage, listening was more than a passive process; it was the means we used to connect with the world. My curiosity could kill us both. I made a conscious effort to ignore what he was doing.

The wall became translucent, and after a moment it faded until I could see through it, as though looking through murky water. "Step inside," ordered my jailor.

I glanced at Conall, and he gave me an apologetic face. Then I did as I was told. Inside, I noticed that the walls of the cell were inlaid with silver metal, covering every surface with the runes of a complex enchantment. My new home was roughly ten feet on a side, with only a stone bench to sit or lay upon. Unlike the regular cells, there was no hole or drain for me to use for elimination. Instead, a chamber pot sat in one corner. I could only surmise that an opening, of whatever sort, had been deemed too risky.

"This looks comfy," I told them, looking back through the murky stone wall at them.

Gareth didn't smile. "You might be interested to know that the last occupant of this place was Jerod Mordan, the wizard who summoned Balinthor and nearly destroyed our world."

That had been just over two thousand years ago. "He didn't do much decorating, did he?" I commented wryly.

If I had been hoping for a laugh, I was disappointed. Gareth was as stoic as ever. Conall's eyes were red, as though he might burst into tears at any moment. My son opened his mouth to speak. "Dad…"

It was then that I finally noticed he was wearing the surcoat I had brought him. "It's alright, son. This isn't your fault. Keep wearing the surcoat. You have nothing to be ashamed of." Then the wall became solid, cutting me off from the outside world.

Darkness covered me as the light from outside vanished and I lowered my head. There was no longer anyone to see me. Lack of light wasn't a big problem for wizards, and the manacles didn't prevent me from using my magesight, although they did diminish it somewhat, but a ten-by-ten stone cell wasn't much of a view. The enchantment in the walls blocked my ability to see anything beyond it.

There were many things I needed to think about, but in that moment, I didn't have the heart for it. So instead I lowered myself onto the stone bench and stretched out. *And I thought being publicly flogged was the most humiliating thing I would ever experience. It doesn't hold a candle to being arrested and put in a jail cell by my own child.*

Closing my eyes against the darkness, I considered sleep. It was a fairly silly notion, since I was nowhere close to being ready for bed. Then I thought about food. I had none, so it was a short thought, but I was glad that I had eaten with Roland right before coming to Albamarl. It was a damn shame that my most recent meal had been dried mutton and porridge, but I had a feeling I might find myself wishing for such luxury in the coming days.

There was no water in my cell, either, which seemed terribly unfair. Then again, the more I drank, the faster I'd fill up the chamber pot, and I didn't want to think about what would happen if that occurred before someone came to empty it.

Finally, I began to examine my shackles. They were pretty much as my daughter, Moira, had described, although these were obviously better made. Apparently, Gareth was no slouch when it came to enchanting. The basic principle was simple—the manacles siphoned away any aythar that I tried to emit. If I didn't exert myself, they only collected the small amount I naturally radiated, but any time I began to consciously try to do something, they rapidly drained the power away.

In a sense, they were similar to the enchantment I had once used to charge my iron bombs, except rather than collecting heat energy, these trapped aythar itself. The key lesson, though, was that they had a limit, just like my bombs. Eventually they would fill up completely, and if the power they stored exceeded that point, they would explode. I didn't think I wanted to be wearing them when that happened.

Given my strength, it was possible I could fill them within a day or two if I bent myself entirely to the task, but since I wasn't feeling suicidal, I decided to shelve that option for the time being. If I avoided emitting aythar deliberately, they would probably last a week or two. It was hard to judge without testing the material, for I didn't know what its energy capacity was, as I did with iron.

They were carved from a crystalline mineral of some sort. Crystals could often contain surprising amounts of power, which was why I had once used diamond to make a set of stasis cubes strong enough to freeze time for an entire city. This material probably didn't have that kind of capacity, but it was also a lot larger than the diamonds.

Either way, it was a dead-end line of thought. Overloading the manacles would surely kill me. The best—and simplest—course of action, would be to use my ability as an archmage and let the material pass through my wrists. There were two problems, however.

One, I didn't know if anyone was watching. If they were, that action might result in a response, and if that led to a battle with Gareth or Tyrion—well, I had been warned of the possible result. The second problem was that there might be a hidden enchantment I couldn't see on the inner surface of the manacles. If I had been the enchanter I'd have implemented something to detect the absence of the wearer's wrists. In other words, they might detonate if I removed them without following the proper procedure.

The only reason I would want to remove them, though, was simply to make myself more comfortable. A quick glance at the enchantment built in to the walls had already shown me that it was of a similar nature. The room was something like the Ironheart Chamber I had once built to trap a god. It would absorb any force thrown against it, and while it wouldn't have been sufficient to hold Karenth, it was more than enough to hold me. To escape, I would have to destroy the enchantment or use my ability as an archmage to pass through it, as Gareth had done to let me enter.

The same two problems that kept me from attempting to remove the manacles applied equally to the enchantment on the room.

What about a teleport circle? Hah! The room had been built to hold mages, and it had been effective at holding Jerod Mordan, who had the same innate ability to teleport that Karen had. Although I hadn't spent enough time to decipher most of the enchantment, I could assume that it would prevent those sorts of shenanigans.

"This is a fine pickle I've gotten myself into," I said the words aloud, more to hear my own voice than for any other reason. The room was deathly still. The silence might be worse than the darkness. It was already beginning to eat at me.

Reaching down, I felt around my waist, wishing I still had my pouches, or even just the belt. They had removed both, guessing, and rightly so, that I might have tricks concealed within them. They had also taken my boots and my jacket. I was clothed only in a simple tunic and a pair of trousers.

And my feet were getting cold.

"You could have left me my socks!" I yelled, wondering if anyone could hear me. If they could, they didn't do me the courtesy of responding. Even laughter would have been nice, or swearing. Anything, just so I knew someone heard me.

How long have I been in here? An hour, two hours? I laughed. It probably hadn't even been twenty minutes yet. How long would it be before the trial? If it was a week, I'd have to wait this amount of time—I did a mental calculation—five hundred and four more times.

What if it was longer than a week? "This is going to be rough," I told myself.

After a while, I retreated into my memories. One benefit of perfect recall is that you can always revisit the past. Doing my best to ignore the hard stone against my back and the chill of my feet, I immersed myself once more in the warm days of summer. Days when Penny had been just a friend, a girl I couldn't imagine being silly enough to love me. Days when Marcus had always had some foolish scheme to while away the hours. Days when Dorian had traipsed around with us on endless adventures.

 **CHAPTER 16**

"Lady Hightower, have you taken leave of your senses?" The speaker was in his thirties, with piercing brown eyes and a pronounced, almost blade-like nose.

Rose answered him calmly, "No. I don't believe so. Have I given you some reason to think so?"

"Frankly, yes," replied Lord Watson, the chief judge of the courts of Lothion. He was also, not coincidentally, the judge who would be overseeing Mordecai's trial. "You have nothing to gain from this and everything to lose."

"I am not the one on trial," said Rose coolly.

"I'm referring to your reputation. Lord Cameron is accused of murdering a prince. Based on the evidence, I am as certain of his guilt as I am that the sun will rise tomorrow. You will do him no favors by representing him and you will only serve to tarnish your own standing. Let someone else take this distasteful task."

Rose's eyes narrowed until they were slits with mere glints of sapphire between the lids. "Would any of your barristers do so?"

Lord Watson chuffed. "Unlikely. They are not fools, but if he offers them enough gold, one of them might reconsider. If not, he can represent himself."

"Do any of them believe in his innocence?" asked Rose.

"Lady Hightower, *no one* believes in his innocence," said the judge emphatically.

"Then if one of them did take his money, how would they represent him effectively?" demanded Rose. "How is that right and just? He has not been convicted yet, but if you allow him representation that already believes in his guilt, then he may as well be."

"Justice will see him hanged, Lady Hightower. That is a fact. But your life will continue. Would you give more fodder to the rumors regarding your relationship to the accused?"

Rose's expression had been relaxed, almost languid, but at the judge's remark her eyes locked on his and they seemed to catch fire with a ferocity that nearly caused the man to flinch in his seat. "Rumors. Tell me, Your Honor, do rumors have any standing in a court of law? Do they have the weight of evidence?"

Lord Watson hesitated before answering, "Of course not."

"Then I would advise you to stick to the facts of this case. Otherwise you may find yourself dealing with another case entirely, and *not* from that side of the bench. I don't think either of us want that. Do we?" she warned him.

The judge looked outraged. "Is that a threat, Lady Hightower?"

"No, Your Honor, merely a statement of intent," she responded, calm once more. "Now, I ask again. May I have the list of witnesses and any other information pertinent to the trial? Time is limited."

Lord Watson grinned maliciously back at her. "Only after I see a signed letter from the defendant, naming you as his counsel." He leaned back, lacing his fingers together behind his head. "You may have trouble obtaining that, however, since the Queen has given orders to keep him confined without visitors."

"Aside from his counsel," corrected Rose confidently.

"Which you are not," said Lord Watson, "unless you already have his signed consent in hand."

Rose kept her eyes on the judge, but held one arm out to the side, toward her maid-servant, Angela. The other woman lifted a leather case and put it in her hand. Opening it, Rose drew out a folded sheet of parchment. "As it happens, I already have that document."

The judge sneered. "You expect me to believe he named you, a woman, in advance?" His expression changed as he read the document she presented to him. "How did you get this?"

She smiled beatifically at him. "If you will notice the date, Your Honor, I was named his counsel over a decade ago, to represent him in the matter of Tremont's destruction. There is no date of expiry on that letter."

With an expulsion of pent-up breath, Judge Watson dropped the letter and turned to a scribe who stood to one side of his desk. "Clerk, please copy out the list of witnesses and any other pertinent information we have for Lady Hightower." Then he took to his feet, towering over the women in front of him. "It saddens me to see you drag your once-proud family into the gutters. If your father were alive today, he would be sorely disappointed. I will see you again the day of the trial." Turning away, he left the room.

Rose waited patiently while the clerk did as instructed. It took the man half an hour to write out everything. The court-room was expansive, with small desks on either side of the room and a variety of other scribes and functionaries continually entering and leaving. She was painfully aware of them, for many stood in small groups, whispering as they cast glances in her direction.

Angela's face colored when one group became loud enough for their voices to carry clearly to her ears, with the words 'slattern,' 'blood-lord,' and 'lady highwhore,' featuring prominently. If Rose heard them, though, she gave no sign of it.

When her maid became so overwrought that she opened her mouth to berate one of the speakers, Rose caught her hand. "Angela, after we return to the palace I'll need you to run an errand for me."

Angela looked from her wrist to her lady's face and closed her mouth. Then she dipped her head respectfully and answered, "Of course, milady."

Half an hour later, they were back in Rose's carriage, returning to the palace. Alone at last, Angela took the opportunity to vent her frustration. "You shouldn't have stopped me. Those dogs had no business saying such things."

Rose's lips quirked upward on one side. "I have excellent hearing, Angela, as I'm sure you're aware."

"Then you should have let me confront them!" protested her maid.

"That would serve no one, least of all me," said Rose. "Do you think I was merely listening? How many of those men did you recognize?"

"One or two."

"I knew fifteen of them, and made note of two others for future study. More importantly, I also know many of their personal details, who they are connected to, who they work for, and who they take bribes from. Rumor-mongers have their uses. Confronting them directly does little, unless one first determines who is behind them. Some are clueless, repeating only what they have heard, but others are deliberate. Discovering which is which is key to taking effective action," lectured Rose.

Angela leaned forward. "Then you'll punish them later?"

Rose laughed. "Heavens, no! One or two, perhaps, but I'll ignore most of them. Once Mordecai is vindicated, their newfound doubts will be useful. Some of them may even become allies one day. Punishment is a goal for the simple-minded. I prefer to pursue more important things, such as leverage."

"Do you really think Lord Cameron is innocent?" asked her maid uncertainly.

"Of course," said Rose, looking out the window. Inwardly, however, she struggled with her doubt. *He has to be. If he isn't...* Softly, she muttered to herself, "Anything."

"What was that?" said Angela.

Smiling demurely, Rose brushed the question aside. "Nothing, dear. Just talking to myself." Then she laughed.

"What's so funny?"

"Highwhore," said Rose. "I haven't heard that one before. It was rather clever, actually."

Her maid frowned. "You shouldn't laugh at such things, milady. I didn't find it amusing whatsoever."

"You have to laugh, Angela. Anger and tears only serve to embolden your enemies," Rose replied. *Besides, it may become truth if things go ill.*

***

The void died, slain by a blinding white light that devoured everything, piercing my eyes. The fantasies of the past vanished and I sat up, hopeful, though I knew it was a false hope. Blinking and covering my watering eyes with one hand, I tried to see beyond the murky stone wall that separated me from the world.

It was fruitless, of course. Though the stone was now permeable, the enchantment that lay upon it still functioned, blocking my magesight, and my ordinary eyesight was not up to the task yet. Footsteps sounded as a man entered the room, and then my magesight identified him. Tyrion.

"Hello, grandson," he intoned cheerfully.

"I liked you better when you were a figment of my imagination," I told him seriously.

My ancestor stared at me curiously. "Having visions already? I suppose the darkness brings them quicker."

Tyrion was well acquainted with the effects of isolation, though his prison hadn't been nearly as silent and dark as mine. He had spent years confined to a small wooden room, seeing others only when his meals were brought, or when he was taken out to fight.

"The silence is worse," I admitted. "Sometimes my heartbeat sounds so loudly in my ears I wonder if it will deafen me."

"Hmm," he said, looking thoughtful. "That never occurred to me. I brought you some water." There was a clink as he placed a metal pitcher on the floor.

"How about food?" I asked.

He shook his head. "Unlike my experience, these people have no intention of keeping you in fighting condition. Prisoners only get one meal a day. You still have several hours to go."

I ran my fingers through my hair, thinking. It made no sense that Ariadne would agree to such treatment. No matter what I had done, we were still family. Surely, she would want me fed properly. "What about the Queen?" I mumbled. "Doesn't she care?"

Tyrion shrugged. "Probably. You know her better than I do. In any case, she is avoiding the matter on the advice of those around her. The chief jailor, Regan, is the one that has set the rules. He feels you should be treated much as the ordinary prisoners are."

"You and Gareth are taking turns keeping watch, right?" I reminded him. "You're a duke. The guards wouldn't dare argue with you if you brought me food, or a blanket."

"That may be," admitted Tyrion. "But neither of us care enough to test the rule. No one wants to be considered a sympathizer. Your life may as well be over, Mordecai. Have some thought for those who survive you. Would you leave a blemish on our reputations just so you could have a blanket for a few miserable days?"

"Considering what you went through, I'd have thought you would have more sympathy," I responded.

Sighing, Tyrion sat down on the bench beside me. "I do, truth be told. That's why I'm here. The water isn't supposed to come until your meal time. Don't you feel grateful?" There was a not-so-subtle sneer in his voice.

"It sounds more like you came to rub my nose in it."

"Guilty as charged!" he barked before pausing. After a moment, he began to laugh. "I suppose prison humor isn't at the top of your list right now."

I glared at him balefully. "What do you think?"

"Gareth said you were making jokes all the way to the cell. I was rather impressed," said Tyrion. "But enough of that. I came to share some news."

"Has my family come?" I asked.

"No idea," said Tyrion. "I'm here to talk about ANSIS. You will be glad to know that my krytek are now reporting that the city is clear of any trace of it."

"Congratulations," I responded in a flat tone.

He gave me a slightly sour look. "You know as well as I do that this is far from over. They won't give up so easily."

"And?"

Tyrion said nothing for a while and he appeared to be struggling with himself. Eventually he went on, "I need your help."

Lifting my arms, I showed him my manacles. "I'm a little tied up at the moment."

He grinned. "That's more like it. What I mean is I need your family."

"Get your own," I said harshly, before adding mentally, *Oh, that's right, you got most of them killed.*

"I don't think you want to see this world fall as so many others have. While you may not live to enjoy it, I know you care about your family and a lot of other people out there. Gareth Gaelyn is a fine mage, but he doesn't have the creativity required to see us through this. With you heading to the gallows, that leaves me—and your children. Help me help them."

The worlds were uttered with a sincerity I had never heard from the man before. In spite of myself, I believed him, but I didn't want to. I hated the bastard.

He continued, "Your oldest son hasn't shown up yet, but the Queen's brother seems to think he's able to pierce the veil between the dimensions. Not only that, I know myself that he's a brilliant enchanter, much like yourself. While I don't understand it, that device he and his mechanical friend have concocted to locate ANSIS is utterly beyond the expertise of the She'Har. I think your son may be the key to all of this. If I'm to have a hope of keeping this world safe, I'll need him to cooperate with me."

"Just him?" I said at last.

"Your daughter has the Centyr gift. Your son's friend is a Mordan. Both of them could be very valuable. There are so few mages in general. All of your children will be important in the years ahead," said Tyrion.

Almost choking on the words, I answered, "What is it you want me to do, exactly?"

"Tell me how to reach Matthew," said Tyrion immediately. "If he returns before your execution, impress upon him the importance of working together with me. That goes for the rest of your offspring as well. They harbor a bit of a grudge against me after our previous encounter. Even Conall out there." He jerked his head in the direction of the entrance. "He's in awe of me, but he doesn't trust me."

"The last thing I could imagine telling my children— is to trust *you*," I told him.

"Mordecai, listen. You're a father, a *true* father. That's why I let you have Lynaralla, not because of that stupid match we had. At some point, I realized you have something I've lost. I was never a parent, not truly. The brief time I had ended too soon. I can't replace you, but I can promise to protect them in your place. What I do know, based on my failure as a father, is that you would do anything to protect them.

"You're going to die. I can't stop that. I don't even particularly care about it, I won't lie. But I respect your desire to ensure a better future for them. Tell them to work with me. Let me finish the job that you cannot."

His false sincerity made the bile rise in my throat. "How do I know you aren't the one that killed Leomund?" I accused.

Tyrion began to laugh.

"It seems awfully convenient for you," I declared. "If I'm locked up, executed, that leaves a neat power vacuum for you to fill. With me out of the way, you can do whatever you want."

When he finally stopped laughing, he replied, "You give me too much credit. I am not so cunning as that."

"Aren't you?" I argued. "Have you forgotten I have your memories of that time? You waited years while you orchestrated the plan for your revenge. You devised not one, but two plans to ensure the demise of the She'Har, and you successfully executed both of them. I know you aren't stupid. In fact, I think this barbaric persona you display for everyone to see may be nothing more than an affectation to make them underestimate you."

"Is that what you think?" asked Tyrion.

I nodded. "Others might mistake you for a violent brute, but I think you're just pretending, inspired by your psychopathic daughter Brigid, perhaps."

His aythar flashed and Tyrion's hand shot forward, stopping close to my throat. It was sheathed in deadly aythar, a product of the tattooed enchantment that covered his skin. "Careful what you say," he warned. "One more word about any of my children and I might just forget my determination to protect this world."

I met his eyes evenly. "Did you do it? Did you kill the Prince?"

Tyrion watched me for several seconds and then dismissed his armblade. "Does it matter? Even if I did, my promise to you is sincere and your options are the same. You'll either help me or die knowing that this world's time is in short supply. I don't think you'll gamble with your children's future like that."

He left without waiting for my reply.

 CHAPTER 17

Another eon passed before light returned to my world again. I almost hoped it was because they were bringing me out for my trial. The isolation was becoming unbearable. My only clue to how much time had passed was the fact that I had only had one meal, so it was improbable that it was the day of the trial already.

I might even have welcomed another visit from Tyrion, but to my surprise the figure that entered the cell was eminently feminine.

"Rose?" I croaked. My throat was dry, for my water ration had run out long ago.

"It's me, Mordecai," she answered softly. Then she turned and called out, "Can someone give me a lantern? It's pitch black in here." She stepped out and returned a minute later, carrying a light. The wall became solid once more and then she gave me her full attention. "You look terrible."

"You shouldn't be here," I told her. "People will talk."

"You aren't allowed visitors," said Rose.

"Then how did you get in?"

"I'm your counsel," she said smugly. "People can say what they like, but I can't do my job if I don't talk to you."

"You're wasting your time. They've already made up their minds. The only reason I can see that they haven't come to hang me yet is they haven't been able to decide which rope they want to use."

Rose gave me a look of disapproval. "We've already been over this, Mort."

"We have?" I asked, surprised.

She nodded. "Yes, the last time you were on trial. Hopefully this time you'll listen more carefully to my advice."

"You're hopeless," I said with a sigh.

She smiled. "I've been called worse." Smoothing her skirts, she sat down beside me.

"I doubt it," I responded. "No one would dare."

"You would be surprised," she muttered, so low I could barely hear her.

"What did you say?"

"Nothing," said Rose. "We have more important things to discuss. I'm only permitted a limited amount of time here."

"You haven't asked the most important question, yet," I said.

She arched one brow. "And what do you think that question is?"

"Did I do it?"

Rose looked disgusted. "If I thought that, I'd be planning your escape, not a futile court defense. No, what I want to know first is *why* did you go there when I expressly told you not to?"

With a boyish grin, I replied, "On a lark."

"As I suspected," she said grimly.

"What did you suspect?"

"That you, Mordecai Illeniel, are a complete and utter fool. Sometimes I wish I could strangle you," she answered seriously.

I shrugged. "Apparently you aren't alone."

"Where did you go after you spoke with me that day?" she questioned.

"I took a stroll through the city and then went to visit my factor, David Summerfield."

"Did you speak with anyone else other than him?" she asked.

I shook my head. "Not until I decided to storm Leomund's hunting lodge."

"Did you tell David where you planned to go before you left?"

"David showed me a map, so I could find it," I responded. "I don't think I told him I was planning to go right then, but I'm sure he could have guessed that was my plan."

Rose nodded. "How long did it take you to get there after you left?"

"A half an hour, maybe? I flew."

"And how long were you there before you broke in and confronted the Prince-Consort?" asked Rose.

"Two or three hours." By now I was sitting as close as possible without touching her, not for some romantic reason, but because I was freezing. I could feel the heat given off by her body and I had to fight the urge to press myself against her.

Rose pursed her lips. "That's unfortunate."

"How so?"

"More time expands the possibility that someone learned of your destination and could have reached there soon enough to frame you," she explained. "Can Tyrion or Gareth fly the same way you do?"

"No," I said. "Not that I'm aware, at least. Even so, there was more than enough time, but I never detected another wizard."

"Could they have hidden themselves from you?" asked Rose.

"No," I said. "My range is as good as or better than theirs. I would have become aware of them if they came within a mile or two. Only a Prathion could have gotten close undetected."

She looked thoughtful. "George is in Arundel still. Do you know where Elaine is?"

"She was staying at my home," I informed her. "I haven't seen her in a few days, but you can't seriously suspect her of being involved in this."

"It's my job to consider every possibility until we discover what actually happened," she said sternly. Then she continued her interrogation. I couldn't fault her thoroughness or her work ethic. She covered every detail, no matter how ordinary or mundane. Rose wanted to know who had arrived with David Airedale, how many servants had been in the house, how many had actually seen me. She questioned me regarding how long I was actually in the building and how much I had said to them. She spent a particularly long time grilling me about the events that occurred after I entered the Prince's bedroom.

When she finished, I asked her a question of my own, "Have you considered those who weren't there?"

"Such as?"

"Those who stand to gain from my removal," I clarified. "Tyrion for example."

She nodded, and a look of discomfort crossed her features. "I've already spoken with him."

"So have I."

She looked surprised, so I described my conversation with my ancestor to her. When I was done, I gave her the obvious conclusion, "He admitted he had a lot to gain, and he didn't deny it."

"He didn't admit it either," countered Rose. "It sounds to me as though he would prefer to torment you with the suggestion."

"So you believe him?" I said, aghast.

"Mordecai," said Rose, "you are too close to this matter. You already hate the man. Your emotions are making it impossible to consider him objectively." Lifting her hand, she brushed the hair away from my ear, then hissed and drew her hand back in alarm. "Your skin is ice-cold!"

I smiled hopelessly. "It's not quite that bad."

"No, it's worse than that," she said angrily. "You aren't even shivering." Cupping my cheeks between two palms that felt almost painfully hot, she stared into my eyes. Then she looked around the cell. "Why don't you have a blanket?"

I shrugged.

"This is unforgiveable," she announced, pulling me close and wrapping her arms around me. I wanted to cry from gratefulness at the sudden warmth. The respite was brief, however. A moment later she pulled away and stood up, putting her back toward me. "Help me unlace this," she ordered.

"Huh?" I said dumbly. It hardly seemed the time.

"Do as I say, Mordecai. This is no time to fool around," she said firmly.

My thought exactly. But I didn't argue. With numb fingers, I used my shackled hands to undo the laces, whereupon she promptly began to wiggle, sliding the dress over her head. Belatedly, I realized what she meant to do. "I'm not wearing your dress, Rose," I protested.

"Of course not, you silly man! I couldn't walk out of here in my undergarments." Then she reached down and began to lift the hem of the soft gown that had been under her dress. I knew quite well there were no more layers beneath it.

I shot to my feet and caught her wrists just as her hands reached mid-thigh. "What are you doing?"

"Making sure you don't die of exposure before I can save your life in court," she replied softly. "Now let go of my arms. This is hard enough for me without you making a fuss."

"But…"

"It isn't anything you haven't seen before," she argued.

When? shouted my inner voice, but then I realized what she must mean. "That was Penny, not—not you."

While she had seemed embarrassed at first, my dramatic reaction had removed her fear. Now she appeared to be enjoying my mortified response. "I meant your magesight. You've told me about it many times. I doubt I have any surprises for you."

Magesight was one thing; seeing a naked woman in the flesh was quite another. I started to say that, but then held my tongue. I would only be embarrassing her further, and she was obviously determined to do this. Slowly, I released her wrists. If I hadn't already been half-frozen, my cheeks would have flushed.

I had expected her to turn around at least. She shifted her weight on her feet for a second, as though she would do so, but then she stilled and lifted her gown over her head without looking away. Aside from her shoes, socks, and garters, she was entirely nude before me.

We stood that way for a timeless second, our eyes locked. I was afraid to look anywhere else, for to do so would be to see something I shouldn't. Her expression was almost challenging. Then she glanced away and to one side, blushing. "You could turn around," she suggested.

"Oh!" I said, startled. Then, a second later, my brain started working. *She could have turned around as well.* Ignoring that thought, I picked up her dress and started to pass it behind me.

"Put the gown on first," she commanded.

Resigned, I did so. It wasn't easy. Rose was petite, but fortunately the gown was rather voluminous, so it was merely tight on me. The sleeves were loose, but the cuffs tore when I forced my hands through them, and the shoulders felt as though they would split at any moment. Behind me, my magesight revealed that she was still standing relaxed, making no attempt at modesty.

I took her dress up again and handed it to her, accidentally seeing more than I intended. *That was no accident,* I berated myself. After a minute, Rose reassured me, "You can turn around now."

I did, and she presented her back, so I could redo the laces. Without the gown, the bare skin of her back seemed to burn my fingers. *Penny's going to kill me for this,* I thought, and then ground my teeth.

She fussed with her sleeves and skirt for a moment and then asked me, "How do I look?"

Unbelievable, I thought, *with or without the dress.* "Uh, fine," I said, fumbling for words.

"You'd never know I was naked beneath it, would you?"

How could I forget? "No," I said, moderating my tone. "Just make sure they don't get a close look at your back. They might figure it out if they look closely."

"Good point," said Rose, and then she stepped forward to wrap her arms around me.

Embracing her was nothing unusual, but after everything that had just happened I felt guilty and awkward. At the same time, I was still desperate for warmth. After only the briefest moment of hesitation, I returned the embrace.

She didn't let go, and I began to wonder how long this would go on. "Uh, Rose? Are you going to release me?"

"I'm trying to warm you up."

"But…"

"Shhh," she told me. "My time is probably nearly up. When they come back for me, I'll let go. Until then, you can have as much warmth as I can give."

That nearly undid me. After nearly two days alone in the cold dark, my spirits were about as low as they could get. Her warmth and affection made me want to weep. Squeezing my eyes shut, I held onto her, hunching forward to bury my face against the warmth of her neck.

We stayed that way for what might have been a few minutes, but whether five minutes or ten, it was too short. The wall changed and Gareth's voice entered the room. "Your time is up."

I didn't want to let go, but I did anyway and the chill of the room immediately struck me once more. It hadn't bothered me as much before, perhaps because I'd given up, but now it felt worse.

Gareth glanced at me, taking in my new attire, but his only comment was, "Interesting." Then he directed Rose, "The lantern too, milady."

She looked defiant for a moment, but then, reluctantly, she picked up the lantern and carried it away with her. "We can't leave him in these conditions," she told Gareth as she stepped outside.

"Unless you can change the jailor's mind, I won't allow anything else within the cell," he said coldly.

Rose cast angry eyes up at him. "I remember my friends, Lord Gaelyn."

He smiled down at her. "Is that an inducement, milady? A threat might be better. What about your enemies?"

She had already turned away, striding down the corridor when she answered, "I make sure they remember *me*."

Gareth looked back at me and then the wall became solid again, cutting off my view. The darkness swallowed me, and I sat back down on my bench, hating the way the stone bit into my sore flesh. My feet were still bare, and they soaked in the chill faster than any other part of me.

"Forgive me, Penny," I said quietly, for all I could think was that I needed Rose to return. *Was this what it was like for you, all those years ago? When the shiggreth held you and Dorian captive?*

***

Rose walked briskly, taking the stairs that led up to the upper levels and nodding to the guards she passed there. When she reached the final station, where the warden, Regan, sat comfortably in his office, she stopped. She knocked on the door and waited.

After a moment, the door opened, and she was free of the dungeon once more. The warden stood close at hand. Regan was a large man with a frame that had probably been impressive at one time, but in the present was given over to a corpulent plumpness that made his appearance almost as repulsive as his personality. He grinned at her through rotten teeth.

"My things, if you will," she reminded him.

"Oh, of course, milady," he answered. He stepped away, entering another room and then returning with a wicker basket in his hand. The top was open, and a collection of items lay within: her daggers, two blankets, a small pillow, and the remains of a meal she had brought. The meat and cheese were gone, with only bones and a small apple remaining.

"You don't care for fruit, I see," remarked Rose.

"Apples hurt my teeth, milady," said the chief jailor.

"The food wasn't packed with your needs in mind. Nor did I intend for you to have it," she said coldly.

Regan shifted uncomfortably. "You was told he couldn't have anything from outside," said the man. "I thought it was for me."

She had already examined the man from head to toe, taking note of everything from his dirty boots to the smell that seemed to emanate from him. Her response was calculated. "If I brought enough for you and Lord Cameron next time, perhaps you would consider letting me bring it to him?"

"No can do, milady. You may be of high station, but rules is rules," said the warden.

"You should think on that," said Rose. "It wouldn't hurt you to have a friend in high places." Her eyes traveled downward. "Wouldn't it be nice if you could afford new boots?"

Regan's face shifted, growing angry. "You may be all high and mighty, milady. But that man down there murdered the Queen's husband. It's worth more than my life if I break the rules."

She had miscalculated. "Please pardon any offense I have given you, Master Regan. It was unintentional." Then she left.

 CHAPTER 18

Sir Gram stood on the battlements of Castle Lancaster, staring out over the open field that lay to the south. The moon was halfway to full, providing some illumination, but to his dragon-bond-enhanced vision it might as well have been full daylight. He didn't like what he saw.

A camp of at least twenty ogres sat in the open field close to the edge of the forest. Calling it a 'camp' might be giving it too much credit, though. There were no tents or cookfires. The massive humanoids slept exposed to the elements. The only reason to call it a camp was that they slept scattered across a small area.

"Why now?" muttered Gram.

Matthew stood next to him. "I have a theory about that."

Gram smirked. "When have you ever *not* had a theory?"

Matt ignored his remark. "When Elaine was trapped in the forest that was swapped with Lancaster, she said that the creatures of the forest were drawn to aythar. Even her invisibility drew them to her, though they couldn't find her exact location."

"That would explain the spiders last night. So, you think they're here for you?" said Gram.

Matthew nodded. "And Karen, and possibly even the magic radiating from your enchanted tattoo and Alyssa's armor."

"If that's the case, then the people here would have been better off if we had never come," observed the young knight.

Matthew sighed. "It's too late now. If we leave at this point, they may try and raid the castle anyway."

Karen appeared beside them suddenly, a look of panic on her features.

The fear alone was enough to tell Matthew what was wrong. "Spider?" he asked. She nodded frantically, still trying to catch her breath.

"I'll go," volunteered Gram.

Karen held up three fingers. "Three of them," she panted.

"I'll go then," said Matthew. "It'll be easier for me." He made no attempt to point out that Karen could have taken them on herself. Since their encounter at the smithy, she had developed an irrational fear of arachnids. *Or perhaps I should say 'rational fear,'* observed Matthew. *They are dangerous, after all.*

Karen took his hand and the two of them vanished, leaving Gram behind. He stared into the empty space for a moment before muttering to himself, "Show off." *Or perhaps you just want to impress your girlfriend. Not that you'd ever admit it.*

Gram took a moment to stare down the length of the wall to the far end, where Alyssa stood guard at the southeastern corner. He knew better than to worry about her. She could handle herself. Even so, he looked in her direction just as often as he looked to his own quarter in the southwest.

***

Manfred studied the heavy pouch in his hand without opening it. He could tell by its weight that it held gold inside. Without a word, he tucked it into his jacket, then reached up and twisted his thin moustache. It was a nervous habit he had never been able to rid himself of. Finally, he said, "You've already paid me for this month. Why the extra?"

"To compensate you for the trouble," said Rose Thornbear. "I'll require much more of you than usual in the coming days. You'll need the money to pay informants and to pay for assistance." She handed him a folded piece of paper. "There are three names at the top. Those are the names of the men I need you to hire. They are familiar with my requirements already, so don't worry that they might haggle over the amount. Below those names you'll find a list with the names of all the witnesses to be examined during the trial."

Manfred's eyes widened. "That sort of thing isn't in my line of work, Lady Hightower."

She smiled briefly, flashing white teeth. "Relax. I just want information. I need to know everything about them—their birthplaces, friends, acquaintances, time of service with the Prince—*everything*."

The man opened the paper and quickly scanned it with his eyes. "What's this name written separately at the bottom?"

"I thought you might know that name already," said Rose, "considering your line of work."

Manfred looked offended. "Only amateurs wind up in the dungeon."

She patted his cheek. "Yet you know his name nonetheless. I want you to handle that matter personally. You can give the rest of it to others."

Manfred frowned. "I'm a purveyor of information, milady. I don't get personally involved anymore."

"Time is of the essence," Rose informed him. "I need this done properly and professionally. I'll compensate you accordingly."

"You need something specific?"

"Find the names of young prisoners who have recently been in his care. Ignore those without families. I'm only interested in the married ones. Get me the names of their wives," explained Rose.

"Young prisoners?" Manfred seemed confused.

"Young men have young wives, Manfred," said Rose. "Young sisters might do as well, but only if they visited them while they were locked up."

"Ahh, I begin to see what you're after," said Manfred.

"Exactly why I want you to handle this yourself," said Rose. "Once you have a good list, visit as many as you can find." She handed him a second purse, this one smaller and filled with silver. "Dole this out as you need. I need leverage."

"How soon do you need it?" asked the rogue.

"Tomorrow."

Manfred let out a long whistle. "Hard evidence will be difficult to come by in such a short time."

"For my purposes it doesn't need to be provable, Manfred, just true. I'm not dealing with a peer of the realm. Trust your instincts and get me the names of the ones that will be most useful."

Their conversation went on a short while longer, as she specified her needs regarding the other names. After Manfred left, Rose washed her face and returned to the main room.

Elise was waiting for her. "Tea?" offered the older woman.

Rose shot her a grateful look. "Yes, thank you." She accepted a small cup and took a sip.

"Why haven't you asked for my help?" said her mother-in-law suddenly.

Few people surprised Rose Thornbear, but on rare occasions it happened. This was one of them. She managed not to choke as she swallowed, then replied in a neutral tone, "What do you mean?"

"You know exactly what I mean," said Elise sharply. "You're proud, Rose, too proud. I suppose it's a fault of your breeding, but then again, that's why I approved of you marrying my son."

It irritated her to hear Elise making judgements about the Hightowers, but then again, the old woman knew that as well. *She's trying to get under my skin.* "Mother," began Rose softly, "it's long past time for you to be getting your hands dirty. Let me handle this."

Elise chuckled and then made a show of looking around the room. "Mother, is it? I don't see any of the children around. Are you thinking to coddle me with sweet phrases?"

Rose took a deep breath. She hadn't had enough sleep over the past several nights, and her control was slipping. *I'm doing this for your sake,* she thought angrily, but her words were considerably calmer. "Did your lunch disagree with you? You seem out of sorts."

"Don't test me, girl. One of my children is in trouble, and I haven't seen you doing much about it. Not that I would expect to, but since you've seen fit to keep me in the dark I can only assume you're in over your head."

By 'one of her children,' she was referring to Mordecai, of course. The old woman had often noted that she considered him like a son to her. When Rose failed to respond, Elise continued, "Does Meredith know they've locked up her son?"

"No," said Rose evenly. "I haven't sent any messages, yet."

"Don't you think she deserves to know?" demanded the old woman.

Rose set her cup to one side. "Actually, I intend to make a trip there today to inform his family. Trust me, Elise, I have things well in hand."

"I suggest you share what you know, lest I take matters into my own hands," warned Elise.

Alarm filled Rose and she leaned forward, almost rising from her seat. "You wouldn't!"

Elise laughed at her reaction. It was rare that she got to see her daughter-in-law lose her composure. "You haven't been sleeping enough, have you, girl? You're starting to imagine things you shouldn't. You know I would never hurt Ariadne. I love Genevieve's children as much as my own."

Feeling foolish, Rose relaxed. Then she grew irritated. The old woman had played her strings with an expert hand. The previous queen, Genevieve Lancaster, had been Elise's best friend and confidante for most of the old woman's many years. "Don't tease me, Elise. I don't have the nerves for it right now."

An evil light appeared in the old woman's eyes. "Who said I was teasing? I would never hurt the Lancasters, but there are plenty around the Queen right now who I would not hesitate to remove."

"Don't get involved in this," said Rose, becoming more direct.

Elise made no pretense at hiding her anger. "Why not?"

Because you're too old! Rose wanted to shout. *What would Dorian think of me, if I continually drag his mother into the muck?* "You've lived a long life, Elise. You deserve to enjoy it in peace."

"How am I supposed to enjoy it with Mordecai facing the hangman's noose?" declared Elise. Then her voice turned dark with regret. "You know how much I owe him and his family. Let me help."

Her tone made Rose wince. Over four and a half decades ago, before Mordecai's birth, Elise Thornbear had taught one of her darkest secrets to a priest. The man had been a member of the Church of Millicenth, the order that trained Elise and other young women like her as prostitutes and assassins. She had been given little choice, but the priest had used the recipe she taught him to wipe out nearly the entire Cameron family, and Elise had never fully forgiven herself for that.

Rose wanted to pull her own hair out in frustration. Her mother-in-law had her over a barrel. If she didn't bring her in on her plans, the old woman might act on her own, possibly spoiling them. "Fine. I'll explain everything to you, on one condition."

"Name it."

"You do nothing without my approval," said Rose. "I won't have you upsetting the applecart."

The old woman chuckled. "Fine."

With the bargain set, Rose began to explain the situation. She left out nothing, aside from her personal feelings on certain matters and persons. She held nothing back, for she did not need to. Unlike most people, Elise Thornbear was more steeped in murder, larceny, spy craft, and the darkest secrets of politics than almost anyone alive. Rose didn't have to worry about being misunderstood.

When she had finished, she felt better for sharing, and simultaneously guilty. *Forgive me, Dorian,* she thought to herself. Elise, on the other hand, seemed animated, almost happy. She eyed Rose craftily. "Do you know who did it?"

"I have a strong suspicion," said Rose, "but it does me little good."

"There are two obvious suspects," observed Elise. "The one who stands the most to gain, and the one who started those rumors."

"Mordecai suspects Tyrion as well," Rose agreed.

Elise frowned. "But you don't. So you think it's Airedale?"

"He was ideally positioned to make the most of the opportunity," observed Rose. "But I fear the truth is much worse."

"Well, spit it out girl! I'm not getting any younger," demanded Elise impatiently.

Rose explained her theory and Elise's eyes grew wide. "You see the problem?" concluded Lady Rose.

Elise shook her head in disagreement. "Politically, this is better. If it were Airedale it would be hard to manage. The ramifications would be too great. But this, this could neatly solve the Queen's problem and save Mort from the hangman."

"But I can't *prove* it," said Rose in exasperation, "and without hard evidence no one is going to believe it."

"You're too hung up on the truth, girl, just like that fool son of mine," Elise said sagely. "Truth be damned, let's just frame someone else."

"What?"

Her mother-in-law rubbed her hands together as she warmed to the subject. "How about Tyrion? He'd be easy enough, and who knows? Maybe he did do it."

"It's unlikely," said Rose. "Besides, we need him. The *kingdom* needs him. If he dies, we have no idea what the She'Har will do, and we're already at a disadvantage dealing with ANSIS. We can't afford to lose the assets he offers Lothion."

"Airedale then," decided Elise brazenly. "He'll be even easier, though not as much fun as Tyrion."

"No," said Rose, primly. "It's not only distasteful, it's unnecessary. I'll do my best to reveal the truth."

"I don't follow your logic," responded Elise. "You'd rather see a good man hang than a wicked one?"

"If he's guilty, yes!" declared Rose adamantly.

"There's no way you can prove your supposition," stated Elise. "And while you waste your time trying, they'll convict Mort and put and end to him. Do you think your moral high ground will make you happy? It won't. If virtues were food, even you would starve."

They argued for the better part of an hour before eventually Rose agreed to a compromise. "Do what you will then," she said with resignation. "But not until after the trial. If we win, there will be no need."

"If your backup plan fails, Mort is dead," said Elise flatly. "They won't wait around with a wizard. It's too risky. They'll march him off to hang straight away."

Rose stared up at her with steel in her icy blue eyes, "It won't fail."

Elise nodded. "Hmph. Alright then." Slapping her knees, she rose to her feet with more energy than Rose had seen from her in weeks. "When you see Carissa, tell her to come find me."

"Carissa?" Rose exclaimed at the mention of her daughter's name. "Don't drag her into this!"

"Relax," said Elise soothingly. "I'm not going to make her do anything *unsavory.* She'd be useless anyway. That girl is much too much like you and her father. I just need her back, and her nimble fingers. As you tried so hard not to mention, I'm getting a little old for this and my hands aren't as steady as they once were. Actually, when you go see Meredith, see if you can find Alyssa. She would be ideal."

"Then you won't need Carissa," said Rose determinedly.

"No, I'll still need her. Alyssa isn't familiar with the social circles in the city. I'll need my granddaughter for at least one thing. She's an excellent distraction."

Yet another reason why I shouldn't have told you anything, thought Rose.

"Tell her to find me at your old house in the city," continued Elise. "And make sure your groundskeeper and housekeeper take the week off. It wouldn't do to have them happen along and see something they shouldn't. We wouldn't want any unnecessary *accidents* to occur to with everything else going on right now."

Having said that, her mother-in-law put on her travel coat, gathered a few necessities, and left. Rose stared at the door for some time afterward. "What have I done?" she wondered to herself. Only time would tell.

She rang the bell for Angela. She needed a bath, though she doubted it would be enough to make her feel clean again.

 CHAPTER 19

Lynaralla was the first to greet Rose when she entered the house. "Lady Rose," said the young woman, dipping into a respectful curtsey. "It is a pleasure to see you."

She smiled approvingly at the girl. "I see you've been practicing. You've improved."

"As have you, milady," replied the She'Har. "One can hardly tell how much you've aged."

Rose closed her eyes and sighed audibly.

"Did I do it wrong again?" asked the girl, her eyes wide and innocent.

"Yes, dear, you did."

"You said I should follow a greeting with a compliment when possible," explained Lynaralla.

"That is true, but you have to be aware of the social context. In particular, when addressing someone of greater age or station you should never presume upon their abilities, whether they are improving or not. You should also never comment on a lady's age unless she is very young," lectured Rose.

Lynaralla frowned. "But I implied that you appear young. Is that not a compliment?"

"Stick to beauty or attire," advised Rose. "Age is too complex a topic. Done improperly, a compliment on an older woman's youthful appearance can be taken as either a backhanded compliment or as superfluous flattery. Neither is helpful, unless that is what you intend."

Moira walked in, a smile on her face. "I keep telling you it's a lost cause. She'll never get the hang of it."

"I've taught more difficult students over the years," replied Rose, turning to give Moira a quick hug. "Lynaralla has the advantage of being highly intelligent. I have faith that she will surprise you."

"Where's Dad?" asked Moira. "I've been wondering when he and Roland would return. He said it would be within a day, but it's been over two now."

A shadow passed over Rose's face. "I have bad news. Is Elaine here? She should hear this as well."

"She's with Millie," answered Moira. "Let me go fetch her."

Rose held out a hand to make her wait. "How is the girl?"

"About as you would expect," said Moira.

"Is she talking? I'll need to ask her some questions after I give you the news."

Moira nodded. "I'll bring her too, then."

Rose shook her head. "After I explain everything. I don't want her to hear some of this."

Moira looked puzzled at the sudden mystery, but she did as she was told. A few minutes later, she, Lynaralla, Irene, and Elaine were gathered in the living room with Rose. By then Moira's expression had gone dark. Humphrey sat beside her, whining and licking her hand, unsure why she was upset.

"You already know what I have to say, don't you?" asked Rose.

"Most of it," admitted Moira.

"What is it?" demanded Elaine. "The suspense is killing me. Some of us aren't mind readers, you realize."

Rose gave them the facts, relaying the events that had occurred after Mordecai had returned to the capital with Roland. She omitted her suspicions, as well as her darker plans to protect Mordecai, either by winning the trial—or otherwise. It felt as though she was walking a tightrope while she talked, for she had to keep her thoughts rigidly disciplined.

Moira stared at her suspiciously when she finished. "You're hiding something. Several somethings, in fact. What aren't you telling me?"

"Rumor and gossip will do you no good," said Rose, dissembling. "Trust me."

Mordecai's oldest daughter grew agitated, rising to her feet. "He's my father, Rose. I deserve to know everything."

Keeping her mind scrupulously blank, Rose replied, "If your father were here, he would tell you to do as I say and trust me. Sit back down."

"That pendant can't keep me out of your head, Rose," Moira threatened. The room seemed to grow darker as the tension thickened. "I'll have it from you, whether you want to tell me or not." Humphrey whimpered, hiding his head between his paws.

Elaine broke in, "Moira, stop it!"

But Moira wasn't finished. "You think keeping your mind blank will protect your secrets?"

Everyone was on their feet by then, aside from Rose. Elaine moved to stand in front of her and did *something*, but she couldn't see what it was. The two young women stared at each other for a long moment.

"Get out of my way, Elaine," growled Moira.

"Stop it, Moira!" yelled Irene, watching them from one side.

Moira snapped her fingers and Elaine collapsed, her body limp as she slid to the ground. "Too late," muttered Moira. "I was already way ahead of you." Then she turned her eyes back to Rose.

Irene started to intervene, but Rose stood gracefully and moved to stand directly in front of Moira. "Take your shield down," Rose said sternly.

"She doesn't have one up," said Irene.

"Thank you, Irene," said Rose, and then she brought one hand up and slapped the older sister with such speed that the slap resounded through the room. "Is this how your mother raised you to act?"

Blinking back unbidden tears, Moira stared at her in confusion.

"Sit down. Now," Rose commanded with a tone of authority that was hard to refuse.

Moira sat.

Looking down at Elaine, Rose asked, "Will she be alright?"

Moira nodded, while Irene answered meekly, "I think so."

Resuming her seat, Rose smoothed her dress once more. She could feel something close to her skin, and when she put her hand on the armrest, she couldn't feel the texture. "Irene, please take the shield down. We're quite safe."

Irene looked warily between Rose and her sister. "But she just…"

"I don't need protection, Rennie," Rose reiterated. "We're having a family talk. A civilized discussion between *human* beings. Your sister isn't going to invade my mind. Are you?" She directed her gaze to Moira and the young woman looked down, ashamed.

"No, Lady Rose."

Rose looked up at Irene, who was still on her feet. "Sit down or go make some tea, Rennie. I don't like people looming over me."

"What should I do, Lady Rose?" asked Lynaralla.

"Take a seat," said Rose. Then she turned to Moira. "I need to talk to Millie now. If necessary, you can use your abilities to keep her calm while I ask the questions."

Moira went and brought out the girl, and Rose spent the next quarter hour interrogating her. She spared no questions in her search for the truth, even asking about delicate matters such as her past abuse at the hands of Prince Leomund. Through it all, the girl remained remarkably calm and when Rose was finished, she sent Millie back to Moira's room.

"What do you think?" asked Moira, hesitantly. She was still too embarrassed to meet Rose's gaze.

"Nothing has changed," announced Rose. "Her testimony as it now stands will do nothing to help your father's case."

"I could..." Moira started to say something, but then stopped.

Rose nodded. "Yes. You *will,* but only this. When she testifies, she will remember that your father put her to sleep *after* he flew away with her. She saw no harm come to Leomund while Mordecai was still present."

"That means they'll let him go, right?" asked Irene, hopefully. "If she says he didn't kill the Prince, that means he isn't guilty. They'll have to let him go."

"Sadly, no," said Rose, shaking her head. "The weight of evidence is still badly against your father. The judge will also be well aware of the fact that Millie has been spending time under this roof, with Moira. It might help, but it won't be enough on its own."

"What about the other witnesses?" suggested Moira. "If I could meet with them, I could find out who did it, or if they don't know, I could at the very least change what they remember."

"You will not even think about going near Albamarl during this time," Rose told her emphatically. "If there's so much as a rumor of you being near the witnesses, the entire case will be thrown into chaos. Gareth Gaelyn wouldn't stand for it, and who knows what your *other* mother would do."

"What if Elaine helped?" added Moira. "With her help, no one would even know I was there."

"You mean the friend whose free will you just violated? The one on the rug here?" Rose said, her tone acidic. "I won't risk it. I have other plans for her."

"Then what do we *do*?" asked Irene, desperate. "We can't just sit here."

"That is precisely what you will do," Rose insisted. "Moira, you will take care of Millie until she's called for the trial. Irene, you and Lynaralla will see if you can get through the boundary and get Gram and the others back. If you succeed, send Karen to me. I need Elaine as well. When she wakes, tell her to go to the capital, but she is *not* to use the portal to the Queen's chambers. Have her take another route—I don't care what it is, so long as no one sees her. Have her report to my city house. Gram's grandmother, Elise is there. She can put her to good use."

Rose let out a long exhalation of air, then got up from her seat. "I was going to visit Meredith to give her the news, but all the excitement here has worn me out. I'll leave that to you ladies. Please give her my apologies."

No one argued with her, but after Rose left the room, she heard them begin to whisper. She picked up Irene's voice just before she entered the portal. "Who knew she could be so scary?"

Suppressing a chuckle, she returned to Albamarl.

 **C**HAPTER 20

Chad Grayson considered his navel, then reached down and squeezed his belly. "I was gettin' fat," he observed sourly. He was a relatively slender man, but the tendency had always been there, whenever he spent too much time on his ass and too little time moving.

That wasn't the case currently, though. Since Mordecai had forced a dragon on him, Cyhan wouldn't leave him alone. The big man insisted on training him, to help him adjust to his newfound strength.

His biggest problem, though, was that the training wasn't much like any training he had done before. Chad wasn't unfamiliar with strenuous activity. He hadn't become a paragon of archery by being lazy. It had required lots of practice, and continued practice. What most didn't realize was that while becoming a decent archer was something a person could attain and maintain without too much continued effort, being a master marksman required continual practice; otherwise the skill would degrade.

Pulling a warbow was no mean feat, either. While most hunting bows had a draw weight of sixty to eighty pounds, warbows generally exceeded a hundred. Chad insisted on hunting with a bow of similar weight to help maintain the musculature needed.

But all of that was pointless now. His bow now felt like a toy in his hands. What was the point of strength training when you could already pull a bow with a draw weight many times greater than any currently made? It had even affected his aim, although he had adjusted quickly.

Cyhan had also complimented him on his speed in adjusting to walking and moving around, but that had been easy for him. As a hunter, Chad was used to moving in unnatural fashion, to paying uncommon attention to how and where he placed his feet. Being excessively strong actually made some of that easier, but it did annoy him that he now had to continually soft-foot as he walked to avoid launching himself into walls and ceilings.

The only real change he had enjoyed had been the enhancement of his sight, hearing, and smell. Those were things he had always wanted more of. For a hunter, they were definitely more important than whether he could draw a hundred-weight bow or a hundred-and-fifty-weight bow.

It was thanks to that improved hearing that he heard the messenger's approach long before the man reached his door. In the past, he might not have noticed until the man was almost at his door, or not at all if he was in the middle of talking or otherwise distracted. Today he was up and waiting to open it before the stranger had even knocked.

"What do ya want?" he asked hostilely after the man had knocked.

"Is this Chad Grayson's home?" replied the other.

Opening his door, Chad eyed the stranger warily. "Well, there's no beer in yer hand, and yer ugly enough I'd as soon piss on ya as look at you. So no, he doesn't live here."

The messenger was taken aback for a second, but then grinned widely. "I was told you'd be surly. This is for you, sir." He held out a small package wrapped in oiled leather.

Chad's eyes narrowed. "What's this?"

"A message for you, sir, from Albamarl."

The hunter sighed. *When will they learn?* He took the package and waited, but the messenger made no move to leave. *Oh yeah, the prick wants a tip.* Reaching into his belt, he pulled out a silver coin and flipped it through the air to the other man, who deftly caught it.

"Thank you, sir," said the messenger gratefully.

"Fuck off," replied Chad. When the messenger continued to wait, he questioned him, "Why are you still here?"

"I was told to wait for your response, sir."

Sighing in disgust, Chad unrolled the oiled leather and opened the envelope within. There was a short letter inside, and at the bottom he saw a familiar name had signed it, 'Manfred.' He glanced up at the messenger. "Tell the asshole I'm not for hire. I'm gainfully employed by the Count di' Cameron now." Going back inside his home, he slammed the door and barred it.

He was tempted to throw the letter into the hearth, but the fire had gone out. Instead he sat down at his table and poured a cup of water from the pitcher that sat there. He swished it around in his mouth to wash away the stale taste of the previous night's ale, then looked at the letter again.

Hunter,

> *Your services are once again needed. Make haste to the capital, bringing those tools needed to accomplish your task. Please ensure that none know of your journey. Even the World Road may be watched. Make certain you are not recognized.*

I know it has been many years since you last accepted work, but do not turn this offer down. The client is important and could be a significant thorn in your side should you refuse. Bear with it and meet me at the Hightower gate tomorrow, mid-afternoon.

There are watchers in the city who are sensitive. Bring no magic into the city, but be advised that the target may require extra effort to bring down. Plan accordingly.

Manfred

"Screw you, Manfred," muttered Chad, but he didn't cast the letter aside. His old associate knew very well he would turn him down. The man wouldn't have attempted to hire him if he hadn't thought there was a reason he would accept. Manfred was also not known for poetic prose. "Thorn in my side, eh?"

Chad studied the middle paragraph, and after a second his eyes widened. "The bitch has gone crazy." Standing up, he went back to the door and flung it open. The messenger still stood patiently in the yard. "Hey, jackass!" called the ranger. "What's happening in the capital these days?"

The man dipped his head in nervous respect, but the excitement in his eyes was evident. "I'm amazed the news hasn't reached here yet, what with the speed of trade on the World Road nowadays."

Chad growled. "Just answer the question ballsack. I've got a headache an' it ain't gettin' any better lookin' at you."

"Prince Leomund was murdered by the Blood Count. They have him in chains waiting for trial. They say that—"

"How the hell did that happen?" interrupted the ranger.

"With a dagger it is said," responded the messenger.

Chad shook his head. "No, shit-for-brains, how did they put him in chains? I know the Count, an' I'm damn sure he wouldn't let them lock him up again."

The stranger was practically vibrating with excitement to tell his tale. "He was arrested by Lord Gaelyn and his own son, the Queen's Champion. I've heard he stood adamant before the Queen, threatening to kill her and overturn the kingdom in civil war, but when faced by his son, he wept in shame and surrendered."

Chad realized he was grinding his teeth. "Spare me the storyteller's embellishments and just give me the details." He listened for several minutes, and when the man had run out of facts and began to speculate, he lost his patience.

"That's enough. Tell the man who paid you I'll be there, wrapped in ribbons and bows."

"Pardon, sir? Ribbons and…"

"Ribbons and bows, ye muleheaded twat!" swore Chad. "Tell him that exactly. He knows what it means. Now get gone before I do yer mother a favor and trim that ugly head of yers off."

He slammed the door behind him again, but he didn't sit down. Instead he went to his room and began collecting his things. He needed to pack light. Mentally, he sent a thought out to his dragon, *Prissy, come quick. We have to travel.*

The beast was out hunting, but she was close enough to hear him. *For the last time, my name is Priscilla.*

It's gonna be 'steak' if ye keep arguing with me, Chad shot back.

He was ready within a quarter of an hour, and he left Washbrook immediately, stopping only to leave a note for Danae at the Muddy Pig so she wouldn't wonder at his absence. Then he was on the road, unremarkable in appearance to other travelers, except for the massive bow stave tied to his back.

***

"How long do we have to wait here, grandmother?" asked Carissa for the second or third time. They had been waiting in the street near the home of Lord Airedale for nearly half an hour.

Elise looked at her with her one good eye. The other had gone white and rheumy, a recent addition that was merely temporary. She was dressed in worn, tattered clothes and carried a heavy basket of laundry as well. With her hunched back and frail appearance, she looked ready to collapse at any moment. "Until that jackanape decides to leave for his assignation with Lady Carmella."

Carissa pursed her lips. "Brendan won't come. He knows Carmella doesn't fancy him. How do you know she made an assignation with him?"

Her grandmother cackled, completing her disguise as an old crone. "Because I sent him a letter asking for a meeting."

Carissa was shocked. "You signed her name? That's, that's…"

"Forgery, sweetheart. It's called forgery," said Elise, patting Carissa's cheek gently.

Carissa Thornbear looked uncomfortable. "He still won't believe it."

"Of course he will, sweetling. Men are fools, and lords even more so. They can't help but think themselves irresistible," Elise said softly.

"I still don't understand why you need me here," said her granddaughter.

"To make sure that chivalry is not dead," replied the old woman. "When he comes out, he'll chance upon you. All you have to do is greet him and say a few pleasantries. I'll have an accident near the door."

"Chivalry?"

Her grandmother nodded. "Self-important lordlings like Brendan have a tendency to forget their manners when no one of importance is around. Your presence is merely to make him remember his nobler attributes." As she finished her remark, the front door to Lord Airedale's house opened and a young man in expensive finery stepped out. "Quick, quick, go now," hissed Elise.

Carissa straightened and began walking hurriedly, she crossed directly in front of young Brendan, pretending not to notice him as he exited. "Carissa?" called out the young lord. "Is that you?"

She stopped and turned her head to look at him. "Master Airedale! I didn't expect to encounter you."

The young man frowned. "Please, my lady, you know I've asked you to call me by my given name."

Carissa covered her mouth, blinking at him coquettishly. "Forgive me, Brendan. It just seems too soon to be so familiar."

Brendan smiled, raking long fingers through the thick mane of hair that covered his head. "Certainly not. Our families have known one another since long before we were born. It's only natural."

It was at that point that Elise Thornbear stumbled, uttering a loud cry as she crashed into the young lord, sending her basket and its varied articles of clothing flying onto the cobblestones. While the young man caught his balance quickly enough, Elise continued downward, falling to her hands and knees so violently that Carissa drew a sharp intake of breath, fearing her grandmother might truly be injured.

"Hag! Watch where you walk!" shouted Brendan, losing his temper. The poor benighted woman at his feet scrambled to collect her basket's contents, while simultaneously muttering an endless stream of apologies.

Carissa was aghast at his lack of sympathy, but she bent immediately and began to help her grandmother gather up the clothing scattered on the roadway. "Are you alright, madam?"

Brendan chewed his lip, already regretting his loss of decorum. Putting on a smile, he bent to assist them. "Pardon me, madam. You surprised me."

"It's nothing, young sir," muttered Elise. "Old Mag is used to it." There were tears in her eyes and blood on her hands from the rough ground. Lifting the heavy basket, she made as though to continue on, but then she swayed on her feet.

Brendan caught her arm, and Carissa moved to the other side to catch her if she fell. "Brendan, she's skin and bones!" cried the young woman. "She probably hasn't eaten in days, and her hands are bloody."

Young Airedale made a conscious effort to hide his impatience, though he only partly succeeded. "Take a rest in my house, madam. I'll see you fed and your hands washed before you leave." Stepping back inside, he called one of his maids and she was soon ushering Elise indoors.

When he came back out, Carissa stood waiting with an approving expression on her face. "That was a very kind thing of you to do, Brendan. That poor woman probably hasn't known a good meal in weeks."

Brendan puffed up slightly, looking to one side modestly. "It's only common courtesy for us to do what we can for the poor."

You probably would have kicked her if I hadn't been here, thought Carissa, remembering his temper, but she smiled sweetly. "You are the very soul of gentility, Brendan. If you don't mind me inquiring, where are you headed?" Her expression suggested she might be interested in company if he wasn't busy.

"Ah," said Brendan, struggling to find an excuse for leaving her without revealing his true destination. "Forgive me, Carissa. Father has an urgent errand for me. I dare not tarry."

Carissa looked disappointed. "Another time, perhaps."

After they parted, she struggled to contain her good humor as she made her way home. *Acting is rather fun.*

It was only an hour before her grandmother rejoined her. "What did you do?" asked Carissa.

Elise smiled mysteriously. "Nothing much, dearest. I only needed to make sure they would be looking for new help in a day or two."

Her granddaughter gasped, covering her mouth. "You didn't!"

"Don't fret, poppet," said Elise, reaching out to stroke Carissa's hair. "It's nothing as serious as that. Several of their staff will come down ill in a day or two, but they'll recover with no lasting harm."

"How ill?" said Carissa warily.

227

"There's a terrible stomach ailment going around," said Elise. "I expect they'll be in bed for a week or two."

Her granddaughter frowned. "It sounds awful. Why would you do that?"

"I need a job," said Elise simply. "It would take ages to find an opening the usual way, so I made my own luck." Rising to her feet, she went to the kitchen. "Come help me with the pot. It's a little heavy for these old bones. I need to finish these extracts before I start my job in a couple of days."

"Nana is a little scary," whispered Carissa as she rose to help her grandmother. *I wonder if Gram knows?*

 **CHAPTER 21**

Lady Hightower stepped into the warden's office, carrying an even larger basket than the last time she had come. Regan looked at it with obvious anticipation, his smile displaying a disconcerting mixture of rotten and missing teeth. "It is good to see you again, milady," he greeted her.

Rose looked him up and down with critical eyes. "I cannot say the same, Master Jailor."

He ignored her insult. "I see you brought me a gift."

"Hardly," she replied dismissively. "This is for Lord Cameron."

"I've already told you the rules, Lady Hightower," began the corpulent man.

Rose cut him off. "Are those the same rules you gave Wilhelmina Baker?"

Regan seemed surprised to hear the name. He stared stupidly at her for several seconds before responding, "Huh?"

"Surely you remember her, Regan. That thick head of yours isn't that slow. What about Martha Taylor? Are you beginning to see a pattern?"

The warden glared at her, furious. "Get out."

"You didn't tell Agnes Morris to get out, did you, Regan? I think perhaps you should be a little friendlier," said Rose, her voice dripping with saccharine tones.

"You can't frighten me with rumors, Lady Hightower," said the jailor. "Whatever those women told you, it was all lies."

Rose smiled, showing him a long row of white teeth in an expression that was anything but friendly. "Do you think I care? Whether you think I can prove it or not is beside the point. Force my hand and I'll ruin you. The best you can hope for is to be thrown out on your ass, but I'll make certain that doesn't happen. I'll see to it you wind up in one of those cells you guard so *virtuously*."

The jailor wasn't ready to surrender yet. "That's it. I'm calling the guard to have you removed."

"Excellent," said Rose. "Call the Royal Guard, I have some things to talk about with their captain, Sir Harold. Did you know he's a friend of mine? The Knights of Thorn were named after my dear departed husband. Harold owes me quite a lot. Or would you prefer to call the City Guard? Oh, that wouldn't be fair at all would it, since their captain answers to me directly. Have you thought this through, Regan?"

The warden's face was ashen. "I'll lose my post if they find out I bent the rules."

Rose reached into her basket and pulled out a heavy purse, then tossed it to him. "That's for your retirement, if such should happen, which it won't. I'm not taking anything sinister in to him. Just food and some comforts to keep him from freezing to death before the trial." She offered up the basket for his inspection. "Feel free to look through it."

Regan made a pretense of pawing through the goods within. Rose studied the room while he did. "What are those cabinets over there?" she asked.

"That's where we keep their belongings." He lifted his necklace, displaying a ring of keys, which he rattled. "Locked up safe and sound. We return them when our guests leave." He laughed as though he had made a joke.

Rose didn't find him funny. "Lord Cameron will be found innocent in a few days. See to it his things are untouched."

The warden snorted. "If you say so, milady."

She snapped at him when he started to pull out the roast fowl she had brought. "That's not for you."

Disappointed, he released it and returned the basket to her. "Very well. You can take this in."

Rose smiled again, this time more genuinely. "Thank you, Regan." She left the office but turned back at the door for one more remark. "By the way, his visiting time is an hour from now on. Half an hour is too short."

The jailor nodded, covering his face with one hand. "Please leave, milady."

She did, but as she walked down the corridor she heard him swear softly to himself, almost beneath her hearing, "Lady Highwhore." Gritting her teeth, she went on. When she reached her destination, Tyrion was on guard, one of his uncannily human-like krytek serving as his backup.

"Lady Hightower," he said, smiling and bowing slightly. "I had a feeling you'd be back soon. How did you get the basket down here?"

"Master Regan has rethought his policies," she responded. "His visiting time has also been extended to an hour."

Tyrion gazed back at her incredulously. "Really?"

"Feel free to ask him yourself if you doubt me," returned Rose.

Tyrion grinned. "You are a force of nature, Lady Rose. Have you thought more about my offer?"

She froze for a moment, caught by her reluctance to answer. She had already thought it through, though. Elise and Carissa were staying in her city house; all she had to do was send Angela away for the evening. *Anything,* she repeated silently to herself. "I have," she replied smoothly. "You may call upon me this evening after you are finished here."

"I look forward to it," said Tyrion.

That makes one of us, thought Rose, refusing to meet his eyes. "Open the cell, please."

***

In the middle of another of my incessant dreams, I was startled when the light washed over me. At first, I thought it was my imagination, but then I heard her voice. "Mordecai? Are you awake?"

I tried to sit up, but my body felt numb and awkward. Jerking, I nearly fell onto the floor, but a warm hand caught my shoulder, steadying me. Blinking in the overly bright light cast by the lantern, I looked up at her. "Rose, you shouldn't have come."

"Gods, Mort! You're so cold," exclaimed Rose. She ran her hands down my chest, then felt my legs and began rubbing my feet. "Your feet are as cold as ice."

"It's not so bad once they stop burning," I mumbled.

"Can you sit up?" she asked.

I gave her a half-hearted smile. "Sure," I said, and almost managed it, though she had to help me part of the way. After that, she rustled around in her basket and drew something out before spreading it part of the way over the bench.

"I need to get you up for a moment," she told me. "Put your arms around my neck."

I did, draping the long chain between my wrists over her head and down her back. What followed were several minutes of awkward shuffling while she tried to steady me and keep me from falling while simultaneously arranging a blanket across the bench. Eventually, she finished and helped me sit down again. I thought she might be done, but then she knelt in front of me.

"Rose, what are you doing?" I asked.

She handed me a second blanket, but remained on the floor. "Wrap that around yourself." Then I felt pressure from her fingers, as she gently rubbed my chilled toes.

I might have cried, but my eyes were too dry to respond to my emotions. "Don't do that, Rose."

She looked up at me but her warm hands never left my feet. "Why not?"

"They're dirty," I said, feeling embarrassed. "Someone like you shouldn't…"

Brilliant sapphires stared up at me fiercely, piercing my soul. "Someone like who? Someone like Lady Rose Thornbear?" Then her expression softened. "Are you saying I'm not worthy to rub your feet, Lord Cameron?" Her tone was teasing.

I looked away. She knew very well what I meant. Lady Rose had been the paragon of proper etiquette and manners for as long as I had known her. What's more, it wasn't a show. She really *was* all those things that so many women merely pretended to be. She shouldn't have been getting her hands dirty to help *me*.

She changed tactics. "What would Dorian do if he were here?"

"That's easy," I replied. "He'd break the wall down and carry me out of here like a sick child. Then he'd defeat the guards with one hand and walk out. He'd probably save a princess along the way somehow."

Rose chuckled. "Alright. Let's amend the question. What would Dorian do if he were here and he couldn't break down the wall or any of the rest of that nonsense?"

I refused to answer.

"How about Penny? What do you think your wife would do, Mort?"

"She'd break down the wall and carry me out of here like a sick child," I said immediately. "I'm not sure about the princess, though. She has mixed views on them."

Rose laughed harder than anytime I could remember. Not her usual restrained, polite laughter, but a genuine belly laugh. There was something odd about the sound of it, however. *Is she crying?* After she had recovered, she spoke again, "You're probably right. That sounds just like her."

The feeling was beginning to return to my feet, sending a burning, painful sensation upward. I flinched as her efforts began to hurt.

Sensing my discomfort, Rose stopped, but she kept her warm fingers wrapped around my toes. "They're gone, Mordecai," she said suddenly. "But I think about them all the time. I wonder what they would do if they were in our shoes. I ask myself whether there's anything I have forgotten, whether I've done enough. When I die and meet them again, I don't want them to tell me I disappointed them."

"That's impossible," I insisted. "They would never think that."

"Really, Mort?" she asked. She was definitely crying. I could hear the tears in her voice. "I'm not so sure. It's never enough. I don't know that I've been anything but a failure at raising Gram. He's become exactly what his father asked me to avoid. And Penny—what would she think of me now? Would she say I've done enough? Or perhaps she would think I've done too much."

"I don't understand," I said, but I did. "Penny loved you, Rose. She would never find fault in you."

"I'm not so sure, Mordecai," she answered. "I don't know what's right or wrong anymore." Then she sighed and reached into her basket once more, pulling out several pairs of wool socks. Slowly, she put them onto my feet, until each had not one, but three thick layers of wool around it. Rising to her feet, she pulled the basket closer and sat down beside me. "Let me in," she said.

"Huh?" I was confused.

"Wrap the blanket around the two of us so I can help warm you up," she explained.

She was fully clothed, so it wasn't nearly as improper as it felt, but I still suffered a pang of guilt. Stretching one end of the blanket wide, I settled it over her shoulder and she scooted close until she was against my side. As cold as I was, she felt like a warm stove beside me.

Rustling around under the cover, she slipped her hands out and unwrapped the roast bird that my senses had spotted there several minutes earlier. It was messy and greasy, and my hands were so clumsy that I dropped it several times, staining the blanket and getting lint on the pheasant. I didn't care.

Eventually I gave up trying to hold it myself and let her feed me, choking down as much as I could hold. When my stomach started to rebel, I told her stop. "I can't eat anymore. You brought too much."

"The rest is for later," she explained. "I'll leave it here." Then she extricated herself from the blanket and brought the water pitcher over, making me drink from it. "Don't spill," she warned. "We'll never warm you up if you get water on you."

"It's almost time for you to go," I told her.

"I'll leave when I'm ready," she insisted.

We resumed our huddled position on the bench, but it really wasn't comfortable. My body was sore and aching in too many places to count. "I can't stay like this, Rose."

She thought about it a moment, and then brought out a small cushion from her basket. "Use this as a pillow," she said firmly.

"How much stuff did they let you bring in here?" I wondered aloud.

"That's not your concern," Rose reprimanded me. "Lie down."

I did as I was told, finding the cushion was just thick enough to serve as a passable pillow for my head. Rose put the second blanket over me and tucked it carefully in along my back and legs, and then, before I could protest, she lay down herself, slipping through the chain and resting her head on my arm. Easing back against my stomach, she pulled the blanket over herself and held it closed.

"Uh, Rose," I began cautiously. I was still holding my right arm out straight, the chain dangling from it in a long loop before it met with the manacle on my other wrist.

"Shhh," she responded. "Put your arm around me."

I lay still, frozen for a moment, trying to decide what to do. Where should I put my hand? It wasn't my first time spooning, of course, but this was *not* Penny. Most of the good options would likely see the death of me. I had already resigned myself to a bad end, but I wasn't ready to commit suicide.

Apparently deciding that I wasn't going to listen, Rose found my hand and pulled it across her body, setting it against her stomach and pressing it firmly in place. Then she repositioned her arm, using it to cover my own. When I let my arm go slack, she warned me, "Hold me firmly, Mordecai. I won't break."

That's not what I'm worried about!

"Or bite," she added, apparently reading my mind.

Then again, if that was the case, I was damned, well and truly. I tried not to think. Fortunately, my body was still so cold there was little danger of embarrassing myself in a more direct manner.

As usual, her hair was pinned up in one of her ridiculously complicated coiffures, so I didn't have to worry about choking on it. Instead, I found my nose close to the nape of her neck. She smelled inordinately good. I didn't want to think about that either, so I focused on the more negative aspect of our situation. I stunk.

I was used to my own stench, of course, being unable to escape it. But I couldn't imagine that she found it pleasant. *Why is she doing this?* The answer was obvious. *To keep you alive, dunderhead.* But I still couldn't help but feel she was doing too much. As well as I knew Rose, I knew this had to be humiliating for her.

"What's happening out there?" I said at last. "Are my children alright? They haven't done anything stupid, have they?"

"Moira and Irene didn't take it well," she answered. "I told them to stay home and they almost mutinied on me. Conall has been suffering as one of your guards, but every time I look at him he makes a guilty face, as though I've just accused him of murdering you. Matthew and Gram still don't know. They haven't returned from Lancaster."

"Good," I muttered. "I was more worried about them than the others. They're liable to do something stupid."

"Hah," said Rose, then she gave a knowing chuckle. "I wouldn't be so sure. Your daughters are in quite a state. I wouldn't be surprised if Moira decided to enslave the entire city to set you free." Then she shifted, pressing her hips backward against me.

Oh, no. "Rose, you have to stay still," I protested weakly.

"Lift your knee a little," she replied, ignoring my remark. "If you're going to get the most out of this, you can't be a prude. Your legs need warmth too."

I was already feeling warmer, and I managed to blush, but I did as she suggested, sliding my right knee up until it was across her left thigh and up against… I stopped my thoughts there. Of course, we had two skirts, my trousers, and the gown I was wearing between us, but that was little barrier to my imagination.

"About Moira," I said, wrenching my thoughts back into line. "What did she say?"

"It wasn't so much what she said," explained Rose. "She wasn't satisfied with what I told her. She threatened to root around in my head to get the answers she wanted."

She described the brief argument, with Elaine and Irene coming to her defense, then she stopped.

I felt terrible, for her and for my daughter. I also worried what would become of Moira if I died. I hoped that in time she would find a balance with her new abilities and her dark compulsions, but if I was gone, she might start down a path she couldn't return from. "So they stopped her?" I asked.

"No, she did something, and Elaine fell unconscious," said Rose. "After that, I struck her and gave her a short lecture on proper behavior."

I choked. "You what?"

"I'm sorry, Mordecai. I was overwrought, and I lost my temper. I've never done that with Gram and Carissa, but she was out of control. I even brought Penny into it."

I couldn't help but laugh. "You realize how dangerous she is, don't you?"

Rose was emphatic. "She's a *child*, Mordecai. Yours and Penny's, and very much like a daughter to me. She may be grown, but I won't let her make that sort of mistake, not while I'm there."

To my knowledge, Rose Thornbear had only used physical force twice in her life. Once accidentally, when she brained her own father to escape from house arrest, and once when she had struck Dorian to snap him out of a murderous rage. "Thank you," I said sincerely. "I'll worry less if you're watching over them after I'm gone."

Her hand tightened over mine, her nails digging into my skin painfully. "You're not going anywhere. I'll see you exonerated at the trial."

"Even the greatest counsel in the world can only do so much," I told her. "Don't blame yourself if it doesn't turn out how you hope."

"You'll be free the day of the trial, Mordecai," she insisted. "No matter what it costs."

I didn't like the sound of that, and I started to say so, but the wall shimmered and became translucent. Our time was done. Rose bolted upright and was on her feet as quickly as a startled rabbit. She gathered her basket, leaving the food behind, took up her lantern, and without another word, she was gone.

With a sigh, I pulled the blanket closely around myself and settled back down. *After they hang me, I'm going to have a lot of explaining to do when I see Penny.* The chill settled around me once more, but for the first time in days I felt warm, and the blankets were thick. I could last another day.

***

Tyrion chuckled as the wall became solid behind her once more. "Have a nice time?"

"A visit to a friend in a freezing dungeon cell can hardly be described so," Rose retorted.

The archmage gave a look of surprise. "Really? The way the two of you were snuggled together in there almost made me think you were planning to spoil my reward before the evening had arrived, but after seeing how chaste you were I began to feel sorry for you."

Startled, Rose looked at him in alarm. "You could see through the walls?"

Tyrion nodded. "When necessary, the enchantment allows magesight to work in a one-directional fashion. What better time to observe him than when he has a suspicious visitor?"

Furious, Rose stepped closer. "I don't like you, remember that. No matter what I do this evening, I do it for *him*."

Tyrion grinned, and a shiver ran down her spine as she smelled the mint on his breath. "We'll see how you feel about that *after* my visit. We didn't have *ladies* in my time—didn't have *whores* either, for that matter." Leaning in, he breathed into her ear, whispering, "We just had *sex*."

Rose nearly dropped the basket, but she recovered it at the last second. Stepping back, she turned and began walking quickly away, her legs taking the longest strides possible. Tyrion laughed behind her. "Make sure you brush off your clothing before you take the stairs. There's dust all over your skirts. You don't need any more rumors going around."

 CHAPTER 22

By the time she had reached her rooms, Rose was already breaking down. She closed her bedroom door and stripped off her dress as quickly as she could manage, which wasn't very quickly. Her hands were shaking uncontrollably. She fumbled with her hair, pulling out pins and undoing the braids frantically, as though by doing so she could dispel the feeling of suffocation that threatened to overwhelm her.

Staring into the mirror, she wasn't happy with what she saw. *Follow the ritual,* she chanted silently in her head. Going to her wardrobe, she selected a simple blue dress and put it on. She had no intention of dressing in her finest for what lay in store. That done, she began redoing her hair, choosing a simple style since her hands weren't up to the task of anything more complex.

When she finished, she looked in the mirror again. Her hands were still shaking, and a tear spilled unwanted down her cheek, spoiling the powder she had just applied. Rage filled her, and unable to stop herself, she unleashed a shriek that by all rights should have shattered the silvered glass in front of her.

The bedroom door flew open, revealing Elise Thornbear's worried features. "Are you alright?"

Rose's scream cut off, only half-done. Her mouth formed an 'o' as she stared at her mother-in-law in surprise.

"Don't just gape at me, girl!" demanded Elise. "What's wrong?"

"Why—why are you here?" she said, tripping over her words uncharacteristically.

"I wanted a bath," snapped Elise. "I probably won't get a chance at one for a week or two after this. Now tell me, what's going on?"

Rose got to her feet and began pushing her mother-in-law out the door. "No, you have to go. You can't be here when he comes. Please, Elise, don't ask me anything else."

Elise refused to be herded. "When who comes?" She caught Rose's hands in hers and her face grew more concerned. "Why are your hands shaking like this? Has someone done something to you? Talk to me, girl!"

With her emotions already out of control, Rose began to cry. Forgetting her usual reserve, she told Elise everything, spilling her secret arrangement with Tyrion to the last person she wanted to know about it, Dorian's mother. The confession was cathartic, while at the same time she knew it would forever destroy her in the eyes of her mother-in-law.

Elise Thornbear's eyes grew hard as she came to understand the situation, but her anger wasn't directed at Rose. "It always comes back to this, doesn't it?" she muttered. Absently, she reached out and stroked Rose's half-braided hair. "Stop blaming yourself, girl. This isn't your fault."

Dejected, Rose sat next to Elise, her head down. "I won't let him die, Elise. Even if it costs me everything."

"Of course you won't," agreed the older woman. "Don't think I'm looking down on you for this. If anything, you should have come to me sooner."

"I didn't want you to think—to know—that I'm…"

Elise shushed her. "Know what? That you're a strong woman, willing to do anything to protect her loved ones? I already knew that. If ever I misjudged you, it would be in thinking that perhaps you valued your ideals above practicality. I'm more impressed with you now than ever. My son chose wisely when he married you."

That ushered in a new round of tears from Rose.

"That's enough, girl," said Elise calmly. "Crying won't solve anything. Let me help you. This doesn't have to be as bad as you think."

"But I've never—you don't understand—Dorian's the only man I've ever…" said Rose, half mumbling.

Elise clucked. "They're pretty much all the same, once you get right down to it, from a functional standpoint. The trick is keeping your heart out of it. That's where all the real pain comes from." Getting carefully to her feet, Elise headed toward her own bedroom. "Wait right there. Let me get something for you."

When she returned, the older woman was carrying a small satchel. She reached into it and drew out a smaller pouch; from that she took out what looked like a tiny bundle of leaves rolled together.

"What's this?" asked Rose, puzzled.

"Nothing exotic," said Elise. "It's an old whore's trick, barely a secret at all. You chew it, but don't swallow. Use it when he gets here and spit it out right before the work begins."

Curious and faintly hopeful, Rose asked, "What does it do?"

"It's a stimulant. I use it now and then to give me energy, but more importantly for you, it produces euphoria

245

and a mild sort of numbness. The euphoria will help keep you from weeping and the numbness will keep any pain at bay, if he turns out to be the rough sort."

"Will it help me forget?"

Elise shook her head. "If anything, it makes you more mentally alert, but you won't hurt, and you won't care as much." When Rose didn't look entirely convinced, she added, "Trust me. When I was a Grey Lady, I helped a lot of the other girls get through this."

"I don't *want* to get through this," Rose protested.

"Then you only have two other options," Elise informed her. "Poison him or drug him. Both are risky, and I wouldn't suggest using poison to an amateur like yourself. If things go badly, he'll force you to take the poison in his place. Potential victims are vengeful like that."

"Drugging sounds better," answered Rose. *I can't believe I said that.*

Elise left again, returning with an unopened bottle of wine. "This is your best bet then."

Rose recognized the vintner's label, for it was a respectable wine she'd had many times before. "What will you put in it?"

"Nothing," said Elise, chuckling. "It's already in there. I made this myself years ago, when my husband was still alive. I only have three bottles left. Don't believe the label or the vintner's mark on the seal; it's a fake. The only drawback is that if you try it on an experienced wine connoisseur, he might notice the difference in flavor."

Rose smiled faintly. "I don't think Tyrion's developed a taste for wine."

"I'm sure he hasn't," agreed Elise. "Try and get him to have a full glass or it will take forever to work. Two glasses won't hurt him, but if he tries to have more, you'll need to spill the bottle to avoid him killing himself."

"What will it do, exactly?"

Elise rubbed her hands together, warming to her subject. "It's nearly perfect, hence why I chose to put it in wine. The effect is very similar to normal inebriation, but it happens more quickly. It also has the benefit of sometimes producing amnesia. Many who take it don't remember what happened the night before. The crowning touch is that it leaves a terrible headache, which helps to further the lie."

Anxious, Rose leaned forward. "When you say quickly, how quickly do you mean? A minute or two?"

Elise began to cackle, perfectly portraying the evil witch planning wickedness, causing Rose to shiver. Then she smiled, the warmth returning to her face. "Heavens no, sweetheart. Drugs aren't magic. Very few things work that quickly, and those that do are as dangerous to the handler as they are to the victim. Besides, working slowly is often an advantage, for it puts time between the act and the onset."

"I think I'd prefer speed at the moment," said Rose.

"Be glad he's built lean," said Elise sagely. "If he was given to fat, it would take longer. As it is, if he drinks a full glass, it will probably take at least twenty minutes to make him sleep. It could be as long as an hour."

"An hour!" exclaimed Rose.

Elise patted her hand, which was still holding the small bundle of leaves. "Start chewing them when he gets here. They'll help keep you awake so you can stay alert until after he's passed out, since you'll have to drink some as well, to put him at ease. If you can't delay him long enough, you may still have to go through with it."

Rose shuddered.

Done with her explanations, Elise took to her feet once more and headed for the door. "I suppose I'll have to skip that bath." She stopped with her hand on the handle, turning back. "One last piece of advice. Don't let him kiss you if you can avoid it, whatever else happens. It's a novice mistake that usually causes more pain than all the rest combined."

Once she was outside, Elise Thornbear's calm façade crumbled. Wiping her face with her sleeve, she began walking, a shadow filling her heart. "Why?" she whispered sadly. "She doesn't deserve this."

***

When the door opened again an hour later, Tyrion was there. He entered smoothly, confidence written in his stride.

Rose looked up from where she sat on the couch. The wine bottle rested casually on the table in front of her. "Is it too much for you to knock?" she asked.

"Why bother?" he said, a rakish smile on his lips. "You were expecting me. I have only come to accept the gifts you have offered." Glancing around the room, his magesight explored the areas his eyes could not reveal on their own. "Where is your family?"

Struggling to hide her nervousness, Rose answered, "I sent them away for the evening."

"That means we can sleep in tomorrow," Tyrion announced. "I appreciate your thoughtfulness. A prize is more properly savored when it can be enjoyed at leisure." Removing his outer coat, he tossed it aside without bothering to hang it up, heedless of the wrinkles it might gather on the floor. Underneath he wore a loose shirt with a plunging neckline, exposing so much of his chest that Rose suspected his navel might be visible at the right angle.

He crossed the room to where she sat, walking almost too slowly. Despite her best efforts, Rose flinched away when he dropped onto the cushions beside her. "Relax, Lady Rose," he told her. "You'll spoil the mood if you remain so tense." Once of his arms was draped over the back of the couch behind her, and his hand reached forward to casually stroke the back of her neck.

Too fast, this is happening too fast! Leaning forward, Rose reached for the wine bottle. "Before we go further, I'd like to clarify your side of our bargain," she said. Attempting to appear nonchalant, she reached for the bottle opener and promptly dropped it.

Chuckling, Tyrion took the bottle from her hand and ran one finger around the top. Then he pressed his fingertip against it and drew it back, removing the cork in a smooth motion, as though it was glued to his skin. Tossing the cork aside, he placed the bottle back on the table. "That sounds fair," he answered. "I'm prepared to do whatever necessary to free your precious friend from his wrongful imprisonment, and I'll be happy to let you decide what that entails."

Rose nodded, and using two hands, she filled two glasses with wine. She took one in her right hand and offered the second to her guest. Tyrion's eyes followed her the entire time, studying her features. Then he lifted his hand in a gesture of refusal. "Thank you, no. I prefer to have all my faculties for this, the better to savor it."

When she put both glasses back down, he spoke again, "Feel free to have some yourself, if that will help you relax."

Nodding, Rose lifted her own glass again, taking the smallest of sips from it. "All I need is your assurance that the krytek will not interfere. In the next day or two, there will be men entering the city bearing enchanted weapons. I want them to be ignored. After the trial, if things go badly, make sure your minions remain passive. In return, I will grant you your desire tonight." She managed to get the words out smoothly, somehow.

Tyrion arched one brow. "Tonight? Tonight is one thing, but it hardly matters. Do you think me fool enough to sell my service for a single night's pleasure? No, Lady Rose, I know all too well how fleeting the pleasures of the flesh are."

Rose felt a faint stirring of hope. "What do you want then?"

"Your service in exchange," pronounced the archmage. "Tonight, tomorrow, whenever I feel the need to quench my blade. Give me your assurance that you will sate my appetite whenever required and convince me with your performance tonight."

Sickened by the thought, something else occurred to Rose. "Is this your idea of—of a proposal?"

Tyrion chuckled. "Certainly not. I have higher ambitions in that regard."

Rose felt his hand on her skirt, travelling upward as he stroked her thigh through the fabric. Startled, she bolted up from her seat and moved several steps away.

Her tormentor laughed. Leaning back casually, he said, "Still afraid of me? That won't do, Rose. I need to see your conviction."

Her mind in chaos, Rose cast about for anything that might offer safety, but there was nothing. *Where are the leaves Elise gave me?* she thought despairingly. She had dropped them somewhere, but she couldn't remember where. Tyrion's eyes were burning into her. *What do I do?*

As if in answer to her thought, Tyrion spoke up, "Take off the dress."

The world went still at his words, and so did her mind. A cold calm stole across her, revealing everything to her with crisp clarity. She had made a devil's bargain, and it was time to pay. Straightening, she stared down at the man leering at her. *Anything,* she repeated to herself, tightening her jaw. Reaching up, she undid the laces at her shoulders.

For once, she regretted wearing such a simple dress. One of the more elaborate gowns would have taken much longer. With the shoulders undone, she shifted slightly so the dress could slide down. Once it had reached the floor, she would be completely naked in front of him.

"Stop!" ordered Tyrion as she started to release the fabric in her hands. She froze, and he began to laugh, long and loud. Then he reached out and picked up his wine glass, downing it in a single long draught. Setting the empty glass down, he laughed again, more normally this time. Then he stood and moved to stand behind her.

Taking the fabric from her hands, he pulled it back up and began retying her laces. "Dear Rose, I wish you could have seen the look you were giving me."

"What?" she asked, stupefied by his reaction. Turning her head slightly, she caught a whiff of his breath, a mixture of wine and—mint.

"You had me the first time I visited," he explained. "I already planned to get my grandson out. I probably would have done so already, just to keep him from freezing to death, if it hadn't been for your faithful ministrations keeping him alive."

"Then this, all this?"

"Just some fun," he teased. "I wanted to see just how devoted you were, and I must say, you didn't disappoint."

Turning, she slapped him so hard that her hand burned with pain. "Bastard!"

He didn't flinch. Licking his lips, he warned her, "Careful. Pain tends to arouse my baser nature, and I know you don't want that. Do you?"

Pushing him back roughly, Rose crossed several feet of space and seated herself gracefully in a chair. "Is this all a game to you?"

Tyrion went back to the couch, pouring himself another glass of wine. Then he offered her still-unfinished glass to her. She took it and made a show of taking another sip. "Not at all," he answered. "To be honest, if you had been more willing I might well have taken your offering, though you're a little more mature than suits my usual tastes. As it is, I couldn't stand watching your reaction any longer."

"Why not?" asked Rose coldly. "You seemed to enjoy it enough."

He sighed. "Because, despite things I did in the past, I am not a rapist. At least, not any longer. I prefer my prey warm and willing."

"You claim that," said Rose, "but your actions dictate otherwise." With one hand, she lifted her pendant, waving it at him.

He laughed. "You think I've found some way around your protections? I gave up such things millennia before you were born. I know women well enough to elicit the reactions I seek, without resorting to such tricks." Then he leaned forward to whisper conspiratorially, "If your blood was burning, if your heart was racing, it wasn't because of magic. It was simply your own wicked desires making themselves known to you."

"If all you have to say is lurid nonsense, you can get out," said Rose forcefully.

"Don't be so angry Rose. Let me finish my drink. In time, I think the two of us could be good friends. You are—by far—the most interesting woman I have encountered in thousands of years."

She eyed the glass in his hand. It was already half gone. If he finished it, she would have to dispose of the bottle to prevent him from having a third glass. "We will never be friends, Tyrion. I don't approve of your methods."

"Oh, I think we will, Rose. Let me stay a while longer so we can chat. The Queen is busy tonight, so I have little to do with my time." His words were noticeably slurred. He poured the rest of the wine in the glass down his throat.

Rose's eyes narrowed. "The Queen?"

He smiled. "Higher ambitions, remember?" Raising his glass, he pretended to make a toast only to be disappointed when he discovered it was already empty. He placed it on the table, then said, "She's a lively woman, unlike yourself."

Angry beyond words, Rose smiled calmly. Leaning over, she picked up the bottle. "More wine?" Not waiting for an answer, she filled his glass to the brim. She remembered Elise's warning vividly, and she wondered if a third would kill him. At the moment, she didn't really care.

"In a second," said Tyrion, waving his hand errantly through the air. "My head is spinning. Let me rest my eyes for a moment." He leaned back, sinking down into the cushions, and moments later he was asleep.

Lucky bastard, thought Rose. She collected the still-full glass and the half empty bottle and carried them away. *You deserve every bit of pain your head will give you tomorrow.*

After that, she stood silently for a moment. What to do? A single glance at the man sleeping on her couch made her certain she didn't want to sleep in her room tonight. Then her eye spotted the small bundle of leaves Elise had left. It had fallen to the floor beside the foot of the couch. Without a second thought she scooped it up and popped it into her mouth, chewing slowly.

Her tongue and lips went numb almost immediately, followed by her cheeks, as a cool but warm feeling seeped through her. Her heart rate increased, but she felt remarkably calm and clearheaded. Returning to her room, she redressed, donning a more appropriate gown for traveling, and redid her hair. It was hardly necessary—her mind was already calm—but the ritual was as much a habit as anything else.

Stepping out, she crossed the room and went to the outer door. On the way, she spied Tyrion's coat, still lying discarded by the door. Spitefully, she stepped on it, making a show of wiping her shoes on the rich fabric as though it were a doormat. She regretted that her shoes were already clean.

Then she left. She would sleep at her city house tonight with Elise and Carissa.

 **C**HAPTER 23

Chad Grayson ambled down the thoroughfare at a leisurely pace. The sun was beating down fiercely, but it hardly bothered him in the wide-brimmed hat he wore. He reached up once more to tug on the brim, angling it downward to obscure his face better from other passersby.

He had already met with his contact and confirmed his suspicions. The job he would be taking on was possibly the most dangerous of his career. It might even be the end of his career. If it had been anyone else that asked, he would have refused. If it had been *for* anyone else, he would have refused. *I've lived long enough,* he thought, resigning himself to his work. *If I die, at least I'll die at the top of my game.*

He was far from suicidal, however. The huntsman had every intention of weighing the odds as much in his own favor as was possible. Glancing up now and then, he studied the buildings around him, noting the elevation of the rooftops. Most of them were useless for his purposes. He kept walking.

The Royal Justice Building was across the street from western side of the palace, with its main entrance facing the palace street. He spent extra time studying the area and the buildings around it. He wasn't happy with what he saw. *Bad line of sight or certain death,* he cursed silently. Once again, he looked up at the palace wall.

"That's where I'd want to be," he muttered. "Everything else bein' equal."

But everything else was far from equal. While the palace battlements provided the best view, they would also be the worst place to try and escape from, once his job was done. That was assuming he could find a way to put himself there without rousing the entire Guard to a murderous fury.

"On the plus side, no one would expect me to be there." Glancing down at the dusty robe that covered his body, he made a decision. "I'll need different clothes." That wouldn't be a problem, though. The trick was acquiring them without too many holes and stains. *Blood tends to spoil a disguise,* he chuckled to himself.

He crossed the street and made another pass in front of the Justice Building, then continued on to do a full circuit around the palace itself. That done, he worked his way outward. He wanted to be familiar with the entire area. Although it was secondary to his goal, knowing the streets would increase his chances of making it out alive afterward.

The day passed slowly as he learned the streets, mapping out several routes to the closest city gate. Not that the gate held any real offer of safety, not with wizards involved. There probably wouldn't be enough left of him to feed the crows. *Sorry, Danae. The odds aren't lookin' good on this one.*

Chad gazed longingly at the taverns and bars he passed. The sun was hot, and wearing out his boot leather had made him thirsty, but he didn't stop at any of them. He was working.

One thing he was grateful for, though. He had insisted that his next meeting be at one of the taverns closest to the Hightower gate, a place called the Green Pony. He was supposed to meet another man there, one hired to assist him in his endeavor.

The hunter didn't particularly want help, though. A second man would only double his chances of being spotted before it was time to draw back his string and loose the first arrow. A second man would almost certainly be useless and might even make escape harder. *I'll give him a fuckoff job and ignore him,* thought Chad. *An' if he won't fuck off, I'll hide his body in an alley somewhere.* Idly, he fingered the long knife at his hip.

It wasn't one of his enchanted knives, the ones given to him by the Count. He had been warned. The new guards roaming the streets could sense magic. His knives, arrows, and bow were hidden outside the city. According to his contact, it would be safe to bring them in the next day. *I wonder how she paid off the Royal Guard?* thought Chad. *It must have cost her a pretty penny.*

He didn't feel sorry for her, though. His own price would be worse, paid in steel and blood. The stench of dung assailed his nostrils, and the hunter covered his nose with a handkerchief. "I hate cities," he muttered.

When the sun began to sink low in the sky, he turned his steps toward the Green Pony, hoping the beer there would be enough to make up for the bullshit he would have to deal with. He was disappointed when he finally stepped inside. Years of carousing at the Muddy Pig in Washbrook had spoiled him. The place was a dump.

Looking around, he searched for an empty table, but there were none. Then his eyes fell on a large man sitting in the corner. "I'll be damned," hissed Chad under his breath. Covering his surprise, he moved over and took the empty chair across from the behemoth pretending to be a man. "I should have known you'd turn up," said the ranger. "Yer like a bad penny."

The big man grunted, lifting his mug as a greeting.

"Ya know this is a death sentence, or does that matter to ya?" continued Chad, waving a hand in the air to attract the attention of a barmaid.

Cyhan shrugged, lifting his brows in an expression that said, 'maybe, maybe not.'

"Well this is just dandy," said Chad, his spirits lifting. "At least I'll be dyin' next to someone uglier'n me. Momma always said to have ugly friends. I'll be the prettiest one at the funeral."

The big knight smiled faintly, his version of a polite laugh.

The ranger glared at him. "Are you ever gonna say anythin'? Act like yer happy to see me at least, for fuck's sake!"

"Got a plan?" asked Cyhan.

After giving the warrior a look that could tan leather at ten paces, Chad began to explain what he had in mind. It didn't take him long, since they were both well versed in the craft, and by the time he finished, the barmaid had brought his first mug.

Picking it up, he finished it in one long, gulping draught, holding up one hand to hold the server's attention before she could wander away. Setting the empty mug down, he told her, "I ain't done yet, darlin'. Keep 'em comin'."

Since he was a new customer and she hadn't yet seen the heft of his purse, she looked askance at Cyhan, presumably because she thought he was paying. The big man nodded and she left.

Chad gave Cyhan a sidelong look and flashed a wicked smile. "Thanks, partner. I'm startin' to like you better already."

The grandmaster knight grunted and then said, "I'll need a bow."

The ranger looked at him quizzically. "Can ya shoot?"

Cyhan raised one brow, answering the question with a hard stare.

"I'm not askin' if ya can hit a target at fifty paces," clarified the hunter. "This ain't target practice. I need ta know if ya can..." He stopped. "Ya know what, never mind. We'll walk by the location tomorrow an' then we'll get you a bow. After that I need to make a quick trip outside the city to collect my tools. Before we come back, we'll warm up our limbs with a little practice."

Crossing his arms, Cyhan stared at the ceiling.

The serving girl returned with his mug and paused for a second to see if he would finish it as quickly as the first. Chad took a long pull, then said, "Find another mug. I'll be done with this one by the time you get back." She left.

Turning back to Cyhan he continued, "It ain't for you, ya thickheaded monster. I need the warmup. All I expect from you is one or two well-aimed shots. But fer the kind of shootin' I do, I need to be at the top of my game, familiar with both my bow and the shafts I'm usin'."

Cyhan nodded. "I knew what you meant."

"Did ya bring yer blades?" asked Chad.

The knight smiled. "The world is my weapon."

The hunter sighed in exasperation. "I can never tell when yer bein' serious or just full of shit." In point of fact, he already knew how deadly Sir Cyhan was. Even unarmed, the man could probably have killed every man in the bar, if he had desired to do so. And that was *without* his dragon-bond strength.

The knight grinned. "That was a joke. Of course I have my blades. Have you ever known me to be without them?"

Chad finished his third mug. "Gods save me from this lethal lunatic!" he swore.

Cyhan's face was deadly serious. "The gods are dead. The man we're here to save slew them, remember?"

The hunter spit out some of his beer. "It's a turn of phrase! Did yer momma drop you on yer head?"

The warrior across from him began to laugh deeply, with his belly behind it. After a minute he paused and winked at the ranger. "Another joke. You're making this too easy for me."

Disgusted, Chad gave the big man a look of fury that was almost entirely an act. "I fuckin' hate yer guts sometimes. Ya know that?"

Cyhan spread his arms wide, then leaned back and laced his fingers together behind his head. "Really, Chad? I was just thinking how much I've missed you."

Chad flashed a smile for a second before hiding it. "Shoulda said that at the start. I swear, one o' these days I'm gonna put an arrow in yer ass."

***

Irene and Lynaralla stood in the place they had last seen Matthew and the others, their attention focused on the area in front of them. "Can you see it?" asked Irene.

Lynaralla nodded. "It's faint, but it's there."

"Do you know what to do?"

The She'Har woman shook her head, causing her silver hair to wave around her head. "No. None of this was included in the knowledge I was born with."

"Well, my brother figured it out, so it can't be that hard," opined Irene. "Want to take turns?"

"No," said Lynaralla. "It will be more efficient if you to move over there a short distance. We can both try in different places until one of us figures it out."

Irene's face lit up. "That does make sense." She followed Lynaralla's advice and moved ten feet to the left, and then both girls began attempting to do *something*.

For the better part of half an hour they succeeded at doing something, just not what they wanted. Lynaralla's experiments were methodical, trying first one thing and another, slightly modifying her approach with each attempt, while Irene was more slapdash in her attempts. They finally called a break and Irene sat down on the ground, heedless of getting dirt on her skirts.

"Why am I so tired?" she complained.

"It looked like you were using a lot of power," said Lynaralla, who was still feeling fine. "I would have collapsed by now if I had tried the things you did."

Irene nodded. "We don't have a lot of time." Thinking hard, she pursed her lips. "It didn't look very difficult when Matt did it."

"I don't think brute force will work."

"There must be a trick to it," agreed Irene.

Lynaralla returned to her attempts, and after a few seconds Irene stood up and dusted herself off. Finding her spot once more, she took a moment to focus her thoughts and relax her breathing. She closed her eyes, for they were only distracting her from the important information being provided by her magesight.

Then she held up her hands and reached outward, pushing her aythar through her fingers. *I want to touch that,* she thought, referencing the faint shimmer. She felt the power rushing out of her, most of it missing the mark, but at long last she felt some of it touch *something.*

Exultant, she latched onto that tiny bit and bent her will to grasping it fully. Grinding her teeth, she worked harder, giving it everything she had. The magic flowed out of her like a torrent, a river, filling the space in front of her, yet she only had the tiniest hold on the strange boundary. It felt similar to holding a heavy blade in the air, one almost too heavy to hold up, yet being able to use only your fingertips to grasp the tip.

And it was slipping away from her.

No! Irene refused to give up, and her aythar blazed like a heatless fire around her, causing her hair to fly outward as though she stood in a fierce gale.

Alarmed, Lynaralla stopped her own effort and stared at the girl who had only recently become her sister. "Irene, stop! You'll kill yourself!" She considered tackling Irene to the ground, but then she saw something happen. The empty air shifted, and a small tear appeared in the hidden boundary, but it lasted only a second in that state before the veil was ripped wide. A massive opening appeared, reaching from the ground to the sky beyond the limit of Lynaralla's senses. It was at least a hundred feet across, and the edges were shifting back and forth tens of feet every second or so.

Lynaralla stepped forward, crossing to the other side, but when she looked back Irene was still where she had started. The blonde girl took a step, then another, before stumbling. She fell, losing consciousness before she struck the ground, and the boundary began to collapse, rushing inward.

Lynaralla knew what would happen when it closed on her sister's prone form. Lashing out with her power, she caught Irene's body and dragged it roughly forward, pulling it to herself just before the tear in reality snapped shut with a crackling roar.

Dropping to her knees, she cradled Irene's head, her magesight questing outward to examine her sister. "Please be alright."

But Irene wasn't breathing, and as Lynaralla watched, her fluttering heart shuddered to a stop. Her sister's aythar was faint, almost nonexistent. She had put far too much into her working.

"No, no, no," said Lynaralla, horrified. "This can't happen." With desperate speed, she sent a tendril of power into the other girl, attempting to feed some of her own strength into her. Then she used another to squeeze the heart itself, trying to simulate its beat.

Most of the aythar that she pushed at Irene bled away, like water from a stone. Transferring power was always an inefficient act, and it required conscious effort on the part of both the giver and the receiver, but some of it seeped in.

Minutes passed, and Lynaralla learned a new emotion. Despair. Tears began to spill from her eyes and she considered giving up, until she felt a sudden movement of Irene's heart. It fluttered in the grasp of her power, a sensation similar to a small bird in the hand. She released it and Irene's heart began to beat once more, erratically at first, but then gradually with a strong, steady rhythm.

Irene coughed, and her eyes slowly eased open to stare up at the silver-haired girl above her. Crinkling her nose in confusion, she asked, "Are you crying?"

"I think so," answered Lynaralla, and then a long line of snot dropped from her nose to land on Irene's forehead.

"Ew," exclaimed Irene. She drew her arm weakly up to defend her face from further debasement. "Wipe your nose."

The She'Har girl leaned back, and then used her sleeve to do just that. "You nearly died."

"Uh uh," argued Irene.

"You did!"

"You're mistaken," insisted Irene.

Confused, Lynaralla asked, "Why?"

"Because you were there," said Irene confidently. "I was safe the entire time."

"Humans really are stupid," replied the She'Har girl. Then she became aware of the figures approaching them, massive humanoids that were far too large to be men. Looking around, she saw that while she had been distracted a group of ten ogres had surrounded them.

Irene also noticed them. "They don't look friendly. Tyrion taught you how to fight, right?"

"I wasn't very good at it," answered Lynaralla, resignation in her voice. Taking to her feet, she studied the drooling faces around them. "You destroyed those metal monsters a few months ago. How did you do it?"

Irene was struggling to reach a sitting position. "I hit them with a really big rock until they quit moving."

"There are no big rocks here," noted the She'Har girl.

"The ogres are pretty big. Use one of them," advised her human counterpart.

Lynaralla had her doubts about that idea. Primarily because she didn't have the same seemingly inexhaustible supply of power that Irene did. If she started throwing one of the massive creatures around to attack the others, she was pretty sure she'd run out of energy before she finished dispatching them.

On top of that, her sister was effectively helpless. Irene didn't appear to have enough strength to stand, much less walk. So Lynaralla needed to budget enough of her reserves to ensure she could levitate her, as well as protect her from stray attacks.

I need to be clever, she told herself, but while Lynaralla knew she was intelligent, cleverness wasn't something she counted among her virtues. For once, she wished she was truly human.

Using a spellweave to conserve her strength, she lifted Irene into the air and made a mental note of the direction the castle should be in. Then she began to run.

 CHAPTER 24

Rose Thornbear rose late the next morning. She had gone to bed early, but the aftermath of her encounter with Tyrion had left her unable to sleep well. It had taken her forever to fall asleep, and once she did, she was tormented by dreams she preferred not to think upon.

The past few days had left her exhausted, in body and mind, but she had more work yet to do. Foremost among them was to interview the servants from Leomund's hunting lodge in the afternoon. If her suspicions were correct, her best hope for Mordecai's acquittal lay with them, assuming she could discover a way to force the information she needed out of them.

She was afraid to return to her place in the palace, unsure whether Tyrion would still be there, so she planned to spend the morning resting with Carissa at her city house. Elise had already vanished somewhere, leaving a note that explained she was not to be sought after.

Rose was still on her first cup of tea when she heard Carissa utter those dreaded words, "I'm bored. With Nana gone, there's nothing for me to do."

With the trial looming in three days, Rose had been considering her daughter's situation carefully. Ideally, she would have sent her to stay with Mordecai's family until the stormy winds of upheaval had passed, but with Mort in prison, that was a poor option. It might even be the worst option. If things went badly the Royal Guard might soon be seeking to imprison anyone carrying the Thornbear or Illeniel name.

Carissa needed to be somewhere even the Queen couldn't reach. Keeping her tone even, Rose broached her idea, "Would you like to take a trip somewhere?"

"Can I stay with Irene? I haven't spent much time with her in ages," asked Carissa hopefully.

Rose wasn't sure where Irene was currently, whether she had managed to reach Lancaster or was still at home, but either way she was certain it wouldn't be any place safe enough for Carissa. "I believe Irene is away," stated Rose calmly. "In fact, her entire family is caught up in various enterprises related to their father's current misfortune."

"I wish I could help them."

"You already have, dearest," said Rose, soothingly. "According to your grandmother, she couldn't have managed her task without your help."

"That was nothing," complained her daughter. "I want to do more."

Rose looked at her tea sadly before setting it down to go to the writing desk. It would be cold before she could finish it. She carefully penned a letter before sealing it and handing it to her daughter. Then she opened a small drawer and took out a small leather purse. Unlocking the strongbox that stood near the desk, she filled the pouch with gold coins and a smattering of silver. Then she tied the top tightly.

"Take these," she told her daughter. "I want you to give them to Angela when we get back to the palace."

Carissa eyed her mother suspiciously. "What's this for?"

"I'm sending you to Iverly, in Gododdin. There's enough in the purse to buy a small house and keep you comfortably until I can send for you."

"Iverly!" exclaimed Carissa. "That's on the other side of the world!"

Rose smirked. "Hardly. These days, with the World Road, it's only an hour's trip. The important part is that you tell no one where you are headed. Angela will understand already."

"Why would I want to go there?"

"It's quite lovely this time of year. The breezes coming off the Gulf of Garulon make it almost idyllic. Every young lady should experience it sometime in her youth," Rose told her.

"And what will you be doing?" asked Carissa.

Rose frowned at her. "You know very well what I'm doing."

"Then I should wait until after the trial and we can go together," suggested her daughter, secure in her logic.

Rose shook her head, then hugged her daughter. "No, dear. That would defeat the point. I'll join you there after the trial is done, or perhaps a week after that."

"Should I write to you? You won't know the address."

"No," said Rose with a little too much emphasis. "Certainly not. I'll find you, never fear. I have a number of friends there."

"Sometimes I think you know everyone in the world," observed Carissa.

Rose smiled. "I try, dear. The important ones, anyway."

"And half of everyone else," added Carissa. Then her tone grew serious. "I know what you're doing. You think this business you and Nana are into is dangerous and you want me out of the way."

"I want you safe," corrected Rose mildly.

Worried, Carissa hugged her mother again. "Can you really prove his innocence?"

"I will."

"And if you don't?" insisted her daughter.

"I'll do whatever is necessary," said Rose firmly.

"It's bad, isn't it?" asked Carissa. "Is the Queen going to arrest you?"

"It won't come to that," said Rose. "Remember the family motto: Only a fool threatens those a Thornbear protects. Everything will be fine, I promise."

Carissa was quiet for a minute, but then she asked another question, her voice muffled by her mother's shoulder, "That's fine for them, but who protects the Thornbear?"

Her mother didn't answer. "Go pack your things."

***

A message was waiting for Rose at the palace gate, a summons from the Queen. Rose thanked the messenger and turned to her daughter. "Go find Angela. I'll see you in a few weeks."

Carissa darted forward, kissing her quickly on the cheek. "What if you don't show up in a few weeks?"

"Wait a year, then seek an audience with King Nicholas. He owes me a few favors. Hopefully by then the furor will have died down." She gave her daughter a push, urging her to leave, then turned away.

Rose moved briskly, but she still heard her daughter's concerned farewell. "I love you, Momma. Don't keep me waiting too long."

Damn it, Rose swore to herself. *Everything will be fine.* She focused on her breathing—that was the key to keep from spoiling her face before she met with the Queen. Spine straight and shoulders square, she proceeded through the palace halls with stately grace, projecting the certainty that she owned every inch of the ground she strode across.

Rose wore her poise like a warrior wears armor, and not even the whispering of the courtiers could shake her reserve. Even when more than one of those whispers carried far enough to catch her sharp ears. "Highwhore."

She didn't bother to spare a glance for the man who said it. She knew enough to ruin him, and most of the others as well. For years their fear of her had kept their tongues silent, but now they smelled blood. In her mind she could sense it: The hounds were gathering around her, waiting to drag her down, anxious for their bloody feast.

Rose heard Carissa's voice once more in her memory. *"But who protects the Thornbear?"*

It was a relief when she was ushered into the small audience room where Ariadne waited. Painting a smile on her face, she knelt quickly. "You asked for me, Your Majesty?"

"We're alone, Rose. No need for formality today," said Ariadne. "I wanted to ask you about Mordecai."

Rising to her feet, Rose met the Queen's eyes. "He is well, for now."

Ariadne continued hesitantly, "I heard you've been visiting him."

"As his legal counsel," said Rose, nodding. "By your orders, no one else has been able to see him."

"I had to do that, Rose. The lords—"

"I already know about political expediency, Ari. No need to make excuses," interrupted Rose, her tone giving away just a hint of her true feelings on the matter.

Ariadne picked up on it immediately, and she flinched as though she had been slapped. "I love him as much as anyone, Rose. He's family."

"Speaking of family," said Rose, "how is your brother, Roland? You must be very pleased to see him again. I'm sure you are very grateful to your cousin for returning him to you." She didn't bother to hide her sarcasm.

The Queen ignored her baiting. "He's as energetic as ever, anxious to return home. He's been after me to release Mordecai, so he could take him home. As usual he's more worried about his own concerns than those of the realm."

"Sometimes we have to choose between the two," observed Rose. "It's rarely a happy choice."

"Exactly," said Ariadne, thinking that Rose understood her. "How are the conditions down there? Are they feeding him well?"

"I wouldn't keep a rabid dog in such a pit," said Rose honestly, her eyes flashing.

Abashed, Ariadne lowered her eyes. "I didn't realize. What can we—?"

"He hasn't frozen to death," interrupted Rose. "I've gotten some blankets to him. He'll live until the trial."

The Queen's patience broke at last. "What would you have me do, Rose? Clearly you blame me for this somehow. What is it that you think I should be doing?"

"Help me!" Rose hissed sharply. "Put pressure on Airedale to testify in his defense. Order him to lie if you have to!"

"Under oath?" responded Ariadne, seeming surprised. "Airedale is an honorable man. He wouldn't do that, even for me."

"The man is a weasel, Ari," Rose snapped. "Just like his father was. Remember him? The one you had to execute for betraying James? The apple hasn't fallen far from the tree. Have him testify that one of the servants did it. His *honorable* word will be enough to see Mordecai acquitted."

"You'd see an innocent man executed for Mordecai's crime?" said Ariadne, incredulous.

Rose wanted to tear out her hair. "He is innocent, Ariadne! I swear it. Have you become so addled by lying tongues you can't spot the truth anymore? Airedale was there to further some plot he and Leomund were working on. Now he's using this as an opportunity to bring down your greatest supporter."

The Queen stiffened. "I am not sad to see Leomund dead. He was a dreadful man. But I won't twist the law to suit my whims, and Mordecai wouldn't want me to. He set that example for me years ago, though he paid for it with his own pain and blood."

"Then how could you believe he would cast the law aside and kill Leomund?" asked Rose.

"Because I know him as well as you do," answered Ariadne sadly. "When he found that poor waif, he lost his mind, and as much as I wish I could give him a medal for ridding the world of Leomund, I cannot set my desires above the law."

"If you had been properly attentive to your duties, this would never have come up to begin with," said Rose sharply.

Ariadne was taken aback. "What?"

Rose had crossed the line, and she knew it, but she wasn't about to retreat. "If you had dealt with Leomund as you should have, it would never have fallen to Mort to do something. The only reason he was there that day was to protect you from whatever plot the man was brewing. If you had exposed the Prince's betrayal sooner and removed his head, it wouldn't have fallen to your loyal vassal to act in your stead. Mordecai went there because I was foolish enough to tell him of Leomund's dark conspiracy, not realizing he would run off and immediately investigate it on his own."

The Queen's face went white, then slowly colored to red as her anger began to burn. "You speak boldly for a woman whose own motives are anything but *pure*."

"What are you implying?" asked Rose, her tone threatening to freeze the air around her.

"Why are you going so far for him, Rose? He's my cousin, but what is he to you?"

"He's as much my family as he is—"

"No, he isn't. That's precisely the point," interrupted Ariadne. "Don't you realize what they're saying about you, Rose?" said Ariadne. "Tyrion told me about your extended *visit* yesterday. What did you think people would say? Penelope hasn't even been in her grave four months yet."

Rose's eyes seemed to turn from blue to steel grey. "I have done nothing to be ashamed of, even were Penny here to ask me today. Unlike someone foolish enough to invite the wolf into her bed before her husband had even died. Have you even considered *Tyrion's* motives?"

The Queen's fury was such that her words nearly failed her. "Get out!"

Rose curtseyed deeply. "With great pleasure, Your Majesty." Then she turned and marched for the door.

"I don't want to see you or even hear your name before the trial!" Ariadne shouted at her retreating form.

 CHAPTER 25

Rose's mind was in such a state that she was hardly aware of her surroundings as she walked, heading without thought for the door to her chambers. Deep down, her subconscious registered that something was off, but she was too angry to pay attention to her instincts.

She was almost to her door when she realized what should have been immediately obvious to her. The part of the palace her chambers were in didn't have the luxury of enchanted lights as some of the more traveled parts did. They still relied on old-fashioned oil lamps set in sconces along the wall.

Lamps that weren't lit.

The section of the hall that her door was set in was in the deepest part of the shadow, dark enough she had trouble seeing the entrance to her rooms. That alone would have set off alarms in her mind, but it was the whisper of steel sliding from leather that told her she had made a serious mistake.

Leaping forward, her foot tangled in her skirt and Rose stumbled. The long knife that been aimed at the spot between her shoulder blades narrowly missed, cutting through the fabric and skin of her left shoulder. Ignoring the pain, she considered reaching for the dagger strapped to her leg, but it would be impossible to get out with her dress bunched up as it was. Instead, she drew out the smaller blade hidden in her bodice, but it was too late.

The assassin wasn't slow. As soon as his first strike missed, he shifted his weight and kicked forward, his boot striking Rose in the side, beneath her left arm. She felt a pop, and pain blossomed through her as the force of the blow sent her crashing to the floor. A second kick found her stomach, sending the air rushing from her lungs and nearly rendering her senseless.

She gasped hopelessly, trying to draw air with lungs that refused to work, as the assassin turned her over onto her back and knelt above her, his knees just beneath each of her arms. He appeared to be clad all in black, although the light was so dim his clothing might have been almost any color.

"If you hadn't been stupid, this would have been over already. You might've saved yourself some pain." The stranger flashed a perfect smile at her as he leaned down. "I don't mind, though. I prefer it this way. Pain is more fun."

He held a shorter blade now, a dagger with six inches of blackened steel emerging from the hilt. Placing it carefully against her right shoulder, he began to bear down, pushing it through the skin, its point high enough to miss her lungs.

Rose jerked, kicking and thrashing, trying to throw him off, still unable to scream, but his weight was too great. Agony tore through her as the blade passed over her collarbone and through the soft tissue until it reached the stone floor beneath her. The assassin pulled it out again with tender slowness, watching her writhe.

Then her fingers found something cold on the floor beside her. Slapping at her assailant with her left hand, she waited until he caught her wrist to stop her before she brought her right hand and the bodice knife up and slammed it into his side, the steel sliding between his ribs and narrowly missing his heart.

"Bitch!" screamed the assassin, his voice gurgling slightly. Her blade had punctured one of his lungs.

Jerking it back, she stabbed again, catching him once more in the abdomen before he could roll off of her. Her third and fourth blows only hit his thigh and lower leg.

She was beginning to draw shallow breaths as she scrabbled backward to lean against the wall. Using the brief respite, she pulled out the longer blade strapped to her leg, but she knew it was futile. The assassin was on his feet, hobbling toward her on his one good leg. He was bleeding profusely, but that was the trouble with knife fights.

People didn't die quickly, unless someone got lucky and struck the heart. Often the winner of such a fight would die minutes or hours after the loser. Rose didn't know if she had given the assassin a mortal wound or not, but it was clear that he would live long enough to make it a moot point.

Then her bedroom door opened, and a lean figure stepped out. "Sloppy," said Tyrion softly. "You're an embarrassment to your profession."

The assassin took half a step, and then he was falling, or rather there were pieces of him falling. His head, right arm, and upper torso fell one way; his left arm and lower torso went the other. His hips and legs made a macabre sight, swaying slightly for a second before joining the rest of him on the floor. A rapidly growing pool of blood flowed outward, threatening to soak into Rose's dress.

Kneeling down, Tyrion gathered Rose into his arms, taking time to gather her blades and lay them in her lap before he stood and took her inside her chambers. The door closed itself behind him.

He carried her across the room and laid her carefully on the couch before sitting on a nearby chair, cradling his head in his hands. "You wouldn't believe my head. It feels like someone took a club to it last night."

Rose gave him a hard stare, as she quietly bled onto the cushions. She couldn't berate him if she wanted to. She could barely draw breath.

"Don't look at me like that. Trust me, my head hurts worse," said Tyrion sourly. "And I would know. I'm an expert on getting stabbed." When she continued to glare at him, he added, "You aren't dying. You've got a shallow cut above one shoulder, a neat stab wound through the other, and a broken rib that's in no danger of poking anything important. Just give me a minute to get my bearings. I only woke up a few seconds ago."

She continued to stare at him accusingly, and after a moment he rose to his feet and stalked away. Rose watched him curiously as he staggered toward her bedroom, then went inside. He returned a moment later with the pitcher of water that she kept on the table in there. She almost forgave him then, thinking he meant to wash her wounds, but Tyrion lifted the pitcher and began to drink, pouring water down his throat as though he were dying of thirst. When the water was almost gone, he lifted it and poured the rest over his head, making a terrible mess on the rug at his feet.

He shivered slightly, then looked at her. "Fine. Stop whining." Kneeling beside the couch, he reached up and placed his finger at the edge of the neckline of her dress. A second later, she felt the fabric part, and he began to peel away the material.

Rose flinched, trying to pull away from him, but he pushed her down with his other hand and tore away the rest of the top half of her dress. "Don't be such a prude," he told her. "You'd think after last night you wouldn't be so easily embarrassed." Dipping one finger into the wound in her shoulder, he tasted the blood, then he put his finger back, and Rose felt a slow burn begin in the injured flesh. She was breathing well enough now to hiss at the pain.

It faded after a moment, becoming a dull throb, and then he moved on to the cut above her other shoulder. Again, she felt the searing pain, but this time it ended more quickly.

"Don't worry," Tyrion told her. "I'm really good at this. In a few weeks there will hardly even be a scar left, but your shoulder is going to be a little stiff for a while. I recommend you stretch it as often as possible." His hand traveled down her chest and to one side, stopping when it was above her broken rib. "The next part will hurt. Do you want me to numb it first?"

"Why didn't you do that first?" said Rose through clenched teeth. "Before you set fire to my shoulders."

He shrugged. "Didn't occur to me. It's not worth the effort for little things."

A strange, cool sensation washed over her torso, so Rose assumed he had taken her remark for an affirmative. She felt some pressure and then a slight warmth, but no pain. A minute later, Tyrion took his hand away. "That should do it," he announced. "I'll leave the nerve block so you won't feel the soreness until it wears off, probably in an hour or two."

"Thank you," said Rose, somewhat reluctantly.

Gazing down at her, Tyrion's eyes roamed across her chest briefly, and then he prodded one of her breasts with his finger. "It was my pleasure."

Her response was instant—her hand rose to slap him—but her shoulder ruined the motion and her blow landed on his shoulder instead of his cheek. "Get off me!" she ordered.

The moment he withdrew, she covered herself with the remains of her dress and with less difficulty than she expected, she sat up. Then she went to her bedroom and shut the door. She removed the ruined dress, looking at it regretfully. It had been one of her favorites.

She used a towel to wipe away the blood that hadn't dried yet, wishing she still had water to scrub away the rest. *No use crying over it,* she thought, and then she pulled on a long wool dress that was as warm as it was comfortable. When she returned to the front room, she found Tyrion sitting on the couch again, apparently unworried that the blood there would stain his trousers. He held her blades in his lap, studying them.

"This is fine work," he commented. "Did Mordecai make them?"

Rose nodded.

"I never noticed them before," remarked Tyrion. "The sheaths are also enchanted, obscuring the magic until they're drawn. Clever." He grinned at her wickedly. "What did you plan to do with them?"

They were part of her everyday attire, a habit she had kept since reaching womanhood, but her reply was severe, "Stab you with them."

Tyrion laughed. "You really are feisty! Though I think if that were the case, you'd have done so already. You've had plenty of chances."

"Give me another and see what happens," returned Rose, feeling slightly better for some reason.

He re-sheathed the weapons and then tossed them onto the table. "Why do you think that fellow wanted to kill you?"

She could think of several reasons. She'd already considered a number of them and promptly discarded them. Over the years, she had made many enemies at court—that was the problem with being successful at politics. Airedale was the obvious suspect, given the current situation, but she hadn't expected the spineless snake to have the guts to try it.

I need time to think, she thought in frustration. She needed Tyrion out of her apartments. Then something occurred to her. "You said he was an embarrassment. What did you mean?"

Tyrion stared at the table, looking at her daggers for a moment, then answered, "He wasted several opportunities. He bungled the approach, then he started kicking. Once you were helpless, he rolled you over to torment you instead of finishing you off. Even worse, he couldn't even do that right. When he knelt down, he should have put his knees on your arms. Leaving them free was his stupidest mistake. I doubt he's ever killed anyone before."

"You saw all that?" asked Rose sharply.

"Of course," replied Tyrion.

Agape, she stared at him. "Why didn't you do something sooner?"

Tyrion sighed. "You underestimate just how bad this headache is. I woke up just as it started, and it took me a moment to collect my wits." Then, he smiled. "Besides, I wanted to see how it would turn out before I spoiled the fun." Rising to his feet, he started for the door. "I need to go take a bath. The Queen's probably looking for me."

"Give her my regards," said Rose acidly.

"Sure," said Tyrion.

"And don't forget our bargain."

He looked uncertain for a moment, as though he was struggling to remember something. "About that…"

Rose released a dramatic sigh, pretending to be annoyed. "Make sure the krytek don't interfere. There will be strangers moving through the city with enchanted weapons. Ignore them. If the trial goes against us, make sure they know to do nothing, no matter what happens."

"Yeah, I remember that part," said Tyrion impatiently. "But last night is pretty fuzzy."

"One night, and one night only," said Rose firmly. "That was the deal, and I don't ever want to hear about it again."

Tyrion looked puzzled, but after a moment he shrugged. "Fine. Honestly, I'm surprised you went so far. I was going to help even if you hadn't been so willing." He winked and blew her a kiss.

For a moment, Rose considered telling him the truth but dismissed the idea. It was better if he thought he had something on her. From what she knew of the man, he was unlikely to brag, and even if he did, she could simply deny it. *Besides, my reputation is already in tatters.* Feigning outrage, she growled, "Leave. Now."

It wasn't until after he was well and truly gone that the shaking started. Rose considered making tea, but decided wine was a better choice. Going to one of the cupboards she pulled out a bottle and after a brief struggle, uncorked it. Thinking of Elise, she hoped it wasn't one of her 'special' bottles, but she knew the old woman wasn't foolish enough to leave such a thing lying around. She had brought the drugged bottle from some hideaway in her room.

She finished the first glass with unseemly haste and poured herself a second before remembering that it was almost time to visit Mordecai. *I just want to go to bed,* thought Rose as a feeling of deep exhaustion washed over her.

It was far too early for that, of course, but adrenaline and her life-and-death struggle had taken a toll on her. Taking a long swallow from the glass, she rose and considered changing back into a more appropriate gown, then decided against it. She was too tired.

Finding her basket, she tucked yet another blanket into it before leaving. She hoped she could find something good in the kitchens to add to it.

 CHAPTER 26

I was sitting up when Rose arrived, swaddled in the blankets she had given me. My hunger had returned, but it wasn't as sharp as it had been before, and being warm made a big difference. My sense of time had long since vanished, but I had had a feeling it was almost time. Rose's visit was the only bright spot in my otherwise bleak existence.

It was obvious something was wrong when she entered, though. Rose's hair was unbound, flowing down to her waist like a wild, dark river. It took me a moment longer to notice that her dress was unusual as well, being a simple wool affair that was completely unlike her.

I had seen her in it before, of course, when she and Gram had lived with us, but only at home. Rose was meticulous about her appearance anytime there was even the slightest chance she would be seen.

"Hello," I greeted her, trying to be cheerful.

Setting her lantern and basket down, she looked at me with tired eyes. "Are you hungry?"

She was definitely not well, and I wondered if it was merely the stress of the past few days, or whether something more serious had happened. Knowing Rose, it would do me no good to ask. She'd tell me on her own or not, according to her principles.

I'd always respected those principles, for she had never violated them—to my knowledge—and she never

289

kept secrets that didn't need to be kept. If anything, I trusted her judgment as much as or more than my own, but this was the first time I had ever seen anything take such a visible toll on her.

When she bent down to retrieve the food from the basket, I heard a faint hiss from her lips. She paused, and then bent at the knees instead. Getting to my feet, I went to her and put my hand on her shoulder. "What happened to you?"

She flinched at my touch, and losing her balance, fell sideways. I heard a barely suppressed whimper when she hit the floor, but after that she said nothing before pulling herself back up to a sitting position. "Please, Mort, sit down. I'm tired today. It'll be easier for me if you don't surprise me."

Surprise her? That hadn't been surprise; it had been pain. I was a little dense when it came to women, or so I had been told, but I knew the difference between the two reactions. Debating my options, I sat down. I was well acquainted with the waiting game.

Today's feast was half of what had been a very large round of bread, and a wedge of hard cheese. Rose hadn't been allowed to bring a knife in, so I made do by simply gnawing on both in turns while she sat next to me. I watched her from the side of one eye as I gobbled down some of the food.

Quiet, she sat with her hands clasped together and her head slightly down, gazing at the floor. She looked pensive, or perhaps resigned. I wanted to comfort her, but I didn't know how. Comfort doesn't really mean much coming from a man waiting for death.

My hand rose twice on its own, wanting to pat her on the back, or smooth her hair, but I caught myself each time and put it back in my lap. We had been friends a long time, but despite our survivalist spooning the night before, it wasn't my place to touch her with such familiarity.

That wasn't quite true either, I realized. A simple touch or even an embrace had never been awkward before. *Whatever's wrong, she needs some distance,* I thought. Finishing another bite of the bread, I wrapped it in a napkin and set it aside with the cheese.

"If you're tired, Rose, go home and get some rest. You don't need to sit here with me. This place would depress anyone," I told her.

Her face turned toward me, and I could see a look of strained desperation in her eyes. "They're watching me, Mordecai. Gareth can see us through the wall, maybe Conall too. I'm not sure how it works," she said quietly.

Immediately, my mind returned to the day before. They had seen us. Our close contact could easily be misinterpreted. I wasn't even sure what to think about it.

Had they started rumors about her? Rose's reputation had always been above reproach. The scandals and gossip that constantly circulated at court never touched her. What might they be saying now? *Is that why she looks so defeated?*

"I'm sorry, Rose. Whatever they're saying, it's my fault. You should definitely go. I'm fed and warm. You don't need to worry about me."

She stood up again, as though she might do just that, but there was tension in her stance, as though she fought an inner battle with herself. "Lie down," she said after a moment.

I smiled in a way that I hoped was reassuring. "I told you, I'm warm enough. Not to mention, I smell really bad. There's no need to torture yourself."

"Just..." she began, and then stopped. Taking a step or two forward, she returned and paced back. "Lie down—please."

"Rose, I told you I'm..."

"Not for you, Mordecai—for me," she said, cutting me off.

"But you said they're watching us. You don't want to—"

"I don't care, not anymore," she replied, her voice thick.

Lying down, I scooted back against the wall, giving her as much room as I could. As before, she took her place, slipping between my arms and nestling herself against my stomach. This time I didn't have to be told to put my hand on her midriff. She pulled the second blanket over us and became still.

Her hair was tickling my face. I had never realized just how much of it there was before. She had always kept it braided and bound, but now it was everywhere. Lifting my chin, I raised it over her shoulder so I could breathe easily.

"Careful of my shoulder," she warned. "It's sore."

That's why she flinched earlier, I realized. "What happened to it?"

She didn't answer for a while, but when I had almost given up on a response, she said, "I tried to do too much earlier. I hurt my back too. Possibly pulled a muscle."

I chuckled. "Getting old isn't much fun."

"No, it isn't," she agreed.

We lay there quietly for several minutes, before I finally asked, "Why are we doing this? What happened today?"

"Please don't ask questions, Mordecai," she responded. Then, a minute later she added, "I just want to feel safe for a while. Just a little while. Is that wrong of me?"

"No," I whispered. "I wish I knew how to help more."

"Close your eyes," she said simply. "This isn't a dungeon cell, it's somewhere else. Better times and better days. Pretend you're Dorian."

Dorian? What does that mean? I was already acutely aware of the heat from her body and the soft pressure of her hips against my… *Don't think about that! Or is that what she's thinking? No, it can't be.* Desire, guilt, and confusion whirled through me. Eventually, I resorted to humor. "I doubt Dorian ever smelled this bad."

Rose laughed. "Armor leaves a terrible smell," she remarked. "But thankfully he usually bathed before coming to bed."

She shifted again, her hips pushing against me once more, and today I wasn't half frozen. Despite my best efforts, I felt a pressure building down there and I was horrified to think she would soon notice my physical response. I pulled away slightly, trying to create a little room between her and my rebellious soldier.

"Hold me closer, Mort," she insisted.

"Listen, Rose, I don't want to embarrass myself, or you, but…"

She laughed lightly. "When I said pretend you're Dorian, I didn't mean quite so literally."

My face turned hot with shame.

"I meant by being so easily embarrassed," added Rose. "I'm a woman, Mort. Hold me like one."

Something broke loose inside me then. My arm tightened, pulling her close while I pressed my body firmly against hers. I no longer cared what she noticed about my condition. I wanted her to notice. I made sure she could feel me. Turning my head slightly, I inhaled the scent of her neck. I wanted her, but I did no more than that.

It was an unspoken declaration of desire, and when I relaxed slightly her hand went back, gripping the side of my hips, urging me to press closer. I did, a low growl rumbling from my throat.

I was almost beyond reason, and my hand ached to reach lower, to pull her skirts up and remove the barriers of cloth that lay between us, but I restrained myself. Instead I used my hand to explore the shape of her thigh and hip, her soft stomach, and then her breast. The soft purr she responded with was an affirmation that only served to increase my passion.

We lay together like that, holding each other and pressing our bodies close in exquisite agony like frustrated teenagers, for the rest of her time there. Neither of us dared do more. We didn't kiss or talk; there were no declarations of love or lust. In the strictest sense, neither of us did anything wrong. We remained clothed, our bodies unjoined, separated by cloth, but in our hearts, we had abandoned any pretense of decency.

I merely held her, in the most concupiscent way possible.

Why we didn't do more would have been a mystery to any stranger observing us, since it was clear what we both wanted. But *we* knew precisely why we restrained ourselves. Penny and Dorian. Guilt held us back. Guilt kept me from kissing her. In the end, all we could do was express our physical desire, without fully acting upon it.

When our time had nearly run out, Rose untangled herself from my arms and we sat together silently, hand in hand. Saying nothing.

We stared blankly into the distance, fearing to look in each other's eyes. Afraid to see the shame and recrimination we had caused each other. Afraid of the feeling, the reason, behind our guilt.

Then the wall faded at last, and Rose gathered her basket and lantern. She left without a word, and my throat refused to unclench enough for me to give her a goodbye.

The darkness returned, and I sat in it. Thinking of the past, of Penny.

 **CHAPTER** 27

Lynaralla ran as fast as her long legs could carry her, towing the spellweave that held Irene behind her. The dress she wore hindered her, so she had cut away the material that hung past her hips. Her body was strong, lean, and limber. She'Har children were born physically perfect, both in form and potential. If she had trained as an athlete, she would have been exceptional, able to compete with the best human runners.

But she had never been given to excessive exercise. She was forced to rely only on the stamina she possessed in spite of her relatively sedentary lifestyle.

Thus far she had killed only one ogre, using a whip-like spellweave that had neatly removed one of its legs, so she could run around the monster. The rest had quickly fallen in behind her and given chase. The effort that had cost her hadn't been too great, but her mental calculation made her doubt she could finish the rest of them off so easily.

Loud grunts and calls in the distance warned her that the ones chasing her were not alone, further reinforcing her decision to run rather than fight. Without knowing quite why, she zigged to the right for a moment. The reason became clear when a massive club sailed through the air to her left, thrown by one of her pursuers.

Warrior's gift, she realized, recognizing what had happened. It was a manifestation of the Illeniel gift that was common among their krytek fighters and somewhat less common among the She'Har children themselves. She had never felt it before.

For a moment, she wished it had come to her when Tyrion had been training her, but after a second, she understood why it hadn't. Only real danger would trigger it, making it useless for practice and training.

With her magesight she could feel the ones behind her growing rapidly closer. Their much longer strides were impossible for her to beat; only their greater bulk had kept them from gaining speed quickly enough to catch her already.

Using her power again, she strengthened her legs, but only slightly. She hadn't practiced running with enhanced speed and she would risk falling if she tried doing too much in such a situation. Lynaralla wasn't particularly powerful as a mage, or cunning as a warrior, but she was no fool.

"Death comes with the first mistake," Tyrion had told her. *"Be cautious and let your enemy win the battle for you."*

He hadn't meant to sit idly by while they tried to kill you, though. She knew that well enough. The key was to give the enemy enough rope to hang himself.

The open road would be her death. The ogres were faster than she could hope to run, and she could sense more approaching from ahead. Darting to one side, she bounded through the tall grass and into the trees on her left.

Her pursuers couldn't change direction as quickly, and once they entered the wood they began running into the trees and bushes that blocked their path. Charging headlong into the greenery, a few of the ogres were stunned when they blundered into trunks strong enough to resist them. The others smashed through saplings and underbrush.

It slowed them down, and Lynaralla stretched out her legs, increasing her lead. She flew along on sprite-like feet, leaping over fallen logs and ducking under low limbs and hanging vines, silver hair streaming behind her like moonlight. Despite the danger, despite her fear, she felt a new emotion: the joy of the hart, eluding the hunter.

Marking their positions in her mind, she raced through wood and dale, across open glens and into thicker copses of trees. Her enemies were everywhere, but they couldn't touch her.

A mile passed, and her heart was pounding in her ears, her breath coming heavily, but fatigue couldn't lay hold of her. When she came to a small stream, she pushed more power into her legs and soared over it. Her landing was less than ideal, for a thorn bush met her on the other side, ripping long tears in her skin, but her adrenaline was such that she hardly felt it. Leaping up again, she continued running with the wind pushing small droplets of blood into crimson lines along her skin.

She almost didn't care any longer if she died. The exhilaration of the chase was enough, the joy of the run. She couldn't stop; she would run until her heart burst.

Through it all she towed Irene along, her sister floating behind her like a dandelion seed. The other girl was unconscious again, and Lynaralla hoped she was still alive, but she couldn't spare a thought to check and see if her heart still beat.

Several miles later, the woodland ended abruptly, opening up to a wide field with Castle Lancaster looming several hundred yards ahead.

For an instant, she felt relief, but then despair caught her. The open ground was too wide. She ran forward without hope, knowing she couldn't cross that distance before they caught up to her.

She tried anyway. Pressing the last of her power into the muscles of her legs, she raced across the field, the grass whipping her thighs as her feet pounded a frantic rhythm on the soft earth. Her lungs were burning, and her mouth was gaping as she tried to pull in more air to sustain her flight, but it wasn't enough.

Behind her, four of them had already emerged, and without trees and other obstacles to slow them they were picking up speed quickly. Running a zigzag pattern might have helped, if there had only been one, but they were spread out, waiting for her to blunder into one of them if she tried it.

Too far. It's too far away. Desperate, she had only one hope left. She stopped the flow of aythar to her legs and used it to propel Irene forward, causing her spellwoven stretcher to shoot ahead, skimming a few feet above the ground. Maybe it would reach the castle before its momentum ran out. If someone was watching, perhaps they would save her sister.

Deprived of the extra energy, Lynaralla stumbled. She felt the danger, but she couldn't escape it. Falling toward the ground, she never reached it. A massive hand snapped her up, dislocating her shoulder and whipping her head to one side with the brutal force of the grab. The world spun around her, and when her eyes came into focus again, she was hanging upside down in the air.

The ogre was holding her aloft by one leg. The other dangled oddly to one side, exerting a painful pressure on her hips and back. It sniffed her with wide nostrils, and then lifted her to its mouth, running a broad tongue up her back and legs, tasting the sweat and blood on her skin. Then the monster's mouth opened wide to receive its first bite.

Red light blazed, and suddenly the creature's head was simply gone. Its hand opened and Lynaralla fell once more, but she was caught by strong hands.

"Is she alright?" The yell came from Karen, who stood just behind Gram and Alyssa, tendrils of smoke drifting lazily away from her fingertips.

The other three ogres were surprised by the sudden appearance of the newcomers, but they didn't remain idle. Clubs the size of tree trunks swept downward with force enough to smash the four humans into jelly. Gram still held Lynaralla, while Alyssa lifted her spear, but they knew it wouldn't do a thing to stop what was coming.

Staring up from within Gram's arms, Lynaralla saw Karen's shield spring out around them, and when the clubs met it, they stopped, sending a shiver through the magic so strong that Karen nearly lost her feet. Wasting no time, Gram turned and deposited Lynaralla at Karen's feet, then with a word he summoned Thorn. "Get her back," he said quickly, and then, with a nod, he and Alyssa faced the ogres.

Karen bent, placing a hand on Lynaralla's brow, and the two of them reappeared on the battlements of Castle Lancaster. Matthew stood a few feet away.

"You should have taken me!" he yelled.

"You weren't close enough," barked Karen. "She'd have been dead if I waited any longer." Then she vanished once again, leaving Lynaralla and Matthew alone.

Matthew knelt beside her and examined her wounds. Before he had even begun to fix her shoulder, Karen reappeared, this time with Irene in her arms. She struggled under the girl's weight, for they were close to the same size.

Lynaralla felt a numbness spread over her shoulder and then heard a 'pop' as he put her arm back in place.

"The rest is superficial," said Matthew, looking up at Karen. "Take me to them."

Karen shook her head. "What about Irene? I can't see anything wrong with her."

"Burnout," mumbled Lynaralla. "She pushed too hard opening the boundary."

Matthew winced. "That's going to hurt when she wakes up." Then, he stared out across the field. Gram and Alyssa were dancing a wide circle around one another, his great sword and her spear disabling one massive opponent after another.

Both were armored, but it hardly mattered. The ogre's clubs were so large that if one connected, it would probably kill them anyway.

Karen stepped up beside Matthew, placing one hand casually around his waist. "See, they're fine."

"For now," muttered Matt. "There's more swarming out of the woods on both sides. We need to go back."

"Where do you want to be?" asked Karen.

"Twenty feet behind them, on this side," answered Matthew immediately. "Kill the one closest to us and give me a few seconds. I'll clear out the others."

"You have to pay the ferryman first," Karen declared firmly.

Matthew appeared startled. Glancing down, he looked at Lynaralla. "We're not alone. Just take us down there!"

Karen shook her head no, then tilted her chin up, puckering her lips.

"Of all the lunacy!" swore Matthew, but he gave in. Leaning down quickly, he kissed her on the lips and they vanished.

Down on the field again, Karen killed the nearest ogre with several sharp blows of pure force, tearing through its large belly and sending it falling to its knees. Matthew held up his metal hand and summoned the enchanted metal triangles he had created months before. They rose into the air in front of him; the spinning black metal seemed to expand as planes of dimensional force stretched out from them, creating a deadly blur that would cut through anything.

He swept his arms outward, and the two discs separated and flew out, crossing the distance in opposite directions before circling back to slice through the enemy. The enchanted weapons wove in and out, controlled by his will. They passed through enemies, weapons, and anything else they encountered as though it were nothing more tangible than air.

Ogres died, and while more kept coming, his deadly attacks cut them down faster than they could reach the field. Those left fighting Alyssa and Gram were isolated, and the two warriors took them apart with almost effortless abandon. Several minutes later, those ogres that arrived last saw their cause was lost, and turned back, running for safety.

Matthew let them run. He called his blades back, and when they returned, the deadly planes of force disappeared, leaving the two metal triangles unscathed—without even blood on them to show their recent lethal efforts. They settled onto his fist and then winked out of existence.

Gram and Alyssa sauntered over to them, grinning, faces flushed from battle. They continually looked at each other, causing Matthew to roll his eyes, mildly disgusted. The two of them enjoyed battle—and each other—too much in his opinion.

"Come along Sir Slaughter and Dame Destruction. Let's return to the castle," said Karen.

Alyssa frowned at her. "I am not a dame." Meanwhile, Gram began to blush.

"It seemed appropriate. Isn't a dame just another term for a woman?" asked Karen.

Matthew had been warning her to stop with his eyes, but at this point he leaned in, whispering in her ear, "Dame is a rank in this world, equivalent to a knight. It's also the honorific given to the *wife* of a knight."

Karen's face lit up with mirth. "So she thought I was suggesting they were going to marry?"

"I don't think she took it that way," said Matt. "She thought you meant she'd be knighted, but the way Gram is blushing means he probably interpreted it the other way."

"Oh." Karen held her hands out to the others, inviting them to form a circle so she could teleport them all together. When they were all close and face-to-face, she looked directly at Sir Gram. "You are going to marry her soon, aren't you?"

Gram was poleaxed, and he began to stammer, "I haven't—we don't—when—asked—yet."

They were standing on the battlements again by the time he finished. Matthew lifted Irene in his arms, and Karen levitated Lynaralla, and together they took them down to the yard and into the keep, leaving the two warriors to continue guarding the walls.

As they walked, Karen brought the subject up again. "He really should marry her soon."

"Could you drop the subject?" growled Matthew, more anxious than he probably needed to be.

Karen gave him a sidelong glance. "You've heard them at night, I'm sure. If he doesn't marry her soon, it'll wind up being a shotgun wedding."

Matthew refused to comment, but Lynaralla spoke up curiously from where she floated beside them. "What's a shotgun?"

Karen took a moment to explain, both the weapon and the meaning of the phrase. When she finished, Lynaralla nodded in understanding. "I don't think she's pregnant, yet." Then she added, "You and Matthew have spent considerable time together of late. Will you be having a shotgun wedding as well?"

Matthew quickened his pace, leaving the two of them behind.

"Did I say something wrong?" asked the She'Har girl.

Karen smiled. "No. You used the phrase correctly. Don't worry, though. We've been careful."

"What does careful mean in this context? Does the act cause injury?"

For once, Karen was caught off-guard. "It means he— we…" She trailed off, turning red as she tried to explain.

***

"What did you say again?" asked Matthew incredulously.

"Your father has been arrested for the murder of Prince Leomund," repeated Lynaralla. She was lying on a bed in one of the guest rooms within Castle Lancaster. Her minor injuries had been treated, but her body was still exhausted.

"That's impossible," protested Matthew.

"Those are the charges," said Lynaralla flatly. "Lady Rose sent me to tell you. She wants Karen to come to the capital."

"Just Karen?" he asked, puzzled. "Explain what's going on."

This was one occasion when Lynaralla's patience and literal nature were a definite advantage as she carefully and meticulously explained everything she knew. With her perfect memory, she was able to replay events in her mind and give Matthew Rose's explanation and message word for word.

"And she wants Moira to stay away from the city," muttered Matthew, ruminating on what he had heard. "I can see how that makes sense. Sending you and Irene here also helps to keep you out of harm's way."

"What do you think she needs me for?" wondered Karen.

Matt smiled grimly. "That's easy. Your gift makes you ideal for getting an escaped prisoner to safety. I'm afraid you'll need to go to Albamarl alone. Meet with Rose and do whatever she asks."

"Why can't you come?" asked Karen.

"Someone has to be here to open the way for you when you return. I'll be camped out where we first entered until you show up with her and Father."

Karen frowned. "In the middle of nowhere? Why?"

"Where's the best place to hide a prisoner from the Queen?" asked Matthew, before answering his own question. "In a castle tucked into a hidden dimension. No one can reach him here, and even if Roland returns, he wouldn't turn him over to his sister."

Karen seemed uncomfortable. "How long do you think we can keep up what we've been doing here? Last night there were more spiders than ever."

"Spiders?" asked Lynaralla.

"Big ones," said Karen emphatically.

"Ever since we arrived, they've been showing up at night, trying to climb over the walls," explained Matthew.

"I have nightmares thinking about what will happen if one sneaks in," added Karen. "Can't we just take him back to Washbrook? Even if the castle isn't habitable, you said the shield enchantment is strong enough to keep out anything."

"They'll lay siege to the town if he tries to hide there. Eventually people will starve, and that's not even considering the damage to the farmers and people in the surrounding areas. Even if we were successful somehow, it would turn into a civil war. I doubt my father would countenance the loss of life that would entail," explained Matthew. "This place is ideal for avoiding those problems."

"What about the people here?" reminded Karen. "We've been protecting them until Roland comes back. Are they willing to stay, or should we try and get them back to Lothion?"

Matthew looked pensive, but after a moment he replied, "We can give them a choice, if it comes to that. For now, I'll keep this to myself."

"What about me?" asked Lynaralla.

Karen gave her a stern look. "You'll be staying in that bed until you're better."

"My injuries are minor," said Lynaralla. "I will be fine within a day or two."

"Irene won't," Matthew stated firmly. "She'll be stuck in bed for a couple of weeks, at least. You can stay here with her and help us defend the castle while Karen is gone."

"How soon should I leave?" asked Karen.

"Now," returned Matthew.

She didn't look pleased. "You seem anxious to be rid of me."

"You know better than that."

Karen sighed. "Fine." She held out one hand. "You'll have to open the boundary for me."

He nodded. "After you go, I'll start watching for you tomorrow. I'll only be out there in the morning and early afternoon. At night I'll return here to help with the spiders, so if you get him free at some other time, wait somewhere else until you know I'll be there."

"Alright," said Karen, then she closed her eyes and lifted her chin.

Matt glanced at Lynaralla. "Not again."

Opening one eye, Karen stared at him. "You have to pay the ferryman."

"This is your trip. I'm just coming to open the boundary. Why do I have to pay?"

"It's for your family," insisted Karen.

Matthew released an exasperated sigh. "Fine." Taking her hand, he dragged her into the corridor. "If you're going to be childish, then the hallway is better." Once he was certain they were alone, he kissed her soundly, and then they were gone.

 **C**HAPTER 28

It was late afternoon before Chad and Cyhan returned
to the Green Pony. They had spent the afternoon reclaiming
their weapons and fine-tuning their marksmanship.

Once they were in their shared room, alone, Cyhan
voiced his complaint about his bow again. "It's too light."

Chad frowned. "It's nearly a hundred-pound draw
weight. You can't find a heavier bow unless you want to wait
half a year for a custom-made warbow. Besides, it'll be easier
for you to aim if you aren't dealin' with a monster bow."

He had been impressed with the big man's aim.
Cyhan's skill had been more than adequate, but he was no
master bowman. Chad figured his friend could manage
one, perhaps two well-aimed shots before the chaos of
battle would force him to switch tactics. Giving him a
heavier bow would only slow him down.

"Just don't miss that first shot," the hunter reminded
him. "I'll handle the rest from there. You'll need to keep
the guards off my back after all hell breaks loose."

"No need to keep repeating yourself," said Cyhan.
"I'd rather hear a practical exit strategy."

"I don't have one," admitted Chad. "As it stands
now, this is a suicide mission. Our contact left a note for
me downstairs, though. Apparently our 'employer' has
an expert she wants us to meet with, someone that can
get us out even with a swarm of angry mages chasin' our
hairy asses."

"It seems unlikely such a person could exist," observed Cyhan, "if Tyrion's krytek are all over the city. With two archmages and Conall guarding him, along with the Royal Guard, which will probably include Sir Harold..." His voice trailed off. "If you have any loved ones, make sure to leave them a long letter."

Chad grimaced. "Most of them are friends of ours, or Mort's at least. It ain't that bleak. Some of them may freeze up, or refuse to act at all."

"Gareth and Tyrion won't freeze," countered Cyhan. "Both are killers, and Tyrion's krytek are bred for battle. Even if the rest fail to act, we have little hope. Our first attack must be decisive."

"Ya mean fatal," said the hunter.

The big warrior nodded. "Our employer is highly intelligent, but she is no warrior. Her compassion has clouded her judgment. If we follow her plan to the letter, we die."

"We'll probably die anyway, or wish we had."

"In that case, at least we will have removed some of Mordecai's most dangerous competitors. Whatever happens after, he will have a stronger hand to play," said Cyhan, his eyes glinting coldly.

Chad sighed. He agreed with Sir Cyhan, but he knew it wouldn't be so easy to kill men he had shared drinks with in the not so distant past. He could do it, but he wouldn't like it. "Fine, which one do you want?"

Cyhan told him and Chad Grayson smiled. "I would have felt bad killin' him. That leaves me the one I can't stand anyway, the smug bastard." Whatever else happened, he figured Penny would approve of his target, wherever she was in the great beyond.

***

That evening they met their third accomplice, the man who would supposedly make it possible for them to escape after their dirty deeds.

The greybeard that sat down at their table was the epitome of the term 'old-timer.' Chad winced and exchanged glances with Cyhan. The man was so skinny and frail that it was painful just watching him ease into his seat across from them.

The stranger grinned, displaying a smile that was missing several teeth. "You boys look like the capable sort. I hear you're planning some murder and mayhem!" His voice was filled with an odd enthusiasm.

Alarmed, Chad leaned forward to put his hand on the newcomer's forearm. "Listen, mister, we shouldn't be talkin' about things like that here out in the open."

The old man glanced around hurriedly, then answered in a conspiratorial whisper, "Oh yeah! Of course. We should adjourn to someplace quieter to plan our jailbreak."

"Shhh!" warned Chad, glaring at the man. "Shut up, ya demented old geezer." Even the man's behavior was suspicious. Other patrons were beginning to look in the direction of their table, sensing something of interest.

The old man giggled. "Mum's the word." He closed his mouth, but his eyes darted back and forth between them with a delighted enthusiasm that made Chad's hand itch for his knife. It was clear that Manfred had lost his mind sending them the has-been that sat in front of them.

Chad and Cyhan's eyes met, and the big man nodded. Speaking calmly, Chad made a suggestion, "Why don't we all take a walk? I know a better place to talk." Leaving a few coins on the table, he rose to his feet. The others followed suit.

The ranger led his companions on a long, rambling walk until he had found a quiet, dark alley where they were unlikely to be observed. Cyhan took his cue and stood behind the stranger as Chad turned and slid his long knife from its sheath. "Sorry about this, old-timer, but I'm gonna have to terminate yer employment with us."

The old man's eyes went wide with shock, and then he vanished.

Chad blinked. The man hadn't darted away or seemed to move at all. He had simply disappeared, as though he had never been there at all. "What the hell?"

Cyhan's response was more direct. Without hesitation, he stepped forward and struck out. His fist connected with *something*. A second later, the old man reappeared, lying on the ground in obvious pain.

Reaching for his back, the old man rubbed it. "That was my kidney, you jerk!" It wasn't the old man's voice that reached them, however—it was that of a young woman, a voice they knew.

"Elaine?" said Chad querulously.

"Who else would it be?" she answered angrily.

Putting his knife away, Chad ran his fingers through his hair in agitation. "I dunno? Anyone else, that's what I was thinkin'!"

Cyhan chuckled, then bent down to help the old man regain his feet. "That was a risky game, Elaine. If I hadn't thought it might be you, it would have been a blade in your kidney instead of my knuckles."

"You knew it was me?" she asked incredulously. Chad's expression was equally disbelieving.

The veteran knight nodded, then tapped his nose. "Your smell was very pleasant. Few old men wash their hair with lavender."

"You recognized my *smell*?"

Cyhan shook his head. "No, I just knew you weren't an old man. That meant it was most likely either you or your brother."

"But you still punched me hard enough to leave what I imagine is going to be a bad bruise," she bit back.

The big warrior shrugged. "If I had thought you were an enemy, I would have struck hard enough to kill. We had to be certain."

Chad looked around nervously. "Let's get off the street."

A short while later, they were back in their room over the Green Pony. Elaine had removed her illusion and sat on the bed, still rubbing the place on her back. "You knew you were supposed to meet a friend, anyway. Why would you want to take them to an alley and beat them up?"

Cyhan merely shrugged, a faint smile playing across his lips, but Chad was more vocal. "Because ya were actin' like a fool down there! It only took us ten seconds to decide ya were gonna get us killed and figure we should take care of you first. Besides that, we weren't there to meet a *friend*. There are no friends in this sort of work."

"You were going to kill me?" blurted out Elaine, outraged.

"He was," said Cyhan. "I was withholding judgment until we knew who you were."

Her eyes were wide. "So, if it *had* been a stranger, you would have just murdered him? Just like that?"

The two men's eyes met for a second, then Chad answered, "Pretty much, yeah."

"That's just wrong!" she spluttered.

Chad leaned closer. "No. Walkin' into a bar and spoutin' off about 'murder an' mayhem,' *that's* wrong. No self respectin' criminal talks like that. That's what ya get from readin' them damn romance books o' yers."

Elaine refused to look at him. Cyhan chose to return to more practical matters. "I am more concerned that your illusion may have drawn the attention of the krytek watchers. They would have noticed your use of magic."

"Shows how much you know," observed Elaine acerbically. "For a normal wizard, yes, but I'm a Prathion."

"You weren't using invisibility," said Cyhan flatly.

"Our gift is more versatile than that. My illusion was magic, yes, but I layered it with a selective type of invisibility to hide the aythar from magesight. A Prathion can fool anyone, if they're skilled enough."

Chad grew visibly excited. He looked at Cyhan. "You know what this means?"

Elaine answered first, "That you're an ass?"

The hunter winked at her. "That goes without sayin', darlin'. What I was goin' to say was that it means we don't have to die."

The young woman gave them both a look of long-suffering. "That's why I'm here. How thickheaded are the two of you?"

"Thick enough to get mixed up into this with you," Chad shot back.

Strangely, Cyhan found himself forced to act as moderator between the two of them as they discussed their plans. It was an uncommon role for him to take, but he handled it with dry aplomb, as he did most things. They sketched out their plan for Elaine and agreed to meet with her again the next day to walk through the area. She had several ideas that neither of them had considered, mainly because they were impossible without a wizard.

As their talk wore on, Cyhan found himself feeling moderately positive they might survive, but he didn't pin his hopes on it. *Death is always close,* he reminded himself. Thinking of his daughter, he hoped it wouldn't be that close. They hadn't had nearly enough time yet.

"When is the trial?" asked Elaine, bringing Cyhan out of his reverie.

"The day after tomorrow," answered the big warrior.

"I need to meet Rose this evening," she informed them. "She has something else for me to do. I'll explain the plan to her then."

"We refer to her as the 'employer,'" growled Chad.

Elaine glared at him. "We all know who she is. What's the point?" The hunter was really beginning to get under her skin.

"In case we're overheard," explained Chad, his tone that of one speaking to a small and possibly very slow child. "At worst, we're found out, but at least she stays safe from discovery."

"I put a ward around the room to keep anyone from listening," said Elaine sharply.

Cyhan rejoined the conversation, "The krytek could—"

Elaine cut him off, pointing at herself. "Prathion. I made certain they can't see it."

"I don't give a damn," said Chad harshly. "Stick to 'employer.' No matter how smart ya think ya are, *missy*, people make mistakes. That's why we follow rules."

Her eyes shot daggers at the ranger. "Perhaps you'd be kind enough to show me the book all these rules of yours are written in. That is, unless you're simply making them up to hide your obvious mental deficiencies."

"Missy, you listen here," began Chad.

"It's Elaine—*Lady Elaine,* to people like you."

"Very well, *Lady,*" said Chad. "I've half a mind to stuff that attitude o' yers straight up yer pompous ass. If it wasn't fer my kindly disposition, I'd probably…"

With a sigh, Cyhan leaned forward to intervene again. He had a feeling he would be doing a lot of that over the next couple of days. He felt a sense of relief when Elaine finally left for her meeting with Lady Rose.

 CHAPTER 29

Rose sat quietly with her tea, deep in thought. It had been a long day, but at least no one had tried to kill her. The night before had been a restless one, in large part because of the violent attempt on her life, but also for other reasons. Her mind kept turning in circles, and around each bend Mordecai's face reappeared, oblivious to her attempts to banish it from her thoughts.

That isn't productive, she reminded herself again, returning her attention to the results of her interviews with the witnesses.

"Vander is the key," she muttered to herself. Leomund's chief servant had lied when answering her questions, and considering what her informant had told her regarding the man's family situation, she had an excellent idea why that might be. The trick would be finding a way to trip him up during his testimony. If she could do that, it should be enough to create more than enough doubt to get the charges against Mordecai dropped. If the man screwed up badly enough, she might be able to reveal the true killer to the court.

Her mind drifted for a moment, and she found herself remembering the feel of his strong arm around her. It had been years since she had felt anything like that. A sensation of warmth and security, of companionship, the knowledge she wasn't alone against the cruelty of the world.

That hadn't been all she had felt, though. A flush rose to her cheeks as she remembered the fire that had blazed within her, a fire she had almost forgotten existed. In the many years since Dorian's death, she had almost banished it entirely, but last night had reminded her that she was indeed still a woman.

"Urgh!" she exclaimed, shaking her head to clear it. "What is wrong with me? I'm not some moon-eyed young girl." *And if I don't keep my mind clear, I never will be. Everything hangs on this trial.*

A knock at the door brought her back to the present. Painfully aware that she was alone, Rose drew out the dagger she kept on her leg and went to see who it was. In the past, she might have opened the door, but today she didn't. "Who is there?" she called.

"Carmella, Lady Rose. A friend of your daughter, Carissa," answered the voice of a young woman.

Rose recognized the voice, but her hand still hesitated before removing the bar. Briefly, she wondered if she would ever be free of the persistent fear left by the assassin. That had been the second time in recent memory someone had tried to kill her, counting the attack by ANSIS a few months prior. She had faced even worse in her youth, but the long, peaceful years had healed those scars. Now it seemed they were back in full force.

Refusing to be ruled by fear, she opened the door, keeping the blade out of sight. "Lady Carmella, what brings you here?" she asked innocently.

The young woman glanced over her shoulder to make sure no one else had entered the corridor. "A matter of some delicacy, Lady Rose. I wonder if I could prevail upon you for some advice. May I come in?"

Rose studied her for a second and then relaxed. "Please do," she told the young woman, opening the door wide and sliding the dagger back into its sheath beneath her skirt. Once the lady was inside, she closed and barred the door again.

Carmella noted her behavior. "Is it really necessary to *bar* it? Surely the lock is enough. This is the Royal Palace after all."

Rose smiled demurely. "I have become rather cautious of late. Would you care for some tea?"

The other woman's eyes lit up. "That would be wonderful."

The pot was still fresh, so Rose poured a second cup and then added a small amount of milk before offering it to her.

Carmella sipped it with obvious pleasure. "Just the way I like it."

Rose nodded in agreement. "Milk and no sugar."

"How did you know?" asked Carmella, mildly surprised.

"Because I asked you to meet me here, Elaine," said Rose, her eyes mysterious.

With a sigh, Carmella's features dissolved, revealing Elaine. "This isn't my day. I'm starting to doubt my abilities. What gave me away?"

"It wasn't your fault, dear," Rose assured her. "It was just the person you chose to emulate. Lady Carmella and my daughter are acquaintances at best. They don't really care for each other. She would never seek my advice, especially not with my reputation in its current state."

"That's really not enough to be certain," argued Elaine.

"Which is why I tested you with the tea," said Rose agreeably. "At that point, the chances were slim I would be wrong. Carmella has a notorious sweet tooth."

"I like your methods much better," offered Elaine, rubbing her bruised back absently.

Rose lifted one brow, sensing a story. "As opposed to whose?"

"Those ruffians your man sent me to help," admitted Elaine. Knowing she couldn't hide the story, she went on, "I met them at a tavern, in disguise, and they decided I was a…" She paused looking for the right word. "I believe Chad called it a 'liability.'"

Covering her mouth with one hand to hide a smile, Rose lifted her cup and took a sip. "I'm sure that didn't go over well."

"They led me to an alley!" declared Elaine with righteous umbrage. "They were planning to kill me!"

Rose set her cup back down gracefully and turned languid eyes on her friend. "Fortunately, you were quick-witted enough to realize their plan and revealed yourself before things got out of hand." Her voice concealed any hint of humor.

Elaine looked down, studying her tea. "Something like that."

"Which one gave you the bruise?" asked Rose. "Cyhan?"

The younger woman nodded. "Good guess."

"If it had been Master Grayson, you'd probably have been gutted. He doesn't have the quite the same reserve that Sir Cyhan displays," noted Rose. When Elaine gave her a shocked glance, she continued, "It's my fault, dear. I told Manfred to warn you."

"He did," protested Elaine. "That's why I used such an elaborate disguise."

"Which you overdid, making them suspicious," put in Rose evenly. "Simpler is always better, dear. We tend to forget, since we know them socially, but those two are barely house-trained. Left to their own devices, they tend to violence."

Elaine snorted in a decidedly unladylike fashion. "House-trained, I'm going to remember that one for later." Then she became serious. "So what do you need me for this evening?"

Rose stood and gestured for her to follow, leading her to the wardrobe in her bedroom. "Burglary," she answered, pulling out a set of clothes sized for a slender man or a tall boy.

The tunic was cut short with tight-fitting sleeves, while the trousers were of knit wool, meant to stay close to the skin. "I think these will fit you," said Rose, and then she went to a large chest and removed a belt and several pouches. She laid them on the bed and began to change her own clothing, trading her plain gown for a more elaborate dress.

"Why do you want me in a man's clothing?" asked Elaine. "Shouldn't we both be dressed similarly?"

Rose paused. "Your clothes aren't particularly important, but on the day of the trial you may need to be able to move quickly. If I had a choice I'd give you mail to wear, assuming you could keep it silent, but the weight might be a problem. In any case, I don't keep armor lying around. The stuff has to be fitted anyway."

"I'll stick out like a sore thumb if I wear this," said Elaine.

Tutting, Rose waggled her finger. "Of course you won't, dear. I envy you your abilities, to be able to change your appearance with a thought. I might never wear a formal gown again if I could do that."

"Really?" questioned Elaine, surprised.

Pursing her lips, Rose changed her mind. "I suppose you're right. I would still wear the dresses. I'm particularly fond of fashion. It would still be nice to have the option, though."

Elaine laughed, then picked up the belt. "What's in the pouches?"

"Not much," said Rose dismissively. "A few coins for weight. They're to serve as a decoy. I tried to get them made to match Mordecai's. They aren't quite perfect, but they're close enough."

The young wizard frowned. "They aren't enchanted. Any mage that's familiar with him will notice right away."

"Fix that for me, would you, dear?" said Rose, sitting down to rebraid her hair. "Nothing elaborate, just enough so they'll pass casual inspection if Tyrion or Gareth look at them."

Elaine gave her a look of despair. "I'm not a very good enchanter, Rose. I couldn't reproduce something like his storage pouch enchantment without studying my notes at home. Even then, it might take me a day or two."

Rose's fingers never faltered in their complex dance as they twined and weaved through her hair. "It only has to *look* like it. I'm sure you can manage something."

As usual when talking to Rose, Elaine felt foolish. Taking out one of her wands, she used it as an improvised stylus. Working from memory she gave the pouches the *feeling* she had observed from Mordecai's real pouches in the past, and then she inscribed a few runes to create a temporary ward that would fix the illusion in place. It wasn't a real enchantment, but the illusion would last for a week or two before it began to fade. "That should do it," she muttered quietly.

"I never doubted you for a second," declared Rose wryly. "Take a seat. Let me fix your hair for you."

"There's nothing wrong with it," argued Elaine. "I like it this way."

Rose pointed at the stool, and Elaine promptly sat. "You're a burglar now, dear. Loose hair can be a distraction and we wouldn't want it to catch on anything." Working quickly and efficiently, she pulled and twisted at the younger woman's hair, braiding it into an elegant coiffure that compressed the hair and kept it close against her skull. When she finished, she tucked the ends under a loop that passed over the ears, and there was no longer a stray hair to be found.

Elaine stared at herself in the mirror, knowing she had no hope of ever replicating what Rose had done. "It's too tight, not to mention I won't be able to do this again without your help."

"Leave it as is," suggested Rose. "You can sleep on it."

"I'll get a headache. I told you it's too tight," whined Elaine, but her breath caught in her throat when she saw a sudden flash of fire in Rose's eyes.

Taking a deep breath, Rose closed her eyes and then reopened them slowly. Gone was the hidden rage and desperation that Elaine had briefly seen, replaced with her usual placid calm. "You can bear with it for a couple of days, dear. We've all had to make sacrifices." Then she straightened and left the room.

Elaine sat still, staring at herself in the mirror. *What was that?* she wondered. If she hadn't known better, she might have thought Rose was stressed, but that couldn't be the case. She had never known the older woman to be anything other than calm and controlled. She sometimes wondered if Rose was human, so perfect was her composure. Either way, she decided not to test Rose's patience.

***

"There's a large man inside," whispered Elaine. She stood beside the older woman, invisible.

Rose paused, her knuckles an inch from the door. "I know, dear. That's why I was about to knock," she replied softly. "Please focus on your job. The pouches are in one of the small lockers."

"How are you going to distract him?"

"Trust me," said Rose, then she rapped smartly on the door before Elaine could ask her anything more.

When Regan opened it, he looked distastefully at her. "You again."

Rose stared at him imperiously, standing in the middle of the open space, forcing him to step back to allow her inside—coincidentally allowing Elaine plenty of room to slip through before he moved back to close the door behind her. "I'm equally pleased to see you, Regan."

The warden grunted before waving at her to hand him her basket. She did, and he began pawing through it with his usual clumsy abandon. Satisfied, he handed it back. "Take it in."

"I have something else to discuss before I go," Rose told him. "Or rather, something to inform you of."

The jailor's face turned sour. Whatever she had to say, he knew he wouldn't like it.

"I'll be bringing two women with me tomorrow to assist," said Rose, pausing to let her words sink in.

"Can't do that," snapped Regan immediately.

"I can, and I will," said Rose firmly. "Lord Cameron's trial will be held the day after tomorrow."

"And what does that have to do with you breaking so many rules that I get tossed in a cell?" demanded the loathsome man.

"He needs a proper bath," Rose explained.

"Do ya think this is an inn?" Regan rebuked her. "Maybe you'd like to have a tailor stop by as well? I bet I can recommend one fer ya!"

Rose lifted one brow. "That would surprise me."

"No shit!" swore the puffy jailor. "Because it ain't fuckin' happening! It's about as likely as me decidin' to throw a fancy ball for the rest of my *guests*."

She smiled sweetly up at him, then replied, "That might be a little excessive, but if you think it a good idea, I'm not opposed. I'm sure they could use some exercise."

Regan wasn't particularly good at recognizing sarcasm. His pale, pink-and-white splotched skin darkened to an unhealthy beet-like color. "Are you fuckin' daft? That wasn't a serious suggestion!"

Seeming disappointed, Rose nodded. "Oh. That's too bad. I'll forget that, then. In any case, my two maids will be bringing a large tub with them tomorrow. They'll need to make several trips in and out as well, to carry the hot water. I'm sure you understand."

Regan's face swelled, and the man looked apoplectic. Rose worried he might die suddenly, which would inconvenience her plans. "Lady, what part of *no* don't you understand?"

Her eyes turned to ice. "The part where you use your position to convince desperate young women to let you shove that shriveled-up turnip you substitute for your manhood into them."

The warden swayed on his feet, his eyes bugging out. "Lies! I said those was lies!"

"Really?" said Rose softly, a dangerous edge to her voice. "Because I have several young women just dying to describe your *turnip* to Lord Watson. If they're lying, as you say, you have only to drop your grease-stained trousers and prove them wrong. I'm sure the court will be very amused."

"I'm callin' yer bluff, Lady. I don't believe you got all them girls to admit to that," warned Regan.

Rose showed her teeth, stepping forward so that the jailor was forced to step back. "It's no inconvenience for me. I've already got the Queen's approval for this. Notifying you was merely a formality. You can check with her while I go to make my report to Lord Watson."

Regan stared at her in silence for a moment, his eyes narrowing with suspicion.

She continued her attack, "Surely you haven't forgotten that the prisoner is the Queen's cousin? Do you think she'd want her own family to appear in court looking like a filthy vagabond?" She paused, eyeing the warden up and down in disgust. "Then again, considering your own hygiene, you probably couldn't tell the difference." Without waiting for an answer, she lifted her basket and made as though to leave. "I'll see Lord Watson in the morning."

Barely a second passed before Regan shouted after her, "Wait! Let's not be hasty. I didn't mean to ruffle yer feathers."

He became docile after that, and Rose knew she would have no further trouble from him in the future. She hadn't been entirely sure he would go along with her wishes, but now she had no doubt she could probably bring live steel into the dungeon without him raising an eye. She knew Regan's type all too well. He was a coward at heart, and once properly broken he would roll over like the gutless dog he truly was.

She spent another minute or two soothing his fears and then made her exit. Once she was outside and away from his office, she spoke to the empty air. "Any problems?"

"That was amazing!" gushed Elaine. "I thought he might piss his pants he was so scared. How on earth did you do that?"

"We all have our talents, dear. I was born with that one. Unfortunately, I've had to practice it far too often. Did you get it?"

"Of course," said the young wizard. "It wasn't too hard. I just had to cover the lockers with an illusion that made it appear they were all still closed. Add in a spell for silence and a moment to turn the lock tumblers and I was done. You gave me a lot more time than I needed."

Rose nodded slightly. "Thank you, Elaine. Leave it on my bed, and then go find your accomplices. I won't need anything else until after the trial—if things go badly." She resumed her walk. When she reached the first set of stairs, she started to descend, then spoke again, "Elaine?"

"How did you know I was there?" asked the young lady's disembodied voice.

329

"Just a guess," admitted Rose. "Don't follow me down there. You need to leave."

"They'll never notice me."

"I have no idea what the magics on that cell he's in are capable of," explained Rose. "I also can't be certain of Tyrion and Gareth's capabilities. Archmages are seemingly capable of almost anything."

"But they can't—"

Rose cut her off. "I won't repeat myself, Elaine. This is too important. Leave now." She made the words a threat, leaving it to the other woman's imagination to come up with what she might do if she endangered her plan.

Her only answer was silence, so, after a moment, Rose resumed her steady descent of the stairs.

 # CHAPTER 30

I stared at the stone wall expectantly, waiting for her arrival. I'd had plenty of time to think about our strange encounter the day before. Time to think was all I had, to be truthful.

The first thing I had figured out was that we had made a terrible mistake. Being locked up in the darkness for days on end had befuddled my wits and weakened my resolve. I knew very well that I found Rose attractive. Who wouldn't? I was also willing to admit that it was more than that. We had been friends for decades, and our moment the day before wasn't the first time I had felt perhaps a little too much attraction to Rose.

That was a lie, I told myself. *You're in love with her.*

Shut up, I swore at myself silently, though I knew it was true. It was my deepest darkest shame, and had been for ages, possibly for as long as I had known her.

But I had always had Penny, and I had loved her just as dearly. Too much to do something stupid. Other women had tempted me over the years, but it had been fairly easy to resist those temptations. Rose, on the other hand, had never shown the slightest hint that she might cross the line. It was something I respected her for.

What had happened yesterday had been an act of pity, or comfort, and I was ashamed to have displayed my animalistic desire. Sure, we hadn't *done* anything, but I had pawed at her like randy beast, and she had been too dignified to embarrass me.

I doubted she would ever have the same respect for me that she had once had, but if I apologized and did my best to set things right, we could hopefully continue our friendship. *At least until they hang me.*

And after I'm dead, maybe Penny will forgive me for that one moment of weakness, I added miserably.

Her voice returned to me. *"I'm a woman. Hold me like one."* I ground my teeth in frustration, thinking, *I'm pretty sure that doesn't translate to 'hump my leg.'* For perhaps the hundredth time, my face reddened thinking about it.

When the wall faded and light flooded in nearly jumped to my feet, my expression hopeful and my head empty of thought. I was severely disappointed when it was Gareth Gaelyn who stepped into my cell.

The red-bearded archmage studied me silently for a long moment, his face a mask. I stared back at him, defiant.

"Your trial will be held the day after tomorrow," he said at last.

"Have you sent out invitations yet?" I asked. "I haven't even finished the guest list."

Gareth stared back without smiling. "You may think I have no pity for you, but that is not entirely the case."

"I'm sure this hurts you as much as me, Gareth," I replied with obvious sarcasm. "I hope you'll remember our time together fondly in the years to come."

"I've come to offer some advice," he answered, ignoring my comment.

That brought me up short. "Huh?"

"Refuse to let Lady Rose defend you. When they bring you before the court, admit your guilt," said Gareth.

"I didn't do it," I told him. "Why would I deliberately put my neck in the noose?"

"For your family's sake, and for hers." I had nothing to say to that, so I waited, and after a few seconds he continued, "While you have been locked away, she has stooped at nothing to find a way to protect you. Her reputation has sunk to a level that rivals your own, and while that might not matter to you, for a woman of her station, it is vastly important. Lady Rose's allies are vanishing quickly, while her enemies are slavering for her blood."

I didn't like the sound of that, but I wasn't ready to capitulate based on a few rumors. "What do you mean, 'stooped at nothing'?"

Gareth turned away, idly fingering his beard, as though he was searching for words. "If one of your children were in danger, or your recently departed wife, what would you do to protect them?"

"Anything," I said immediately.

"But you're an archmage, and a man," observed Gareth. "You have countless options. What if you were a woman of high station, with little besides your reputation, wealth, and beauty? What would you do?"

"Wealth and high station can do an awful lot," I noted.

My visitor nodded. "They can, but some things cannot be bought, and rank's privileges are dependent on the crown. Without that support, summer friends begin to find better ways to spend their time. In such a situation, a woman might be forced to trade on her reputation—and her beauty."

Something in my chest tightened painfully. "What are you saying? Spit it out."

Gareth faced me, his eyes burning into mine. "I have always held Lady Hightower in the highest regard. I still do, despite recent events, but her actions have lowered her in the eyes of her peers. She has angered the Queen with her reckless efforts to see you freed. Others in the court have taken note and begun to act accordingly. There are no friends left for her to call upon, yet she has continued to barter on your behalf, with whomever might aid you.

"Your plight has driven her into the arms of your ancestor, and while she may think her efforts there will pay some dividend, I think it unlikely, for he spends most of his free hours in the Queen's bed, not to mention how much he stands to gain by your removal," explained Gareth.

"That's bullshit!" I swore. "You can't believe court gossip…"

"I don't," said Gareth evenly. "This information comes from my own agents. There have been three attempts on her life of late, though she is only aware of one."

"Attempts on her life?" I exclaimed, shocked.

He held up a hand. "Let me finish. One of my men has been following her. He foiled two attempts merely by showing himself at moments when it appeared her assassin might make an attempt, but on the third occasion he was too far away to do anything but observe by the time he arrived. Lady Rose was stabbed and beaten yesterday, just a few hours before her visit."

I frowned. She had been sore, but I had seen no sign of blood or a stab wound.

"She was saved by Tyrion's arrival. He emerged from her apartments to dispatch the attacker. I presume it was he who healed her injuries. Also of note, he had been within her rooms since the previous night, after she sent her family away to stay elsewhere."

Shaking my head, I tried to make sense of it. *She wouldn't do that. She's too proud. She wouldn't do that, not for me.* No, I knew better. They must have been conspiring together to free me. It was as simple as that.

"Tyrion visited her rooms twice before," continued Gareth relentlessly. "And if that were not enough, she has been seen frequenting the slums and shadier districts of the city. I assume this was for some purpose related to your case, but I doubt others drew the same conclusion."

Outraged, I glared at Gareth. "I've known Rose for nearly thirty years. This is all circumstance and hearsay."

"You don't need to convince me, Mordecai," said Gareth. Then he waved his hand in a wide circle. "It's them, the rest of the city, the courtiers and rumormongers. They have already convicted her of the worst crimes in their imaginations." His hand stopped over my bench, where a small, stale crust of the bread she had left behind sat wrapped in a napkin. He picked it up and showed it to me. "How do you think she got this to you?"

"What does that have to do with this?"

"My agent looked into a few of the people she met with in the city," said Gareth. "Several of them were young women who had husbands that spent time in the dungeon. Apparently, they were able to bribe the warden to convince him to let them bring food and other comforts to their loved ones.

"These were poor women, Mordecai, and the warden here is one of the slimiest, pox-ridden whoresons I have ever seen. How do you think they paid the man for his assistance?"

Mortified, I sat down. Assassination attempts? Tyrion? It was too much. My brain shut down trying to comprehend it all.

"Cut her loose, Mordecai, for her sake. She won't thank you for it, but it would be a mercy to her." Then he left.

***

When Rose appeared an hour or two later, I struggled to meet her eyes.

"Feeling guilty?" she asked in a light tone. She placed the basket on the floor in front of the bench and smoothed out the blanket there before taking a seat.

"Yeah," I admitted. "I think I've made a mistake."

"More than one," she opined. "Come try some of this. It will make you feel better. I brought some fruit." Reaching down, she plucked an apple from the basket and gave me what was meant to be a comforting smile.

"How much did that cost you?" I asked bitterly.

She took a small, delicate bite from it. "Not much. Apples are cheap in this season."

"You aren't supposed to be able to bring these things to me, are you?"

Rose stood, and taking a step toward me, she lifted the apple to my mouth. She waited, staring at me until I opened it, and then she pushed it in, forcing me to take a bite. "That's better," she said softly. "The warden and I have come to an arrangement," she said nonchalantly. "He won't be any trouble."

Reluctantly I chewed, though the flesh of the apple tasted like ashes in my mouth. When I tried to swallow, I choked and the coughing that resulted made my eyes water.

"Try not to waste your food, Mordecai," cautioned Rose. "We need you healthy for the trial."

Taking the apple from her hand, I put it back in the basket, and then I held her out at arm's length, studying her face. She stared proudly back at me, but I caught a hint of something in the depths of her eyes. Reaching up with one finger, I wiped at the skin beneath one eye. It came away with a light coating of powder. The skin was dark beneath her lashes.

She hasn't slept, I realized.

Pushing my hand away, she daubed at her undereye, trying to redistribute the powder evenly, though she didn't have a mirror to guide her. "That wasn't very kind of you, Mort," she said, rebuking me.

"Let's stop this," I told her suddenly. "I don't like what this is doing to you."

"Nothing a little sleep won't cure," she replied reassuringly. "You should have a care for yourself." Moving sideways, she stepped around to approach me from behind. She slid her arms under mine and clasped her hands in front of me, squeezing lightly.

My resolve began to melt. I didn't want to push her away, but I clenched my jaw and grasped her hands firmly. Pulling her hands apart, I stepped away from her. "I've been lying to you, Rose. I can't do it anymore. You deserve better."

337

She looked at me carefully, tilting her head to one side. "You may have your doubts. Yesterday was sudden, and perhaps foolish, but I am not so flighty. If anyone understands the pain of losing someone, it's me. I'll wait as long as it takes, but I won't change my mind."

"It isn't that," I argued. "Or rather, it isn't *just* that. I lied about Leomund. I killed him, Rose. When I saw what he had done to that girl, I lost my mind. He was unconscious, but I hardly cared. I took my dagger out and put it through his heart. I plan to tell them that at the trial."

I expected her to look shocked, or at least disappointed, but she displayed neither expression. "Then I suppose it's pointless for me to defend you in court," she said simply. "Very well. I'll move my other plans forward."

That sent a chill through me. Worried, I asked, "Other plans?"

She nodded. "To free you, of course. You didn't think I put all my eggs in one basket, did you?"

"But I did it," I insisted.

"Of course, dear," she said condescendingly. "That just means we'll have to do it the hard way."

I shook my head. "You don't understand. I'm guilty. I want to pay for my crime. You shouldn't do anything foolish on my account."

"Foolish?" she said, looking askance at me. "Foolish, like trying to lie to me? Leomund died, but not by your dagger. It was his own blade that was put through his heart."

My face colored slightly. Ordinarily I wasn't a bad liar, but something about Rose always made me falter. "Yes, his dagger," I said, agreeing with her. "That's what I meant. I was so worked up at the time I must have misremembered."

"People don't lie to me, Mordecai, not successfully. They may sometimes lie *about* me, but lying *to* me doesn't work. Why don't we get down to the heart of this? Are you trying to protect me?"

"Damn it, yes!" I roared. "Someone has to. I heard about the attempt on your life."

Rose relaxed slightly then. "That. I should have known he'd tell you."

"You're damn right he did," I said angrily.

"I didn't expect that," Rose admitted, "but since then, I've taken precautions."

Like Tyrion? I thought, cruelly, but I kept the words back. Angry as I was, I couldn't hurt her for what she had done trying to protect me. Instead, I moved closer, glaring down at her and forcing her to step back, until she was brought to a halt by the wall. *Why is she so damned beautiful?* I felt hungry just staring at her, and not for apples.

The normally indomitable Rose seemed to wilt slightly before my visible wrath. She stared up at me, eyes wide and nostrils flaring as she fought to control her breathing, but it wasn't fear I saw in her face.

From the depths of my belly, the beast rose, shouting at me to take her. The thought of what Tyrion might have done had aroused some territorial instinct that wanted to wipe him from her memory—by making her my own.

She lifted her chin and her lips parted slightly, while her eyes bored into mine, challenging me.

Gods be damned! I swore silently. Pushing off from the wall, I stalked away, fighting to get my thoughts under control. "Whatever you're planning, forget it," I told her. "I won't cooperate. I won't have you or my family dragged through the dirt over this."

"Then your best hope is to do as I say," she responded, fire in her voice.

"What does that mean?" I asked suspiciously, sensing a hidden threat.

"It means your best hope for keeping your family out of this is to testify truthfully and make my job easier. If I lose your case, I can't make any promises about what comes after," she said coolly.

"You can't win this one," I reminded her.

"I can, and I will," she replied. "And if you want to keep your children out of it, you'll hope that I do."

"Don't you dare bring them into this," I growled.

"Sit down," she responded, and then she took a seat on the bench. "Let me explain this to you."

I did, and then she continued, "If we lose the trial, several things will happen. I've already arranged things to keep the children away, yours and mine, but if you fight me on this I'll be forced to alter my plans."

Glaring at her, I asked, "Are you threatening me?"

"I don't make threats, Mordecai," she said smoothly. "I deliver on my promises. Even if we lose at the trial, I will get you away from here, and I can do so without involving the children. If you decide not to cooperate, however, that will make things much more difficult. I have already had trouble persuading them not to intervene. The only reason they haven't already done something stupid is because they trust me. If you won't help, I'll tell them. All bets are off then."

"That's a threat, Rose, even if you couch it in pretty language," I said bitterly.

She shook her head. "No, it isn't. As I said before, they trust me. The reason they trust me is because they know I won't lie to them. If you decide my help isn't good enough, I will keep their trust by telling them the truth."

Exasperated, I put my head in my hands. "Why are you doing this to yourself?"

She said nothing for a while, but after a moment I felt her hand questing for mine. Despite my better judgment, I took it. In a small voice, she asked, "Are you angry with me?"

I thought about that, then admitted, "No. I'm angry with myself for getting you into this, for being helpless to protect you."

"Then you know exactly how I feel," said Rose. "This isn't the first time, either. Do you know why I hate Sir Egan?"

Egan had been the one who had held her back when Dorian died, preventing her from throwing herself under the massive gate that had crushed him into dust. I hadn't been there, but Penny had, and she had told me the story several times. "Yeah," I said.

Leaning sideway, Rose put her head against my shoulder. "No, you don't. You may think you do, but it isn't that simple. I know that what he did was to protect me, and I'm also well aware that I couldn't have made any difference. What I hated him for was the knowledge I gained that day. The feeling of helplessness. That day I became intimately aware of the fact that I had no power. I watched him die and I couldn't do a thing.

"Since then, I swore I wouldn't let that happen again," she said, her voice thick with emotion.

Putting an arm around her shoulder, I nodded. "I understand."

"That isn't all, Mort. Not by far. This situation is the same thing all over again, and I will do *anything* to stop it, and no one, not you, not Egan, or even the Queen will stop me from saving you. And if it turns out I can't, I'm going to be beside you under that stone."

Her conviction was humbling, all the more because I didn't feel as though I deserved it, but I accepted it nonetheless. She had backed me into a corner. Refusing to acknowledge her determination would only hurt her more.

I looked at her again, watching the tears roll down her cheeks. They didn't last long, and when they stopped, she wiped her face and glanced up at me, a wan smile beneath red eyes. My heart went out to her, and the words began to bubble up from within me. "Rose," I said seriously. My mouth opened again, but nothing came out. I couldn't say it.

I love you. Why was it so hard? I had told her a dozen times over the years. The casual declaration anyone might make to a friend or family member. But it was different now.

She pressed a finger to my lips. "Not yet. I've had years alone to come to terms with it. Your loss is still too fresh. Don't push yourself."

We didn't talk after that, but when she left a short while later, she gave me one final message. "Be prepared tomorrow. You're getting a bath."

"What?" I blurted out, but she left without answering, a mysterious smile on her lips.

 # CHAPTER 31

"There's good news and bad news," Manfred began. As usual, they were in her bedroom, since that was where the secret passage opened up.

With Elise and Carissa gone, that wasn't strictly necessary, but it wasn't as though Rose could alter the layout of her rooms on a whim. "What's the bad news?" she asked, anxious to hear the worst first.

"My contacts haven't been able to identify your assassin," he answered smoothly. "None of the usual players have gone missing recently either, so it's a safe bet he was from outside the city." Manfred sat down on the corner of her bed.

She frowned. "Don't sit there," Rose snapped immediately. "If you're that tired, use the stool." She pointed toward the dressing table. After the man had regained his feet, she went on, "So then it may well be that he was an amateur after all."

Manfred nodded. "Either way, it will be almost impossible to link him with whoever paid him to kill you."

Unless it was you who brokered the deal, thought Rose. She had no illusions about the man's loyalty. They had worked together for many years, but Manfred, by his very nature, could not be trusted. With her base of power eroding by the day, it was only a matter of time before her tools began to turn against her. Now that the winds had shifted, she knew he was likely to sell her out to the first bidder who offered him enough.

"My best hope is that his disappearance will give his employer cold feet," observed Rose. Tyrion had eliminated the remains after he left. Even the blood had been gone when she checked later, though how he had managed it she had no idea. "What's the good news?"

"Your last piece has stepped onto the board," answered Manfred.

Rose looked sharply at him. "You saw her?" Her paranoia was ratcheting up to its highest level. She had told Manfred nothing of her final helper. The man should have been completely ignorant of her.

He nodded. "She went to your city house looking for you. One of my men recognized her and made contact—on your behalf."

"How do you know her?" asked Rose. "She doesn't run in your circles."

Manfred smiled. "She's made a business of carrying messages over the past year. I have found her services quite useful."

Rose grimaced. If she was well known enough for one of Manfred's scabs to have recognized her, then there could be others who knew her well enough to identify her. *And if word gets back to Gareth, my plan will be at risk,* she added mentally. "Where is she now?"

"I'll bring her by later," said the rogue. "She's never been to your rooms, so I thought it would be best to bring her unseen."

"I can't fault your efficiency, Manfred," complimented Rose. Reaching into her dressing table, she pulled out a small pouch and tossed it to him.

The rogue touched his forehead and dipped his head respectfully. "It's been a pleasure working with you over the years. However, I'm afraid I'll need more this time."

Her brows rose. "Extortion? That's unlike you. I've been your most devoted client for ages."

"There's blood on the ground, Lady Rose. I've received several attractive offers lately," he answered enigmatically.

"How much?" she demanded.

"More than you can afford. They have deep pockets."

Rose watched him carefully. "You should have taken their offers then. Why tell me this? Doesn't it run against your financial interests?"

"Patience is a virtue, Lady Rose. If I delay accepting their offers, they'll pay more later. In the meantime, I can earn a premium with my current client," he explained.

Rose went to her storage chest and opened it, removing a small iron strongbox. Using a key to unlock, it she withdrew two more small leather pouches, both of them heavy with gold. She tossed them to her shifty-eyed companion. "Don't be so certain of yourself. My pockets are very deep as well. Give me their names."

"Cantley and Airedale," said the rogue.

She had expected Airedale, but Cantley was a surprise. Both men were exceedingly rich, and if they were both making offers, Manfred stood to make a lot of money. Rose felt a chill run down her spine. *One more day. That's all I need.* Meeting Manfred's eyes, she wondered if he knew what she was thinking. *Possibly.*

It wouldn't be his hand that put the knife in her back, of course. Manfred didn't do that sort of work, but he would probably be the one who paid the holder of the blade. He made his living brokering deals for information, or whatever else the client desired.

"How long can you give me?" she asked.

Manfred gave her an apologetic look. "It doesn't work like that, Lady Rose."

Translation, he won't give away his hand and spook his future target into doing something foolish, she thought. "I understand your business, Manfred, and I've always admired your dedication to your work. What's the best you can do?"

The rogue pretended to give it some thought for a moment. "A week perhaps. After that I'll no longer be able to assist you. It could damage my reputation if I was known to be working for both a potential target and those paying for—well, you understand."

"How much do you want?" she asked, feigning desperation, which wasn't all that hard, considering her situation.

"How much do you have?" he said without shame.

"I can give you ten times what you just received," she said anxiously. "Give me a few hours to gather the money."

"Have it when I bring your friend," he suggested.

She nodded quickly.

He left after that, and Rose went to the front room. She paced back and forth for several minutes, thinking furiously. *If he's offering a week, it will be much sooner, possibly even before the trial tomorrow.* She had no illusions about her associate's honesty. She even admired his brazenness, even though it was at her expense.

She ran through her options and penned a quick letter before finding a page to deliver it for her. Then she made herself another cup of tea, silently wishing she could find some way to calm her nerves.

***

It was nearly three hours before Manfred returned. Rose was still sitting in the front room, but she had left her bedroom door open and the entrance to the hidden passage unlocked. Her chair was positioned so she could see when he entered her room.

She didn't usually make such particular arrangements, but she couldn't bear the thought of being in her room alone when he returned. There was always the risk that it wouldn't be him coming through the door. From where she sat, it would be simple enough to bolt for the corridor if another assassin showed up instead.

But it was indeed Manfred who stepped into her bedroom, followed by Karen a second later. That was almost as bad, for it meant she would be following through with her first idea. *Anything,* Rose chanted to herself mentally.

Rising from her chair, she went to greet them, giving Karen a hug in the process. "I'm so glad you came," she told the younger woman.

Karen grinned. "I could have teleported here straight away, but I'd never been in your rooms before."

"A useful talent to be sure," Rose agreed. Her heart was beginning to pound, and she started to fear it might be loud enough for everyone else to hear. "Excuse us for a moment, Manfred. I'll be right back."

Leaving the man in her bedroom, she shut the door and escorted Karen to the door that led to the corridor. "Would you mind stepping outside for a moment?"

"Into the hall?" asked Karen, puzzled. "What if someone sees me?"

Rose took a cloak down from a hanger on the wall and handed it to her. "Put the hood up. I'll let you back in soon."

"I don't understand."

She smiled at Karen. "There's a privacy ward on my rooms, dear. I want to speak with him without fear of you overhearing."

"Oh, I wouldn't do that!" insisted Karen.

"Humor me, dear," said Rose. Then she opened the door and ushered Karen outside. Keeping her steps even, she headed back toward her bedroom. The door seemed to loom in front of her, seeming larger than it ever had before. *Breathe,* she told herself.

She opened it and went in, closing it once more behind her. "You have it?" asked Manfred, his features pinched with greed.

"Have I ever let you down before?" she returned, giving the rogue a haughty look. Feigning innocence was too difficult, but superiority was an act that was second nature to her. Moving to one side of the room, she opened the storage chest again and tried to lift the strong box she usually kept her money in. It moved slightly, but then fell back into the chest.

"It's too heavy for me," Rose apologized. "I forget how heavy gold can be. Can you help me?"

All too glad to help with such a task, Manfred hurried over, leaning down to grasp the box in question. Rose put her left hand on his shoulder encouragingly as he bent down, while her right slipped through the hidden slit in her dress.

The man's arms were stretched out, and as he began to lift, he called out in surprise. "Why it's not heavy at…" His words cut off as the long blade of Rose's dagger went into his chest, just below his arm. He jerked, releasing the strongbox and standing upright before stumbling away from her, a red stain forming beneath his arm.

Manfred tried to speak, but his lungs weren't working properly. He wasn't dead yet, however. Drawing out a six-inch knife, he glared at her with furious eyes. Unsteady on his feet, he held the weapon in his left hand and advanced on her.

Rose snatched up the stool from her dressing table and held it out defensively. When her one-time associate rushed toward her, she dodged sideways and shoved him hard with the stool, causing him to fall.

Manfred struggled to rise, but his legs were beginning to fail him as he gradually weakened. Rose continued to keep the stool between them as he crawled after her, leaving a bloody trail across the rug. What followed was a slow chase in which he managed to bleed all over the floor and at one point, her bed. When he finally collapsed and grew still, she approached him cautiously.

He had dropped the knife, so she used her foot to kick it away and then checked to see if he was finally dead.

He wasn't.

Nothing is ever simple, thought Rose as she observed his labored breathing. Putting the stool down, she took up her dagger again and positioned it between his shoulder blades and to the left of his spine. Then she tried to push it through.

Manfred jerked at the pain, causing her to leave a bloody cut across his back. Fear and adrenaline kicked in then, and Rose panicked. Stabbing and sobbing simultaneously, she finished off her previous associate. By the time she was sure he was dead, and everything was still once more, she was covered in blood.

She didn't want to move. Her nerves were a wreck and her stomach twisted rebelliously, but she couldn't afford to waste time. Getting to her feet, she stood unsteadily for a moment, then stripped off her gown, dropping it on top of the corpse. In her wardrobe she found a clean linen shift and pulled it over her head, then studied herself in the mirror.

With a towel and some water, she wiped away the spots of blood on her cheeks, then washed her hands, turning the water in the basin pink. *Karen's waiting,* she thought.

When she got to the door, she opened it and stepped outside. *She'll notice the body in the other room if she comes back within my privacy ward.* It was something she hadn't considered before. "Something has come up," she told Karen quickly. "Go back to my city house for now. You can visit me late tonight."

Karen stared at her. "You changed clothes? I thought you were just going to talk to him for a minute."

Self-conscious, Rose realized she must look strange wearing the simple night gown. Her feet were bare, and she looked as though she was about to retire for the evening, even though it was still mid-afternoon. The conclusion Karen would draw was obvious.

Better that than the truth, thought Rose. "I can't talk now. Just teleport straight to my rooms tonight. I will need to fill you in regarding the plan for tomorrow."

Karen smirked, then winked at her. "As you wish." Then she teleported away.

Closing the door, Rose stood inside for moment. A million things passed through her mind, but she couldn't focus on any of them. "Tea," she told herself at last.

Filling the kettle and setting it over the hearth was more difficult than usual, but by the time it was ready, she was shaking so badly that she spilled the hot water on her wrist. Hissing in pain, she dropped the kettle and stumbled backward, tripping over a chair and falling to her knees.

It wasn't her first time using a knife, or even a sword. Over the years she had been forced to defend herself on several occasions, but this was the first time she had killed a man in cold blood. Rolling onto her back, she held up her hands, studying them. She was still trembling, and she thought she saw small amounts of blood still trapped beneath her nails.

She lay there for a long time.

 CHAPTER 32

When a knock finally sounded on her door, Rose was still lying on the floor. It had been at least an hour. She didn't really feel any better, but at least her heart was no longer racing. She got to her feet slowly, letting the habits of a lifetime guide her feet and hands. Tyrion stood outside the door when she opened it.

He took one look at her attire and grinned. "I appreciate your enthusiasm, but I'm not really in the mood right now."

"Come inside," she told him, standing away to allow him to enter.

He did, and she took his hand, leading him toward the bedroom. A smirk grew on his face. "I suppose if you insist," he said drolly. His expression changed when he saw the state of her boudoir. "By the gods!" he exclaimed.

There was blood everywhere, on the walls, the floor, the bed, and a large pool of it was congealing around the body at the foot of her bed. "I had no idea your tastes were so...exotic. Was he a friend of yours?"

"Business partner," answered Rose, her voice numb.

"I'm guessing he overcharged you," responded Tyrion dryly.

"Can you get rid of him?" she asked, too tired for banter.

Tyrion stared down at her for a moment, then sighed. "I'm not in the business of disposing of bodies. I've already cleaned up one mess for you."

Rose didn't answer, looking over the scene with dead eyes.

"Fine," said Tyrion. Moving over to the corpse, he lifted her soiled dress and examined it. "What in the world were you doing? It looks like he was stabbed to death by a deranged child."

"He wouldn't die," she explained.

"Where did you stab him first?" asked the archmage, but then drew his own conclusion. "Under the arm here? Your blade wasn't long enough."

Rose shrugged.

"You barely nicked his heart. That's why he took so long," continued Tyrion. "If you had gone under the other arm, it would have worked better."

"I'm right-handed."

He pointed at his shoulder. "Then a downward strike here, between the clavicles."

"He might have seen me, then."

Tyrion pursed his lips. "A valid point. Next time just stab him in the kidney. It won't kill him instantly, but the pain is so great he won't be able to fight."

Rose nodded mutely and turned away, heading for the door.

"Wait!" protested Tyrion. "What about your things?"

"You can get rid of anything that's stained—the bed, the furniture, I don't care anymore." She closed the door.

When Tyrion emerged from her bedroom ten minutes later, she was drinking tea. She offered him a cup, but he declined. "Are you alright?" he asked, a hint of sympathy in his voice.

"No," she replied. "But I'm functional."

"If you'd like my advice—" he began.

She cut him off, "No."

Tyrion's expression soured, but he gave up on the idea. Moving toward the door, he announced, "I have other places to be."

"Can you heat water?" she asked suddenly.

"What?"

"Can you heat water?" she repeated.

He gazed at her suspiciously. "As in for tea?"

She nodded. "Something like that."

"I can burn a man to ashes in seconds. Warming up a kettle is nothing," he responded.

He took a step toward her still-hot kettle, but she waved him off. "Not now. I just wanted to know. You can leave," she told him.

Bewildered and muttering under his breath, he left. "Strangest woman I've ever known."

***

Rose appeared that evening and, as promised, she had two women and a large copper tub with her. The look on my face made it clear that I thought she'd lost her mind. "I'm not letting you bathe me."

"Fine," said Rose. "Lillith and Janice have plenty of experience. I'll wait outside."

Her two accomplices were busily moving in and out, carrying buckets of steaming water to fill the tub. They had a businesslike air about them, and their rugged shoulders and strong backs made it apparent they had spent their lives handling difficult labor. I didn't fancy stripping in front of them, either.

"I can bathe myself," I protested.

Rose nodded. "Do a thorough job or I'll turn you over to their tender mercies." Lillith chuckled evilly at Rose's remark.

They carried in countless buckets of steaming water, and I wondered how they had gotten it all down here. My cell was on the fourth and lowest level, so carrying it all by hand would have been an epic chore, even for such sturdy women as Rose's companions.

The obvious conclusion was that one of my wizardly jailors had heated it for them. *Probably Conall,* I assumed. Gareth and Tyrion weren't that sympathetic.

When they were done filling the tub they left soap and towels, then stepped out, Rose following in their wake. She returned a moment later with Gareth standing behind her. "You can't leave him alone," said the surly archmage.

"What do you think I'll do, drown myself?" I asked him, exasperated.

"That's one possibility," he agreed. "In any case, prisoners can't be left alone with contraband." Then he leaned close and whispered in my ear, "You hang tomorrow. Use your time wisely. Your son and I will give you your privacy today."

Shocked, I watched him leave. *Did he really just say that?* "Unbelievable," I muttered.

"What did he say?" asked Rose.

"They won't be watching," I answered. "Take that however you want."

She flushed, then went to the side of the room and sat down.

I watched her, feeling awkward. "Can't you at least turn around?"

Rose smiled faintly. "Whatever for? It's nothing I haven't seen before."

"I'm not Dorian," I growled.

"You realize that Elise and I both bathed you while you were ill a few months ago," she informed me, a malicious mirth in her tone.

"I thought it was just Elise and Penny."

"And Alyssa, and Elaine..." She paused. "Oh, and Lynaralla, Irene, Moira, my daughter Carissa, Angela. I think there were a few more, but it's hard to recall everyone."

I goggled at her, stunned. "What did you do, invite the castle staff as well?"

Rose covered her mouth with one hand as she laughed politely. "Of course. We made quite an event of it. It was the most humorous thing to happen since that band of comedy players visited Washbrook."

I knew she was putting me on by then. "I'm sure there were lots of puns about my 'wizard's staff' as well."

Her expression switched to one of pity. "It's more of a wand, dear, let's be honest."

Pretending at outrage, I turned around and began to remove my dirty clothing. "It's a staff," I insisted.

"Whatever makes you feel better, Mordecai," she remarked. "We all have little lies we tell ourselves."

Amused, I stepped into the tub and lowered myself into water that was almost too hot for comfort. Almost. A long sigh escaped from my lips as the heat soaked into muscles that had been cramped and sore from a week spent sleeping on a cold stone bench. The thought of dying tomorrow seemed a distant worry.

Lathering and scrubbing, I washed away the sweat and grime, but when I started to wash my hair, I felt Rose's hands on my shoulders. "Let me," she said softly.

357

"You don't have to do that," I protested, but she had already stolen the soap. The next few minutes were a delight as she massaged my scalp, and after she rinsed my hair with a fresh bucket, she told me to lean forward.

Scrubbing my back was completely unnecessary, and it caused a host of reactions in me, but thankfully the water was opaque with soap by then. Gareth's words kept returning to my mind.

Rose didn't linger at it, though, and she surprised me again when she reached into her basket and brought out a razor. The edge glinted dangerously in the orange light cast by the lantern. "I know what you are thinking," she informed me.

By all the dead gods, I hope not! "What's that?" I asked nervously.

"That it's too dark for you to shave," she replied. "And that you need a mirror."

I nodded immediately. "You read my mind."

She smiled. "You don't have to worry. I'm very experienced. In spite of his skill with a sword, Dorian was forever cutting himself, so most of the time I was his barber."

That made a perverse sort of sense, though I wondered if it was strictly true. While Dorian had been hopeless at lying, he hadn't been above feigning something like that to spend more time with his wife. I resolved not to reveal his secret. Even though he had passed on, I would keep his trust.

And what would he think about your situation now? my inner voice asked. *Shut up,* I told it. Sometimes my inner voice is an asshole.

Cold steel touched my throat, and then Rose's breath tickled my ear. "I won't hurt you."

The flinch that resulted from that might well have slit my throat, if she hadn't been holding the back of the razor to my skin. Somewhat annoyed, I spoke up, "I wasn't nervous before, but now you have me worried."

She laughed and then began applying lather to my chin. When she brought the razor back this time, she was all business. "Keep still."

Her strokes were smooth and sure. Something occurred to me then, and I wanted to warn her not to shave off my nearly recovered goatee, but I didn't dare speak, or even swallow. I feared she might shave off my Adam's apple. Within a few minutes she was done, and when I felt my chin everything was as it should be.

"Thank you," I told her. "Penny always used to threaten to take off my beard when she was angry." A cold chill swept over me as the words left my mouth. I still didn't know what had happened that day when I had lost control of my powers while in a drunken stupor, but I was fairly sure that it had been Penny who had left me clean-shaven. *I should be figuring that out. Not whatever it is I've been doing.* Guilt ate at me.

Rose wiped my face, and she was probably quite aware of what I was feeling, but she said nothing. Putting away the razor, she stood and moved away, turning her back this time. "You can dry off and get dressed now. Your clothes are in the basket."

I did as I was bid, and when I reached into the basket I found a grey velvet doublet with soft leather boots and well-made trousers to match. I recognized them. "How did you get these?"

"Tyrion," she answered. "He said they were in his closet in your old house."

The house he had resumed ownership of. That still annoyed me, but not as much as hearing his name on her lips. "I want you to stay clear of him, Rose. He's dangerous."

Her eyes flashed a warning. "I'm well aware. I don't need your reminder."

There was no point in fighting with her about it, so I took a moment to dry my manacles and the skin beneath them with the towel, then I took a seat on the bench. Rose joined me. "Don't you think you should share your plan with me?" I suggested.

"Do you really believe no one is listening?" said Rose.

She had a point. We sat hand in hand, until the wall faded, and her assistants came in to carry out the tub. Rose was the last to leave and I grabbed her hand before she could exit. "Rose, wait. I need to thank you, for everything."

"I already know," she said reassuringly.

"No," I said, shaking my head. "I…" My treacherous throat closed up again. I couldn't say it.

Once more she put her finger to my lips. "I already know. Give yourself time. You aren't done grieving yet." She turned away, but before she stepped across the threshold, she delivered one more statement, a knowing smirk on her face. "I also know you weren't thinking about it being too dark to shave earlier."

I gaped at her, embarrassed once more.

"Someday—after the trial," she told me, her expression turning serious. "It might be a year or two before you're ready. I can wait."

Then she was gone, but I stared at the stone wall where she had been for a long time. *I doubt I'll ever be ready for you,* I thought somberly. *In fact, Dorian probably didn't realize how far in over his head he was until it was too late.* I went back to studying my manacles, and for the first time in many days, I looked forward to the 'morrow.

 CHAPTER 33

When they came for me in the morning, I was already up and pacing the floor, feeling very much like a caged lion. To my disappointment, it was Gareth and Tyrion who arrived to take me to my appointment with destiny.

"You look eager to get your neck stretched," said Tyrion jovially.

"Anything to get out of this damned cell," I responded, refusing to let him dampen my mood. "Though of the two of us, I'd say you're the one who could use another inch or two in height," I added, referring to the fact that I was at least an inch taller.

Sure, it was petty, but no man likes to be looked down on. Tyrion was relatively tall, but I still had a slight advantage, and I knew it had to irritate him.

For once, Gareth smirked, giving away the fact that he wasn't completely devoid of humor. So I turned to him. "I don't know why you're so happy. Fall colors went out of fashion two thousand years ago."

Both of them gave me looks of confusion. They didn't get it. Lifting my manacled hands, I tugged at my well-trimmed goatee. "His beard," I said with a sigh.

Gareth shrugged. "Red isn't a fall color."

"I beg to differ. Your beard is exactly the shade some leaves turn in the autumn. You just don't want to admit how much that remark stung," I told him.

Tyrion frowned. "Trees aside, fall colors are brown, green, grey, some blues…"

"And burnt orange," I insisted. "Don't try to pretend you know anything about fashion."

"Ask your girlfriend," suggested Gareth. "She'll be able to decide the matter. Maybe the judge can issue a ruling, if he doesn't have anything else more pressing to attend to today."

Gareth had surprised me. "I didn't think you had a sense of humor."

He grinned maliciously. "Gallows humor is my specialty."

There was no winning, so I kept my mouth shut. Not because I had been defeated, but rather because my audience was too limited to appreciate my humor. I told myself that several times as we climbed the stairs. It wasn't until we emerged from the dungeon that I realized I had forgotten to deny the most important point. "She isn't my girlfriend," I insisted belatedly.

"Mine either," said Tyrion with a sinister chuckle. "More of a passing amusement."

That did it. Furious, I whipped my hands up and to one side, causing the long chain that linked my wrists to whistle through the air. Tyrion's reflexes were fast, and he caught it, but the end of the loop continued onward, putting a red weal on his cheek.

He jerked the chain, causing me to stumble, bending forward, and then he planted the toe of his boot in my sternum. I felt his aythar ignite, and something sharp pressed against the back of my neck. "You do not want to test me today, boy, unless you'd like to have a tragic accident before you reach the courtroom."

Coughing and wheezing, I was forced to bite back my anger, but it left a bitter taste in my mouth. *Someday soon,* I vowed silently, *I'm going to make you pay for that remark.* I owed him several debts already.

Grabbing my elbows, they hauled me to my feet and dragged me along until I was able to get my legs working again. When we finally stepped out of the palace and into the morning sun I was nearly blinded by the brilliance. They didn't wait for me to adjust, though. Urging me on, they walked me through the yard and into the main gate.

"Your admirers are waiting outside," said Tyrion wryly.

And they were. The street between the palace and the House of Justice was packed with people, and by the sound of their calls and jeers, they weren't very happy to see me. I hadn't been popular in the capital since the night I had slaughtered Tremont's loyalists in a killing spree that had later earned me the nickname 'The Blood Count.' People who recognized me in Albamarl usually lowered their eyes or walked in the opposite direction if they saw me coming, but the chains on my wrists had emboldened them to make their true feelings known.

Those closest spat at me, while the ones further back threw rotten fruit and other things too unspeakable to think about. Fortunately, my escort didn't fancy being covered in filth, so they erected a shield to keep the three of us free of detritus.

We were about to enter the courthouse when I heard a new cry go up behind us. "Highwhore!" screamed the crowd. Turning, I saw Lady Rose begin to cross, and to my horror, she was unescorted.

The mob had already used up their choicest missiles, so they didn't have much left to throw, which was a small mercy. Head held high, Lady Rose strode forward with such a commanding presence that the people at first spread apart to make way for her.

But the mob mentality was only given pause for a moment. One particularly brave woman leapt forward from the crowd and spat in her face. That was all it took, and the fragile order dissolved into a howling chaos.

I tried to reach her, but my noble escorts refused to release my arms. They jerked me back, and I began to throw myself from side to side, begging them to let me go. I might have lost my mind entirely if it hadn't been for Conall's arrival.

He had just emerged with Harold and the Queen, and when he saw what was transpiring, he left his royal charge and leapt into the crowd. A moment later, I saw a spherical shield appear, pushing the people back as he helped Rose back to her feet. He waited, took her with him back to the Queen, and then the four of them crossed the street together.

Show over, my captors led me into the Halls of Justice. Not content to remain silent, Gareth leaned close to my ear. "Now do you see the price she's paid for you? Once this sham of a trial is done, what do you think will happen to her?"

Burning with shame and fear for Rose, I answered him honestly, "Please protect her."

Gareth looked solemn, and he gave me a slight nod, but Tyrion's answer roused me to new heights of rage. "Don't worry, boy. I'll take care of her," said my ancestor, a faint leer on his face.

I hadn't wanted to kill anyone that badly since the day he had shamed me in front of Penny. Or perhaps since the day I had caught Leomund whipping Millie. Or the day that Celior...well, to be honest, I'd had a lot of moments like that, but just then Tyrion was at the top of my list of people who needed to die.

"Calm yourself, Mordecai," ordered Rose from behind me. "If you walk into the court raving like a rabid dog, it won't help our case."

I glanced back at her, taking note of the faint streak of dirt on her cheek. Despite what had just happened, she looked serene, almost regal. Her eyes held a warning, but beyond that was an icy blue steel that reminded me of a granite promontory in a storm. *Adamant* was the word that popped into my head. She would weather the slings and arrows that might lie ahead.

I'd be damned if I didn't do as much myself. Straightening my back, I marched into the courtroom as though the two men on either side of me were my escorts, rather than my jailors.

Normally there would have been a delay after I (the accused) was brought in, but with the Queen already in the building, Lord Watson was under some pressure to begin promptly. No sooner than we were seated, we were forced to rise and acknowledge 'His Honor' before resuming our places. Ariadne then entered, and we did it all over again, with more reverence. Everyone stood and bowed as she was escorted to her place.

In Lothion, the ruling monarch reserved the right of justice, which meant that technically she could overrule the judge or anyone else if she so chose. In a case as important as mine, though, she wouldn't dare exert her power. Doing so would risk rebellion and civil war. I had encountered that drawback years before, when I had been tried for ushering Andrew Tremont into the afterlife and turning his estate into a haunted wasteland.

The royal box was at the far end of the courtroom, behind and slightly above the judge's bench, highlighting her rank as the final arbiter. It wasn't until she was seated that the rest of us were allowed to sit down once again. There were a few more formalities, but it wasn't long before Judge Watson called the court to order and summoned the royal prosecutor to come forward.

"Lord Oswald, please present the charges," ordered Lord Watson.

Brandon Oswald was a minor noble from a small house, and he was a second son at that. A successful career as a barrister was all he could reasonably look forward to unless his older brother died suddenly. Striding toward the middle of the floor, he puffed up his chest with as much self-importance as he could muster, unrolled an unnecessarily ornate scroll, and began to read, "In the matter of the sovereign nation of Lothion against one Mordecai Illeniel, the Count di' Cameron, the charges are as follows: Lord Cameron did by force enter the residence of Leomund, husband of our Queen and Prince-Consort of the realm. In so doing he trespassed against the Prince, willfully destroyed his property, and then proceeded to assault the Prince's person. As if this were not enough, he then slew the Prince while he was unconscious and stole his property, in the person of a young serf named Millie."

Lord Watson looked down, turning his eyes in my direction. "How does the accused plead?"

Lady Rose stood, responding in a loud clear voice, "The defendant admits guilt to all charges but for assaulting the Prince. To the charge of murder, we plead not guilty."

A faint smile played across the judge's lips. "Lady Rose, perhaps you are not aware, but even if all the other charges are proven false, laying hand upon a royal person is itself a capital crime."

She bowed her head deferentially. "I am aware, Your Honor, but there are mitigating circumstances. The defendant encountered the Prince in the commission of a crime. He struck the Prince in order to protect the life of the serf, Millie."

"Have you any proof of this supposed crime?" asked the judge.

"Yes, Your Honor, the witnesses gathered today can confirm the details of the Prince's abuse and torture," said Rose.

"Very well, let us proceed," began Lord Watson, but a clerk stepped up to his side and whispered something in his ear. He glanced back at the Queen's box and then made a surprise announcement. "The Queen has, in her mercy, decided to dismiss the charge of assault given the circumstances and her personal knowledge of her late-husband's proclivities. What remains to be proved is the charge of murder. Lord Oswald, you may proceed."

Oswald didn't seem too happy with that announcement, but he swallowed his disappointment and called his first witness, Lord Airedale.

David Airedale took the stand with arrogant aplomb, and the prosecutor's questions were simple and to the point. He recounted his experience at the hunting lodge and made sure to describe the look of fury on my face when I burst onto the scene in great detail. He was done in less than five minutes. Then it was Rose's turn to question him.

"Count Airedale," she began, "I will not belabor the facts of your testimony, for they are not in question. But I do have questions regarding your presence at Prince Leomund's hunting lodge that day. Would you mind telling the court why you were there?"

Airedale shifted uncomfortably in his seat. "It is no secret that the Prince and I were friends. My reason for being there was no more complicated than that."

Rose smiled coldly. "Perhaps I should be more specific, Your Excellency. While I am sure it is true that you were friends with the Prince, *close* friends in fact, did not your purpose there also include the intention to arrange for the sale of one of your serfs?"

Airedale's face paled slightly, but he recovered quickly. "I don't recall. The events that followed were so traumatic that I have forgotten."

"Are you telling me that you have forgotten the fact that you offered to sell Prince Leomund a serf named Lucy Brimmon, a girl living under your protection who is currently age ten?" asked Rose pointedly.

The look on David Airedale's face was priceless. He gaped at Rose for several seconds, then answered, "Listen, I don't know where you got that information, but it is no crime to sell property to another lord of the realm." His eyes darted toward Oswald, hoping for support.

The prosecutor spoke then, "Objection, milord. This has no bearing on the case at hand."

Before Judge Watson could rule, Rose raised her voice. "It has everything to do with the credibility of the witness, who, as I can show, was complicit in Prince Leomund's crimes."

Lord Watson was firm. "Sustained. Lady Hightower, please return to the matter at hand."

Someone in the gallery hissed, and despite being forced to move on, Rose smiled faintly. Without pause, she asked her next question, "Lord Airedale, do you know any of the other witnesses personally?"

David Airedale shrugged. "I have visited Prince Leomund on several occasions. I would probably recognize his servants, but I do not know them on a personal basis."

"Even though two of them were also purchased from you by the Prince?" asked Rose, "Specifically, Millie and the Prince's head servant, Vander Brimmon."

"Objection!" shouted Lord Oswald. "The provenance of Prince Leomund's servants has no bearing on the question of murder."

"Sustained," said Lord Watson, his response so quick that it was obvious he didn't really care.

Unfazed, Rose launched into her next line of questioning. "Your Excellency, you said earlier that when Lord Cameron appeared, you were downstairs warming yourself before the fire, is that correct?"

"Yes."

"But Prince Leomund was upstairs. Do you know what he was doing?" she probed.

David Airedale shook his head. "How should I know?"

She didn't relent, however. "When you first arrived at Prince Leomund's lodge, did the Prince come down to greet you?"

He nodded. "Yes, of course."

"According to my client, he asked you up to the bedroom where the murder later occurred, where he then reintroduced you to Millie. Is that true?" asked Rose.

Angry, Airedale fairly shook as he answered, "You mean while he *spied* on us. Yes, the Prince called me up to show me the condition of the girl he had bought."

"He didn't offer to have her show you her new talents as a sex slave?" asked Rose.

"No!" shouted Airedale.

"Then why did you go back downstairs, leaving the Prince alone with her?"

"They weren't alone," Airedale said instantly.

Rose raised her brows in interest. "Would you explain to the court then, who was in the room?"

Eyes darting from one side to the other, David Airedale looked for support from Lord Oswald and even the judge, but he found none. Despondent, he answered, "He was going to discipline the girl, for what purpose I don't know. He called the rest of his servants to watch. I have no stomach for such things, so I left."

"Then by your own admission, you were aware he was about to whip the girl," accused Rose.

"I had no way of knowing he planned to whip her!" blurted out Airedale.

Lord Oswald was on his feet again. "Objection. Prince Leomund's method of punishment is immaterial."

"Sustained," said Lord Watson. "Lady Hightower, may I remind you, Lord Airedale is not on trial here today."

"Perhaps he should be, Your Honor," said Rose in an even voice.

"Objection!" shouted Oswald again.

The judge held up his hand. "Lady Hightower, please get to the point."

Rose bowed her head deferentially once more. "Certainly, Your Honor. Lord Airedale, is it possible, given your knowledge of Prince Leomund's activities, that you felt an overwhelming sense of guilt at being complicit in his crime, a guilt so powerful that it compelled you to murder the Prince when you found him unconscious and alone?"

"Absolutely not!" cried Airedale. "I don't give two figs what he did with his property!"

Lady Rose smiled, raising her voice. "That, my lord, is very apparent. I have no further questions, Your Honor."

David Airedale was led away fuming, while those in the gallery muttered. Whatever else occurred, his reputation had suffered greatly.

Rose sat down beside me, keeping her face forward. Leaning over, I whispered in her ear admiringly, "You nearly ruined him up there."

Her lips quirked upward in a faint smirk. "I'm just getting warmed up."

"Do you really think he did it?" I asked.

She glanced at me briefly. "He doesn't have the spine, but he may know who actually did do it."

Even more curious now, I asked, "Do *you* know who did it?" But Rose remained silent, her eyes intent on Oswald's next witness.

 # CHAPTER 34

The next witness was one of the servants who had been present in Leomund's lodge. Lord Oswald's questions were perfunctory, again merely serving to confirm the story already told as well as to paint me as a raging madman when I entered the house. Rose's cross-examination was fairly simple as well. She confirmed the timeline and had them verify where they were before and after I entered the house, but she also asked several strange questions, mainly concerning the servant's relationships to one another.

She also asked each of them about the Prince's behavior, but after the first one eagerly began to tell of Prince Leomund's cruelty, Oswald objected and as usual, the judge supported him. By the time they got to the last servant, I was beginning to get nervous, for the only people left to take the stand after him were myself and Millie, and I knew neither of us could say anything that would clear my name.

Rose was practically chomping at the bit to examine the last servant however; a man named Vander Brimmon. When her turn came, she shot forward onto the floor with alacrity. "Vander Brimmon," she started, "may I call you Vander?"

He bobbed his head. "Yes, milady."

"Vander, as I established earlier, you were once a serf of Lord Airedale's, were you not?"

Vander seemed anxious, and his head turned from side to side, as though looking for someone to answer for him.

"Please answer the question," said Rose. "You originally belonged to Lord Airedale, yes?"

"Yes, milady."

She nodded. "What was your position in the Prince's household?"

"I was his chief servant, milady," answered Vander.

"A position of responsibility," observed Rose. "Very much like a butler, wouldn't you say?"

Vander blushed. "No, milady. I am not a freeman. I wouldn't presume to claim such a title."

"But you were in charge of the other servants?" she pressed.

"Yes, milady."

"Then you must have been very aware of his treatment of them," suggested Rose. "Is that true?"

Lord Oswald was ready for her. "Objection, we've been over this. It isn't relevant."

"Sustained," pronounced Judge Watson, for perhaps the hundredth time. "Lady Hightower, I have warned you before, we are here to examine evidence of Lord Cameron's guilt or innocence, not to dredge up possible past crimes of Prince Leomund."

Rose bowed her head in acceptance. "Very well, Your Honor. I bow to your wisdom. I believe you will see the merit of that question shortly, however."

"Stick to the case at hand, Lady Hightower," growled Lord Watson.

She turned back to the witness. "Vander, you have a family, do you not? A wife and children?"

Vander lowered his head. "I was not allowed to marry, milady."

"Nevertheless, you were in love, and you had three children before being sold to Prince Leomund, correct?"

The prosecutor threw his hands up in exasperation, but didn't bother objecting.

"Yes, milady," said Vander.

"And they still live on Lord Airedale's estate?" she prodded.

Rose's face shone with imminent victory, making me wonder where she was going, but I could only watch, like everyone else in the room. When she asked her next question, the pieces began to fall into place in my mind.

"Lucy Brimmon is your daughter, isn't she?" asked Rose, carefully enunciating every syllable.

Vander's eyes went wide in obvious fear, then his jaw clenched.

Rose was relentless, however. "Answer the question, Vander. Lucy Brimmon is your daughter, isn't she?"

A muttering rose from the gallery, as some people began to talk, some of them confused, while others had begun to grasp where Rose's questions were leading. Lord Watson was forced to use his gavel to quiet the room. Then he turned to the witness. "Answer the question, Mister Brimmon."

Vander's face was red, but at last he answered, "Yes. Lucy is my youngest."

Rose's face was a vision of triumph. She made a show of pacing across the floor in front of the bench, then asked, "Were you aware that Prince Leomund had just agreed to purchase Lucy from Lord Airedale?"

Lord Oswald's face was apoplectic as he screamed, "Objection!" The gallery began to shout as Lord Watson held up his hand for order, but several voices yelled out, "Let him answer!"

After banging his gavel loudly for almost a full minute, Lord Watson eventually regained control of the room. Then, after careful thought, he said, "Overruled. I believe Lady Hightower's question may have serious relevance. Mister Brimmon, please answer the question."

Vander sat still, paralyzed, so Rose asked him again, "Vander, you knew the Prince was about to buy your daughter, didn't you?"

Stammering, he finally answered, "H—he never told me that."

Rose wasn't about to surrender. "Your hesitation tells me you knew something, Mister Brimmon. I'll ask you again, did you know the Prince had arranged to bring your daughter to his private estate?"

Vander's resolve broke, and tears began to roll down his cheeks. "I overheard them talking about it."

Lady Rose's face became sympathetic. "I know this must be difficult for you, Vander. You were well aware of the Prince's tastes. What did you suspect would happen to your daughter Lucy once she entered the Prince's service?"

Vander's answer came out in a whisper, "What he always does."

Rose lifted her chin and addressed Lord Watson directly. "Your Honor, I would ask the court to remember that according to Mister Brimmon's own answer to Lord Oswald a few minutes ago, he was the first to enter the bedroom and discover the Prince's body."

The courtroom was so quiet I imagined I could have heard a pin drop. I certainly heard the rustle of Lord Watson's robe as he nodded assent. Then Rose turned back to the witness.

"Vander, when you went into the bedroom, you found the Prince, but he wasn't dead yet, was he?" she asked him directly.

"He was," cried Vander, his voice nearly unintelligible through his tears. "The knife was in his chest."

"I think you're lying, Vander," said Rose sternly. "What man wouldn't commit murder to protect his own children?" she asked rhetorically. "Who wouldn't take the opportunity to protect his child from the depraved attentions of a sadistic child rapist?"

Judge Watson stepped in then. "Lady Hightower, please save your rhetoric for the closing statements and stick to examining the witness."

She nodded. "Vander, did Lord Airedale encourage you to take revenge on Prince Leomund?"

"No!"

"Did the other servants know you murdered him? Did they promise to keep your secret for you?" she added.

"No! I didn't kill him!" yelled Vander.

"No one would blame you, Vander," said Rose, waving her arms at the gallery. "Any man or woman in this room would have killed him under those circumstances. Could you have done any less?"

"I didn't do it," he answered, his voice nearly a whisper.

"Your fellow servants didn't blame you either, which is why they promised to protect you, isn't that true?"

Vander Brimmon began to sob uncontrollably, and after several minutes it became apparent he wouldn't answer. Rose addressed the judge again, "Your Honor, let the record show that Mister Brimmon refused to answer the question." Then she headed back toward me. "No further questions."

As I watched Rose sit down beside me, my own emotions were a confusing mix of admiration, surprise, and horror. I couldn't help but feel enormous sympathy for Vander as they led him away from the witness stand, while at the same time I was relieved. My own trial wasn't over, but it seemed almost certain they would have to acquit me.

And after they did, Vander would very quickly stand trial for murdering the Prince-Consort. From my perspective, he had done nothing wrong, but I knew the law wouldn't find it that way. Killing a prince, for whatever reason, was a capital crime. No matter how compelling the mitigating circumstances, Vander would be executed.

Looking at Rose once more, I saw a faint tremor in her hand, and I knew she must be feeling the same. Without caring about the glares from my two guards, I reached out and covered her hand with my own, but Rose didn't meet my eyes.

She was quietly muttering to herself. "Anything." She said it several times, and while I didn't know the context, I understood her meaning.

***

After a short recess everyone returned, and the trial resumed. I was to be the next witness to take the stand, though to my surprise, not at Rose's behest. It had never occurred to me before, but I learned later that in Gododdin the defendant can't be compelled to testify if they choose not to do so. If someone had told me that before my trial, I wouldn't have understood. But within moments of facing Lord Oswald, I knew very well why Rose hadn't wanted to examine me on the stand.

The prosecutor ran through the obvious questions rather quickly, having me identify myself and give a quick recount of what I remembered. I answered honestly, with one exception. Rose had counseled me to feign confusion over one particular of my last moments in Leomund's bedchamber. Brandon Oswald was quick to leap on that discrepancy.

"Lord Cameron, according to witness statements, including that of Her Majesty, when you arrived in Albamarl with Roland, you stated that you cast a spell to put Millie into a state of slumber *before* you left Leomund's bedroom. Are you disputing your previous account?" asked Lord Oswald.

I shook my head. "No, I did say that, but I misspoke at the time."

Lord Oswald's face grew stern. "Then you admit to lying to the Queen?"

"No, sir," I said confidently. "My memory of events was muddled by my emotions at the time. When I first recounted what happened, I was in a hurry. It was a simple mistake."

"You said something that wasn't true, Lord Cameron. I believe everyone would agree that that is the very definition of a lie. Don't you agree?" insisted the prosecutor.

I could see Rose tensing. If she could have, she probably would have liked to answer my questions for me. *Don't worry, Rose,* I thought silently. *I've got this one.* "No, sir, I don't. A lie is a false statement with the intention to deceive. I had no such intention. As a barrister, surely you're aware of this?"

"Your intention is still very much in question," said Lord Oswald. "When you first returned with Duke Roland, you admitted to spying on Prince Leomund and then forcing your way into his hunting lodge and then assaulting him. You very nearly convicted yourself with those statements, so it seems strange that you would suddenly change this one detail, a detail that neatly prevents the only witness in the room from coming to your defense. I find that curious. Don't you, Lord Cameron?"

I was ready for this one. "No, Lord Oswald, I don't. When I met the Queen, I freely admitted to everything I knew, because at the time I had no knowledge of Prince Leomund's murder. If I had intended to lie, my story would have been different from the beginning. My statement that Millie was asleep before I left was a simple mistake, one I would not have made if I had been trying to conceal a crime."

Lord Oswald looked unhappy with my response. "A convenient answer," he replied. "Let's move on to something more pertinent. You weren't very fond of Prince Leomund, were you?"

"I barely knew him," I said honestly. "I only met him on a few occasions, but he definitely did not make a good impression on me."

"You're understating your animosity toward the Prince, aren't you, Lord Cameron? Others have said you hated the Queen's husband with a fierce passion."

While that was essentially true in the present, I didn't actually recall feeling so strong in the past, nor had I ever said as much to anyone else. Giving the prosecutor a look of puzzlement, I asked, "Which others?"

"I ask the questions, Lord Cameron. Please answer."

"I'm trying to," I replied. "To my knowledge, I have never displayed or communicated such a feeling of vituperation toward the Prince, so for me to address your question you need to specify who made such a claim, unless you're simply fabricating rumors to further your position."

Lord Oswald's face turned purple, but Judge Watson leaned forward. "Please inform the court of the sources of your claim, Lord Oswald. I'm curious."

"I'm sure there were several," said the prosecutor, let me check my papers. He stumbled as he went to his table, causing a titter to rise from the gallery. After a moment he lifted a sheet of parchment. "Yes, here it is. Lord Airedale. Now answer the question, Lord Cameron."

I smiled. "I have never spoken to Lord Airedale regarding the Prince. His only basis for making such a claim would be the fact that he saw me break into the Prince's lodge. At the time, I was furious over the abuse occurring there. I suspect he may have other reasons for remembering conversations that we didn't have in the past."

The prosecutor moved on from there, and while I felt good about what had gone on so far, things began to get ugly. "Lord Cameron, you're very fond of the Queen, aren't you?"

"She is my cousin," I answered immediately. "I love her dearly."

"Your first cousin, once removed, to be precise. Is that correct?"

"Her mother, Queen Genevieve, was my grandmother's sister," I said firmly.

"Would you describe her as beautiful?" asked Lord Oswald.

I had no idea where he was leading, but apparently Rose did. Before I could answer, she leapt to her feet. "Objection. The Queen's appearance has no relevance."

The judge nodded. "Sustained."

Lord Oswald smirked, then moved on. "Your wife died recently, did she not?"

"Almost four months ago," I said firmly. "I believe everyone is aware of that already."

"Have you considered remarrying, Lord Cameron?"

His questions were beginning to make me angry, but I knew better than to let it show. "Certainly not. I loved my wife more than I can say. I have not recovered from her loss yet."

"With your obvious knowledge of the law, you are doubtless aware that first cousins once removed are legally allowed to marry, are you not?" asked Lord Oswald.

Frowning, I replied, "Yes, but the Queen is like a sister to me. It had never occurred to me, plus she was married already."

"*Was* is the operative word here, Lord Cameron. You have had tender feelings for our Queen for a long time, haven't you, Lord Cameron?" said Lord Oswald accusingly.

"Not of the kind you suggest," I insisted.

"Yet you created a special portal to allow the Queen to visit your home whenever she wished, did you not?"

"Well, yes," I answered. "Are you accusing the Queen of impropriety?"

Lord Oswald smiled. "I'm just establishing the situation for the court's enlightenment. You created a portal between your home and the Queen's chambers. She occasionally used this to sleep in your home, is that correct?"

"My wife and family were all aware of the portal," I declared. "We built an extra room for her convenience. There was nothing improper about it."

The gallery was awash with whispers and muttering now. Then the prosecutor continued, "Lord Cameron, if there was something improper going on, do you think your now-departed wife would have dared challenge you on it?"

Furious, I stood up. "Lord Oswald, if you had ever met my wife, you would know better. She was no shrinking violet. She'd have had my balls if such a thing were occurring."

That brought a loud round of laughter from the gallery, and it took Judge Watson several minutes to restore order. When calm had returned, Lord Oswald asked his next question. "You claim your wife would have stood up to you, Lord Cameron, yet she allowed another unmarried woman to live with you for a considerable length of time, didn't she?"

"Objection," said Rose. "The Count's family matters are irrelevant."

Judge Watson gave her a look of undisguised glee. "Overruled. Please continue, Lord Oswald."

The prosecutor nodded. "Let me clarify my question, Lord Cameron. The unmarried woman who lived with you and your family is here in the court today, is she not?"

Slowly, I nodded. "Yes."

"Please name her for the court, Lord Cameron."

The words were like ashes in my mouth. "Lady Rose Thornbear."

Lord Oswald leered at me. "Did you begin having sexual relations as soon as she moved into your home, or did you wait until after your wife had died?"

"Objection!"

"Overruled," snapped Lord Watson.

My eyes burned as I glared my hatred at Lord Oswald. "I have never had sexual relations with anyone other than my late-wife."

"That seems difficult to believe, Lord Cameron, given that you have had upwards of at least three different unmarried women living at your home at any given time, not to mention occasional nighttime visits from our Queen. You expect us to believe that your relations with all of these women are innocent?"

"I do."

The prosecutor continued, "Are any of your family in the courtroom today, to show support?"

The sudden shift made me blink. "Just my younger son, Conall."

"Who also happens to be one of the men who arrested you," pointed out Lord Oswald. "Lord Cameron, why do you think the rest of your family was too ashamed to be seen here today?"

"My older son, Matthew, is still in Lancaster, protecting the duke's estate. My younger daughter Irene is there with him," I explained.

"And what of your adopted daughter, Moira?"

"She's currently at home," I admitted.

"Even though she could have been here today?"

"Yes," I replied. "I prefer she not have to witness this."

Lord Oswald leaned forward, inches from my face. "But you haven't spoken with her, have you, Lord Cameron? In fact, she is not present today of her own choice."

"Not directly, no."

The prosecutor shifted his line of questioning once more. "Lord Cameron, after murdering the Prince, did you

386

hope that the Queen's familial love for you would become something more? Perhaps enough to garner you a new place in the palace?"

"No!" I exclaimed.

"No, you didn't hope to marry her, or no you didn't kill the Prince, Lord Cameron? Which is it?"

"No, to both," I answered, struggling to calm myself. "I didn't kill the Prince, nor have I ever wished for a marital arrangement with the Queen. I've never loved anyone other than my wife."

"Lord Cameron, if your devotion to your wife was so great, why have you been meeting with Lady Hightower?" asked Lord Oswald.

My eyes went to Rose. "She's my legal counsel, and a good friend."

"Did any of your other friends visit you for an hour every evening this week, Lord Cameron?"

"Objection!" shouted Rose.

But Lord Oswald wasn't waiting for my answer, he bulled onward. "Did any of your other friends offer to bathe you before your day in court, Lord Cameron? Is that what good friends do?"

Belatedly, Judge Watson responded, "Sustained. Lord Oswald, please refrain from speculation."

"Forgive me, Your Honor. I have no further questions," said the prosecutor, a look of victory in his eyes.

It was Rose's turn after that, but all she could do was force me to recount my story once more, in the hopes it would wash away some of the stain from Lord Oswald's leading questions. From the mutters in the gallery, I held out little hope of that. After a few minutes, she sat down and I was released from the stand.

 CHAPTER 35

Back in my seat, I looked around the room. Almost everyone was engaged with those beside them in hushed conversations. When I looked to the Queen, she met my eyes, but her expression was cold. Conall stood to one side of her, and he refused to meet my gaze. I could only wonder what he was thinking.

"If there are no further witnesses, I will adjourn to make my deliberations," said Lord Watson, beginning to rise.

Rose was on her feet immediately. "Begging your pardon, Your Honor. I would like to call one further witness."

The judge gave her a disapproving look. "Your witness is not on my list."

"I only received a response last night, Your Honor," said Rose. "If it please you, I would like to call Millie, the girl rescued by Lord Cameron, to the stand to testify." Turning, she directed his attention to the back of the room.

I followed her eyes, and there I saw Karen standing, with Millie beside her. They began to make their way down the aisle toward the bench.

Lord Oswald was immediately alarmed, and he stood to protest. "Your Honor, I have not been given an opportunity to meet with this witness in advance of the trial. Her testimony should not be allowed."

Rose dipped her head apologetically. "Forgive me, Lord Oswald. I only managed to contact her last night.

Given that she is one of the principal witnesses, I feel it is of importance we hear what she has to say."

Lord Watson shifted his eyes between the two of them for a moment, then took to his feet. "Lady Hightower, Lord Oswald, please join me in my chambers." He walked away and the two of them followed him, leaving the courtroom. Loud whispering broke out and soon rose to a cacophonous discussion as everyone talked at once.

With nothing to do and no one to talk to, I kept my eyes forward, unsure what to do with myself, but Gareth leaned toward me, his eyes on Karen. "I'm starting to understand what Rose is thinking."

I kept my face blank. "I have no idea what you're talking about."

He grinned at me. "I think you do, so I'll give you a word of advice. The indomitable Lady Rose has made a mistake in her planning. What she's considering won't work. It will only lead to her imprisonment after your execution."

I didn't answer, but I felt my jaw clench.

"Make no mistake," said Gareth. "As I said before, I'm not entirely unsympathetic. If I were, I would point out that your surprise witness has spent the past week in the company of your daughter. While that means little to these people at present, if I wanted, I could easily inform them that she's a mind-witch. Little Millie's words would count for nothing then."

"What are you saying, Gareth?" I asked.

"You'd better hope that abomination of a daughter you live with did a good job. If the girl's false testimony isn't enough to sway the judge, you're going to hang. And if Rose attempts to get you out of here with Karen's assistance, she will likely hang as well." He straightened up then and proceeded to ignore my angry glare.

Giving up on Gareth, I returned my eyes to front, but my mind was working furiously as I considered what he had said. It didn't take me long to remember that he had been the one to craft my enchanted manacles. If it had been anyone else, it might not have mattered, but Gareth had been born during the golden age of magic. Mordan mages were plentiful then, and any method of imprisoning a wizard would have to take that fact into account.

Closing my eyes, I focused my magesight on the manacles again, but I didn't learn anything new. I had already figured out the proper method for opening them, though it would require another mage to do so. Aythar had to be channeled into each manacle at the proper points, creating a link between the two cuffs. Only then could the proper command be given so that they would open without killing the person wearing them.

Beyond that, I had studied the runes worked into them, but I couldn't see any obvious reason why someone wearing them couldn't be teleported. Gareth's confidence wasn't a show, though. I knew the red-bearded archmage well enough to know that he didn't bluff. If he thought that an attempt to teleport me away would fail, then it probably would.

This just keeps getting better, I thought to myself. I was still lost in thought when the judge returned to the room.

Lady Rose took her place beside me as he stood behind the bench. "I have decided to allow Lady Hightower's final witness to testify. Lady Hightower, please seat your witness."

Karen led Millie forward, and moments later she was in her place, looking shy and very uncomfortable with so many eyes on her. She was dressed in one of Irene's old dresses, a pretty yellow outfit that covered up most of her scars. I wondered for a moment if that was wise, since it might help for everyone to see just what the Prince had done to her, but I felt ashamed of myself immediately afterward. She had suffered enough.

Since Rose had called her, she was the first to examine Millie. She stepped confidently onto the floor and faced the girl. "Please state your name for the court."

"Millie, milady."

"And your surname?"

Millie stared at her feet. "I don't know it, milady. I was taken into the Prince's service when I was very young."

"But you originally came from Lord Airedale's estate, is that correct?" asked Rose.

Her answer was almost too quiet to hear. "Yes, milady."

"How old are you now, Millie?"

"Twelve I think, milady," said the girl.

"And how long have you been in the Prince's service?" continued Rose.

Millie hesitated. "I'm not sure. Five or six years, maybe."

Rose asked her next question with visible reluctance. "I know this is hard for you Millie, but it's important for the court to hear. How old were you when the Prince began to abuse you?"

Millie shook her head. "He didn't abuse me, milady. I was his property. He could do as he pleased with me."

The crowd in the gallery broke out in angry whispers. They weren't loud enough for Judge Watson to bother with, however, so Rose went on. "And what did it please Prince Leomund to do, Millie? Did he hit you?"

The next ten minutes were painful and awkward, as Rose forced Millie to detail some of Prince Leomund's favorite punishments, which frequently involved whips. Millie also admitted that the Prince used her for more intimate pleasures, though Rose kept her questions in that regard vague. It was enough that the court knew the truth, without embarrassing the girl with specific descriptions of his depraved acts.

Once Rose had established the extent of Prince Leomund's perverse entertainment, Rose directed her questions to Millie's relationships with her fellow servants. "Did the chief servant, Vander Brimmon, know about what the Prince did to you, Millie?"

The girl became visibly distraught, more so even than she had been during the previous questions. "Vander is a nice man," she said loudly. "He didn't do anything wrong. He was always kind to me."

"Millie, please answer the question. Did Vander know about the Prince's treatment of you?" Rose pressed.

Millie's eyes were desperate. "Will he get in trouble for being kind to me?"

Ever patient, Rose shook her head. "No, dear. Kindness is never a crime. Will you answer my question? Did Vander know about the Prince's treatment of you?"

In a voice so low it was practically a mumble, Millie answered, "He took care of my cuts, after the Prince was done. Sometimes, if I was told I couldn't eat, he would sneak bread to me in my room."

"Do you think Vander hated the Prince for the things he did, Millie?" asked Rose.

The girl shook her head.

"You have to answer out loud, Millie, so the court can hear," Rose explained.

"Yes, milady. But he never would have done anything to him. Vander wasn't like that," insisted the girl.

Rose's face grew sad. "Sometimes good men do violent things, Millie, to protect those they love." Then she addressed Judge Watson. "I submit to the court my theory that Vander was the man who drove the blade into Prince Leomund's heart. He had more than one reason to hate his lord, both the abuse he witnessed daily, and the threat that his own daughter might soon fall victim to it."

Millie's face turned pale at Rose's words, and she began to tremble. Judge Watson remained more practical. "Lady Hightower, please finish your questions."

She nodded. "Millie, after Lord Cameron came in and struck the Prince, he fell unconscious, correct?"

The girl nodded, tears running down her face. "Yes, milady."

"Please tell the court what you saw after that. Did Lord Cameron treat your wounds and take you away?" asked Rose. "Was Prince Leomund still alive when you left?"

Millie was visibly shaking, and it took more than a minute before she could answer. When she did, it came in the form of a shout. "No!"

Astonished, Rose stared at her. "Please explain, Millie. Do you mean Lord Cameron didn't hurt the Prince before leaving?"

"No!" shouted Millie once more. "H—he was so angry. It scared me. He made my back feel better, and then I saw him take a dagger and stab the Prince. It wasn't Vander, I swear! Lord Cameron did it right in front of me."

Rose flinched as though she had just been slapped, but she didn't give up. "Please tell the truth, Millie, what happened?"

Millie jumped to her feet, screaming, "I am telling the truth. He stabbed the Prince!" Her finger was pointing straight at me.

"Millie, don't lie," said Rose desperately. "Did…"

But Judge Watson had heard enough. "Please don't torment the witness, Lady Hightower. If you have no more questions, please step aside so Lord Oswald can examine your witness."

Rose looked up at him with pleading eyes. "But, Your Honor."

"Sit down, Lady Hightower. Lord Oswald, the witness is yours," said the judge.

Lord Oswald stood, then with a flourish he bowed in the direction of the bench. "No further questions, Your Honor."

The room was dead silent as I watched Rose. She was still standing in the middle of the floor, but before my eyes I saw her square her shoulders and lift her chin. She stared proudly at the judge before turning to look at the rest of the room. Her gaze was an accusation, or perhaps a statement of defiance, but when she sat down beside me once more, she seemed utterly calm.

After that the judge called for final statements, but I barely heard what was said. Lord Oswald got up and blathered on for a moment, already sure of his victory. I had a sense that Rose's remarks were more poetic, but I wasn't really listening as she made her final, impassioned plea. When she sat back down, I could tell by the look on her face that even she didn't believe it had been enough.

Judge Watson stood and struck his gavel once more. I had a feeling the pompous bastard got a kick out of that. Then he began to speak. "Given the circumstances I don't feel a long deliberation is necessary. Lord Cameron, I find you guilty of all charges. The punishment for the murder of a prince of the realm is death. I order that you be taken from this room and hanged without delay." Then he banged his wooden hammer again, the twat.

Rose was up again immediately, protesting. "Your Honor, please allow some time. Lord Cameron hasn't even been allowed to see his family."

Lord Watson wasn't moved. "Murderers do not merit the court's sympathy, Lady Hightower. Keeping a wizard imprisoned is no easy task and has been an undue hardship on Lords Illeniel and Gaelyn. The sentence will be carried out immediately."

I stared up at him as he said it, tempted to give him a piece of my mind. But I had no idea what would happen next, so I restrained myself, cursing him silently, *Fuck you too.*

 # CHAPTER 36

Chad Grayson stared down at the steps leading from the Justice Building across the street. He stood atop the palace wall, and according to his calculations his targets would be at less than thirty meters when he eventually began to loose his arrows. Of course, shooting down from elevation, he didn't have to worry nearly as much about drop. The wind was his only real concern, but the breeze was relatively mild.

The part he couldn't quite get used to was the fact that he didn't have to worry about the other guards. His original plan had been to steal uniforms and wait until it was nearly time before pretending to patrol the wall. It had been a good plan, though its main flaw had been the fact that the palace guards weren't equipped with longbows—they carried crossbows. He hadn't worried much about it, though. Most people weren't particularly observant. As long as they waited until just before time, it would have been fine.

But with Elaine, none of that was necessary. He and Cyhan stood in the middle of the wall, peering between the merlons without a care in the world. He had thought she would make them invisible at first, but Elaine had explained the impracticality of that proposition. If they had been invisible, they wouldn't have been able to see, making observation difficult.

Instead she had covered them in a double-layered illusion, disguising their clothes and faces. Even their weapons appeared normal, although she cautioned them that when they actually nocked arrows and made a full draw, it would probably look strange unless she was close by to adjust their illusion. She had been confident that her efforts would fool the krytek, as well as the other mages who would soon be exiting the building across the street.

The only thing that made him nervous was that Elaine wasn't with them now. She had left thirty minutes earlier to prepare for their escape. She had picked out a spot within the walls that didn't seem to be frequented by the patrols. It was in the corner where two walls met, and it was there that she was making a circle to teleport them out once their job was done. Like their personal disguises, she planned to cloak the circle in a double-layered illusion as well.

She had promised to return as soon as she was done, but that was half an hour ago, and Chad worried that the trial would finish before she got back. He looked over at his companion, wondering if he was nervous.

Cyhan stood still, imitating a statue.

Nah, the ugly bastard wouldn't know how to be nervous, thought Chad.

They'd had one close call a few minutes before, when a patrolling guard had stopped to ask what they were doing, but Cyhan had run the man off. His uniform was marked by a sergeant's stripes. "We're not on duty, guardsman. We're just here to watch the show." That had been all he'd had to say.

The big man hadn't really had to act, either. He was used to commanding men. His usual looming menace combined with his obvious experience meant he probably could have said almost anything and the guard would have left them alone.

Let's just hope he doesn't talk to his buddies, though. Chad rubbed his brow and turned his attention back on the street below. He wanted a drink. His nerves were strung tighter than his bow, but it was something he was used to from past experiences. *Never killed an archmage before, though. That's something new.*

Rose's instructions had explicitly stated he should kill his targets if possible, but that only showed her inexperience in these matters. *No fucking way I'm going to wing one of the bastards. That's just askin' for a horrible death.*

A murmur began in the crowd below, and he knew it was almost time. People were beginning to emerge from the building. The first ones out were unimportant. Reflexively, Chad checked his arrows again, arranging them in front of himself. *Ten shots,* he reminded himself. There were more in the quiver at his waist, but by the time he got to those, he and Cyhan should already be running.

"Where is that fuckin' girl?" muttered the hunter.

"There they are," cautioned Cyhan, lifting his bow and rolling his shoulders to loosen the muscles.

Four guards were on the stairs now, spreading out to keep the crowd back. Behind them, Mordecai emerged into the sunshine with Tyrion on one side and Gareth on his other. Lady Rose followed close behind them. *Wait for the signal,* Chad reminded himself silently. *We don't know what happened.*

He fervently hoped she wouldn't raise her arm. The best possible ending would be for him and Cyhan to simply leave quietly.

Rose was glancing up at the sky, and she started to move, but Gareth Gaelyn turned suddenly and grabbed her arm, shaking his head and saying something. *Did he just stop her from signaling?*

Then one of the guardsmen said something to the crowd, and a roar went up. "Hang him!"

Good enough for me, decided Chad. "On the count of three," he announced to his companion. Lifting his hundred-and-twenty-weight bow, the hunter began to pull, drawing it to its full extension. "One, two…" Lining his arrow up with Tyrion Illeniel, he said his usual silent prayer, *Fuck you, asshole.*

***

The sun was blinding as I stepped outside, held tightly by my two captors. I could feel Rose's presence behind me, which for some reason terrified me. I didn't know exactly what she had planned, but with all the guards, two archmages, and countless people around, I couldn't help but feel she was standing naked in a sea of predators. If anything happened now, there was no telling who might die.

Then Gareth released my arm and leaned back, grabbing Rose's wrist. "Don't even think about it," he warned.

Had she been about to signal something? I wondered. My eyes scanned the crowd and then went to the palace wall across the street from us. There were quite a few guards there at various places. Most of them appeared to be watching the commotion in the street as much as guarding anything. Two of them in the center seemed a little odd, though, holding their crossbows at an odd angle.

Tyrion and Gareth both had simple shields around them—nothing special, but enough to stop an arrow. It didn't do them any good, though. Tyrion's body jerked as a massive war arrow ripped through his chest with such force that it completely exited the backside of his body and nearly impaled my knee. A similar arrow hit Gareth, burying itself in his left shoulder and ripping through his shoulder blade.

Absently, I noted that the bodkin points on the two arrows were ones I had enchanted and given to Chad Grayson before our first trip into Lancaster. I also realized that two more arrows were already standing out from Tyrion's chest, just as a second arrow found Gareth.

Both men were reeling, not just from the shock of the arrows, but from the feedback that destroying their shields had caused. Even so, Tyrion's aythar flared and his tattoos came to life, creating a much more powerful enchanted shield around his body. Three more arrows shattered against it as he fell to his knees.

Gareth was not so fortunate, though his assassin seemed a bit slower. A third arrow passed through his belly as he fell.

Nine arrows had been fired in the span of less than three seconds, and each of my captors had at least three feathered shafts sticking out from their respective bodies. It was at that point that the crowd finally took notice, and people began screaming.

The guards on the steps finally drew their swords, seeming to move in slow motion, then began to fall as arrows took them in their legs. Apparently, whoever was shooting wasn't as worried about killing them, and he had the skill to attempt it. I knew enough about archery to know hitting their legs was much harder than the much larger target of their chests. Someone was tugging on my arm, and I looked up to see Rose's anxious eyes on me. "Step back!" she urged.

Karen appeared from nowhere and placed her hands on each of us. Her face took on a look of concentration for a moment, and then—nothing happened. Holding up my hands, I shook my manacles in front of her. "They drain away aythar, including yours when you try to teleport me. Take Rose and go!" At last I understood what Gareth had meant, and I felt stupid for not realizing it earlier.

Karen nodded, looking torn, but Rose slapped her hand away. "No! Get the manacles off of him!" she yelled.

I felt aythar moving, from several sources, one of which was completely unexpected. Elaine was somewhere nearby, and it was her power that raised a mist, shrouding the street and limiting our vision to no more than five or six feet.

The other sources were more frightening. Tyrion was moving, and I felt him using his power to stop the bleeding within his body. His action was impressive, for he was using regular wizardry to stop several major arteries from causing him to bleed to death. He was still fatally wounded, but he had bought himself a lot more time, and he had done it while already being in a lot of pain.

Gareth, on the other hand, was a more horrifying sight as his flesh began to melt and flow. What he was doing was a mixture of ordinary magic and metamagic, as he simultaneously healed and transformed his body into something *else*.

I observed all that as I hurriedly tried to explain to Karen what to do. "You have to touch both manacles at the same time, here and here." I pointed to the correct position on each manacle as I spoke. "Channel a small amount of power through those points, and when you feel it connect, say '*Estus*.'"

"What does that mean?" she asked, nervous.

"It means 'off,'" I explained.

"Not much of a password," she muttered.

"It isn't meant to be," I nearly shouted. "Just hurry up and do it."

Several guards came out of the court building, stumbling toward us through the fog. Karen noticed them and threw up one hand, creating an impressive wall of flame.

Just put them to sleep, I thought, but I didn't have time to be critical. I shook my wrists at her. "Hurry up."

I watched Tyrion nervously while she fumbled with my chains. He was still on his knees, protected by his enchanted shield while he struggled furiously to keep himself alive. With Gareth transforming close by, he couldn't risk healing himself as an archmage would. He stared at me the entire time, his eyes boring into me with an all-consuming hatred.

Then Gareth was gone, leaping forward and upward to punish the archers on the wall. His body was a confusing blur of wings, scales, claws, and teeth. Tyrion smiled, and then his wounds began to melt away.

"Estus," said Karen at last, and I heard a click and felt the manacles fall away. I caught them with one hand and tucked them into my belt. She reached out toward us, but before she could act, she seemed to vanish, her body thrown violently to one side.

From the corner of one eye I saw Karen strike the side of the courthouse and slump to the ground.

"You took too long, grandson," said Tyrion's menacing voice, sending chills down my spine.

"Rose, run," I called over my shoulder. "Please."

"No," she said firmly. "Never again."

She was standing behind me, but with my magesight I saw her draw a long dagger from her dress. At the same time, I felt a sudden warning of some sort, and I jumped to one side as one of Tyrion's armblades swept across. I almost made it, but the tip still cut a shallow, bloody groove across my chest. Desperate, I reached for my power, and found—almost nothing.

My magical reserves are normally quite impressive. Penny used to tell me so all the time, and not always as part of some weird wizard sex humor. But today they were almost dry. A week of wearing those damned manacles had left me drained and feeble, magically speaking.

This left me in an awkward position, facing my ancestor, who was freshly healed, as powerful as ever, and armed with enchanted tattoos that would have been difficult for me to deal with under the best of circumstances, while I had next to nothing. No equipment, no weapons, no enchanted pouches, and very damn little magic.

Pretty much a normal Monday for me, but I wasn't ready for it. It was still Sunday, after all.

I backed away, pushing Rose as I went, since she stubbornly refused to run. "Let's talk about this, Tyrion. We can still be friends," I said, using my best charm.

"It's too late for that, Mordecai. I would have helped you, but I'm in no mood now," he threatened, stalking forward slowly.

I held my hands out in a non-threatening manner. "What's a few arrows between friends?"

Tyrion growled. "The difference between having your balls and being cut into so many pieces you're only fit to feed the dogs," he snarled.

Rose stumbled slightly as she reached the stairs to one side of the courthouse, then she caught her balance and put her arm on my back, as if to help guide me down. I could sense them already with my magesight, but I didn't have time to tell her that. Tyrion was still coming forward.

"You can't escape, Mordecai," he hissed. "Your Mordan mage is unconscious, your allies lost in the fog, and you don't have enough strength left to defend yourself, much less that trollop behind you."

We reached the bottom of the steps and kept going, backing along the side of the street. "Watch your language," I warned. "There are ladies present." If I couldn't beat him with magic, I figured perhaps I'd have more success with the rules of etiquette.

I felt another of those strange warnings, but I couldn't dodge; it was coming straight for me and Lady Rose was behind me. I turned to push her away when a wide surge of force flung me directly into her, and we were both tossed twenty feet down the sidewalk, tumbling and rolling. Wrapping my arms around her, I managed to create a light shield to protect us from the cobblestones.

When we finally came to a stop, I remembered the dagger in her hand and I felt fortunate not to have been impaled by it. "He's going to kill me, Rose," I whispered to her as we tried to regain our feet. "Please run. I'll try to keep him busy long enough—"

"No!" she said, nearly shouting. "I've come too far. We leave together, or we die. I no longer care."

"Such sweet lovebirds," said Tyrion, still walking toward us. "Be wary, Mordecai. That bird may sing, but she has venom in her songs."

"You know nothing about her," I bit back.

His eyes went wide. "Me? I know everything about betrayal, grandson, as both a victim and as a master in its commission, and *that woman*"—he pointed at Rose—"has shown me tricks even I didn't expect. I've tasted her fruit and found it bitter indeed."

My initial plan was to try and keep him talking. The more time that passed, the better the chance that something might distract him, not to mention my power was recovering, albeit too slowly to offer much hope. The fruit comment, though, that stung, and my anger was rising.

He saw it on my face, too. "So *that's* what bothers you the most, isn't it?" he sneered. "Don't worry, our arrangement was fair and equitable. I made sure she tasted what I offered as well."

White-knuckled with rage, I wished desperately that I had a weapon, but the only weapons available to me were my words. "I see why you're so upset now," I told him. "I've never had a lover so disappointed in my performance that she felt the need to have me murdered. What stings more, your pride, or was it the arrows?"

"Mordecai!" warned Rose, though I wasn't sure if it was because my remark concerned her, or whether she was worried I'd push him too far. I was almost too angry to care.

I felt a surge of danger and I stepped right, narrowly avoiding the armblade that swept through the space I had just been standing in. At the same time, I bent forward, and his other weapon swept just over my head, so close it trimmed some of the hair from my head. Tyrion surged forward, while I backpedaled, trying desperately to avoid his lethal attacks.

He was fast, way too damn fast, and his movements weren't wild or sloppy, despite his fury. Tyrion's attacks were lightning quick, like a striking cobra, and despite their speed, I could tell there was a cold, calculating mind behind them. Even with the advantage of my strange warnings, I couldn't quite avoid them all. Step by step, I retreated, gaining a collection of minor cuts that bled, painting my new clothes in fresh crimson.

It would have been nice if I could have fought back. As it was, it took everything I had just to avoid the murderous sweep of his arms. I could sense his aythar flowing, not into the air, but through his body, increasing his strength and speed.

He didn't want to kill me, or he would have already done it. He had power to spare. He could have simply set me on fire or blasted me to pieces, but he was choosing to enhance his body instead, which told me his plan. Tyrion wanted to bleed me, to make me suffer, humiliating me in front of Rose.

Thinking his anger had made him careless was a mistake in itself, though. Tyrion steered me across the street, using his aggressive attacks to direct my retreat, until at last we passed a few feet from where Rose was anxiously watching. As the line of his shoulders passed her, she leapt forward, dagger in hand, hoping to drive her blade through his back.

It's worth noting that although her dagger was enchanted, the shield protecting his body was also the product of an enchantment. While an enchanted weapon will almost always tear through a protection crafted from raw magic, when two enchantments are put into opposition it's largely a matter of strength. I had already witnessed Tyrion's shield tattoos shattering enchanted arrows with the power of a warbow behind them, so I knew Rose's dagger didn't have a hope of hurting him—but she didn't know that.

Tyrion did, and in fact, he had planned on it. I saw it in his eyes as she leapt at him. As her blade skittered away from his impervious back, he spun, his left arm sweeping sideways in a blow that would cut her body in twain. Rushing forward, I tried to stop him, but I knew I wouldn't make it in time.

 CHAPTER 37

Chad's first arrow landed slightly left of where he had intended, missing Tyrion's heart. It was no fault of his own, simply bad luck. The man had shifted his stance purely by chance as the arrow left the string. The hunter didn't pause to think about it, though. He already had a second and third arrow in the air before he even knew the result of his first shot.

Thoroughness counts, and Chad Grayson didn't do anything in half measures, whether it was drinking or killing. In his peripheral vision, he saw Cyhan release his second arrow as he reached down to claim three more shafts. *Not bad for an amateur archer,* he thought. The ranger finished his second set of three shots and then started laming the guards on the steps with his last four arrows.

By the time all ten of the arrows he had set out were gone, Cyhan was just beginning to reach for his fourth. Chad was impressed nonetheless. The big man had done better than many veteran archers the huntsman had trained over the years. Despite the stress of the situation, all three of the knight's arrows had found their targets.

Guards were running toward them from both sides, while below people were screaming as the knowledge of their attack finally registered on the crowd. Cyhan dropped the arrow he was holding and used his bow like a short spear, jabbing one end of it into the belly of the first guard, bringing the man up short.

Chad winced at that, not out of sympathy for the guard, but for the bow. The guardsman's sword swept down, a second too late to prevent the jab, but in plenty of time to leave a deep cut in Cyhan's bowstave. *The bastard has no respect for craftsmanship,* swore Chad silently. Borrowing Cyhan's remaining arrows, he began shooting at the guards coming from the other direction of the wall, aiming for their legs with mixed success, since their movement meant the arrows were almost as likely to glance off their thigh guards as they were to penetrate.

Chad ran out of the arrows Cyhan had set out when the last guard reached him, but he lifted the bow and drew anyway, causing the man to flinch and dodge backward. Grinning, Chad dropped the bow and used the brief respite to draw his two long knives. Starting a swordfight with only knives in his hands wasn't on Chad's list of preferred activities, but with his newfound strength and speed, he didn't think it was as hopeless as it would otherwise have been.

The ranger nearly jumped out of his skin when Elaine appeared beside him, her invisibility melting away. He stopped his knife just inches from her belly before swearing, "Scarin' me ain't really wise right now!"

Elaine blanched, but then spoke a word, *"Shibal."* The guard that Chad had been facing crumpled, asleep before he reached the ground. The young woman looked out from between two merlons and then added a few more words, creating a thick mist to conceal Rose and Mordecai. That done, she turned to the ranger. "Sorry I'm late. The circle took longer than I expected."

Glancing behind, Chad saw that the guards who had charged Cyhan were now down. Two appeared to be unconscious, while the third was sitting down, nursing a broken arm and leg. "Why didn't ya just knock 'em off the damned parapet?"

The big man glanced down, then shrugged. It was twenty feet to the ground. "Would have killed them," he said simply.

"This ain't the time fer bein' squeamish," Chad said, rebuking him.

Cyhan pointed down the other section of wall. "If you hadn't been shooting for their legs, that last one wouldn't have reached you."

Chad ground his teeth. "I don't have time fer yer shit right now." Reaching down he recovered his bow and then took several fresh arrows from his quiver as he looked over the edge. Unfortunately, the mist made it impossible to find a target. "They're on their own now. Time to go."

Elaine pointed in the direction of the corner Chad had been shooting toward. "The stairs over there will put us closest to the circle." She started to move in that direction, but then stopped, a strange look on her face. "Harold."

The ranger pushed her from behind. "Don't stop."

She pointed down at the mist below. "Harold's down there." Waving her hand, she caused the mist in that area to clear so they could see him.

Chad glanced down, then kept pushing. "Good thing he's down there and we're up here. Keep movin'." As they went, he couldn't help but wonder, "What is he doin'?"

Cyhan was behind him, and he answered, "He's thinking of jumping."

Chad's eyes went wide. "It's more'n twenty feet!" Then he looked at Cyhan. "Can we jump that far?"

The big knight shrugged. "Maybe. I wouldn't advise it. I always tell those I train not to try it."

"Why not?" asked Chad, but Elaine was still moving, so he followed her, looking back every second or so to see what was happening. Cyhan stopped over one of the men that had been shot in the leg. The man was still conscious, but he was bleeding heavily, and it was obvious he didn't have any fight left in him.

"It's risky," answered the knight, bending down to grab the wounded soldier by the belt and collar.

Harold made his move, bending deeply at the knees he launched himself skyward. If he had been unarmored, he might have sailed completely over the merlons, but as it was he barely reached them, just catching one of the capstones with his right hand. He firmed up his grip, and then, using the incredible strength in his arm, pulled himself upward with a jerk that sent him flying into the air again.

Sir Cyhan lifted the wounded soldier, holding him just above his chest, and as Harold arced gracefully over the top of the merlons, he heaved the man into the air. The poor guard who had become his makeshift missile screamed as he struck Sir Harold square in the chest, and the two of them tumbled headlong toward the street below.

Cyhan turned around and resumed marching toward Chad and Elaine. "I've warned him before. He'll remember his training next time."

If he's still alive, thought Chad. *So much for yer humanitarian impulses.* Then the wall in front of Elaine exploded as something like a golden meteor struck it. "What the fuck was that?" yelled the hunter.

Elaine answered with a single word, "Conall." Then she shrieked in alarm as Cyhan snatched her up and jumped down to the palace yard.

"You said we wasn't supposed to jump!" shouted Chad.

Cyhan grinned briefly, then began to move toward the corner where Elaine's hidden teleport circle was waiting for them.

Looking down nervously, Chad jumped just as the wall beneath him exploded, throwing fragments of stone and masonry in all directions. The landing was easier than he expected, but he rolled rather than trust his knees and ankles to take all the force. Wiping what he thought was sweat from his face, he found a bright red smear of blood on his hand. A stone fragment had torn his cheek open.

Wasting no time, he caught up with his associates. An idea had come to him, and he leaned closer to Elaine. "You can make illusions out of sound too, right?"

She nodded, and he whispered his idea to her. A few seconds later, cries sounded from the other side of the wall, "Protect the Queen! Assassins in the Justice Building!"

Chad smiled wickedly. *That'll get Conall off our backs.*

They were still thirty yards from their destination and it seemed they would make a clean escape, but then something horrific, a shifting ball of flesh, teeth, and scales, *boiled* over the top of the wall. "Fuck me," swore Chad. "Run!"

He didn't follow his own advice, though. He still had his bow in his hand, and quick as thought, he had it up and drawn. There were fifteen enchanted arrows still in his quiver, but they didn't remain there. Firing with blistering speed, Chad Grayson sent them all at the horror that came over the wall. They tore through the shuddering flesh, causing the monster to scream in pain as it settled at the base of the wall.

It didn't die, though. Legs sprouted from its sides and a massive head began to appear. Reflexively, Chad reached for his quiver, but there was nothing left to fire. *This is why I fuckin' hate wizards,* he thought. Then Elaine's hand caught his shoulder and the world vanished into darkness.

"Don't move," cautioned Elaine. "We're invisible. Take my hand and we'll start walking slowly."

"Won't it hear us?" asked Chad.

"I've covered everything," said the young woman. "Sight, sound, and magesight. We're completely undetectable."

"I can't see shit," muttered the hunter. "What happens if we bump into it?"

"That would be bad," said Elaine. "Gareth doesn't appear to be in a good mood right now."

"Gareth? That thing is Gareth Gaelyn?" hissed Chad. "No wonder he doesn't have any friends."

Cyhan chuckled beside him in the darkness. "He ate all his friends two thousand years ago. Give him time. He'll make more."

Not like that he won't, thought Chad sourly, then he turned on Cyhan. "Why are you laughin'? Are ya still gonna be chucklin' when he rips yer innards out?"

The big warrior didn't answer, but he laughed a little more anyway.

"Do either of you know which way to go?" asked Elaine. "I got a little turned around while we were running back for you."

Disgruntled, Chad responded, "Keep yer hand on my shoulder. The wall is this way. If we keep goin' 'til we find it, we can follow it left to get to yer magic circle." Then he added mentally, *Fuckin' amateurs.*

They walked cautiously for several minutes, and Chad was beginning wonder if they would ever reach the wall, when he felt several solid vibrations through the soles of his boots. More followed, growing stronger with each passing second. "He's close. How is he followin' us? He doesn't know where we're headin'." Then something bad occurred to him.

Chad had been a consummate hunter for most of his life, and while it wasn't usually a consideration when hunting men, most animals possessed an incredible sense of smell. "He's trackin' our scent." Grabbing Elaine and Cyhan's wrists, he began to run. Their only hope was speed.

"Why are we running?" exclaimed Elaine. "It's dangerous. We can't see!"

The hunter didn't answer. *Scent tracking is slow. If we move fast, we can stay ahead of him.* He had just finished that thought when they slammed into the wall. The darkness vanished, showing them the courtyard again.

Elaine was on her knees, nursing a bloody chin. Cyhan pulled her to her feet as Chad got a fresh look at the massive wolf that was Gareth Gaelyn. *I've seen warhorses that weren't that big,* thought the hunter, feeling his mouth go dry.

Gareth charged toward them as Elaine grabbed their hands and covered them in her veil once more. Running parallel to the wall, they hoped that the wolf wouldn't know which way they were headed.

Chad made sure he was in the lead, not from any particular sense of chivalry, but to make sure Elaine didn't knock herself silly when they found the next wall. If she lost consciousness, they were all dead. When he judged they were close, he slowed, turning so his shoulder and back would discover the boundary first.

His guess was pretty good, though it still hurt like hell when his shoulder slammed into the hard stone. Elaine nearly knocked the wind from his lungs as she smacked into him. As usual, Cyhan somehow managed to avoid hitting either of them, or losing his balance.

Chad held onto Elaine for a moment, grateful that she hadn't lost her grip on the invisibility veil this time. In the pitch black, he shifted his hands to try and sort out what he was holding, and he felt something soft. *That's definitely her ass,* he thought wryly, giving it a firm squeeze before pushing her away.

"Seriously?" exclaimed Elaine, outraged. "Are you insane?"

The hunter shrugged in the darkness. "Well, if I'm about to die anyway…"

"Shut up," barked Elaine. Gathering her will, she sent feelers of aythar out, making sure they were all within the circle, then with a word, she took them elsewhere.

CHAPTER 38

My newfound sense of danger was screaming at me as I tried to stop Tyrion, but I ignored it. As I rushed forward, he stopped his swing and punched forward, impaling me with his right arm. I felt the blade that extended from his hand pass completely through me, exiting somewhere near one of my kidneys. I froze in place, gaping at him while the pain blinded me to everything else. Glancing down, I could see his hand was entirely inside me.

The look of fierce glee on his face as he withdrew his hand and I fell to my knees was something I wouldn't ever forget. Horrified, I clutched at my stomach, trying to keep my entrails from falling out as he loomed over me.

It was several seconds before I realized the sound filling my ears was Rose's scream. Somehow, she had gotten to my side and she was clutching my arm, her face a picture of despair. *Don't,* I thought, *you'll get blood on yourself.* My eyes went downward, watching the blood running over my hands to spill onto the ground.

"Sorry about that, Mordecai," said Tyrion, gloating. "I wanted to go slower, but it's hard to control myself sometimes. If you haven't realized yet, I'm not really angry with you. It's *her* I want to punish, which is why you have to die first, while she watches."

My hepatic artery was completely severed. I'd be dead in ten seconds or less, but I frantically grasped at it with my power, pulling the ends together and knitting the vessel back into one piece.

Tyrion was kind enough to wait. "That's it. Don't let me kill you too quickly."

Then my eyes lit upon the one hope I had left. Rose's hands were still on my arm, so I used the physical contact to send a quick message to her. *Get around the corner, behind that wall. I can't kill him if you're too close.*

He must have sensed the extra use of aythar, for Tyrion used his foot to kick Rose soundly in the stomach. She fell back and rolled onto her side, clutching her belly, but when she looked up at me, I saw her eyes. She had understood me.

My tormentor walked slowly around me, igniting just the tip of his armblade, which he then ran slowly up my back, cutting a deep gash in my skin and muscle. "Don't heal too quickly," he intoned cruelly.

Behind him, Rose stumbled to her feet, still holding her bruised belly, and began to run. The corner of the nearest building was only ten feet away.

Tyrion chuckled as he watched her go. "I told you, grandson. That one knows much about betrayal. Don't worry, I'll fetch her back in a moment. You'll be dead, but rest easy that your betrayer will die soon after you."

Slowly, almost languorously, he turned to send a tendril of aythar out to catch her. The moment his attention was off of me I released my belly, heedless of my spilling guts. Grabbing the manacles from my belt, I took one in each hand and whipped the chain up and over him in a wide loop. With what aythar I had, I launched myself upward into the air, just as he reflexively cut the chain with his still-active armblades.

The enchantment in those chains had been storing my excess aythar for nearly a week, and the explosion that resulted turned the world white as it ripped through him, crushing Tyrion's shield and shredding his body. As close as I was, I fared only marginally better, already slightly above him. I was flung skyward by a shockwave so powerful that it ripped the skin from my face and legs. It destroyed my eyes, shattered my eardrums, and it was several seconds later, as I cartwheeled through the air, that I realized my right arm was entirely gone.

But I was somehow still conscious, which was probably a good thing. *Mondays,* I thought, forgetting that it was still Sunday. Weakly, I grabbed at the air with my aythar, trying to slow my fall. I didn't succeed—my power was still too feeble—but I managed to orient myself so that my head was uppermost as I fell. *This is going to hurt,* I thought as the ground rushed up at me.

I wasn't disappointed.

The world hit me like an angry battering ram, causing me to lose consciousness for a few seconds. I might not have woken up at all, but when awareness forced itself upon me again I discovered Rose was beside me, twisting a strip of her dress around the stump of my arm to stop the blood that was rushing out of me.

It was kind of silly of her, honestly. My intestines, which had been spilling out of me before the explosion, were mostly gone, along with much of my face and quite a bit of blood. I wouldn't even have known it was Rose beside me if not for my magesight. By all rights, I would be dead in less than a minute, no matter what she did.

But Tyrion was nowhere to be found, and for the first time in a week, I was the only archmage around. Opening my mind to the earth, I let it take away my pain as my consciousness expanded and I became something *more*.

The void was closer, its voice loud, tempting me. It would have been easier, especially as close as I was to death already, but I forced myself to ignore it. It was too dangerous. If I allowed myself to draw upon it, I would almost certainly kill Rose shortly afterward to replenish my lost aythar.

Rose gasped, stumbling back as my broken body changed, becoming stone-like.

I pulled at the earth below, and cobblestones flowed upward, joining my body and replacing my lost mass. It was enticing me to go further, to grow more and wipe away the pain and suffering of the human world, but over the years I had had much practice at ignoring that urge. Contracting inward, I reminded myself of my humanity and envisioned my body as it had been.

The world grew warm and true light broke in on me as my human eyes returned. Moments later I was myself, whole and unharmed.

And naked, let's not forget that—for I hadn't thought to recreate my clothes. *This is definitely a Monday,* I decided. *Whoever made the calendar screwed up.*

Rose's arms were around me, getting my old blood on my new skin, but I didn't particularly mind. Figuring out how my arms worked took me a few seconds, and then I returned the embrace, holding her tenderly against me. So far, it was the best moment of the day.

She was crying softly, her face buried against my neck, but after a minute or so her quiet sobs stilled, and I felt her lips on my shoulder. She worked her way up my neck and kissed the line of my chin and my hands dropped lower, instinctively pulling at her hips.

Uh oh. "Rose, wait, hang on," I told her.

She stopped immediately, then said, "Oh!" A rather appropriate remark, in my opinion. She started to push me away, but I held onto her, turning her around and pulling her hips back toward me. It wasn't for the reason she initially assumed, however, as she slapped at my hands and protested my lewd behavior. A second later, she saw the reason for my actions.

Several people stood nearby, drawn by the sound of Tyrion's explosion, and they were watching us curiously as I used Rose as a sort of human fig leaf to hide my embarrassing portions.

"Oh!" she said for the second time. "Can't you make an illusion to cover yourself?"

"I still have to recover my aythar," I replied. I did have enough to make an illusion, most likely, but I was loathe to use it. In the distance I could sense several strong sources of aythar, either mages or some of Tyrion's krytek. Using what little power I had would make me more visible and render me helpless again.

Ever practical, Rose took her dagger out again and used it to cut around her waist, turning her dress into what was essentially now a separate skirt and blouse. Then she stepped out of the skirt. Beneath it she had a linen shift that reached halfway down her thighs, so she wasn't exposed, but she looked damn funny.

She handed the skirt to me and began to rummage through a handbag that she had somehow managed to hang onto through all the chaos.

"What am I supposed to do with this?" I asked.

"Put it on, stupid," she answered, using a tone she probably reserved for slow children and mentally deficient wizards. Then she pulled out my leather belt, complete with its enchanted pouches. "After you get the skirt up, put the belt around it and roll the edges down over it so it doesn't slide off. Your hips aren't up to the task by themselves."

"Fucking Mondays," I muttered, but I did as she suggested. After an awkward minute, I was done. From the waist down, I was now clad in a beautiful blue skirt with gold embroidery decorating the panels. It was trimmed at the bottom edge with delicate lace, and I was almost certain that it didn't go well with my complexion.

Rose wasn't a tall woman, and that fact, combined with the necessity of using several inches of fabric to roll over the top of my belt, meant that the skirt only reached to my mid-calf. "Nice ankles," remarked Rose, complimenting me.

"Nice knees," I replied, reminding her of her own mostly bare legs. Then I took her hand and we set off. The gathering crowd parted as we moved, probably from shock. I doubted there was a mob in the world that could maintain its righteous fury when faced with two people as ridiculous looking as we were just then.

After we passed through the first ranks, we picked up speed. With my magesight I made a note of the probable magic users in the area and tried to choose a direction that would lead us away from them.

"Any ideas?" I asked her. Several of the potential mages seemed to be heading toward us, coming from different directions, though they were still out of sight due to the buildings.

"Your house," answered Rose immediately. "There are circles there."

She was right, though it wasn't technically *my* house anymore, since Tyrion had claimed it. Then again, maybe it was. I had seen no sign of him since the explosion. I fervently hoped it had ended his miserable life, but I wasn't ready to take bets on it yet.

Either way, the door should still open for me. I was still of the Illeniel bloodline. The big problem was that it was at least a twenty-minute walk from the part of the city we were currently in. We started running.

"How do you run in these things?" I complained. The skirt kept catching between my legs, threatening to trip me up.

Rose slowed slightly. "Ordinarily, we don't. Try lifting them above your knees so they don't catch your lower legs."

Feeling ridiculous, I did as she suggested, which worked. *If anyone sees me like this, I won't have to worry about them calling me the 'Blood Count' anymore,* I thought sourly, *so there's at least one bright side to this.*

We ran, our feet fairly flying over the cobblestone roads. Rose still wore her cloth slippers, but my feet were bare and within less than a hundred yards I was leaving bloody footprints on the stone. The pain of my torn feet was awful, but worse was the fact that I could sense our pursuers closing in. We weren't going to make it.

"They're close," I yelled to Rose.

"They can't enter the house, can they?" she responded.

They couldn't. My house in Albamarl was practically a fortress, but we weren't going to get there. "It's too far. Go ahead, I'll try to lead them away. I don't think they're following you," I told her.

Many years before, I had attuned several of my friends, giving them access to the house in Albamarl. If Tyrion hadn't changed it, Rose should be able to open the door. Looking ahead, I saw a lane that branched off to the right. If I took it, the krytek or whoever it was that was coming would likely follow me.

Rose's hand caught my wrist. "Together, Mordecai. Don't make me say it again," she told me, a fierce look in her eyes.

I was staring back at her, trying to decide how to lose my fanatical savior, when I saw a shimmer pass through her hair. A shimmer I recognized. Pulling to a halt, I stopped and looked back. Several feet behind us was one of the faint dimensional boundaries.

She pulled and tugged at me. "Don't stop!"

Shaking my head, I held firm. "There's a way out." Walking back, I held my other hand up, trying to feel the faint difference in the air where the boundary was. "Trust me," I added.

A member of the Royal Guard rounded the corner half a block away, running toward us, but I knew it wasn't a real guard. It was one of Tyrion's human-like krytek. *Please let me have enough power to do this,* I thought silently.

Pushing my feeble reserves out, I focused on the boundary. I had done it before, I could do it again, but I didn't have any aythar to waste.

The krytek slowed down as he neared us, then drew a sword that appeared to be wrapped in a lethal spellweave of some sort. "He's almost here, Mort!" said Rose, pulling her dagger out once more.

There! Gripping the boundary with my will, I pried it apart, producing a hole that was perhaps three feet in diameter. "Jump through!" I told her.

"You first," she responded. "Or I won't go."

Damn, stubborn woman! I swore to myself, but I knew she wasn't bluffing. Stepping back, I leapt through, trying to make myself as small as possible. On the other side, I looked back, only to catch Rose's feet with my face as she made good on her word. Falling back, my head hit the ground with a resounding thud, which saved me the trouble of releasing the portal. The blow had broken my concentration. It snapped shut behind us.

"Are you alright?" Rose said, lifting my head and staring down at me anxiously.

"Yeah," I muttered. Touching my lips, I picked dirt from my mouth. "But I've learned at least one thing today."

She looked askance at me.

"If we can't find food, I'm not eating your shoes. They taste terrible," I finished, grinning at her through bloody lips. Looking around, I saw we were on what appeared to be a beach. The ground beneath me was a mixture of sand and fine gravel. The sound of waves reached my ears, though I was facing the wrong direction to see them with my eyes.

"Where are we?" asked Rose.

"Damned if I know," I said honestly. A short cliff rose eight or nine feet high at the edge of the beach, and we could see trees behind it. It appeared to be some sort of coastal forest. As I turned around, I saw that the ocean stretched out as far as our eyes could see, reflecting glints of light from the waves. Wherever we were, it was idyllic, almost a scene from a storybook.

Anxious, Rose asked me, "Do we need to keep running? Can they follow us?"

I shook my head. "I don't think so. Tyrion's krytek are technically Illeniel krytek, but if they were produced by his tree, which they were, they don't have the gift. Only Lyralliantha's children will have it."

She gave me a funny look. "You could have just said 'yes.' Now I want you to explain all of that to me."

So I did; we had time now. Rose Thornbear, while not a mage herself, had a sharp mind and a keen memory, and she had spent years around my family and other mages. It didn't take long, though my explanation of the Illeniel gift was new to her.

"But how do you have it?" she asked at the end. "From what you've said, only Penelope's children should have it, and Lynaralla, since she's Lyralliantha's child."

"I'm not sure," I hedged. I had my suspicions, but I wasn't ready to face that yet. Rose pursed her lips, knowing I wasn't telling the full truth, but she said nothing. Then she shivered, rubbing her shoulders. The breeze coming off the ocean was chilly.

Ordinarily, I'd have just created a warm bubble of air around us, but I was well aware of how dangerous this world could be. It might seem safe where we were, but I wasn't willing to trust to that. Remembering my pouches, I opened the largest one and carefully extracted one of my cleverest items—a large wool blanket.

It wasn't enchanted, or special in any other way. But given the circumstances, it was now my most prized possession. I've been accused of paranoia in the past. My special pouches are filled with a variety of miscellany for use in unlikely situations. Most of the items are enchanted, many for violent purposes, but I had also set aside space for things like the blanket, which I hadn't used in years.

Digging around inside the chest my pouch was linked to, I felt a paper-wrapped package. Hopeful, I pulled that out as well. It was a dried packet of travel bread. Handing the blanket to Rose, I unwrapped the paper, but I was disappointed to find that the bread had gone moldy. Such was the fate of even the best long-term foods, when left alone for ten years in a dark space. I made a mental note to create a small stasis box that would fit within the chest, so I could store food indefinitely.

The next time I'm marooned on a strange beach, this won't be a problem, I promised myself, chuckling softly.

"What is it?" asked Rose, who had been watching me.

"Just laughing at myself," I admitted. "I'm thinking about what to store in here for the next time I'm lost in a wilderness."

Rose waved her arms at the beach surrounding us. "Doesn't seem like such a strange idea at present."

"Penny always said I was paranoid," I told her.

She pulled the blanket tighter around herself. "Where did you get the blanket?"

"Penny bought it for me."

"And your moldy biscuits?"

I shrugged. "Penny."

Rose's eyes crinkled at the edges as she smiled faintly. "I don't think she thought you were paranoid. She just enjoyed teasing you." She sniffed at the blanket, then picked off what appeared to be a few dried twigs. "Lavender?"

"Yeah," I answered, my eyes misting. "She said it would get stale in the chest, so she folded the lavender

427

in with it to keep it fresh." My throat tightened at the memory and I bent my head, putting my face between my knees. The past few days all I had cared about was surviving the week, but now, with the sun in my hair and a fresh breeze in my face, it all came crashing down again. I struggled to suppress my tears, but my shoulders began to shake despite my best efforts.

Soft wool enfolded me as Rose settled one end of the blanket around my shoulders, pulling me close. She didn't say a word, or even try to hold me. She'd been a widow long enough to know that words don't really help, and the arms of another would only be more painful while I was missing my wife. Instead, she sat close beside me, keeping the blanket pulled tight around us while resting her hand on my back.

For that, I was grateful.

When my storm had passed, and my cheeks had dried, she spoke, staring off at the waves. "It never goes away, not completely. Sometimes I go weeks or longer without it happening, then something will remind me and it all comes back, almost as painful as the first day. It could be anything, the smell of leather, or the shape of a shadow cast by a tree. It will trigger an old memory and suddenly I'm lost."

My chest ached. "How do you bear it?"

"I don't," she replied. "In the beginning, I shared it with my children. It seemed natural. They were grieving too, and I wanted them to remember. But they were young, and their memories of him have faded over time, and with it their grief. I finally realized I was making it worse for them—they were healing, but I was just reopening old wounds, so I stopped letting them see it.

I'd lock myself in my room and stay there until it had passed. As the years went by, I became convinced I was the only one. Dorian's memory was my burden to bear, and it felt as though if I let go of that sorrow, it would be as though he had never existed."

"That's not true," I told her. "I think of him often, and even if your children have forgotten, I'm sure Elise's sorrow is as great as your own."

Rose nodded, sniffing. "As a mother, I understand that. But for the lonely and broken-hearted, the truth is an inconvenience. We nurse our pain close to our hearts and pretend we're the only ones who feel it."

Thinking of Rose crying alone in her room, I wished we had done more for her over the years. Penny and I had kept her and her family close, trying to ease the burden, but it was impossible to save people from their private pain. I had spent enough nights in my dark and empty bedroom to understand that very well.

I took her hand in mine. "From now on we'll remember him together. Next time it happens, don't be afraid to share it with me."

Rose leaned her head on my shoulder. "Alright, but only if you let me do the same for you."

 # CHAPTER 39

Light returned to Chad Grayson's world as Elaine released the invisibility veil around them, allowing the world to flood in, overwhelming his senses. They stood in a woodland glade, which to Chad's mind was just a frilly way of saying a clearing in the trees. *More importantly, where are the trees located?*

"Elaine…" he began.

"Mm hmm?" she responded. By all appearances, Elaine was feeling pretty good about herself just then, though Chad couldn't be certain. It might have also just been her normal 'I was just nearly killed but now it turns out I'm still alive' face.

He decided to be diplomatic, just in case. "I might be wrong. But this isn't Mordecai's house, is it?"

"Unless it's the forest near his home," suggested Cyhan helpfully. "But there's no slope and the air smells wrong."

"Of course, it isn't," said Elaine. "Rose thought it might be a bad idea to go there. It would be the first place they would look. We're in the forest east of Albamarl."

Chad glared at her. "Then the water I'm hearin', that's the Myrtle River?"

She nodded, a satisfied look on her face.

"How far east of Albamarl?" asked Chad, grinding his teeth.

"Not far, a mile or two. You don't look very happy about it. I thought you'd be pleased," she said.

The hunter turned and started off at an angry jaunt, heading in the direction of the river. The tips of his ears were turning red and gave the impression that 'jaunt' was perhaps a bit too whimsical a term to describe his walk. He was seriously irritated.

Elaine and Cyhan followed him, she with a puzzled face, while Cyhan appeared bemused. The big man already knew why his friend was angry. The situation might have irritated him as well, but he had given up on such things in recent years. He preferred to enjoy watching Chad be angry enough for all three of them. *He's better at it anyway,* thought the knight.

"What's wrong?" asked Elaine. "You're a woodsman, aren't you? Well, welcome to the woods!"

Chad didn't look back. He continued striding forward, but he put one finger up in the air. "First, we are still within spittin' distance of a whole passel of gods-be-damned wizards who all want us dead! Second, we're in the fuckin' woods, with fuck all to eat or drink." He spun in place to face her, while walking backwards. "Emphasis on the word *drink*, sweetheart." Then he spun back and resumed facing forward as he marched angrily along. "Third—"

"I should have known you'd be bitching about alcohol," interrupted Elaine.

"Actually," said Chad, his voice rising in pitch, "I wouldn't mind a pull of McDaniel's finest right now, you can bet yer magic ass on that one. But that wasn't what I meant, unless yer referrin' to a fuckin' double entendre, an' I know how much you fuckin' wizards love fancy shit, make no mistake. What I meant was not only do I *not* have any whisky, but we also do not have any water."

432

"There's a river just ahead of us," pointed out Elaine.

"Which we can't drink, princess fancy-pants!" swore Chad. "Unless you like shittin' yerself fer a week."

She sighed. "We just have to make a fire and boil it first."

"I'm sure you can make a fire, since I'm fresh out of flint and steel, seein' as I didn't expect to be on a long-distance trek through open wilderness," bitched Chad, "but do ya have a pot to piss in?"

"Piss in?" said Elaine.

"It's an expression. Do ya have a pot to put the water in, so we can drink it after ya boil it?"

"No, but I can hold it in a temporary shield, I guess. It's not perfect, but we can manage," she replied.

"Fuckin' wizards," swore the hunter. "That brings me back to my third point. We are not equipped for this shit. No tools, no weapons, no supplies, no tent,"—he rattled his empty quiver—"no fuckin' arrows."

"The world is my weapon," intoned Sir Cyhan, a faint smirk on his face. He had been enjoying the ranger's tirade immensely.

"Shut the fuck up!" said Chad, cursing the big knight. "I do not need that shit from you right now."

"You can make arrows, though," suggested Elaine. "We're surrounded by trees, after all."

Chad didn't dignify that stupidity with a response. *Not that she'd know how to appreciate my diplomacy anyway.* He kept walking, but a sudden noise, actually more of a roar, brought him up short.

Elaine stared at him. "What was that?"

"Your teleport circle, it faded or died or somethin' after we left, right?" asked Chad. He knew that

Mordecai sometimes created temporary circles to prevent being followed.

"No, it was invisible, even to mages," Elaine informed him. "It would fade after a week or two. I was going to erase the circle on this end after we arrived, though, just to be safe." Her face went pale.

"And did you?" asked Chad urgently, but her expression had already answered the question. "Damn it all!" He started running for the river.

"Wait! I'll make us invisible!" shouted Elaine, chasing him.

Cyhan passed by her, his long legs outpacing hers. "He can smell us," he reminded her as he went by.

She was ten feet behind the knight when he reached the river's edge. Chad had already waded in, but he wasn't crossing. Instead, he was wading upstream. "Hurry up!" he yelled back at them.

Cyhan proceeded to follow, but Elaine hesitated, then began to follow them on the bank. The big knight leaned over and grabbed her wrist, pulling her into the muddy water.

"Why aren't we crossing?" she asked.

Chad wasn't paying attention, though. He was busy muttering to himself. "We made at least two hundred yards before he showed up. If we stay in the water for a half a mile and he doesn't catch sight of us…"

"Dragons fly," mentioned Cyhan.

"He's got to stay on the ground if he wants to track our scent," said the hunter. "Besides, if she makes us invisible, he can't spot us from the air."

The three of them gathered together and Elaine settled a three-layered veil of invisibility over them, shielding them from detection by sight, sound, or magesight. Wrapped in darkness, the water rushing over and around their legs felt colder than ever.

Cyhan took the lead. Being the largest and heaviest he was able to forge ahead through the water with relative ease while Elaine and Chad followed in his wake. Each of them had a hand on the big man's belt to make sure they didn't get separated. It was still a slow slog, however.

"Shouldn't we get under the water?" asked Elaine after a minute. "He can still smell us if we're only half under the water."

Chad's teeth were already chattering. "Y—yes, and n—no. If he's close enough and downwind of us he could, but we have enough of a lead that isn't likely to happen. Plus the wind is blowing from the north side of the river, the side he's on. Mainly we're tryin' to keep him from trackin' us. There's no scent trail over water."

"Oh, good," she replied. "I'm too cold to do that anyway."

"I prefer breathing air myself," said Cyhan drolly from the front. He was the only one not already shivering.

"Can't you warm us up?" asked Chad hopefully, directing his question to Elaine.

"Not with the water rushing past. As soon as I warmed it, it would be gone. Also, there's a kind of light emitted by objects, depending on their temperature. I don't know if it's true or not, but Gareth once told me he could see it. If we leave a stream of warm water behind us—well you get the picture," she explained.

"Freeze or get eaten," observed Sir Cyhan.

"I wish the weather was hotter," said Elaine.

"Wouldn't matter," returned Chad. "The Myrtle is fed by snow-melt from the Elentirs. It's fuckin' cold all year 'round."

With the rushing water and no ability to see, they had trouble gauging their progress, and they had no idea whether Gareth had come close to them. For all they knew, he might be right beside them on the river bank. Their only choice was to continue slowly making their way upstream.

"Next time, pick a city," said Chad out of the blue.

"T—then we wouldn't have the river," remarked Elaine.

"A few thousand other humans plus the usual sanitation problems in a city would more than make up for it. Scent trackin' is a lot harder than most realize, even for a bloodhound. By now we could have been sitting in a bar, havin' some hot mulled wine," explained the hunter.

"Not beer?" put in Cyhan.

"I'm too cold to think about beer," admitted Chad. "I'm pretty sure my balls have shriveled up to the size of peas by now."

Time passed, though whether it was a half an hour or a full hour they couldn't be sure, but eventually Chad and Elaine couldn't take the cold water any longer. Their muscles were cramping from the continual shivering. Elaine removed the sound shield and opened the light shield in one small section, allowing them to survey the riverbank, which appeared to be clear.

At that point, the river had a deep, well-defined edge, so Cyhan got out first and dragged his companions up and onto the bank, since their arms and legs weren't cooperating anymore. Once they were all ashore, they huddled together, and Elaine restored her veil.

The wind, which had seemed so pleasant before, was now a brutal knife cutting into their wet, shivering bodies. In spite of her previous warning, Elaine used some of her magic to warm the air around them, though it didn't seem to sink in. She was cold all the way to her bones.

"Take off the dress," suggested Chad, who was pulling off his jacket and boots. Though he couldn't see her in the darkness, he could feel her angry glare anyway. "That wool has probably soaked up fifty pounds of water."

She hesitated, and she grew yet more nervous when she felt Cyhan's skin brush up against her. He had already removed everything but his trousers. Being mostly undressed in a dark bubble with two old men wasn't really how she had imagined spending her afternoon. Reluctantly, she began to work her way out of the wool dress, which was so heavy it almost seemed made of lead. She had a lightweight linen shift on beneath it, which she knew would dry much more quickly.

Wrapping her arms around her knees, Elaine did her best not to come into contact with either of her companions. It wasn't that she didn't trust them, or at least Cyhan, but the entire situation made her uncomfortable.

In contrast, the two men struck up a meaningless conversation with each other, which seemed odd given Cyhan's usual verbal reticence, but after a while Elaine realized it was simply their way of dealing with their own awkwardness. While neither of them particularly minded her, the two men weren't used to being mostly bare-skinned and in such close proximity to each other.

Somehow that fact made her feel slightly better.

"Next time, a city would be nice," said Chad, repeating his statement from earlier. "Surencia, for example. I know an inn there that makes the best meat pies you ever tasted."

"Surencia smells," countered Elaine. "They don't have proper sewers. I don't know how they stand it."

"I heard they were building sewers," said Cyhan. "The World Road has been transporting ideas as well as trade goods."

Chad snickered. "That reminds me of somethin'. Last year, Gram and I were stuck in a root cellar in Halam. We were stuck in close quarters fer quite a while, an it was pretty dark just like this."

"Why would sewers make you think of that?" asked Elaine.

He shared the story with them, modifying it slightly. In his version, it was Gram who had been suffering stomach problems, rather than himself. "The smell was ungodly!"

They laughed, and then Elaine made a wistful observation. "Think this will ever be a fond memory like that?"

"I don't know that I'd call it a *fond* memory," said the hunter. "But it was funny." Then, after a moment's silence, he gagged. "Oh damn! Ya didn't have to take my tale as a challenge!"

Embarrassed, Cyhan answered, "It's never too late to make a new memory."

Then the smell struck Elaine and she pulled her hair around to cover her face. *Next time I go on some crazy mission, I'm going to insist that it's just women,* she thought sourly.

 CHAPTER 40

Mosquitos are a sure way to ruin any outing. Living in a mountain valley for most of my life, I had always thought of them as an annoyance related to forested areas, not the beach, but as evening fell, they descended on us with a furious bloodlust that forced me to reconsider my previous notions.

Unlike most of the bizarre animals I had encountered in the region that replaced Lancaster, these were just normal insects, but that was probably because mosquitos had already reached the pinnacle of evil. They couldn't get any worse.

"Is there anything you can do?" asked Rose.

There definitely was. I could erect a shield-like barrier that would allow air to pass but not small insects, something like a fine mesh. But that would take magic, and I was still conserving my energy. A simpler, yet infinitely more dangerous option would be to call on the void. Once, when I had been a shiggreth, I had discovered that my very presence killed everything near me, insects, plants, or anything else that got too close. It definitely wasn't a viable option with Rose present. It really wouldn't have been a wise option even if I were alone, but I might have made an exception for mosquitos.

Eventually we settled on simply rolling ourselves into the blanket and trying to keep our heads covered with it. As romantic as that sounds, it wasn't. With the cloth over our heads, I began to feel as though I was being smothered. Not to mention that caused my feet to stick out the other end. Whether the mosquitos knew that or not, my imagination made me think they were all over my toes.

At some point, our insect oppressors found somewhere else to be, and our little world grew peaceful. The stars were brilliant overhead, and the ocean filled the air with a constant noise that soothed my nerves. The air was cool enough that we weren't sweating. Rose made a pillow out of my arm and we slept.

We awoke some hours later, before dawn, when I discovered that someone had amputated my arm during the night. After sitting up, it became apparent that my arm was still there, but it was completely nonresponsive. As an additional bonus, I was covered in small bites. *Are there fleas on the beach, or did the mosquitos sneak into the blanket with us?* I wondered.

While I waited on my arm to return to active service, I realized my aythar had partially recovered. I wasn't entirely back to normal, but I didn't need to worry about conserving energy as much now. Generally, my natural rate of replenishment is faster than what I use in all but the most stressful of situations.

I was also hungry.

Rose sat close by, swaddled in the blanket. I turned to her and asked, "Are you hungry?"

She nodded. "Unless you're referring to those moldy biscuits."

Glancing around, I decided the ocean was probably the easiest and safest route. Standing up, I unbuckled my belt, and then, before dropping my makeshift skirt, I warned Rose, "You might want to look away."

True to form, she simply smirked, keeping her eyes on my back. *Women,* I thought. *If I did that, they'd call me a pervert.* I didn't really mind though. Dropping the dress, I gave her a quick shake and then ran toward the water.

I was a passable swimmer, but not great. I quickly discovered that flying and swimming are not too dissimilar. Slipping beneath the waves, I created a shield around myself and using my aythar to grip the brine closest to me, I shot forward through the water. It was a marvelously refreshing experience. I felt as though I had been reborn as a fish.

I had to surface regularly to breathe, but my speed was such that I could cover long distances between breaths, and my magesight was easily able to pick up a wide variety of life around me. Not having lived near a seaside, there were a lot of things that I wasn't sure if we could eat, so I decided to stick to fish.

There were small sharks and large rays, but I didn't know much about eating those. There were also numerous small fish, but I didn't want to have to spend time cleaning more than one, so I took my time and finally located a large silvery fellow that was too beautiful to not be edible.

My prey was over two feet long and showed no fear as I glided up beside him. He was probably surprised when I sent a precise bolt of force through him and pulled him to me. Fish in hand, I shot upward, and we emerged from the water. Then I flew back to Rose and proudly displayed my catch. "Dinner is served, madam!"

She smiled, then smirked, and I remembered I was naked. I dropped the fish and hastily redressed myself. *Heh, redressed,* I thought, then wondered if women made that pun mentally to themselves whenever they put clothes on. *Probably not,* I decided, making a mental note to ask Penny later. She hated puns, so I saved them up to torment her.

The thought brought another stab of pain, but I did my best to ignore it and set about cleaning the fish I had caught. I quickly learned that enchanted blades are awful for scaling a fish. They're simply too sharp. My knife kept slicing through the skin rather than scraping the scales off. Eventually I was forced to use the back of the knife instead, which wasn't ideal, but worked.

Focused on my task, I lost track of what Rose was doing. Realizing she was gone, I felt a moment of panic before I spotted her with my magesight. She was already returning, a load of deadwood in her arms.

"Don't wander off," I told her, my tone perhaps a bit too harsh.

"I didn't go far..."

"This place is dangerous, Rose. There could be all sorts of predators hiding nearby," I said, reprimanding her.

She lifted one brow. "You'd have noticed them with your magical senses. The wood was just over there, near the tree line."

"We didn't need wood. I can cook it without," I insisted. "Some of the predators here are very hard for me to spot. There's burrowing spiders that look almost like rocks. I missed them last time, when Penny..."

Her face softened. "Her arm?"

"No, that was bears," I said at last, but I realized my fears were all mixed together. Angry and confused simultaneously, I just glared at Rose.

The indomitable Rose Thornbear studied me for a moment, then conceded, "I'll be more careful in the future."

I began arranging the wood in a small pile. In spite of my fears, I had to admit it was a good idea. The smoke would make the fish taste better than if I simply heated the flesh to cook it. "I'm sorry I snapped at you," I apologized.

There was a strange smile on her face when she replied, "It's alright. I would have done the same if you wandered away. I can't hold you to a higher standard than myself, so fair's fair."

Using my magic to set the wood aflame, I soon had a blaze going, though I would still have to wait a while for it to burn down a little before I put the fish over it. I made myself busy trimming one of the spindly limbs into a spit. "We make an odd pair," I said as I worked.

"People are strange overall," said Rose. "We aren't that different from everyone else," she opined, then got to her feet and walked toward the surf. "I'm covered in sand. I think I'll take a quick dip while you cook." Then she removed the top of what had once been her dress and began pulling the linen shift over her head. "Feel free to watch."

My cheeks grew hot and I looked away, causing her to laugh. "Fair's fair," added Rose, before she began a long, languorous stroll into the water. I knew this not purely because of my magesight, but because I turned to watch her, once I knew she was no longer looking at me. Even with permission, I felt rather wicked for doing so, as though I was a boy trying to steal a pie, instead of a man of well over forty years.

Some things never change.

Later, after she had dried off and we were eating our fish, she brought up something that had been much on my mind. "You haven't asked me about Tyrion," she said.

My face didn't change. "It's none of my business."

Her expression turned to one of curiosity, as though she had found something interesting to study. "Really?"

"Really," I affirmed. "I don't have the right to judge you, Rose. If anything, I should be thanking you. You stuck with me despite everything." My words were true on one level, and I certainly knew I owed her a debt, but deeper down, thinking about the things she had been forced to do made my stomach churn.

"Such a noble sentiment," observed Rose. "I've always admired that about you. Most men would tie themselves in knots with jealousy."

As a matter of fact, my stomach was already in knots, and her words weren't helping. "Let's not talk about it," I responded. "I admire your tenacity. We can leave it there."

She sighed. "Very well. Let's talk about something else. Was it this easy for you to be noble after Dorian and Penny were freed from captivity?"

Many years before, Penny and Dorian had been captured by the shiggreth and used as leverage against me. They were kept for some time, chained up, naked, and probably very cold. Afterward I had told Penny that whatever had happened, I didn't blame her. People are people after all, and desperate situations make everyone long for comfort, but inwardly it had secretly bothered me. Rose's tone was innocent, but the topic was a sensitive one for me, something she had to know if she was bringing it up now.

I had never mentioned it to Rose, and Penny and I had never discussed it after my blanket statement of forgiveness. *Dorian told her,* I was sure. *He was always too honest to keep a secret, even if it hurt someone to tell*

444

it. "I never blamed Penny," I answered at last. "Human beings are frail, and they were alone, thinking they might be killed at any moment."

"But it bothered you anyway, didn't it?" Rose probed.

I glanced at her, then back at the fire. "A little, but I put it aside. What they suffered was far worse. They didn't deserve to return to pettiness on my end."

Rose nodded. "That's good to hear. That's what I told Penny as well."

My head jerked up. "What? You talked to her about it?"

"Mm hmm," answered Rose. "A few months afterward. Dorian confessed as soon as we were alone, in great detail. He never had much sense in that regard. I think I would have rather he left it unsaid, as Penny did. I waited to talk to Penny, to give her some time to recover."

Astonished, I gaped at her. "So, you talked about it with Dorian, and with Penny? I was the only one left out of the conversation?"

"I always thought you were the smartest one of us all, at least in that instance. I forgave Dorian, but I eventually felt the need to clear the air between Penny and myself," said Rose. "I think she felt relieved, but despite me telling her that all was forgiven, it took me some time to truly get past it."

I laughed at the irony. "If only Dorian had been able to keep his mouth shut. He could have saved you that bit of anxiety. Still, it wasn't that bad, was it?"

Rose grimaced. "My husband was painfully honest." Then she held up three fingers.

Until that moment, I had never been certain. I hadn't known for sure that *anything* really happened, and I had carefully buried my questions on the matter. "Three times?" I blurted out.

She nodded. "If she hadn't already been pregnant, you might have wound up raising Gram's half-brother."

For a moment, I was stunned, but then I let the feeling slide away. It didn't change anything. I still didn't blame either of them, and it was in the distant past anyway. But one of the principals involved was sitting right across from me. "Why did you talk to everyone else, except me?"

"That's simple, Mordecai. Think about it. For me to talk about it with Dorian, or Penny, that's one thing, but discussing it with you was never an option."

I frowned, still not understanding.

Rose went on, "If the two spouses meet and discuss the perceived wrongs against them, what does that lead to?"

"Ahhh," I said. "Now I see your point."

"I was angry, but I wasn't ready to ruin my marriage," said Rose.

"For some reason, I always thought you'd deal with it better than I did," I admitted. "You've always had such composure."

Rose laughed lightly. "You didn't have Dorian apologizing to you every day for weeks on end, or admitting to his deeds in great, unnecessary detail. It's a miracle I didn't kill him."

I winced. "Ouch. He really was a little dense." We didn't talk for a few minutes, enjoying the sound of the waves. For some reason our strange conversation made me feel as though a small weight had been lifted from me. "I wish we could have them back, though," I said finally.

"Me too," Rose replied wistfully.

"That day, when I was in the dungeon. You told me I wasn't ready."

Rose nodded.

"How will I know? How long did it take you?" I asked.

"I don't know," said Rose honestly. "Even after all these years I'm still not sure. I think I might be now, but I've never tested the waters."

Confused, I looked over at her. "But what about…?"

"So it does bother you. Not so noble after all, are you?" she said with a malicious grin.

I frowned. "It does bother me a little, but as I said before, I can't judge. Whatever you did, with Tyrion, or the jailor, or that other fellow—you did it for me. If anything, I'm ashamed for putting myself in such a situation. If I had been in your place, I would have done anything necessary to help you, or any of my other family. It's noble really, if you think—"

She held up one hand. "Wait. What other fellow? You didn't have a chance to talk to Karen."

So it was true. "The man in your room that day, when I came by to talk." *Actually, now that I think about it, that was before I was locked up. Had he been an actual lover, rather than someone she had had to…?*

Rose began to laugh, not her usual lady-like laugh either. It was a deep belly laugh, punctuated by odd, high-pitched nasal sounds. Eventually, she managed to reply, "You honestly thought I slept with *Manfred*? And the jailor? You must really think poorly of my taste in men!"

Off-balance and confused, I resorted to humor. "Well, you seem to fancy me, so you're obviously not all there."

That only earned me one of her polite laughs, then she grew serious. "I didn't sleep with any of them. I managed to find other solutions, though honestly, if it had been necessary to save you, I would have."

A sense of relief washed over me, followed by a feeling of guilt. It shouldn't have mattered to me, either way. Sometimes being noble is hard work. There was still one nagging doubt, though. "Not even Tyrion?"

Rose's eyes glittered fiercely. "Oh, there was no sleeping where that man was concerned. He was far too primal, too animalistic, to be easily satisfied. He kept me fully engaged. I don't regret him at all. In fact, it's something of a shame you killed him."

"A simple 'yes' would have been enough," I said, jealous and angry. "If you liked him so much, you didn't need to bother saving me."

She moved over to where I sat, then patted my cheek, answering with absolute sincerity, "Oh, a brute is handy for satisfying the passions of the flesh, Mordecai, but you're *nicer*." It was several seconds before her façade crumbled and she began to laugh again.

It was then that I realized she had been putting me on. "That was mean," I said, feeling foolish.

"Would you like to know what really happened?" she asked.

At that point, I wasn't sure. "I don't know. Do I? Think about Dorian before you decide."

She smiled. "You definitely want to know." Then she began describing what she had been through over the past week, leaving nothing to spare.

Some of it made me angry, particularly with Tyrion, but when I learned how she had tricked him, I couldn't help but feel both glad and a little sorry for him. He had felt genuinely betrayed at the end. I would have still blown him up, though. Overall, I felt terrible about the stress she had been under and amazed at how she had dealt with it all. Manfred's murder was a shock, and I could tell that out of all of it, that had been what bothered her the most.

The wind was blowing hard by the time she finished, and the sky over the ocean was dark with heavy, ominous clouds. A storm was coming. Leaning back on my elbows, I looked over at her. "And here we are. Outlaws. I'm wanted for murder, and half my friends want to arrest me, while the other half have become accomplices to keep me free. I almost wish we could just stay here. The seaside is a lot nicer than the real world."

Rose was studying the horizon. "I don't know. I think we're about to get wet."

"Let me show you some magic," I offered, then I stretched out fully. Opening my mind, I stretched, expanding my sense of self to encompass the sand beneath and around me. Unlike normal wizardry, this cost me no aythar, just a little of my humanity, which hopefully would return. The sand boiled around me, then began to rise, climbing upward to form thick walls that supported a thin roof of fused silica. I left the structure open in the front and back, so the wind would be able to pass through it, but it would keep the rain off.

Finished with my project, I began to contract once more. And as my mind became more human again, I thought of Penny. *She would have loved this.* Then the world went black.

 # CHAPTER 41

Dawn found Elaine cold, stiff, and generally displeased with life. After they had finished drying off and getting warm the day before, they had started hiking. Chad had thought it unlikely that Gareth would pick up their trail by then, so they had stayed in the forest, which was good, since none of them had the energy left to face the cold water again.

They had walked far into the night, using a veil to hide them from magesight. The trees already protected them pretty well from aerial view if a certain dragon happened to be searching for them from the air.

Since there were three of them and only one blanket, Chad had insisted they spread it out and sleep on top of it. His reasoning had been that the ground would sap their body heat faster than the modestly cool breeze. Whether that was true or not, Elaine couldn't tell, but her body felt bruised from her continual shivering during the night.

The two men had slept back to back, but she had refused to participate. Their pungent time while drying after the river had been more than enough bonding for her tastes.

She regretted it now, though. Keeping a veil up while sleeping was impossible, so she hadn't been able to use magic to warm herself either.

It was a new day, though one with no breakfast. A fact Chad felt no shame in reminding her of at every opportunity.

"Can't you just catch something?" she asked him at last, tired of his complaining.

"Not without fuckin' arrows, I can't!" he swore.

"We could set snares," suggested Cyhan peaceably.

"An' sit on our asses for a day waitin'," replied the hunter. "No thanks. The sooner we're gone from here, the better." Then he looked at Elaine. "Since you think it's safe to use a little magic now, just kill the first thing you see. Rabbit, squirrel, I don't care."

He marched onward, and Elaine glared daggers at his back. She didn't want to kill anything, certainly nothing as cute as a rabbit. She had eaten them many times, sure, but she hadn't had to kill them. *I'm not a farm girl,* she thought bitterly. *Next he'll be asking me to wring chickens' necks.*

Not that they were likely to see a chicken, though. If they did she might very well attempt to kill one. Chickens seemed less repugnant to kill than rabbits. Objectively, she knew her logic didn't make sense, but she didn't feel like examining it. *Certainly not on his account, anyway!*

As they walked, she noticed Chad bending over to pick something green. The hunter offered it to Cyhan, but the big man held up one hand, declining his offer.

Elaine watched him chew for a moment before finally asking, "What's that?"

"Sheep sorrel," replied the woodsman. "You don't want any."

"I might," she retorted. "Let me try some."

He handed her a handful of green leaves. "It won't fill yer belly, but it's better than nothin'."

Tentatively, she put a leaf in her mouth and chewed. The flavor was shockingly sour, so much so that she spit the leaf out and dropped the rest.

Chad snickered, leaning over to reclaim the fallen leaves. "That's my breakfast. Next time just hand 'em back."

"You can't really live on those, can you?" she asked.

"Probably not," said Chad. "Even if ya could, who would want to? At best they just help keep my stomach from growlin' too much."

"Maybe we should try the snares Cyhan mentioned," she put in.

"I'd rather wait until we get to the next town. It'd be quicker," replied the hunter.

Elaine frowned. Something didn't add up. "Next town? Did we pass one already?"

Cyhan spoke up, "A couple of hours ago."

"Why didn't we stop?"

Chad turned on her. "Since you're so keen on questions, I'll tell ya. If you was a pissed-off archmage, huntin' fugitives along the river, where would you look after ya gave up trackin' 'em?"

"Oh."

"Not only that," continued Chad. "He prob'ly went home and had a nice nap last night, while the Royal Guard rode out and took up positions in every village within ten miles or more."

"Then why are we following the river? We want to go north, don't we?" asked Elaine.

"We'll die of thirst if we go north with no water. I know ya said you can boil water and all that, but without something to carry it with us, we won't find any until we cross the northern branch of the Myrtle River, an' who knows how long after that," he explained.

Every time Elaine thought perhaps their situation might improve, Chad came along and burst her bubble.

The hunter went on, "So we follow the river, 'cuz that's where the villages are. And once we get a pot and some skins, we can carry water with us. Then we can think about headin' north."

"Are you going to steal them?"

He gave her a sidelong look. "Ya really have a high opinion of me, don't ya?" Then he showed her his purse. "I think I can trade some o' these shiny coins fer what we need. Assumin' the guards aren't there waitin' on us."

Then he smiled wickedly. "If there are guards, *you* can sneak in an' steal what we need. Ain't that what *Prathion* means? Wizard sneak-thief?"

"It's a shame we can't just make a circle and go back to the Count's home," said Cyhan suddenly.

They all understood why that was a bad idea, but Chad felt the need to vocalize it anyway. "Yeah, Moira's probably up to her tits in guards an' questions by now."

"Do you have to be so vulgar?" snapped Elaine.

Chad and Cyhan both began laughing, then Cyhan put in, "She has a point."

The hunter looked at the big man in surprise, but Sir Cyhan wasn't done. "You're a bad man." He grinned as he said it.

"You! Of all the people in the world, you're gonna take her side? You're worse than me! You were a damned assassin before you took service with King Edward," exclaimed Chad.

Cyhan smiled faintly. "You've killed more men than I have."

Elaine watched with interest as the two of them argued. That last remark surprised her. She had always assumed the knight was the more dangerous of the two. She still thought he was, but if so…

"In wars!" bit back the hunter. "It was all honest killin'—well, most of it."

"Honest is face-to-face, not from fifty yards away," opined Sir Cyhan.

"What about in the dark, with a dagger?" asked Chad. "Or when they're sleepin'?"

"You've done as much," accused Cyhan.

Elaine stared at the two of them, then asked, "One of you was an assassin?"

Cyhan and Chad each pointed at the other, answering in unison, "He was." Then they both started laughing.

"Let's go," said Chad after a moment. "We'll never get anywhere if we stand around jackin' our jaws all day."

Elaine followed, but she kept a little extra distance. She had known the two men since her teen years, but she had always known them as heroes, even if Chad's reputation was a little more mixed. Now she was beginning to doubt her assumptions.

***

Moira was on her knees, staring at the floor. In front of her stood Ariadne, Queen of Lothion. With the Queen was a host of soldiers, though some of them were actually krytek. Their progenitor and leader, Tyrion, was also with the Queen. None of them seemed very happy.

"Where is he?" asked the Queen once again.

"I don't know," said Moira truthfully.

"Lies!" shouted Tyrion. "You helped plan this, didn't you? Admit it!"

Moira kept her tone meek. "No, Your Grace, I knew nothing of it. My father kept me in the dark. I haven't spoken with him since before he was arrested." Humphrey whined beside her. The young dog didn't understand what was happening, but he knew something was wrong.

"Shut that dog up!" yelled Tyrion.

Moira's head came up, a defiant look in her eyes, but Ariadne spoke before she lost her temper. "Leave the dog out of it, Tyrion. He's surely innocent if anyone is in this sordid mess."

Something changed in Tyrion's face, and he nodded. Then he bent down and stroked Humphrey's head. "Forgive me, my Queen. My anger has been out of control lately." He turned his head to look at Moira. "If you're lying, I'll see you strung up beside your father."

"I believe her," said the Queen suddenly. "I know my cousin. Killing a bastard like my late-husband is just like him, but he wouldn't want to drag his family into this with him. That's why he kept Conall and the others out of it."

Tyrion growled, "Not that bitch, Rose Thornbear, though. He had no qualms about turning his slut loose to handle his problems."

"Rose isn't like that," began Moira.

Ariadne interrupted, "Mind your tongue, Lord Illeniel."

Standing back up, Tyrion nodded. "Very well. I agree. The girl is probably innocent, but it matters little. You should lock her up, Your Majesty."

"If she has done nothing, I couldn't conscience such a thing," said Ariadne.

Tyrion strode across the room, stopping at the mantle, where he idly picked up a small porcelain cup, one of Penny's many knick-knacks. "Innocence isn't the point, my Queen. If you wish to catch my descendant, we need to bait the trap. Lock his daughter up and he'll be forced to come to us."

Ariadne glanced to either side of herself, then issued a sharp order to the guards and krytek, "Leave us." Once they were gone she said softly, "You make the mistake of thinking I *want* to apprehend my cousin. He may have broken the law, but he did a service to all of us by ridding the world of that man. My only goal is to prevent a civil war. Putting chains on Moira will only serve to create more conflict. As long as Mordecai stays well beyond my reach, the lords will have no cause for complaint."

"He didn't kill him," said Moira.

"How would you know?" said Tyrion. "Every child wants to believe their father is a saint."

"I looked into Millie's mind, before the trial," said Moira evenly. "She didn't believe he killed the Prince, no matter what she said on the stand."

The Queen looked thoughtful. "That may be. Rose made an excellent case for one of the servants being the true killer, and she might have lied to protect him. Unfortunately, the judge ruled against your father, Moira. As Queen, I have to serve as the enforcer of Lothion's justice."

"It's not justice to execute an innocent man," put in Moira.

"Then make sure I do not find your father, for I will have no choice," said Ariadne, her voice sad.

Tyrion leaned in close, until his nose was almost against Moira's. "Our Queen is soft on your father, but I fully intend to ensure that your father's punishment is carried out. Two men died during his escape, though the thing that has really has lit a fire in my heart, was the attempt on my own life."

"Tyrion!" warned Ariadne.

But he ignored her. Straightening up, he added, "That goes for Rose Thornbear as well. Once I find them, I'll make certain their insides are outside."

"I won't warn you again," said the Queen.

Tyrion looked back at her, then assumed a look of innocence. "Your Majesty has issued an order for their immediate execution. I merely intend to do my duty." Then he returned his attention to Moira. "By the way, Her Majesty has also issued a proclamation stripping both your father and Rose Thornbear of all titles, land, and privileges. Make sure to pass that along to your dear father when you see him next."

Ariadne spoke hurriedly, her tone one of reassurance, "I will pass the title to Conall."

"What of my older brother, Matthew?" asked Moira.

The Queen frowned. "Given his absence, as well as Irene's absence, they are under suspicion of aiding and abetting your father's escape. I cannot pass the title to either of them. Your younger brother is the only one whose loyalty is still unquestioned."

Tyrion sneered. "Your brother and sister must present themselves before the Queen within a week to make an accounting of themselves. Otherwise they will be declared outlaws as well."

Moira remained on her knees until they had left, but she was inwardly fuming. The krytek and guards remained, ostensibly to wait in case her father returned, but within a quarter of an hour she had picked up enough from their minds to know their second purpose.

They were searching for the dragon eggs.

Returning to her bedroom, Moira shut the door, then checked to make sure the privacy ward on her room was secure. Retrieving her stylus and her notes on teleport circles, she made a new one that lead to the transfer house at Castle Cameron.

She couldn't go herself, of course. Her absence would be noticed, but she had an easy solution for that problem. Passing a large portion of her aythar to her alter ego, she and Myra separated.

Moira and her spell-twin stood facing each other for several moments. Then Myra stepped into the circle and was gone. Moira settled onto her bed to wait, absently scratching Humphrey's ears.

In the yard of the new and still vacant Castle Cameron, Myra went to the makeshift control chamber that had been set up in a temporary building by the gatehouse. Once there, she went inside and activated the shield that would seal the castle off. Washbrook she left open. The people there would need their freedom, but the castle, and more importantly, the Ironheart Chamber beneath it, would remain beyond the Queen's reach.

Myra created a new teleport circle within the control room itself, then went back to the transfer house and spent several minutes obliterating the circles there. When she was done, there was only one way left to enter the castle grounds. The circle she had just created, and only she knew its key.

Satisfied, she returned to Moira's room. As soon as she was back, the two of them erased the keys from the circle on the floor and added new ones. Then she teleported to the dragon cave hidden in the mountains above and behind Castle Cameron.

Myra destroyed the circle there and created a new one leading to the castle yard, then began carefully transporting the dragon eggs there. It took a multitude of trips, since each egg was nearly a foot in diameter, but once she had finished, she levitated them and went into the newly created castle.

The heat would have been nigh unto unbearable for a normal human, but for Myra it wasn't a concern. She followed the corridors until she found the stairs down and began descending into the depths. Myra passed through storage rooms and cellars, until she found the secret entrance to the stairs that led even farther down, to the Ironheart Chamber itself. Once there, she stored the eggs inside and sealed the chamber, locking the door enchantment.

Even if Tyrion found the chamber, he would be unable to open it without the code, and if he tried to force his way in, by damaging the enchantment itself, the Ironheart Chamber would explode, releasing the stored power that had once belonged to Karenth, the former god of justice. Myra didn't think even Tyrion would foolish enough to try that. There was enough power stored within the chamber to destroy everything for miles in every direction.

Worse, if the eggs themselves were destroyed, they would release their aythar as well, and since each egg contained nearly as much as the Ironheart Chamber— the results would likely be catastrophic. It might even be worse than the event that created the Gulf of Garulon, when the Dark God Balinthor had been destroyed.

"Desperate measures for desperate times," muttered Myra.

Her tasks complete, she went back above ground and used her circle to return again to Moira's room. Then they completely erased the circle. The only way to enter Castle

Cameron now would be to create a new circle, and that could only be done with knowledge of the proper key.

Myra merged with her creator and then asked, *Do you want to know the key?*

No, answered Moira. *Keep it to yourself. They don't know about you. If I don't know it, I can't reveal it, even if they get desperate and try something stupid. In the worst case, I'll have you escape and give it to Father.*

Myra thought the logic sound, but it made her uncomfortable. Moira was a Centyr mage, so getting the information from her mind without consent would be impossible, which meant that 'something stupid' could only be old-fashioned torture. She wasn't sure she could stomach escaping and leaving her sister to suffer such a fate alone.

"I'm hungry," said Moira suddenly. "I think I'll go cook something."

You aren't actually hungry, said Myra to her mentally.

Moira smiled. *It's time to go to work. There are at least ten krytek here. It will take time to subvert them all without alerting them to what I'm doing.*

I don't think that's wise, cautioned Myra.

Don't worry, replied Moira. *I'll go slow. I have nothing but time. Give me a week and they'll be eating out of my hand.*

 # CHAPTER 42

Rose watched in fascination as the house of sand and what appeared to be glass climbed upward, growing as if of its own accord. It happened over a span of a few minutes and then came to a halt, finished. When she turned her eyes back on Mordecai, her fascination turned to shock.

Lying on the sand in his place was a woman, and though the night was dark, the fire provided enough light to recognize her by her features. It was a face she knew well—that of Penelope Illeniel.

"Penny?" asked Rose, when her shock had faded enough for her mouth to begin working again.

The woman sat up slowly, seeming somewhat dazed as she stared back at Rose.

"Is that really you?" asked Rose, feeling her heart begin to move as emotions flooded through her.

"How long has it been?" asked Penny.

Rose stared at her, dumbfounded, before finally responding, "Since what?"

"Since I died."

Standing up, Rose began to back away. "Who are you?"

Penny grimaced. "That's a tough question. Technically, I'm Mordecai, I suppose, but I prefer to think of myself as Penny, at least for now."

Rose sat down, though it was nearly a fall. It felt as though the very world had shifted beneath her feet. After a few seconds, she gave some thought for her guest.

Penny was still clad in the bottom half of her dress, the one Mordecai had been wearing. Consequently, she was naked from the waist up. Gathering up the blanket, Rose took it to her friend and settled it around her shoulders. Then she asked, "How is this possible?"

"It's complicated," said Penny. "First, how long have I been dead?"

"But you aren't," said Rose.

Her friend's eyes grew sad. "Don't get your hopes up, Rose. I'm about as dead as it gets. This is just sort of a little break from it. How long?"

"Four months."

"How are the children?"

"Which ones?" said Rose, still struggling to process what was happening.

Penny smiled. "All of them, yours and mine. They're well?"

Rose nodded. "As far as I know. We've had some excitement of late. Gram, Matthew, and Irene are in another world, where Lancaster is. Actually, I think it's this world, but we haven't found it yet."

"They found Roland? What about Moira?" Penny's questions were endless, and Rose spent the next half hour catching her up on recent events. The story of Mordecai's arrest and capture upset Penny quite a bit, but Rose did her best to explain everything as well as she could, though she left out some of the more intimate moments she and Mordecai had been through.

Penny studied her while she spoke, and when Rose finally came to a finish, Penny asked her, "You left out some things, didn't you?"

Rose looked away, staring into the fire. "It's been rough."

464

Getting up, Penny moved over beside her friend and offered to share the blanket. "You're on a beach wearing half a dress and I'm in the other half. I know you shortened the story. You must have been through some terrible things."

Rose simply nodded, not trusting herself to reply.

"Thank you," said Penny, genuinely grateful. "Being dead isn't so bad, not as long as I know you're still here to look after them."

That did it. Overwhelmed, Rose felt her eyes begin to brim with tears. "You shouldn't thank me. I don't deserve it."

Putting one arm over her friend's shoulder, Penny hugged her. "Don't be so hard on yourself. Your standards were always impossibly high. Sometimes it made me feel like I would never be good enough to be worthy of a friend like you."

Helpless to stop herself, Rose began to cry uncontrollably while Penny tried to comfort her. Penny seemed genuinely confused and worried, which only made things worse. "What's wrong?" she asked.

Rose was only able to choke out a few words, "You don't understand."

But then she did. Penny's eyes widened slightly and she withdrew her arm. "Is it Mordecai?"

Rose couldn't answer, or even look into her friend's eyes.

Taking a deep breath, Penny seemed to steel herself, then said, "I know you love him. You always have."

Rose looked at her then, but her vision was so blurry that she could barely make out Penny's features.

Penny continued, "And I know he feels deeply for you too. That's part of what's kept us all together over the years. It's only natural, with me gone." Her voice was calm, but she couldn't completely hide her own pain as she made the pronouncement. "How far have things—progressed?"

"Not much," said Rose, her voice numb. "But we've talked about it. He's not ready to move on yet."

"I would think not," said Penny. "It's only been four months. I waited a year."

That didn't help Rose's guilt at all. "But he came back for you. And you're not really dead, Penny. This changes everything."

"Not really," said Penny sadly.

"It does," insisted Rose. "And I feel terrible now."

Penny squinted at her. "You said all you've done is talk."

"There have been some harrowing moments," said Rose. "And when he was in that awful cell, we got closer than is proper."

"Have you kissed him?"

"No," said Rose truthfully. "And I won't, now. I feel like the worst friend possible."

Penny chewed her lip for a moment, torn between conflicting emotions. "That won't do, Rose. I don't want him to wind up like you."

Confused again, Rose glanced up. "What does that mean?"

"You spent ages suffering after Dorian died. I don't want that for him," said Penny.

"But you aren't dead!" responded Rose.

Penny shook her head. "I am. I'm just sort of borrowing his body for the moment."

"You really need to explain that," replied Rose. "You make it sound as though you're possessing him."

Penny nodded. "That's a fair description of it. When I was dying, he tried to save me. To do so, he used that strange power of his to *become* me, so he could heal my body. But there was something he couldn't fix, and that was my aystrylin. That's what the wizards call the wellspring of life. Where their magic comes from, and what keeps people alive."

"I remember," said Rose.

"Anyway, mine was almost gone, and while he was me, or I was him…" Penny stopped. "It's really confusing. I don't even know what pronouns to use." She took a breath. "While I was in control of whatever we were, I took what was left of my aystrylin and wrapped it around his. My body died, but that little piece of me is still there, around his heart, so to speak."

"Did it hurt?" asked Rose. "Why did you do it?"

"It hurt like nothing I can remember when I did it," admitted Penny. "Worse than childbirth. I had a reason, but if I'm being honest, I think I had selfish reasons as well."

"You didn't want to leave him."

Penny nodded, her eyes glistening. "But the reason I told myself was because he was broken inside. There were cracks in his aystrylin. He never truly recovered from his time as a shiggreth. There's something left, a sort of evil that is clinging to his soul. In some ways it's made him stronger. His aystrylin is huge. According to his memories, it's much larger now than it was before, when he was younger. I think the lives he stole have caused it to grow. If he keeps doing it, he might live forever."

Rose sensed a qualifier. "But?"

"But it's also killing him. Maybe not in the sense that he could die, but it's killing his true self. I think if he draws on that dark power, it gets stronger too. If it goes far enough, all that will be left is a shell, something evil wearing his skin and bearing his memories and knowledge, but it won't be him."

"And what you did fixed it?" asked Rose, horrified.

Penny shook her head. "I think I made it better, but the seed of corruption is still lodged within him. I'm not sure it's possible to get rid of it completely. Essentially, I turned what was left of me into a bandage, but if he uses it again, it will eventually tear him apart, and me with him." As if to punctuate her remark, Penny winced, putting her hand over her chest as though she felt a sudden pain.

"What's wrong?" asked Rose.

"I'm running out of time," said Penny. "This has happened a couple of times before. Each time, it starts to hurt after a while. Eventually I get too tired and fall asleep. I guess he wakes up afterward, wondering what happened."

Rose caught her hand. "Tell me what to do."

Lifting her chin, Penny tried to look earnest. "Take care of him. Don't hate yourself because of me. He needs you. My children need you. I need you, Rose."

"You can't honestly feel that way," said Rose, surprised. "It isn't fair. You must hate this, or hate me, at least."

"No!" protested Penny, but then she sighed. "I'll be honest. I do hate it. The first time I came back unexpectedly, it seemed like a blessing. I thought to myself, maybe I'll have the chance to see my children finish growing up, even if it's just a glimpse now and then. But now I wonder if it's just a way to torment myself."

"It could be a good thing," said Rose, hopeful. "I won't interfere. Now that I know what's happening—"

"Rose!" snapped Penny. "Don't make me order you. It's hard enough handing him over. Don't make me tell you to do it. Be happy if you can."

"But…"

"Listen. After Dorian died, I watched you. We tried to help, Mort and I both, but I know it was hard on you. Raising your two children with no father was a terrible strain on you," said Penny.

"I couldn't have done it without your help, Penny, and Mordecai was almost like a father to Gram."

Penny nodded. "Exactly. My children, Conall, and especially Irene, they still need a mother, and if any woman is going to step into my shoes and take on that job, I want it to be you. Do you understand?"

"I would do that anyway, Penny," insisted Rose. "I don't have to marry your husband to take care of them."

"Don't argue with me," said Penny stubbornly. "There aren't many women who could handle my stray dog of a husband, and I doubt I would like any of the others if I met them. Don't do what you've been doing since Dorian died. If someone else snuck in and stole him out from under you, I wouldn't forgive you."

"This is insane," replied Rose.

"Think of it this way," said Penny. "I don't know how long it will be before he messes up and summons me out of my bottle again, but I really don't want to wake up in his bed one night and find a stranger there."

Rose frowned. "That's terrible. I'd die of shame."

"No, you won't," insisted Penny. "We'll have a slumber party and you can tell me what's happening with our children."

"What's it like?" asked Rose. "Can you feel things, or hear?"

"No," said Penny. "It's like falling asleep. I close my eyes and everything disappears. I don't think I even dream. That's why I had to ask you what's been going on."

"Does he know?"

Penny seemed surprised. "He hasn't said anything? No, I guess not, since you were so shocked. I left him a note."

Rose remembered then the moment when she had seen Mordecai suspiciously tucking a letter into his jacket. "What did it say?"

Penny's face took on a look of chagrin. "I don't remember the exact wording, but it was something along the lines of, 'mess up again and you'll regret it.' I shouldn't have written it."

"You could have told him how you feel," suggested Rose.

"I did that before I died," said Penny. "And he already knows how I feel. What would it do to him if I started leaving love letters lying around? It would destroy him."

"But he already knows, since you left one letter," Rose reminded her.

"Let him pretend to ignorance," replied Penny. "And if he gives you trouble, tell me and next time I'll leave him a note telling him he'd better straighten up."

Rose began shaking her head again. "I don't think I can do this."

"You have to," said Penny insistently, then her eyes lit up. "I know. We'll make some rules. As long as you follow them you won't have to feel guilty about it."

"What sort of rules?"

"Number one, you can't marry him until a full year has passed," started Penny.

Rose glared. "I wouldn't have done that, regardless!"

"Says the hussy who started getting friendly with my husband less than four months after I died," Penny shot back.

Mortified, Rose put her hands over her face.

"It was a joke!" said Penny quickly. "Mostly. Alright, rule two, no kissing him."

Rose peeked between her fingers. "Ever?"

"Ever," agreed Penny, giving a firm nod of her head.

"That's not fair either," said Rose.

Penny smiled. "That's better. Show some spine."

"How about until the year is up?" suggested Rose.

"That won't do," said Penny. "You've already started *something*. He'll think you hate him if you wait that long. We don't want him wandering off. Let's say six months, so two months from now."

Rose nodded. "What else?"

"You have to take care of our children."

"I was going to do that no matter what," said Rose.

"And I don't want to know anything about the romantic end of things. If we get to talk again, just pretend you're friends who live together," said Penny. Her eyes were watering again.

"You can't be alright with this, Penny," said Rose. "It's too much."

"I'm not!" said Penny, choking out the words. "But we don't have a choice, do we? So you do this for me, and leave out the details I don't want to hear. Even if you break our rules, don't tell me. I don't think I could bear it."

"I'm not Dorian," said Rose jokingly.

"Oh, that wasn't fair," said Penny. "That was a long time ago, and you forgave him. Also, you shouldn't speak ill of the dead."

"Says the dead woman who wants me to marry her husband," returned Rose.

"Keep it up," warned Penny, "and I'll go find him in the afterlife just to get revenge for all of this."

They both laughed at that, until their laughter turned to tears. They hugged and cried, and for a moment it was almost like the old days. Eventually, Penny pulled away. "I'm getting tired. I need to sleep."

"Please don't go, Penny," said Rose, sad all over again. "Stay with me a while longer."

Penny shook her head, then wiped her face. "Every dream has to end sometime." Leaning over, she put her head in Rose's lap. "Just let me lie here. When he wakes up, he'll be happy to see you." She closed her eyes, squeezing still more tears from her eyes.

And then she was gone. Rose felt the change, sudden and surprising, as the head in her lap became heavier. Looking down, she saw Mordecai's face there, asleep.

Rose wept silently, fighting to keep from shaking him awake, but in that she failed. When Mordecai's eyes opened, they were met with a soft rainfall of sorrow. He wondered what was wrong, but Rose refused to say.

 CHAPTER 43

Waking up to a woman crying over me wasn't exactly a new experience for me, but usually it happened as a result of an extreme event, such as being tortured by a god, almost being murdered during a hunting trip, or being blown to pieces. And those weren't simply examples, they were all things that had happened to me over the course of my life. Making a sandcastle house had never struck me as a particularly traumatic event, but women are strange.

I asked Rose what was wrong, but she wouldn't answer. I tried to console her, but she seemed averse to my presence. When I put my arm around her, she cried harder, then got up and created some distance between us.

All of this left me confused, but that was nothing new. I considered myself an expert at being confused. Call it a life skill. Being married for a long time had given me quite a bit of experience to hone my skills. It had also taught me to leave women alone when they don't want to talk. Nothing good comes of it. In Penny's case, that could mean broken limbs, but with Rose I worried more about her tongue. Women in general often have a knack for using words as weapons, but for a woman of Rose's intelligence, I feared she might be capable of rendering me unfit to live in civil society.

Of course, Rose almost never used her wit to browbeat her fellow man, not without cause anyway, but I didn't want to become her first murder by verbal assault. So, I did us both the courtesy of letting her have her space.

The storm that had been on the horizon made good on its promise of rain, as well as delivering a spectacular light show. The wind, already strong, picked up until it was whipping spray from the wavetops all the way to our new camp at the upper end of the beach. When the rain started to fall, it was a downpour. Despite the perfection of our roof and the thick nature of the walls I had created, the sandcastle house might have fallen apart, but I reinforced it with spells to keep the sand from washing away.

On the plus side, the mosquitos didn't have rain gear, so they stayed home. Rose and I retreated to our new shelter and, after an hour or two of silently watching the storm, we lay down to get some sleep.

She still didn't want me close, though, and there was only one blanket. I tried to be chivalrous and let her have the blanket, but Rose was in a self-sacrificing mood. Every time I offered her the blanket, she pushed it back at me.

It was an odd argument, since we didn't talk during it. We just kept pushing the blanket back and forth. But I knew how to win this sort of war. Wizards have their advantages. *"Shibal,"* I said, putting her to sleep. Then I carefully wrapped her up in the blanket and retreated to the other side of the room to stretch out.

Sleeping on even a slightly chilly beach in a storm is no easy feat, especially when you're wearing half a dress. Since we hadn't encountered anything dangerous yet, I decided to risk using some magic to make myself more comfortable. I created a screen to keep out mosquitos if the storm left, then encapsulated myself in a bubble of warm air.

The spell to do that wouldn't last the whole night, but it was good enough for a few hours. I had used it before. When I woke up cold later on, I'd just reapply it and go back to sleep. I closed my eyes and tried to drift off, but then I started to worry about all the magic I had used. If the aythar-sensing predators we had encountered near Lancaster were present here, they might show up during the night.

So, with a sigh, I got up and went outside. I drew a wide circle in the sand around our sand house, then charged it with a spell to alert me if something crossed it. The circle wasn't strictly necessary, but it would help the spell last long enough so that I wouldn't have to redo it during the night. Then I went back in and fell asleep much faster than I thought possible.

I woke later, not from cold, but because Rose had woken up and moved closer. She draped one end of the blanket over me before settling in against my side. Thinking she had forgiven me for whatever my transgression had been, I tried to offer up my arm as a sacrificial pillow, but as soon as I moved and tried to slide it under her head, she flinched away.

"Don't," she warned.

"What did I do?" I asked, no longer content to wait for my punishment.

"Nothing," she replied.

Shit. I knew then that it must be something serious. *Was it the fish?* No, that was stupid. *Maybe she saw me watching her swim?* That made no sense either; she had been practically flirting with me at the time. 'Nothing' implied something really bad, like being discovered murdering puppies.

I tossed and turned, but only metaphorically, because with Rose close by I didn't want to keep her awake. Eventually an idea came to me. *Maybe it's because I didn't do anything.* Despite our growing intimacy over the past weeks, I had been unable to even admit to my feelings. Rose had told me she understood, that she'd wait until I was ready, but maybe she had really hoped I would do or at least *say* something.

Trouble was, I still wasn't ready. Every time I considered something, a kiss, or just telling her that I cared, I was overwhelmed by guilt, or grief. The two things were inextricably linked within me these days.

I couldn't say anything. That just wasn't possible, not yet, maybe not ever. But I could *do* something, even if it made me feel bad later. *A kiss, maybe.* That would reassure her.

Something told me it was a bad idea, but I've never had any luck second-guessing myself, so I rolled over to face her. The dim light was enough for me to see her eyes were open, even without my magesight, and for a brief second, we were almost nose to nose, gazing at one another. Then I shifted, to bring my lips in line with hers.

"Mort, no!" she cried, pushing me away. Then her eyes watered up again.

My heart was doubly skewered, first by her teary gaze and rejection, and then again by thoughts of Penny. "Sorry," I mumbled, feeling awkward. "I don't know what's wrong or what I'm supposed to do."

Rose dried her face with her sleeve, then replied softly, "That makes two of us."

"It would help if I knew what was wrong," I told her.

She chewed her lip for a moment, then answered, "Survivor's guilt."

I already knew I was suffering from that, not that giving it a special name helped much. "I meant you. What's wrong?"

"Survivor's guilt," she repeated.

I squinted at her in the dark. "Penny was my wife, not yours. You shouldn't feel bad about it."

"She was my best friend," countered Rose.

"You haven't done anything wrong," I said dismissively.

"Haven't I?" said Rose darkly. "I've been thinking over my actions during the past weeks. Would I have done all those things if I wasn't selfishly trying to make something for myself out of her loss?"

That made no sense to me. "So, trying to keep me from getting my neck stretched is a bad thing?"

"That's not what I mean," she responded. "I've lost perspective. I've only been thinking about myself, when I should be thinking about others."

"Well, from my perspective, you've only done what you have always done, the right thing. Even if you didn't give two figs for my twig and berries, you would have done the same thing. If you had an extra motive, well, who doesn't? We're human. People want things. That's how we are," I said somewhat eloquently, at least in my own opinion.

"Did you just say, 'twig and berries'?" asked Rose, incredulous.

I grinned. "It's a euphemism."

She laughed. "I know what it means. I'm just surprised you would call it that. And for your information, I am not at all interested in your 'twig and berries.' I was just saying that I was thinking of myself. Saving you was a selfish effort to cure my own loneliness."

I was relieved to see her mood had lightened and also offended on behalf of little Mordecai. "First," I said, beginning my rebuttal, "being lonely is no sin. You deserve happiness as much as anyone else. Second, I am shattered to learn you find me unattractive. I thought you liked me because of my irresistible physical appeal. Now I have to rethink everything I ever believed about myself."

She smirked. "I didn't say you were unattractive, merely that I'm not interested in you because of your meaty bits. Contrary to popular male belief, most women don't generally sit around thinking about men's winkles."

"Winkles?" I exclaimed, shocked. "Did you just say, 'winkles'? Lady Rose, I am scandalized by your language. I can't wait to inform the court of your wanton words."

She winked at me. "You'll never prove it, and if you try, they won't believe you." Then she rolled over and put her back to me. "I'm going to sleep."

That effectively ended the conversation, so I lay down as well, making sure to keep a small space between us. Rose was obviously feeling better now, but I didn't want to press my luck.

"I'm cold," announced Rose.

For a second, I considered repeating my warming spell, but then discarded the notion. I knew what she meant, and I wasn't feeling particularly noble at the moment anyway. Scooting closer, I draped one arm over her and conformed my shape to hers.

"Just be careful," said Rose. "I don't want that twig poking me, or you'll be over there with no blanket."

***

478

If the early part of my sleep had been rough, the second part was deep. I slept like a rock, probably the first good rest I'd had since escaping from a death sentence. Rose must have been tired as well, because when we woke, it was already morning.

My arm was dead again, but that wasn't what bothered me the most. As my sleep-addled brain slowly began to work, I realized that the snuffling sound in my ears was the product of something large sniffing at my leg.

Adrenaline is a wonderful thing at moments like that. My awareness exploded, and in an instant of severe clarity I realized several things. First, we had overslept, and my alarm spell had worn off, or perhaps the rain had washed away the circle, ending it sooner. Second, our remaining fish, which I had hoped to have for breakfast, was gone. Last, we were surrounded by a pack of very large wolves, and apparently one fish wasn't enough to satisfy them.

The one sniffing my leg had probably been trying to determine if I was dead, and if so, whether I was I still safe to eat. As my heart jumped and my blood began to race, its keen nose registered the difference and it decided to take the initiative. The wolf's mouth snapped open and it lunged for my obviously tasty calf.

A shield probably wouldn't work. I knew that from my experience with the bears that had ruined Penny's arm. Instead, I put as much force as I could into a battering ram to thrust the predator away from me. Much of the energy was wasted, sliding off the wolf's back like water from a duck, but enough made contact to push it back several feet.

With seven more wolves almost as close, a dead arm, and no weapons, I didn't have many options. With a thought, I created a small shield around Rose and myself, in the shape of a bubble, then I reached out with my power and collapsed the sandcastle house on top of us.

That was the part that woke Rose, and she was not very happy about it. She sat up suddenly, and when she saw the sand and roof coming down, she grabbed my dead arm with such strength that I almost felt it. Sometimes numbness is a blessing.

"What?" she shouted in my ear.

I replied with equal loquacity, "Wolves." I was too busy digging through my magical pouches to give a better explanation. Having only one useable arm made it much harder, but eventually I got hold of what I wanted, my staff.

Pulling a six-foot length of wood from a belt pouch with only one arm, while trapped in a bubble under a lot of sand, isn't an easy task. That's when you really want something smaller, like a wand. The upside is that once you finally have it out and in hand, it's a damn sight better. The difference is rather like comparing a dagger and a sword. Both will cut, but a sword will take off an arm or a leg if you use it with enough enthusiasm. And I was certainly feeling enthusiastic.

Shifting and flopping about, I had the staff halfway out before I realized our bubble wasn't big enough, so I took a moment to enlarge it, pushing the sand farther away. Meanwhile, Rose figured out what I was doing and used her two good hands to get the staff the rest of the way out for me.

The wolves were all around the perimeter of our collapsed sand pile, digging underneath the edges of the glass roof to get at us. Changing my shield into a half-dome, I used it to keep what was above us above, while leaving the area around us free for me to attack.

Then I turned my fear and annoyance at the rude awakening into a burning line of intense, red fire, using my staff to channel it. Turning in a circle, it burned through the sand and did much more interesting things to the wolves, cutting them into a varied mix of scorched wolf pieces.

Once I was sure the wolves were dead, I stopped. Rose and I stood in our sand-enclosed bubble for a moment, catching our breath. Then I used my power again, lifting the glassine roof from over us and displacing enough sand so we could walk out.

"I have some bad news," I told Rose.

Worried, she asked, "What is it?"

"The fish is no more," I answered. "Would you care for some wolf instead? I have several options available and all the choicest cuts."

She blanched. "I'll pass, thank you for the offer."

With all the dead animals, our once-idyllic camp seemed more like a slaughterhouse now. "I seem to have lost my appetite as well," I agreed. "We should probably start moving."

"The question," said Rose, "is where do we go?"

"Well, it's a pretty good assumption that we're in the same half of the world that Lancaster is located in, but we have no idea which direction it's in," I said, laying out what we knew.

Rose nodded.

"We could also go back through the boundary, which would put us back in Albamarl. I'm in better shape and the pursuit probably isn't expecting us to reappear there. We could try for the house again," I offered.

"Except that it's probably guarded by now," pointed out Rose. "And if Tyrion somehow survived, he will very likely have reset the enchantment to keep you out of the house."

I pursed my lips. "It would have been difficult to survive that explosion. I barely did, and I wasn't as close. If he lost consciousness for even a few seconds afterward, he would be dead for sure."

"Exactly how much can you survive?" asked Rose, suddenly curious. "You came back from death itself, didn't you?"

"That was different," I explained. "My body was dead, but my soul was chained to it. Gareth made me a new one while Walter kept me from drifting into the afterlife. Aside from that, I can heal almost any wound, so long as I'm conscious and able to use my power. After that fight with Tyrion, I had a really severe case of feedback sickness, which kept me from doing anything. Otherwise I'd have been fine."

"What about during the Ungol attack?" Rose inquired. "You took an arrow through the heart. Something different happened there, didn't it?"

Damn, she's perceptive. Then again, Rose hadn't been present during that attack, or even seen me until later. How could she know about my transformation? "How do you know about that?" I asked sharply.

"Penny," Rose said simply, but she didn't offer any mention of when they had talked.

"She probably exaggerated how bad it was," I replied, wanting to drop the subject.

But Rose had the scent, and she wasn't ready to surrender the chase. "I don't think so, Mordecai. She said you changed. That you still held something from your time as a shiggreth within you."

I winced, but there was no sense denying it now. I nodded, then said, "She always talked too much."

"So back to the original question," said Rose, forging on. "Is what you did unique to you, or could any archmage do it?"

"I think they *could* if they knew how to hear the void," I admitted. "But as far as I know, I'm the only one who's ever been through the experience, so it's probably just me."

"If someone stabbed Tyrion through the heart, would it kill him?" she asked.

"I think so. He would lose consciousness too quickly. I imagine that or cutting off his head would do the trick. If he was already unconscious, or if he had feedback sickness, it would be a lot easier."

"And what about you?" said Rose pointedly.

I shrugged. "It's tricky. If I had feedback sickness, I think almost anything could kill me. Otherwise, it would be safest to burn my entire body to ash—quickly. It's sort of a choice, though. If I refused to change, I would probably die. It's hard to explain."

"Then let me be clear," said Rose emphatically. "Unless you're about to die, I don't want you to use that other power, under any circumstance."

"Why?" I asked, suddenly suspicious. I already knew it was risky, that it might be doing something terrible to me, but Rose didn't. Or at least, she shouldn't know. Even Penny hadn't known that, although she might have learned it at the very end.

"Call it a hunch," said Rose. "Besides, I'm in charge of you now, so you have to listen."

I gaped. "In *charge* of me? What does that mean?" I stopped myself just short of saying she wasn't Penny.

Rose nodded. "Penny left me instructions long ago telling me that if anything happened to her, I would be in charge of managing your stupidity," she added, telling a half-truth.

"Stupidity?"

She smiled innocently, batting her lashes at me. "Oh, forgive me, I meant to say, 'reckless behavior,' but it amounts to the same thing, doesn't it?"

I huffed. "I'll manage myself, thank you very much."

"Tell yourself whatever you like if it makes you feel better," stated Rose. "But first promise me you won't use that dark power you mentioned unless you're about to die."

"Fine," I growled. "But I had already decided that on my own."

She smirked, but I knew I would have the last laugh. No one had yet managed to bridle my stupidity when I put my head to it. She might fool herself thinking she could predict the stupid, but it was a force of nature in its own right. In fact, I wasn't sure I could predict it either. Stupid never dies.

"Back to where we started," I said, changing the subject. "I think we should try flying. Lancaster might be closer than we think, and if not, we'll learn something about this other half of our world. In the worst case, I'll find another boundary and take us back."

Rose looked nervous. "I'm not sure about flying…"

"Just turn around," I told her. "I'll explain how it works." When she didn't move, I walked around and stood behind her. "The important thing to remember," I began, wrapping my arms around her waist, "is that you don't have to do anything." Then I launched us skyward.

She screamed as though someone was sticking a knife in her, twisting in my arms so she could latch onto me with her own hands, while I laughed. It had been a little cruel of me, perhaps, but sometimes my capricious moods get the better of me.

I figured she would forgive me later.

 CHAPTER 44

Matthew had just stepped through the boundary to begin another day's waiting when Karen appeared just a few feet away. She appeared glad to see him. "There you are," he said calmly. "Where are the others?"

Her expression of relief faded quickly. "I don't know."

"What happened?"

She gave him a brief description of the failed rescue attempt of his father, and for once Matthew's normally impassive features darkened with worry. It wasn't something a stranger would have noticed, but she knew him well enough to see the signs. From what she had just told him, it was highly probable that his father was now dead.

"What about the others?" asked Matthew, remaining practical despite his inner turmoil.

Karen didn't have any good news to relay. "I don't know. After Tyrion knocked me unconscious, I didn't see what happened. "I came to almost an hour later. They had me locked in a room with two krytek and several human guards. They must have known I was a wizard, but neither Tyrion nor Gareth was around, so they must not have realized what I could do. I teleported out a few seconds after I woke.

"I was supposed to try and meet Elaine and the others in the forest if everything went well, but by the time I got there, I found no sign of them. I waited a while and even went back to Albamarl a few times, thinking I might find some sign of them, but no luck. Every time I went to the capital, the krytek started making a beeline for me. After a couple of days, I gave up and came here," she finished. "I considered going to your home, to check on Moira, but..."

"You did the right thing," said Matthew quickly, shaking his head. "That's the first place they would go. Moira's probably under watch right now, if not an outright hostage."

"We have to get her out then," said Karen anxiously.

Matthew smiled mysteriously. "I don't think so. She'll be fine."

Karen was shocked. "She's your sister!"

Matt sat down, picking at the grass nearby. "She's also the one person best suited for being a hostage. In fact, I would almost say Rose arranged things so that she was the only one there when they came looking. There's only two reasons for it, to be honest."

"What's the second reason?"

He shrugged. "Someone has to feed Humphrey."

"She could have brought the dog with her," argued Karen.

"Someone also needed to be there to lock things up," added Matthew. "But I still think she makes an ideal hostage." When Karen started glaring at him, he explained, "Aside from me, she's probably the most dangerous wizard alive. Maybe more so than even our father. Unless they use extraordinary measures to lock her up, she'll be able to subvert any guards they use. If she gets loose in the capital, who knows what she could do? She might take over the whole kingdom. In the worst case, we might even have to try and kill her ourselves if she gets too far out of control."

"Moira?" said Karen, outraged. "She's one of the nicest people in your family! I'm probably even closer to her than I am Irene. I can't see her doing any of that."

"A year ago, I would have agreed with you, except for the nice part," said Matthew snidely. "But after Dunbar, she changed."

"But she's all alone."

He shook his head. "No. She's never alone. She's an army all by herself. Let's just hope she doesn't get out of hand."

Karen wasn't sure what to say to that, so she switched topics. "What about Gary?"

"What about him?"

"Isn't he at your house as well?" said Karen.

"No," answered Matthew. "He's in my new shop, inside the yard of Castle Cameron."

"Just there? Doesn't he move around?"

"He said he doesn't need to," offered Matthew. "As far as I know, he's still there, listening for ANSIS broadcasts."

"Shouldn't we go get him?"

Matthew's face took on a look of concentration, then he answered, "Not yet."

"Why?"

"Same as with my sister. Either she's locked down the castle, in which case he's safe, or she hasn't, and they've taken him. If he's safe, we might as well let him keep up his work. If he isn't, we might just be kicking a hornet's nest if we pop in suddenly. Waiting a week or two will reduce our risk. We may get more news in that time. I don't want to make any reckless choices if we can avoid it. I'll continue to keep watch here for a few weeks. If no one shows up, then I'll do something," said Matthew.

Karen sat down next to him, then scooted over until their shoulders were touching. "You don't act very upset, but I know you have to be worried sick. It's ok to show it."

He took a deep breath. "Hopefully I won't have to show it."

"Huh?" she said, nonplussed.

"Because there's only one way I can think of showing it right now. If my father's dead, or Moira, I won't get upset. I'll get even," he replied.

"That isn't ominous at all," said Karen wryly.

"It's not ominous. It isn't an omen. I don't intend to give them any signs or warnings. If they've hurt my family, I'll make those responsible pay for it," said Matthew coldly. "By whatever means necessary."

Karen felt a cold chill run down her spine. Shaking herself, she stood up again. "I'm hungry. Want to go to the castle and eat?"

"No," said Matthew, shaking his head. "I have to stay here in case Elaine or my father show up. I'll open the way for you. They're serving porridge again today."

She shuddered. "Ugh."

"There's dried mutton if porridge isn't to your taste," said Matthew, smiling slightly.

"Pass," said Karen. "I'll go to Dalensa. I know a lovely inn there that serves the most delightful pastries." As soon as she said the words, an idea came to her. "Actually, do you have any money?"

Matthew shook a small purse that held a few coins. "Some."

"Give it to me," she commanded.

He sighed. "I knew this day would come. First you insist on sleeping in my room, now you're taking my money."

"I'll make you eat those words," said Karen. "Literally." Lifting her own purse, she shook it in his face. It was fairly bulging with coins. "I'll buy as much as I can and bring it back for everyone. Your coins will just add to my noble sacrifice."

Matthew frowned. "Porridge is fine. We aren't starving."

Karen laughed. "You are the oddest man I have ever known. Maybe you don't care if you eat the same thing every day, but I know for a fact that most of the people in Lancaster are probably about ready to gnaw their arms off just for a change of pace. Besides, it isn't healthy to eat one thing all the time."

"Why not?"

"I'll explain vitamins later," said Karen. Plucking the purse from his hand, she vanished.

***

It was a week later when Chad, Elaine, and Cyhan arrived. Matthew discovered them waiting outside the boundary when he opened it that morning. "Took you long enough," he said dryly.

"I'm glad to see you too, ya twat," responded Chad. "It ain't like I walked across half of Lothion to get here or anythin'."

Elaine pushed Chad aside. "Is there anything to eat? We haven't had a decent meal in forever."

The hunter protested, "We had crow and wild onions fer stew last night, ya crybaby."

"Crows aren't food," said Elaine stiffly.

"Says who?" asked Chad.

Cyhan spoke up, "It needed salt."

"Everybody's a fuckin' critic these days. Next time I'm lettin' both of ya starve."

The big knight gave him a flat look.

"What?" said Chad. "I'm a hunter. You keep sayin' the world is yer weapon or whatever, but the world is my damned stew pot, so ya'd best keep that in mind if we're stuck in the woods again."

"As long as I never have to eat lotus roots or cattails again, I don't care," said Elaine, shuddering at the memory.

Matthew finally stepped in to end the debate. "If you'd shown up a week ago, you might have been disappointed. All we had was porridge and dried mutton, but over the past week Karen has been making trips all over Gododdin to restock the larder. We had roast pig last night. I'm sure there's still some in the kitchen if you can convince the cook to let you have it."

Chad grinned. "At this point I'd sell Elaine to him for a bit of pork."

Elaine sniffed disdainfully. "Thankfully, I'm not yours to sell."

But Chad ignored her, continuing, "Hell, a few more days and I'd pay to have Elaine cooked and just skip the pig altogether."

Matthew laughed. "What about Sir Cyhan? He's got more meat on him."

"It ain't about the meat, boy. It's about the fat. This girl's got plenty on her hips. Cyhan's old and nothin' but muscle. I'd probably break a tooth tryin' to chew his gristly ass. A hunter learns to judge his prey. Trust me, she'd be better eatin'."

Elaine looked imploringly at Matthew. "Please tell me there are women at the castle. Another minute with these two and I'm liable to commit a crime."

Sir Cyhan glanced at Chad. "I didn't do anything."

The woodsman shrugged. "Don't ask me. I just gave her a compliment and you'd think I insulted her."

 CHAPTER 45

It's impossible to overstate just how beautiful the world is when you can get up to an elevation that allows you to really see it. Nature is beautiful at ground level too, but from the sky, it's an entirely different beauty, one that changes depending on altitude. Just above the tree tops, it's still very close, but the horizon is visible in every direction. Farther up and the landscape starts to reveal its contours, and if you go even higher, the things that were previously details become part of the mixture of colors on what looks like a gigantic artist's canvas.

As I may have mentioned previously, flying is probably my favorite part of being a wizard, and on this day, I got to share it with someone new. Rose overcame her fear more quickly than I expected. Some people never do, as I had learned with Roland years before. Once we got higher and the ground seemed too far away to be a credible threat, her mouth opened up into an 'o' of wonder and awe, a feeling I could still appreciate despite how often I had seen the view.

I took us as high as possible, using some of my strength to maintain a tight bubble of air around us. The coastline we had been on turned out to be just the edge of a massive landmass that went on seemingly forever, to a horizon that was now considerably farther away than it had been before. In the distance I could see mountains, though I had no way of knowing if they were related to the Elentirs or some entirely different range. Between us and the mountains was a verdant tapestry of forest and grasslands, occasionally broken up by rivers that glinted with reflected sunlight.

The only bad thing was that in none of that impressive vista did I see anything that looked remotely like our dislocated destination, Lancaster. After several minutes of looking, I took us back down to a more tenable altitude, one at which I didn't have to make a constant effort to keep our precious bubble of air from bursting and leaving us without anything to breathe.

We headed straight inland at a ninety-degree angle to the coast behind us. It was a good bet that Lancaster wasn't in the ocean, though it was perfectly possible that we weren't even on the right continent. There was just no way of knowing.

The plan was to fly until we spotted something interesting, such as Lancaster, or night fell. We could afford to do that for a few days, assuming we found food and water. I figured that if we hadn't found any sign of it after a week, we could just cross back over and if we were somewhere unknown in our own world, we would have to risk using one of the teleport circle destinations that I knew.

I was hoping we wouldn't have to do that, though. By now there was a very good chance that most of them were being guarded.

As we flew, we saw vast herds of animals on the grasslands, and from that height it was impossible to see if they were as strange and ill-tempered as the other animals I'd encountered before. My default assumption was that they were, since almost everything else had tried to kill me thus far.

I felt a vicarious pleasure watching Rose admire the landscape, and a boyish pride from showing her how fast I could fly, though I refrained from the blistering speeds I sometimes used when I was alone. It's funny how the presence of just one person can turn even someone like me into a responsible person.

In less than two hours, we were over the mountains and passing over a wide plain. It wasn't all plains, of course, but a lot of it was. Still there was no sign of anything familiar, or even interesting. I had half expected to see shining metal everywhere, a testament to the presence of ANSIS, but from our vantage point it appeared to be just untouched wilderness.

Another five hours and the plains still continued, but a new mountain range was beginning to show its head on the distant horizon.

We were also thirsty and in need of some time on the ground to manage our more human needs. My bladder felt as though it might burst. So I took us down close to a river. The land nearest it was greener, thick with lush grass and small copses of trees.

I was wary, though. Water is also a magnet for animals, and more importantly, for the larger animals that eat them. This time we didn't encounter anything, but Rose wasn't happy about my rules for waste elimination.

"I can't pee with you standing over me," she insisted. "Go over there."

My response was short and succinct. "Spiders."

She frowned. "Do you sense any?"

"No, but last time I missed them, and they killed several men before I could help them. And they were wearing armor and in the company of several mages and dragons. What if there's something super sneaky here, like a giant, rabid ant-lion?" I warned her. "If I'm not close, you could be dinner before I could do anything."

She looked at me archly. "Do you really think there's something here?"

I honestly didn't. I had been examining the area carefully, above and below ground, with a paranoid obsession that only comes to people who've been ambushed by monster trapdoor spiders, which I had. "There might be something I haven't seen before," I said. "You stay here and I'll move to the other side of that bush."

"You can still see me with your magesight," she pointed out.

I let out a sigh of exasperation. "That's been true for most of your time in Castle Cameron, as long as I was within a mile or two. I won't be paying attention to your *particulars*, trust me."

"Very well," she said, pointing. "Over there. And don't talk. I'm going to do my best to pretend you're miles away."

Another thought occurred to me. "One second. Let me make sure this bush isn't carnivorous." Brave beyond words, I shoved my arm into the shrubbery and shook it to see if it became enraged or would try to eat me. It didn't. "Alright, I think you're safe," I told her.

"You are ridiculous," said Rose. "Go."

Contrary to my expectations, nothing terrible happened. Once our biological necessities had been taken care of, I used some of my power to levitate a portion of the river water, and then I heated it to boiling before allowing it to cool so we could drink it.

Luckily, I still had a small pot stored in my pouches, so I left the remaining water there and then plucked some fish from the river for an impromptu lunch. I couldn't help but feel a little guilty catching fish in that manner. As a boy, one of my father's favorite activities had been fishing. He hadn't gotten to do much of it, since he was kept pretty busy at the smithy, but whenever he had the chance, he would sneak off to the river and spend hours staring at the water.

Some days he had brought home several; others he would get nothing for his effort. Remembering that, my use of magic felt like cheating. As always, though, I preferred to cheat than go hungry, and even the fish wasn't enough to fill us up. A few more days of this and I'd probably start having dreams of vegetables.

Chad Grayson had once told me something interesting. *"At least half the plants you see are edible in some form or fashion."* I had asked him why we didn't eat more of them, and his reply had been sternly pragmatic. *"Because almost all of 'em taste like shit."*

Putting aside my yearning for carrots and onions, Rose and I returned to our journey into the unknown. As we got closer to the next mountain range, something began to stand out. A forest hugged the foothills and lower slopes, and in the midst of it, there was a tree that rose much higher than the others.

As we drew closer, it soon became apparent the tree in question was a giant that dwarfed its cousins, and I had a sneaking suspicion it was no normal tree. It looked suspiciously familiar to some I had seen in my memories. It also looked much like the tree that had until recently been Tyrion's body.

"I think we've found civilization, of a sort," I told Rose.

She had been studying it as well and she asked, "Is that?"

"It's a She'Har elder," I responded. "Unless I'm much mistaken."

"You told me they had gone extinct, except for Tyrion and Lyralliantha."

"That's what I thought," I said. "But it appears I was wrong. It's just one tree, though, which means unless there are others that we can't see, it can't reproduce. I wonder how long it's been stranded here?"

"Seems strange to think of a tree being stranded," commented Rose. "Since they don't move. Can you tell if it's male or female?"

"Not without being much closer," I answered. "I'd have to examine its—"

"Don't say it."

"—twigs and berries," I finished.

"It's a miracle you managed to have children," remarked Rose.

I laughed, then returned to more serious matters. "I think I should get closer. See if I can talk to it."

"Doesn't that take a lot of time?" she reminded me.

Usually, yes, but I knew that at certain times the She'Har elders could speed their perception of time up to match our own. Generally, that only happened if you tried to set one on fire and it needed to defend itself, but there were other rare moments in which they did so voluntarily. Deep down, I had a feeling this might be one of those times.

If asked, I couldn't explain my feeling. Perhaps it was a premonition, or maybe it was some strange instinct passed down to me through the loshti, but I felt strongly that finding the elder wasn't an accident.

I was meant to be here.

Naturally that triggered my paranoia. "Let me find a safe place for you," I suggested.

Rose gave me a hard look. "We've been over that."

"Rose, listen. A She'Har elder, while usually dormant from our perspective, is enormously powerful. If I bring you with me and it becomes hostile, I might not be able to protect you."

She looked thoughtful. "Could you kill it, if you had to?"

I chewed my lip. "Maybe. Tyrion killed several, back in his time, but every situation is different."

"Well, it's probably friendly anyway," said Rose. "If things get out of hand, I'll put my money on the deranged wizard that's been doing the flying."

Rather than argue, I gave up. We had been through so much lately that I just couldn't imagine things getting any worse. We needed help, or at the very least, directions. The elder would probably be grateful to learn that some of its relatives survived, back on our side of the boundary. Also, my strange feeling of intuition was urging me forward.

We flew on, and as we got closer, the smaller trees thinned out, until they left a small clearing around the base of the She'Har elder. I was also able identify its type.

The She'Har are not a single race, as I had once assumed before examining my memories. They were in fact five separate species of the sentient trees. Once we were close enough, the shape of the branches was enough to tell me this was an Illeniel tree.

My feeling of anticipation grew, and a strange sense of déjà vu came over me. We landed just beneath the edge of its massive canopy and began to walk closer. Almost immediately, I felt the presence of a powerful mind.

I had thought I would need to go all the way to the trunk. If it had been in its normal state, I would have, but this elder was awake and aware of us. I could feel its attention focusing on us.

The seed has returned, and with it the time of beginnings arrives.

Not the most auspicious of greetings. I filed the phrase away. It might come in handy the next time one of my children came home after doing something stupid. *I have news from the other side of the boundary,* I responded.

Come closer, that we may be joined, said the Elder.

I frowned. *Sorry, I'm not in the mood. We can talk just fine at this distance.*

There was no warning. The danger sense I had only lately begun to trust failed me completely. The elder's mind fell on me like an avalanche. It was massive, powerful, and all but irresistible.

But if there's one thing I had had plenty of experience with, it was dealing with things that were supposedly irresistible. I had earned the name 'godslayer' for good reason. Strengthening my shield, I took my staff and used the tip to draw an impromptu circle around us. Then I used that as the foundation for a much stronger shield.

Rose was already unconscious, and the sight of her collapsed at my feet made me angry, which helped to bolster my native stubbornness. I put as much of that as I could into my shield, but it still wasn't quite enough.

The elder's will seeped through my shield and was still strong enough to make my knees feel like jelly. I couldn't even respond with my usual witty repartee. Any effort to communicate would have opened me up even further to its oppressive domination.

You must be examined. The words echoed through my mind, making it even more difficult to think. But I didn't need to think much; it wasn't my first time in such a situation. Marshalling my concentration, I prepared to seek the mind of stone.

A flash of pain struck as something pierced the soles of my feet. Horrified, I discovered thin white, root-like tendrils had gone through the skin and were winding their way up my legs, on the inside.

The fruit has matured. Relax child. Together we may yet save this world.

My defense collapsed. With direct contact the elder had bypassed every defense I possessed, and I could barely think beyond its powerful compulsion. Its roots were growing upward, lacing and twining through my legs and into my torso. In short order, they would reach my brain and I had little doubt what would happen then.

"You're killing me," I gasped.

Tyrion's power, the Illeniel gift, and Thillmarius' corruption have met and joined in you, child. Only through this sacrifice may the world be saved. Rejoice at the honor you have received.

Abandoning my efforts to resist, I opened my mind and reached out for the earth, seeking the solace of stone. My pain faded to insignificance and my *self* grew. Calling out, I drew the bedrock up, severing the roots beneath us and surrounding Rose and me in a massive stone dome.

But the elder wasn't giving up easily. With roots that seemed harder than iron, it bored into the stone, tearing and crushing its way toward us. *Tyrion's power will not suffice, child. Only Thillmarius' corruption can save us,* said the elder.

I needed more, but if I went too far I might lose myself, or worse, kill Rose through sheer negligence. *I need space,* I realized. So I began walking forward, toward the tree, letting my flesh and blood body pass through the shell that protected us.

Beneath the mountains were rivers of fire, I would call them if necessary.

Still you fail, warned the elder. *Burn us and the world dies, for I am Kion.*

Kion? That name gave me pause, for it was the Erollith word for 'gate.' The Dark Gods had been called the kionthara, or gatekeepers.

Now you begin to see, said the elder in my mind. *Kill me and the world will be shattered. Nothing will survive. You bear the corrupted fruit. Give it to me that I might fulfill the destiny of ages. Only through your death will the world be saved.*

I needed to think, and that was getting difficult, so I contracted, withdrawing from the deeper parts of the earth, shrinking until I was just a man—and a small amount more, balancing myself between being human and the mind of the stone. The elder's roots found me again and began boring into my flesh, but my mind was beyond its reach. I was a thing of pure reason and little emotion.

Several things clicked together in my mind. If this elder was the gate, then it might well be the lynchpin that controlled the dimensional boundary that divided the world into a multitude of pieces. Destroying Kion might cause the entire thing to unravel, which would very probably lead to a catastrophe. The elder's warning might not be hyperbole.

The corruption he kept referencing was probably the taint of the void, that lingering trace of the shiggreth I had never quite been able to erase. For some reason the elder wanted it, and consuming me seemed to be its preferred method of attaining it.

Very well, I thought. *You want the void, I'll give it to you, but I'll do the devouring.* My physical body was mostly gone now—it had become a confusing collection of meat, bones, and vines—but somehow, the heart was still beating.

So I turned my attention to the song of death and let my heart stop. As I felt the cold touch of the void, my mind became more human, oddly enough. Death is a part of life, a thing that lies at the end of every existence. It was no stranger. The mind of the stone faded, and my anger returned, bitter and cruel.

Yes! cried the elder. *Feed it. Give us the fruit of corruption.*

I've always been a people pleaser, but today I decided to branch out and become a tree pleaser. *I'll be happy to share,* I announced mentally. *But not as you expect.*

Latching onto the roots of the elder, which were now throughout my body, I began to drink in its life, consuming it like a man dying of thirst.

In the past, I had thought devouring a human life to be the ultimate pleasure. Just the memory of it had given me nightmares. Horrifying dreams that I feared and simultaneously craved. Devouring a She'Har elder was much more satisfying.

Kion struggled, first attempting to withdraw its roots and then screaming into my mind, begging me to stop. *Do not! If you do this, the woman dies!*

505

The elder didn't understand my mindset, though. In the void, other people weren't much of a moral concern for me. In fact, if I'd had some time to think about it, I would probably have given Rose a new name, 'dessert.' At that moment I cared about very little, other than drowning myself in the elder's life.

But my reason remained, and I knew I didn't really want her death, though it seemed illogical to me at that moment. *Let us leave, or I will kill both of you,* I warned.

I felt the elder's surrender, but it took a significant effort of personal discipline to stop feeding on it. Perhaps the only reason I managed it was that I had taken in an enormous quantity of its aythar already. The void was always hungry, but just then, I wasn't truly ravenous. Somehow, I stopped.

I studied Kion with my magesight and something darker—the lifesense that became so vivid whenever I allowed the void to have its way with me. The Illeniel elder was badly weakened. If I had gone on much longer, it would have died, whether I stopped or not. The aythar that had thrummed so powerfully around it before now vibrated feebly.

By contrast, I felt positively wonderful. The power singing in my veins was so strong that I had no doubt that if I surrendered the void and attempted to return to my old human self I would probably burn up in a flash of aythar, leaving my body little more than a pile of ash. *Good thing I don't need to be human,* I thought to myself. "Why be human, when you can be a god?" I muttered with a wicked smile on my face.

You have doomed us all, said the elder. *The machines are coming.*

"You doomed yourself, Kion," I said. "You should never have touched me." Then I remembered Rose. With a thought, I cracked open the stone dome surrounding her. Some part of me wanted to go to her, but I didn't dare get too close. With as much power as I currently had, I could probably avoid draining her life, but I feared the slightest touch might incinerate her.

I was a being of light and fire intertwined with a hunger for more. No matter which way I used my power, to give or take, it would destroy her. Turning my gaze to the massive tree, I commanded, "Take care of her. See that she is healthy and whole, fed and maintained. I will return. If she is not sound of mind and body, I will finish what I have begun with you."

Then I launched myself into the air.

Where are you going? asked Kion weakly.

To find the machines, I answered. *I need something to burn.*

 EPILOGUE

Matthew was waiting outside the boundary between Lancaster and what he thought of as the 'real' world, even though he knew they were one and the same, when he felt something strange. His stomach lurched, and a sensation of vertigo washed over him. The dimensional boundary *shivered* next to him, and then it started to fade. To his normal eyes, he began to see flashes of both places intermittently, but it wasn't just the boundary that flashed.

The ground he stood on was shifting back and forth as well. In principle, it felt a bit like an earthquake, except nothing was moving. Reality was shifting and warping, back and forth. The feeling was so intense that he became nauseated, but before he started to vomit, it stopped. He found himself swaying on his feet even though the ground below him was perfectly stable.

He studied the boundary again, but the shiver that had passed through it was gone. *What was that?* he wondered. *Is it starting to fail?* The bigger question in his mind was what would happen if it did.

"Reconstructing the original world is one thing," he said to himself, "but if the boundary collapses all at once…" His mind refused to give him a satisfactory answer, but he knew it would be bad.

***

David Airedale went to bed tired and irritable. Several more of his staff had come down ill over the past few days, leaving his household understaffed, but that wasn't what bothered him. To be honest, he didn't know what was bothering him. He just felt out of sorts.

Normally he preferred to go to bed late, but tonight his fatigue wouldn't be denied, so he retired early. The few servants he passed all seemed to be yawning, so it wasn't just him. Then again, they were all lazy—he knew that. It was the bane of the nobility, being forced to manage the activities of the vulgar and lazy common class.

For himself, though, he was bone tired. *Perhaps I've been working too hard,* he thought as he entered his bedroom.

A glance told him that Marcella, his wife, was already fast asleep, which was something of a relief. He didn't have the energy for her mindless chatter. Wearily, he struggled out of his clothes and dropped into the bed beside her. He dragged the heavy blankets over himself and was asleep almost before his eyes had closed.

When he awoke, it wasn't morning. There was no light coming from the expensive windows that Marcella had insisted upon. The glass was black, with no hint of sunshine. *I was so tired I forgot to pull the curtains,* he thought groggily. That would have been annoying. Their bedroom windows faced east, and given their late habits, the morning sunshine was rarely welcome.

I should close the curtains, he decided.

Sitting up proved to be a monumental chore, however, so he settled for propping himself up against the headboard. "Marcella," he said, his tongue strangely numb. "Wake up."

His wife didn't move, though, so after a few more repeated verbal attempts, he shook her shoulder with one hand. Her body was limp and unresponsive. "How much did you drink?" he mumbled.

"Not too much, Lord Airedale, never fear," came a woman's voice close to his ear.

He jerked his head around in alarm, or rather, he tried to—everything seemed to happen slower than it should. There was a figure sitting unnoticed at his bedside, an old woman who appeared to have borrowed his wife's dressing table stool. She gave him a friendly smile as their eyes met. "Who are you?" he asked, wishing he could put the proper emphasis in his voice. He was too numb to vent the outrage he felt.

"An old friend," she answered. "You'll understand soon enough." Leaning forward, the crone lifted a damp cloth and wiped something from his lips and chin. Then she stood and went to the hearth, where she tossed the cloth into the fire.

As he watched, he realized two things. One, someone had put extra wood on the fire; otherwise it would have been embers already, for he hadn't added any when he came to bed. Second, the old woman wore a pair of heavy leather work gloves. After burning the cloth, she removed her gloves and added those to the fire as well, taking time to arrange them so they would burn completely.

"I don't know who you are, but I'm about to call for a guard," said Airedale. "You'll be whipped for entering my bedroom unannounced."

The old woman laughed. "Go ahead. They are about as likely to appear as your wife is to wake up. Everyone is sleeping very soundly tonight, my dear Count."

Not to be cowed, he did, yelling as loudly as he could. David Airedale was a man of voluminous lungs, and though he didn't quite have the strength of voice he normally possessed, he was still quite loud. Everyone in the house would show up in a moment.

But they didn't. After his voice died away, the halls were ominously silent. The old woman returned to her seat by the bedside, then drew on a second pair of gloves. They were a closer-fitting pair of doehide gloves more suitable for a lady than this woman.

Then he recognized her. It was the new laundress they had hired a week ago. "I know you!" he exclaimed. "Where did you steal those gloves?"

The old woman smiled again, then held up her hand to admire the fine leather. "Oh, I've had these for years and years. My late-husband had them made for me. I wouldn't ordinarily wear them for something like this, but they're just a precaution."

Something about her manner, her lack of fear or respect, and strangely, the gloves, sent a shiver of fear through Count Airedale's heart. "Who are you? What do you want?" He tried again to rise, but the woman pushed him down again before he was halfway up. He felt as weak as a kitten.

"An old friend of your father's," she replied enigmatically. "He was a customer of mine for a while, though I doubt he mentioned me. Few men brag about their whoring to their sons."

"My father's dead," protested David, "and he wouldn't have been interested in an old hag if he were alive."

The crone began to cackle. "Oh, I was much younger back then. This was decades before the Queen decided to *shorten* your departed father's life."

David Airedale's father had been executed for treason against King James, and he didn't like to be reminded of it. "Whatever game you're playing, witch, your insolence will only increase the punishment."

The woman reached out and lifted Airedale's left hand in her own, then examined it in the light. He was surprised to see he had a slight tremor. "It won't be much longer now," she remarked. "The drug is beginning its work."

"You poisoned me?" he sputtered, then glanced at his wife. "And Marcella?"

The hag waved a hand dismissively at Marcella. "She's only sleeping soundly. She'll wake up feeling just fine in the morning, unlike you."

David Airedale sat up once more and this time she didn't stop him. Lurching forward, he stumbled out of bed before falling to his knees on the floor. "You'll be hanged for this," he said bitterly. "Give me the antidote. I can pay you whatever you want."

"Please, call me Elise," said the woman. "As an old acquaintance of your father's, we should be on a first-name basis."

Staring up at her again, he studied her features, and slowly, understanding began to dawn on him. "Thornbear?"

"That's better," said Elise. "The poison is beginning to wake up your mental faculties, counteracting the soporific I used to get you to bed early. That's why you have that tremor. Eventually, it will begin to burn."

"Why?"

"You've been very naughty, David. You should know why," Elise said mockingly.

"The rumors?" he mumbled.

Leaning forward, she patted the top of his head, as though he were a dog. "Good boy. The rumors were bad. I really don't appreciate people taking advantage of my daughter-in-law's kind nature. She isn't crass enough to bring it up herself, but I could tell you hurt her feelings."

Desperate, he began to beg, "Please, forgive me. I can fix things for her. You don't have to do this."

"Would you really?" asked Elise with what seemed to be genuine curiosity. Then she stood and went to the dressing table, taking the stool with her. "Come over here and sit down."

He tried to stand, but his legs were too unsteady, so he crawled instead, his face burning with humiliation. When he reached the stool, Elise got behind him and putting her hands beneath his arms, she helped him up far enough that he could sit down.

"There's a sheet of paper there. Sign it and I'll consider saving you," said Elise.

On the table he could see two pieces of parchment, one atop the other. He started to lift one, but she pushed his hand aside. "No, you don't get to read it. You just sign the bottom one," she told him. "Then I'll give you this." She held up a small glass vial filled with an amber fluid.

"I'm not signing anything," he argued.

"That's a pity, David," said Elise Thornbear. "I hoped you would be smarter. You don't have much longer to decide. In a little while, the tremors will get much worse. You won't have the option of signing when that happens. You'll start to feel as though your body has been set on fire, with every nerve raw and aching. Eventually you'll begin to seize. I imagine it's very painful, but no one has ever been able to communicate well enough after the seizures start to describe the sensation for me."

"I'd rather die," said Airedale proudly.

Elise smiled maliciously. "Oh, you won't die. Not right away, at least. The seizures will go on for hours. If you're lucky, you'll die, but there's a fair chance you could live. You won't be the same afterward, of course. The poison causes irreversible nerve damage. You'll be crippled for life."

"You're lying."

"Did you know that the brain is essentially a giant collection of nerves, David?" Elise informed him. "Not only will you be weak and crippled, but inside, you'll be a vegetable. You'll spend your remaining days staring off into space and wondering when they'll come to clean the feces out of your pants, if you're capable of thinking even that much."

Airedale felt a faint burning sensation in one of his legs. "Give me the antidote!"

Elise went to a side table and picked up the pen she had laid by there. Dipping it in an open inkwell, she held it up. "Sign it, David. You don't have long before it's too late."

"Alright! Fine! I will!" he screamed.

She brought the pen over to him and placed it in his hand. "Make it as neat and legible as you can. I know your signature, David. Try to cheat me and you'll regret it." Then she assisted as he got his arm into position.

The top sheet of parchment covered all but the bottom portion of the sheet beneath it. Once he had signed, she took both away and then put them on the side table. Ignoring him, she sprinkled some sand over his signature before shaking it off.

"Give me the antidote!" he cried again.

Carefully, Elise laid the bottom sheet on top, making sure it was well displayed. Then she went to Airedale and handed him the vial. "Here you are. A sweet treat for a very wicked boy."

Unstoppering the vial, he held it up and waited while the thick viscous liquid dripped into his mouth. It was surprisingly sweet—like honey. "What is this?" he asked.

Elise winked at him. "Honey. I'm afraid there's no antidote for the poison I gave you. It's nasty stuff. That's why I had to wear gloves. Even a drop on the skin can cause terrible damage or even death, not to mention stains. There's only one true solution to the pain you're about to experience, Lord Airedale, if you're brave enough."

The burning had spread to his arms, and his shaking was growing steadily worse. "What?" he asked.

She went to where he had left his clothes and sorted through them for a moment before retrieving his belt and handing it to him. His knife was still in its sheath. "Slit your wrists," she told him coldly. "Or if you've really got balls, stab yourself in the heart."

"I can't!" he said, horrified. A sudden jerk of his back and legs sent him tumbling to the floor. Painful spasms were starting in his muscles.

"You should hurry," said Elise compassionately. "Once you start to convulse, you won't have the option."

She waited. It was more than a quarter of an hour before Airedale finally jerked the blade across his wrist. Though she hadn't used the poison in several decades, she had already known what the outcome would be. They always chose to end the pain. The lie about the seizures just helped them decide sooner.

While David Airedale bled out on the floor, staring at her with hateful eyes, she collected the vial that had held her fake antidote and then examined the room once more to make sure she had left nothing undone. Wistfully, she looked at the letter on the side table. "Suicide," she said sadly. "What a terrible thing to do, and it looked like you had everything a man could want." She moved to the door, before glancing back. "It just shows, you never know what sadness lies in the hearts of others. Say hello to your father for me, when you see him."

Then she left. Ordinarily, she would have stayed, to make sure her target met his end, but in David Airedale's case, there was no point. Even if someone found him and bound up his wound, he would be unable to tell them what had happened. Dying was the best he could hope for, and in any case, no one in the Airedale household would be waking up to save him until morning. He would be cold and stiff long before that.

As she crept out of the house that morning, carrying a large basket of dirty laundry, Elise reflected on her past. Since marrying her late-husband, she had led a relatively peaceful life, largely free of the things she had been forced to do in her youth, but tonight was a dark reminder. Her only consolation was that at least now, *she* was the one who decided who needed to die, and she felt very little remorse for David Airedale.

Coming in the Summer of 2018:

Transcendence and Rebellion

Stay up to date with my release by signing up for my newsletter at:

Magebornbooks.com

Books by Michael G. Manning

Mageborn Series:

The Blacksmith's Son
The Line of Illeniel
The Archmage Unbound
The God-Stone War
The Final Redemption

Embers of Illeniel (a prequel series):

The Mountains Rise
The Silent Tempest
Betrayer's Bane

Champions of the Dawning Dragons:

Thornbear
Centyr Dominance
Demonhome

The Riven Gates:

Mordecai
The Severed Realm
Transcendence and Rebellion (Summer of 2018)

Standalone Novels:

Thomas